undecided

Julianna Keyes

ISBN: 0995050716
ISBN-13: 978-0995050716

chapter one

To be fair, it's really not my fault this time.

The ad I answered looking for a "studious, responsible roommate" promised one in return. And the location was perfect: a quiet, older building on one of the many tree-lined streets that edge the perimeter of the prestigious Burnham College, preferred living quarters of retired folks. No temptation here.

It's the words "studious" and "responsible" that have me dressed in a pair of creased gray slacks, a white button-up shirt, and a prim black cardigan when I knock on the door of 203 Fir Street. I've even tied my unruly dark hair into some semblance of a respectable bun. And it is precisely this outfit that makes me cringe when the door is opened not by my socks-and-sandals, starch-collared future roommate, but Crosbie Lucas, uber-jock and renowned campus party boy.

I step back. "I think I have the wrong address."

His brown eyes rake me over. "Definitely."

Oh God. Only I could knock on the door of the wrong house and find Crosbie Lucas on the other side. He's got a stocky build, just a few inches taller than me, but broad enough you can picture him having to turn sideways to fit through the door. With dark auburn hair and a smattering of freckles he's not textbook hot, but everyone on campus knows he's never had trouble finding a date.

Having gone to more than my share of frat parties last

year, I've seen him in action. Hell, if you've been anywhere in the vicinity of Burnham College in the past twelve months, you've seen Crosbie Lucas. He's the life of every party: loud and obnoxious, making out in corners, carting in keg after keg, pouring drink after drink. He's the consummate party boy, and though I'd done my very best to be his female equivalent last year, it hadn't exactly worked out for me. Hence the cardigan.

I'd printed out the email supplying the address, and now I tug it out of my purse and unfold it, looking up at Crosbie suspiciously when the address in the email matches the address beside the door. "This is the right place."

He scratches his chin. "Is it? Hmm."

My eyes narrow. "Do you actually live here?" Now that I think about it, I'm pretty sure Crosbie lives in a frat house and always will.

"Technically? I—"

A voice from inside interrupts. "Cros, what are you—? Oh, shit. Ignore him. Ignore him. Please don't leave!" Then things get a million times worse, because even as I hear the thud of socked feet running down hardwood stairs, I recognize the voice of Kellan McVey, Crosbie's best friend, campus stud, and my one-time drunken closet hookup.

Oh fuckity fuck.

"Hey, hi, hey!" Kellan skids across the floor before coming to a halt in front of me. His wool socks are bunched around his calves beneath a pair of shiny black soccer shorts and a matching T-shirt. His dark hair curls around his ears and sticks out adorably, his blue eyes sincere and pleading as they meet mine, willing me not to run away.

"I—" I begin, feeling my face heat.

"Ignore him, please, I'm so sorry. You're Nora, right? Nora Kincaid? I'm Kellan. We've been emailing."

He extends a hand and I shake it automatically, even as his expression remains wholly pleasant, not a trace of recognition dawning on his handsome features. He has no idea who I am. Sure, I was wearing a shiny red corset and a leather mini-skirt during our…interlude at the Alpha Sigma Phi frat party last spring, but I'm wearing a cardigan now, not a *mask*.

He just doesn't remember me.

I retrieve my hand, even as my fingers attempt to linger in his for as long as they can. "You said your name was Matthew in the email." I try not to sound accusatory, even though it's most definitely an accusation. If I'd known I'd exchanged half a dozen "I do laundry on Tuesdays—what's your policy on recycling?" emails with Kellan McVey, I never would have shown up today. I'd never have responded to "Studious Homebody Looking for Same" in the first place.

"It's my middle name," he says, managing to look genuinely apologetic. Although anyone would look sweet standing next to Crosbie, who folds his beefy arms across his even beefier chest and smirks gleefully as he watches the awkward exchange. But Kellan doesn't need to put on a puppy dog stare to look guilty and forgivable, because he's just…so…handsome.

Gah. No. Forget about handsome. I'm looking for serious. Responsible. Didn't-have-sex-with-and-then-forget-me. Hell, he said *he* was looking for most of those things. But even as I resent him for lying, I understand why he did it. If he'd put out an ad saying "Kellan McVey looking for a roommate" he'd have gotten a million replies. An ad that includes the line "strict curfew, very few guests, loves homework!" probably only enticed…me.

"Crosbie doesn't live here," he says, elbowing his friend in the ribs. "He was helping me move some furniture, and now he's leaving. He probably won't even ever come back."

"Actually, I thought I'd stay and help with the interview," Crosbie says.

"Er, no." This year is about making good decisions, and faced with my first challenge, I am not about to participate in an "interview" with Burnham College's two resident manwhores. Despite my last academic transcript and recent police record, I *do* have a brain and it does recognize a bad idea when one is presented. Last year I'd done my best to squash my Nora Bora high school persona, but this year she is back and here to stay. Or at least graduate and not get arrested again.

"Get lost," Kellan orders, shoving Crosbie toward the door. I shuffle to the side as Crosbie tumbles out, laughing. He smells like sweat and lemon-scented laundry detergent, and when he bangs into my shoulder he grabs my hip to steady me, his big fingers digging in just a little too hard before letting go.

"Sorry," he says, making a face at his friend. "His fault. You should probably reconsider living here. He's an asshole."

I don't know what to say so I say nothing. Then Crosbie's gone and it's just Kellan and I.

"Sorry about that," he says. "Do you want to come in? Please come in."

I should leave. He lied to me, he has a stupid friend, and he doesn't remember that we had sex. If I'd been having any doubts about the wisdom of that hookup, they were cemented forty-five minutes later when I spotted him getting a very public blowjob from a very willing blonde.

The mortification of that moment should be enough to send me running. And I swear I would, if only I hadn't met with four other potential roommates yesterday and failed to click with any of them. And if only I didn't need to move out of my cramped room in summer residence by the end of the week.

"Sure," I say.

It's a nice, predictable apartment, arranged in the same style as all the others in the neighborhood. The front door opens to a tiny foyer and set of stairs leading up to the living area. The main space features an open kitchen with a small breakfast bar, and one wall is taken up with three doors—two bedrooms and one bathroom, according to Kellan's ad.

It's bright and airy, with the original hardwood floors and large windows. There are no special upgrades, just standard-issue appliances and white paint on the walls, and it's in the process of being furnished as Matthew—Kellan—had explained in his emails. In an effort to keep him away from the party crowd, his parents agreed to pay for this place on the condition he keeps his grades up, but they're not paying for anything else, so he's getting a roommate to cover his living expenses. Before today I'd assumed that "Matthew's" biggest expense would be cat food and brand new board games. Now...not so much.

"Have a seat," Kellan says, gesturing to the tiny wooden table that, for the moment, is sitting in no-man's land in the space between the front door, living room, and kitchen. More of a hallway, really. Or, in Kellan and Crosbie's book, a dining room.

I sit stiffly, crossing my legs then uncrossing them and crossing at the ankles. I tug at my collar, certain my shirt is trying to strangle me. The last time I wore it was during my party girl phase when I'd paired it with a lacy magenta bra and four undone buttons. Today, however, I had to wear a sports bra just to get it to button up over my boobs. A petite frame and a D-cup does not make getting dressed easy.

"Want a drink or anything?" Kellan asks. He waits for me to shake my head before sitting down and resting his arms on the table. He smiles shyly, his teeth white and even, mouth quirking up slightly more on one side than the other to reveal the dimple in his left cheek. Yes, I know Kellan McVey has a dimple in his left cheek. Everyone does. Just like they know he benches 280 and runs a five-minute mile and came in third in last year's national track meet and is in the second year of a four-year sociology degree. He's basically Burnham's resident celebrity, and here I am, in his living room. Dining room.

Our dining room.

No. I can't even consider this. It's an exercise in failure, and I have had enough failure in this past year to last me a lifetime. In fact, I won't even have a life or a future if I repeat last year's poor performance, hence the commitment to my new prim and proper lifestyle. Nora Bora 2.0. Emphasis on the bore.

I force myself to return the smile, then study my plain fingernails, trying to figure out what, exactly, to say in this situation. "You said—" I begin, at the same moment Kellan says, "I know I—"

We both break off, then laugh awkwardly. "You first," he says.

"Your ad said you were studious and responsible," I say, hating how lame I sound. "I didn't really picture, you know…you."

He winces. "I know. I'm sorry. But it's one hundred percent true. At least, it's going to be. Last year things got a little carried away, I had too much fun, and it cost me. Not just my grades, but nationals. I should have won and—" He interrupts himself with the shake of his head. "That's not important. The point is, this year is going to be a fresh start. I moved out of the frat house and I want to live with someone who wants the same things. Feel free to party your ass off wherever you want—just so long as it's not here." He laughs a little then, and I realize it's the idea of me partying that he finds amusing.

Ha ha, Kellan, it's a freaking cardigan, not a chastity belt.

"Sorry," he says, reading the irritation on my face. "I, uh… I just thought it would make things easier for me and my roommate if there was no…temptation. Like, you know. To complicate things."

I try not to let my jaw drop. Did he just call me ugly? Or at the very least, un-tempting?

"I mean—" He cringes and runs a hand through his hair. "Shit. I'm so bad at this. Just listen to me. I mean, I asked for someone studious and responsible so we could keep each other on the straight and narrow, you know? If you're not bringing people here to party, and I'm not bringing people over, then we'll just…study, right? And, I don't know, watch the news and…read. Ugh." His head falls back. "I'm such an idiot. I'm sorry, Nora, this must sound as appealing as prison. Basically I emailed with like, half a dozen people, and you were the only one who sounded any good at all. Like, normal and smart, with a sense of humor. And a strong stance on recycling."

I smile reluctantly and he looks relieved.

"Come on," he says, standing. "Let me give you the grand

tour so I can try to keep my foot out of my mouth."

I stand too, then neither one of us moves.

"Well," he says, clearing his throat. "This is the dining room."

I nod and try not to laugh. This whole thing is so stupid and weird. I'm not going to be roommates with Kellan McVey. Not only is he the antithesis of everything my ideal new roommate is supposed to be, we've had sex.

And he doesn't *remember* it.

"This is the living room," he continues, gesturing behind him. Because we're pretty much already standing in it, neither of us moves, I just peer over his shoulder. There's a wooden entertainment unit set up on one wall with an enormous flat screen TV positioned in the middle.

"Full cable," Kellan adds when I don't react. "Including HBO."

I nod.

"Um..." He scratches his shoulder and points behind me. "That's the kitchen. I know how to cook and I clean up, too. My mother was a housekeeper, and the last thing she wanted to do when she got home was clean up after four boys, so I know how to wash a dish and take out the trash. That whole bit was true in the email. I wasn't just trying to lure you here."

"That was a big part of your appeal."

He smiles, and there's the dimple again.

"Hand to God, I'm tidy. Let me show you the rooms." He heads for the door closest to the kitchen. "They're the same size, same layout. I already put my stuff in this one, but if you'd rather be in here, just say so and I'll move over. Honestly, I think Crosbie just didn't want to carry the mattress another three feet."

I peek past him into the bedroom. It's a decent-sized room that easily fits a queen-size bed, desk, and dresser, and a bunch of boxes that have yet to be unpacked. Given Kellan's reputation, I'd kind of expected red walls, mirrored ceilings and zebra-print pillows, but maybe he's serious about turning over a new leaf. Or maybe he just decorates his room like a normal person and not a porn king.

"Next one," he says, opening the other door and showing me an identical unfurnished room. More hardwood, a large window that looks over the back parking lot, and bare walls painted white. Plenty of room for my things and good for studying— No, no. What am I doing? I can't consider moving in here, even if the bathroom is surprisingly spacious. I'm going to endure the tour, tell him I'll think about it, then go home and write a polite email declining the offer. Those other roommates weren't so bad, were they? Even if two were thirty minutes away, one was a chain smoker, and the other had four cats.

This place is the cheapest too, given Kellan's parents are the ones really covering the rent. And Kellan doesn't have any cats and he doesn't smoke, which I appreciate, and he says he washes his own dishes, which—No. No pro list for this place. Cons only.

"So that's the tour." Kellan steps back and takes a seat on the arm of the brown leather sofa positioned opposite the television. "And this is me. I swear I pay my bills on time, and I'm going to use this place to sleep and study, no parties. No girls. I know I said that in my email and you probably thought I was lying—"

More like I thought no girls would be tempted to come home with Matthew, who said his favorite food was mac and cheese—

"—but I'm totally serious. This would be our home, and I'd completely respect your boundaries. Fuck. Boundaries? Did I just say that? You know what I mean. And please don't worry about Crosbie. He's really not that bad, but I'll keep him away if he annoys you."

I force a smile. The place is great. And if not for Kellan, I'd be all over this deal. But telling people I live with Kellan McVey is like telling them I live in a candy store or a bank vault—they're going to be friends with me for the wrong reasons. Not to mention my own…temptations. I'd like to say I'm above it all and I'm the one girl on campus who isn't dying to date Kellan McVey, but I'm not. Even with the very offensive I-don't-remember-having-sex-with-you issue, he's still super hot. And he seems nice. And kind of dorky, which makes him surprisingly down to earth, and—

No. What am I doing? I can't justify this. There's nothing he can say—

"I can give you a break on the rent too," he offers hastily. "How about until January, no rent? I already told you my parents are paying for this place, and I have some savings. You said in the emails you work at a coffee shop, right? So you can use that money for books or Christmas presents or whatever, and then in January, if you still like it here, you can pay. If not, no hard feelings. It'll be like a trial run."

Did I just hear him correctly? Free rent?

"Is it the bedrooms?" he asks, misinterpreting my hesitation. "You can totally choose—"

"The bedrooms are fine," I say.

Don't do it.

"Everything looks great," I hear myself add.

Nice apartment, free rent, hot roommate?

I can't.

"So… Are we doing this?" He shoots me a tentative grin, dimple flashing.

Stare at something besides the dimple.

I look at his chest and stick out my hand.

"We're doing this," I say.

chapter two

Okay, so today didn't go exactly as planned. It went *mostly* as planned, in that I have to move out of my current place by the weekend and I found a great, free, apartment, but obviously my roommate is not the bookworm I'd been anticipating. And we once had sex in a closet and then he forgot about it.

I drop onto the edge of the twin mattress in my shoebox-sized dorm room and sigh, trying to convince myself I made the right decision. I mean, if I make a pros and cons list, the pros obviously outweigh the cons. And what's the worst that could happen? I have a crush on my roommate for a while? Big deal. People live through crushes all the time.

The tiny dorm window is already open, but I still shove it up an extra half inch, as though it will make breathing any easier. After last year's debacle I'd had to sign up for summer classes and move into Henley, the lone residence they keep open for summer students. The rooms are barely big enough to house a bed and an average-sized human, and the building is nearly deserted. Of its ten available floors only five are in use, and there are four other people on my level. Not that I've had a lot of time for socializing, with three classes, a full-time job, and three hundred hours of community service.

I wrapped up my summer courses and community service last week, and now all that's left is my job at Beans, the coffee shop in town. I'd loved working there last year, but now it's painfully awkward. The awkwardness is entirely my fault, but after nearly flunking out and getting arrested, I'd had to make some changes. One of those changes was ending things with my best friend and co-worker, Marcela Lopes. After getting my ass chewed in the Dean's office, I'd flipped the switch on any fun and frivolity, and that meant getting rid of any bad influences in my life. Unfortunately Marcela fell squarely into that category, and she did not take being "shunned" too well.

I know I made the right choice in changing my circle of friends—more like, deleting my circle of friends and opting to have none—but I really miss Marcela. She's smart and funny and a little bit insane, and she's the only one in the world who knows about my hookup with Kellan. She'd die laughing if she heard about today's events, but I can't call her. And when I go into work tomorrow, I can't tell her, either. She's not speaking to me, and it's for the best.

I'm pretty sure.

I strip out of the constricting interview clothes and toss on a pair of jeans and a long sleeve shirt. I unwind my hair from its bun, relieved when it falls in nice waves down my back instead of its usual tumbleweed nest. Though we technically have a small kitchen on our floor, it's just a filthy microwave and a stove with one working burner, so I forgo eating in, grab a jacket, and head to the small campus strip mall, which has been a ghost town all summer.

There are two days left in August but no one gave Mother Nature the news, and the trees in northern Oregon are already starting to change, greens giving way to muted yellows and reds, the air already taking on the crisp feel of autumn.

Classes officially resume on September fifth, the day after Labor Day, and students are allowed to move in on the third. Until then it's just me and a handful of other summer students lining up for burgers and fries at the Hedgehog Grill, one of the few campus restaurants that stay open year-round.

"Hey, Nora," calls Franco, the owner. "Lemme guess. Burger. Mushrooms. Bacon. Vinegar for the fries. And...an orange soda?"

"Sounds good," I say, getting out my wallet. It always

sounds good, since I always get the same thing when I come here. I pay and find a booth along the wall, grabbing my archaeology textbook from my bag, determined to cram every bit of knowledge about matrices and excavation processes into my brain by the end of dinner. Even though I have no intention of being an archaeologist, I'd failed this course last year and the only way to ease the bruise of an F is to re-take the class.

I'm halfway through a page about strata when I hear my name. Looking up, however, it's not Franco calling me over to pick up my food, it's Crosbie Lucas approaching with a tray of his own.

"Trying to go incognito?" he asks, gesturing to my loose hair and non-cardigan. "Look more like a college student than a nanny?"

"I guess it didn't work."

"Can't fool me." Without waiting for an invitation, he slides into the far side of the booth and munches on a fry. "What are you reading?"

"I'm studying."

"I figured. What?"

"Archaeology."

"*You* want to be Indiana Jones?"

"I just want to pass."

He shrugs. "Sure. Fair enough."

My eyes dart around and I catch several people looking our way. Despite last year's irresponsible antics, I'm a small fish in a big pond, and I don't have much of a reputation. Crosbie Lucas, however, does, and though I've just agreed to move in with his best friend, I have not agreed to be friends with Crosbie by extension. Every girl Crosbie hooks up with gets added to a list called the "Crosbabes" and no way do I want to join their ranks, rumored or real.

Before I can think of a polite brush-off, Franco shouts that my food is ready. I head up to collect my meal, then return to the table and sigh when Crosbie shows no signs of leaving.

"What are you doing on campus?" I ask. "I thought you

lived on the Frat Farm." The short strip of old Victorian homes converted into Burnham frat houses on the west side of campus has more than earned its name, thanks to the wild parties and rumors of crazy behavior that's more fact than fiction. I should know, since I'd been a frequent flier there last year.

Crosbie speaks around a mouthful of food. "Just working out. They keep the Larson gym open all summer."

"I thought they had weights at the frat houses."

"Oh yeah? You spend a lot of time there?"

"No," I lie. "Just a guess." Though Crosbie and I were never officially introduced last year, we'd been at a lot of the same parties, and it's more than a little offensive that he doesn't remember me.

He stuffs a couple of fries into his mouth. "I've got an elliptical and some weights in my room, but it's not enough. And the gym here's quiet in the summer, so I like to use it when I can."

"Makes sense."

"You staying on campus?"

"Yeah. I was taking summer courses."

"Trying to get a leg up, huh?"

Ha. "Yep," I lie again.

"Kell says you're moving in."

I hesitate. I already know it's true, but hearing it from someone else feels weird. Like it's more true, more permanent, more wrong, somehow. Like how you know streaking down Main Street is a bad idea, but hearing your parents say "You ran naked down Main Street, Nora!?" makes it sound even worse.

"September third."

"Should be interesting."

"What does that mean?"

He shrugs. "It means, Kellan's got good intentions about being a model student this year, but I don't think it'll happen. And something tells me you're the kind of girl that doesn't want to be corrupted."

I nearly choke on my burger. "Corrupted?"

"Yeah. You ever go to a party? Get drunk? Mess around? That's what Kellan's into—hell, you've got your nose buried in a book, but even you must know that. I just think maybe you're going to be…scandalized a little bit this year. It's why I said you had the wrong address. So you didn't make a mistake."

I try to keep a straight face. "Thanks for looking out for me."

He points at me with a fry. "I see you're not taking this seriously. I'm just saying, don't get your hopes up."

"What would I be hoping for, Crosbie?"

He grins. "What every girl hopes for. Happily ever after with Kellan McVey."

"I'm just trying to graduate."

"Same here," he replies, distracted by a commotion over my shoulder. "But sometimes…we get a little off track."

"Hi, Crosbie!" A gaggle of girls dressed in tiny summer dresses and heels totters past, each shooting Crosbie their most endearing smile.

He gives them a nod. "Ladies."

"Join us?" one asks, as though I'm invisible and Crosbie's dining alone. Seems to be the theme for today.

"Sure thing," he answers, watching them giggle and make their way to a corner booth.

"You just went off track pretty easily."

He laughs and swipes one of my fries, since his are gone. "I'll get back on track tomorrow. Nice talking to you, Nora."

"Yes," I agree. "It's been fantastic."

* * *

Most people hate moving, but for me it's really no big deal. All of my earthly possessions fit into a pair of large duffel bags and two pilfered milk crates, all of which I strap to my bicycle and painstakingly wheel over to Fir Street the day before Labor Day.

It's strange to see Burnham bustling again after it was a virtual dead zone all summer, but today is the official first day of move-ins, and campus is buzzing with new and returning students. Everywhere I look there are tearful parents and anxious sophomores, everyone doing their best to put on brave faces. Frosh leaders wear obnoxious neon T-shirts and carry megaphones, rallying their nervous young troops with promises of the best years of their lives.

I keep my head down and maneuver my unwieldy load through the crowds, breathing a sigh of relief when I make it to the shady pathways that wind around the edge of campus. It's quieter here, the canopy of old trees dotting the pavement with light and shade. The sun found its way back to Oregon and it's warmer than it has been, enough so that even in jeans and a tank top, I'm sweating when I reach the apartment.

I pause on the sidewalk and take in my new home. The apartments are more like tiny townhouses, each with a door that opens onto a tiny front lawn. They have red brick faces, green doors, and a single window on the second level. It's...homey.

The home I'll be sharing with Kellan McVey.

The front door bursts open and Kellan and Crosbie elbow each other as they stumble out, dressed in sneakers, shorts, and matching Burnham Track T-shirts. They stop when they see me, and I smile uncomfortably and wheel my bike up the short path to the front door.

"You got more?" Kellan asks, taking in my load.

"This is it."

"That's it?" Crosbie looks perplexed. "Where's your bed? Your desk?"

"They're coming," I say. "I was in residence last year, so I don't own any furniture. It's supposed to arrive on Tuesday." Today's Sunday and tomorrow's Labor Day, so that's the earliest it could get here. I don't mention that it's coming from Ikea, so odds are I won't figure out how to get everything built until the following weekend, if ever.

I wave off their offers to help bring the stuff in, but they insist, and after one short trip, my bedroom is fully equipped with two milk crates of books, and two duffel bags of clothes and toiletries.

"Home sweet home," I say when they linger.

"You, uh, want to come for a run?" Kellan asks. "We were just leaving."

I definitely do not. Athletics are not my forte. "Thanks," I say, "but I have to be at work in an hour. I'm just going to hang some stuff in the closet and head out."

"Oh yeah?" Crosbie asks. "Where do you work?"

Though Kellan already knows this from our email exchange, I tell them about Beans, located in the center of Burnham's tiny downtown.

"I've been in there a bunch of times," Kellan says. "I don't think I saw you."

I do my best not to roll my eyes. I'm invisible. I get it. "I must not have been working."

"They have open mic nights, right?" Crosbie asks, looking interested. "Like, for any type of talent?"

Kellan makes no effort to hide *his* eye roll. "Dude. No."

I'm expecting him to make a joke about his lap dance talent or something, so it's a total surprise when Crosbie says, "Do you ever have magicians perform?"

My eyebrows shoot up. "Magicians? Er, no, not that I've seen."

"Huh."

"No one has time for your tricks," Kellan mutters, clearly embarrassed for his friend. But Crosbie doesn't appear to care. "Illusions," he says. "You don't have time for my *illusions.*"

I'm too surprised to laugh, but I do make a strange sound that's half snort-half snicker. Kellan looks at me in confusion, but Crosbie grins and I feel my mouth twitch. Anyone who can quote *Arrested Development* can't be all bad.

"There's a sign up book at the register," I tell him. "Come in any time and put your name down."

"Maybe I will."

"Don't encourage him," Kellan pleads, dragging Crosbie

from the room.

"No encouragement necessary," Crosbie says. Just before he lets Kellan win the tug of war he adds, "We'll see you."

That would be a first, I think, watching them go.

* * *

Speaking of invisible, I wish that were the case at Beans. Because almost everyone who works here is a student, we have pretty set schedules and I normally work alongside Marcela and our boss, Nate.

Nate and Marcela are polar opposites. Nate is the tall, blond, hipster-type with skinny jeans and dark-rimmed glasses, and Marcela is the kind of girl who beats up hipsters. She favors thigh high boots, short skirts, and too-tight tops. Paired with her bleached hair and signature red lipstick, she looks like a cross between a fifties movie star and a naughty schoolgirl who hates me. I'd ended things right after my arrest in May, and I'd sort of hoped that her summer away from Burnham would help calm her vitriol, but it didn't. She returned two weeks ago with the same amount of burning resentment she'd left with.

"Hey," Nate calls when I rush in through the kitchen, tying my apron around my waist. I'd parked my bike in the alley and now I wash my hands and pretend not to notice Marcela ignoring me as she takes a tray of muffins out of the oven. "You're late," he adds, propping himself up against the counter.

"It's three minutes," I point out, drying my hands. "I didn't account for the travel time."

"You've been making the same trip for a year."

"Not today. I mov—" I try to stop myself, but it's too late. Not that it's a problem if Nate knows where I live, but it's obvious I can't afford one of those apartments by myself, so the next obvious question is to ask about roommates, and I don't want to have this conversation now.

Or ever.

Especially when Nate might not know about the Kellan McVey thing, but Marcela does.

"Wait," he says when I try to hustle up front. "You moved?"

"Yeah," I call over my shoulder. "I think I heard the bell. Time to work!"

I elbow my way through the swinging doors to the front of the shop, inhaling the familiar smells of coffee, vanilla, and pastry. The owner of Beans is a huge patron of the arts and every square inch of the shop that isn't devoted to coffee, snacks, and seating is committed to displaying artwork. We've got everything from paintings on the walls to handmade furniture, sculpture, jewelry, and a very popular set of Russian nesting dolls painted to look like famous movie characters.

I recognize the woman waiting at the counter. She comes in often and is nice enough, but she's got increasingly complicated drink orders and despite the fact that she looks only a couple of years older than me, insists on wearing fur coats year-round. Marcela nicknamed her Mink Coat and the name stuck.

"Ready to order?" I ask.

"Yes, please. I'll have a small iced half-caf double non-fat peppermint mocha with coconut milk. No whip."

Nate's lingering at my side and she shoots him a shy smile he barely notices. For once I'm grateful for her complicated order. Welcoming the opportunity to avoid follow up questions, I take an absurdly long time to make sure the cup is perfectly full before sliding it across the counter.

"Thank you." She flicks another glance at Nate, who's carefully restocking a tray of brownies, and leaves.

"So," Nate says when Mink Coat is gone. "You moved?"

"Yeah." I add the extra change to our tip jar. "Just to the edge of campus. Off campus. Barely."

His brow furrows. "Just off campus is a pretty nice area."

"Safe and studious."

He rolls his eyes. He knows all about my life changes, and while he wasn't exactly cheering when I got arrested last year, he does think I'm taking things way too seriously. That's just the way I am, though. Always have been. I'm hot or I'm cold, never in between. Invisible or under arrest.

I started to develop when I was thirteen, cringing at the newfound unwanted attention my boobs were getting. Because I'd gone from being an awkward, gangly teen to the subject of catcalls and leers with no transitional stage, I'd rebelled the best way I could: baggy sweatshirts and jeans, sneakers, no makeup. And for the most part, it did the trick. I got no attention. I also got no dates. No one asked me to the Christmas dance or homecoming or even to prom. I had to go with my neighbor Charlie, who was a grade behind. When I moved to Burnham from my home in Washington, I decided it was time for a change of pace. I wasn't going to bury myself in oversized clothing I found on the discount racks, I was going to come out of my self-imposed shell and live my life. When I met Marcela on my second day at school, I knew she was the ideal accomplice and the perfect guide to the Burnham party scene. And it wasn't like I was particularly shy or awkward—I'd just never embraced my outgoing, sexy side.

Until last year.

Repeatedly. Endlessly. And sometimes illegally.

I went from zero to sixty without ever tapping the brakes, and eventually I spun out. So here I am, back to zero, hunkered down, paying for all my fun. Was it worth it? Yes, I'd say so. Am I completely aware that I'm reversing course, going from sixty to zero without ever finding a reasonable middle ground? Yes again.

I got good grades in high school, but high school wasn't hard. College is. Burnham is my dad's alma mater, which is the only reason I got in, and it's prestigious for a reason. Their alumni boast two presidents, a Nobel Peace Prize winner, and a Supreme Court Justice. Professors will fail you if they don't think you're trying hard enough or if they think you're phoning it in. It's not enough to show up and complete all your assignments—they want to know you tried. And last year, I did not try. Hence my scholarship getting slashed in half, my parents kicking in for the missing tuition this year, and me moving in with Kellan McVey, my new study buddy.

I may have gotten a C- in Stats last year, but even I know the odds of this arrangement failing.

chapter three

Okay, so it's possible I've been making a bigger deal out of this "Kellan McVey's my roommate thing" than is strictly necessary. I mean, he's just a guy. A guy who comes home after a mid-morning soccer game in the rain, strips off his soaking wet jersey as he crosses the living room, and grins at me before disappearing into the bathroom.

Have I mentioned that Kellan is ripped? Like, how-is-that-real ripped? Because he is. And while I'd like to pretend it's the peanut butter sandwich I'm eating that has my mouth watering, it's not. The heated feeling spreading through my belly has nothing to do with mealtime, either, and everything to do with the fact that I haven't actually been with anybody since that time in the closet with Kellan.

Four long months ago.

I firmly close and lock the door on the dirty thoughts trying to penetrate my studious haze, and focus on taking my plate to the sink when Kellan comes out of the bathroom in shorts and…that's it. Just shorts. His dark curls wet and shiny, a tiny drop of water working its way between his pecs and down over his six pack and—

"Any plans today?" Kellan asks, joining me in the tiny kitchen and pulling a leftover bowl of mac and cheese out of the fridge. He sticks it in the microwave and punches a few buttons, the soft whir of the fans filling the air.

"Ah, just work," I say. "I start at two."

"No last act of rebellion before school starts?" It's Labor Day, and classes officially begin tomorrow. I've got five courses and two tutorials, and juggling school and work should be more than enough to keep me out of trouble.

I shake my head, since forming words poses a greater challenge than I'm up for. I've already seen Kellan's soap in the bathroom, but smelling it on his freshly washed body is its own brand of olfactory torture. I rack my brain to think of something witty or intelligent to say, but can only come up with, "What are you going to do?"

"Eat," he says promptly, the microwave obeying the command and politely beeping. Kellan removes the bowl, stirs, and takes a bite, nodding his satisfaction. If I have learned one thing about Kellan in our three days as roommates, it's that he wasn't lying when he said he loves mac and cheese. He buys it in bulk and one of our four kitchen cupboards is stocked with boxes of it. I mean, I like a bowl of mac and cheese as much as the next girl, but in this quantity it's kind of gross. Though it's hard to think of mac and cheese as anything but sexy and delicious when it's being forked into the mouth of a shirtless Kellan McVey.

"Well," I begin, ready to make my escape and hopefully not embarrass myself by drooling.

"What'd you say you were studying?" Kellan asks, boosting himself onto the counter and settling in.

Is this happening? Are we…talking? Just me and Kellan McVey?

"I'm undecided," I hear myself say, my voice blessedly normal. "I've got a bit of everything this year. You're doing sociology, right?"

"Yeah." He shrugs carelessly. "It seems like a safe bet. A good base. You can go a lot of ways with it."

"Sure." I take a sip of water and try not to look like I'm loitering in my own home. I want to have a conversation with Kellan. I want this to be a thing we do. I tossed the cardigan into the back of my closet the second I unpacked, and though the corsets and leather mini-skirts are stuffed back there too, I don't want him to see me as the uptight budding librarian he met at our first meeting.

In deference to the rainy weather, I'm wearing jeans and a turquoise flannel shirt, which fits well and shows off my figure, not that he seems to notice. After a lengthy moment of awkward silence, I sigh and turn to go.

"Hey," he says.

I stop. "Yeah?"

"You pass the Frat Farm when you go into town, right? For work?"

I pretend I have to think about it, that I haven't spent a lot of time at the Frat Farm. "I guess so."

"Any chance I can get you to drop off something for Crosbie? He needs it first thing tomorrow, but I'm not heading there today."

It's like, fifteen minutes from here to the Frat Farm, but whatever. It's on my way. "Sure," I say. "But you'll have to give me the address." This part is true—I know Crosbie lives in a frat house, but not which one. They're all the same in the dark.

"Thanks." He hops off the counter and jogs into his room as I try not to ogle the shifting muscles in his back. He returns a second later carrying a box with a familiar shoe company logo. "Sneakers," he explains. "Special order. A guy I know works at the store and Crosbie's been waiting for these forever."

"A shoe guy," I say, studying the box. "Who knew?" When I think of Crosbie Lucas—and to be fair, it's not often that I do—I think of three things: loud, muscles, and Crosbabes. Only one of those things floats my boat, and it's not enough to make up for the other two.

Kellan shakes his head. "Don't get him talking about shoes, he'll never stop. And no matter what, don't let him convince you to participate in any magic tricks. You'll never get out alive."

Illusions, I think. *Don't participate in any illusions*. "Duly noted," I say. Then, for some reason, I salute.

Kellan stares at me for a second, then wrinkles up his nose and lets loose with a heartfelt belly laugh. And by belly laugh, I mean six-pack laugh, because that thing ripples and shifts in a way that does something to my own stomach and a certain spot beneath it.

* * *

Twenty minutes later I'm leaning my bike against the front stoop of the Alpha Sigma Phi frat house. It's a peeling green Victorian on a shady, tree-lined street of similar houses painted in muted and respectable earth tones. Because it's the day before classes start, things on the Frat Farm are relatively tame—guys are moving in, there are several parents hanging around, and everyone's still on their best behavior.

Alpha Sigma Phi is quiet, the front door closed, a large potted plant blooming cheerfully beneath the mailbox. It's the kind of plant that says "Trust us, mom—your son's in good hands!" The kind of plant that'll be dead a week from now.

I ring the bell and hear it chime inside, and a few seconds later the door opens to reveal a tall, thin black guy wearing a suit and tie and a nametag that says "My name is Dane." He does a double take when he sees me, and I realize they're expecting new roommates and are hoping to make a good impression on the parents. This is positive news for me— Alpha Sigma Phi is aptly named. The guys are all athletes and take the "Alpha" part of their title very seriously, each one determined to be the man of the house. If they're still in "impress mom" mode, I'm unlikely to stumble into an orgy.

"Hey," I say.

"Hey." He glances at the box in my hand.

"Does Crosbie Lucas live here?"

"*Oh.*" Dane smiles and nods knowingly. "Yeah, yeah. He lives here. Right up there." He steps aside to reveal a large staircase leading to the second floor. "Go ahead. Do your thing."

I blink. Flannel, jeans, and one o'clock on a Monday?

There's nothing sexy or suggestive about me. "I don't need to go upstairs," I say, suddenly a little less confident I won't see anything I can't unsee. The last thing I need is to walk in on Crosbie and his newest Crosbabe. I thrust the paper bag holding the shoebox toward Dane. "Could you just give him this? It's from—"

"Tell him yourself," he says. "I'm not going to be responsible for whatever 'gift' you brought for the guy."

"It's not a gift—"

But Dane's already walking away. So much for best behavior.

I consider just leaving the bag inside the door and asking Kellan to call Crosbie and tell him it's there, but I think about how irresponsible frat houses are and figure I'll just hurry upstairs, find his room, cover my eyes and knock on the door. No chance for any sort of miscommunication or awkward encounter.

Okay. Enough stalling. I have to be at work in forty minutes, and I left early so I'd have a bit of time to amble around town while it was still quiet. Because it's Labor Day and everybody's busy moving in and preparing for class, the small downtown will be mostly empty, just a few shops and restaurants open for locals. Quiet solitary walks—how's that for rebellion, Kellan?

I wipe my sneakers on the welcome mat—I expect this mat will go the way of the plant—and climb the old wooden staircase to the upper level. Last year the guys' rooms had names on them, and this year is no different. Though without blaring dance music, a hundred writhing bodies, and sticky splashes of alcohol on the floor, it's nothing like my past experiences.

There's a long hallway that stretches toward the back of the house, lined with doors on either side. A couple are open but most are closed, and I can hear music and voices filtering through the thin walls. I make my way down the hall, scanning names until I find Crosbie second from the end.

I inch closer and try to listen for warning sounds—

mattress springs squeaking, heavy breathing, cheesy porno music—but there's just a strangely rhythmic thud and whir noise. I give serious thought to hanging the shoes on the knob and getting out of here, then I tell myself to suck it up and knock. He's not going to answer the door naked—I'm pretty sure. Like, fifty percent sure. Thirty.

I knock. The thud-whir combo slows, then stops, and after a second the door is wrenched open to reveal Crosbie on the other side, a small towel in one hand as he wipes his neck. He's wearing a white wife beater with a large V-shaped sweat mark down the front and gray sweatpants. His forehead is slick and shiny, and every one of his overdeveloped muscles is on display.

He's alone.

And very surprised to see me.

"Nora," he says, eyes comically wide. It's actually kind of cute, especially now that I can breathe easy knowing I'm not about to walk in on anything that will give me nightmares.

"Hey," I say.

For a second we just stare at each other. It's weird—like seeing an animal in the wild you've only ever seen at the zoo.

"Um." I shake my head and thrust out the bag. "Kellan asked me to give you these. They're sneakers."

"Right. Okay. Thanks." He takes the bag and then we just stare some more. "What are you doing right now?"

My heart thumps in my chest. It's embarrassing to admit it, but that line worked on me a couple of times last year with other guys. But today my answer is different. "I'm going to work. I start at two."

"Yeah? Two?" He's got an mp3 player in his pocket and now he pulls it out to check the time. Then he nudges the door open a bit wider and glances behind him to where I can see a haphazardly made bed. "Come in here for a minute."

"I beg your pardon?"

It takes a second, then his whole face changes, confusion shifting to surprise then amusement. "Just lay on the bed for a bit," he says, trying to keep a straight face. "This won't take long."

I roll my eyes, feeling foolish. "Shut up."

He laughs. "Seriously, come in. I need someone to quiz me and those ass hats won't do it."

"What do you need to be quizzed for? Classes haven't even started."

"I've got Bio with McGregor tomorrow." He opens the door more and gestures for me to enter. And for some reason, I'm entering. "Everybody knows he drops a pop quiz first thing on day one and I'm going to be ready for it."

I'm trying to listen, but mostly I'm taking in Crosbie Lucas's bedroom. It's small and cramped, with a queen bed against the wall on the right, its blue plaid bedspread rumpled on top. The desk is home to a laptop and piles of books and school supplies, and the rest of the room is devoted to sports. The source of the thud-whir is an elliptical machine on the left side of the room, next to which sits a small weight stack. Even though Crosbie's only on the track team, same as Kellan, there are hockey sticks, baseball bats, soccer balls, volleyballs…pretty much anything you'd need to play any game on the planet.

A wardrobe, its doors left open, reveals an explosion of clothing, much of which is heaped in the corner, on the desk chair, and on the floor by the bed. A garbage can holds a couple of empty beer bottles, but the window that overlooks the front lawn—and which is propped open with a ruler— keeps the room from smelling as bad as it looks.

"Here." Crosbie snatches a textbook from the elliptical and sticks it in my hand. "Have a seat and start asking me questions about the first chapter."

The only free space to sit is the bed, and when I shoot a longing look at the clothing-covered desk chair, Crosbie laughs at me. Given our first cardigan-clad encounter, he must think I'm a terrified prude. "Just sit on the bed," he says. "It's not like I knew you were coming. I don't exactly bring a lot of girls up here to 'quiz.'"

"You don't need the air quotes," I say, taking a seat at the very edge of the mattress. "I'm actually just going to quiz you."

He makes a finger gun with his hand and shoots me. "I knew you were smart." He grabs a bottle of water from the cup holder on the elliptical, chugs half, and climbs back on the machine. "Okay. Start."

I flip open the book and skim the first page, raising my voice to be heard over the thud-whir. "You ready?"

"Bring it."

"First question: head and shoulders, knees and…?"

"Toes!" He fist pumps the air.

"That was just a warm up. Question two: the toe bone's connected to the foot bone, the foot bone's connected to the…?"

"Ankle bone."

I laugh and dodge the bottle cap he throws at my head.

"Now ask me some real questions," he says. "At this rate I'll be the smartest guy in the class."

"I never knew you were so studious."

"I'm full of surprises." He uses a small set of weights to do bicep curls as he runs backward on the elliptical. I try not to watch his muscles move. He's much bigger than Kellan. Kellan has a traditional runner's physique, tall and trim. Crosbie looks more like a wrestler, shorter, broad and stocky.

"All right." I force myself to concentrate. I'm supposed to be quizzing Crosbie on biology, not obsessing over his body. I don't even *care* about his body. But as I start to ask him real questions and he does his very best to answer correctly, I start to care about this, just a little bit. Because he's completely and utterly sincere, no trace of the brash bravado he normally exhibits. No sign of the guy who dances on tabletops and adds Crosbabes to the list scrawled on the bathroom wall on the fourth floor of the Student Union building.

He's not a genius but he tries hard, and he's obviously been paying attention because he gets about seventy percent of the answers right without any prompting. Sometimes I give him hints and his brow wrinkles as he considers things, then bobs his head arrogantly when he figures it out, never once breaking his stride on the elliptical. The only time he sets down the weights is to take a drink of water, then he's right back to it. He's certainly committed.

Speaking of committed—I have a job to get to, and nine minutes in which to make the ten minute trip. "Work," I announce, standing. "I have to go."

"Oh yeah." Crosbie powers down the machine and hops off, snatching the towel and mopping himself up. Sweat runs in rivulets down his neck, his shirt is soaked, and I remind myself to keep my eyes on his face. "I'll walk down with you," he says, reaching past me to open the door. The elliptical did a good job of blocking out the noise from the rest of the house, but without it I can hear raised voices downstairs—certainly more than just Dane, and certainly having more fun than they were half an hour ago.

"You don't have to do that," I say hastily. Because even though we were only "quizzing," absolutely no one will believe it, and how unfair would it be to have my "good" year tainted before it even begins?

"I don't mind." He's too close now, holding the door and waiting for me to pass through. He smells like sweat and...man...and it should be off-putting, but it's not. That's confusing enough to have me hustling out the door.

"Really," I say, putting up a hand to stop him when he tries to follow. "Don't. It's a flight of stairs. I can handle it."

"I think the guys might say—"

I shoot him a terse smile. "I think they 'might' too," I interrupt, my meaning clear. He's worried they might make some sort of generally inappropriate comment; I'm worried about a more specific type of rumor. And I see the dark and offended look shift into his eyes when he realizes what I'm implying.

"Right," he says, stepping back and folding his arms across his chest. "Suit yourself."

I feel bad, but I don't change my mind. "Good luck on your test tomorrow."

"Yeah. Thanks." Then he closes the door in my face.

chapter four

I arrive at Beans for my shift, entering the kitchen just in time
to see Nate and Marcela laughing as they arrange pre-made
cookie dough on a baking sheet. In itself, that's hardly
incriminating. The suspicious part is how Nate leaps away as
though the cookies are radioactive and he's only just now
remembering it.

I've always known that Nate was in love with Marcela.
The three of us are the same age—twenty-one—but Nate's our
boss and often acts like an old man. He tries to be professional
and grown up, and apart from a two-month period last spring
where he sent her gifts from a "secret admirer," I don't think
he's ever acted on it. I think the fact that she never figured out
it was him was pretty discouraging, and since then I assumed
he'd given up the dream.

"Hey," I say, pausing mid-stride to peer between them.

"Hey," Nate says, rubbing a hand over the back of his
neck. He has a handsome, model-like face—too pretty,
Marcela used to say—and super blue eyes. Right now those
eyes are having a difficult time meeting mine, though Marcela
appears completely oblivious. Though it could just be her
determined effort to give me the silent treatment.

I arch a brow at Nate as I walk past, then head out front.
The shop is pretty low-key, and there are half a dozen patrons
seated randomly around the room, reading, texting, and
drinking coffee. I grab a bus bin and amble around clearing off

tables, and when I get back to the counter Nate is standing next to the register, looking uncomfortable.

"Did I interrupt something?"

"No," he says quickly.

"No?"

We both glance over as Marcela comes out with a tray of clean mugs and starts to stack them with the rest. Nate's eyes linger a second too long and I harrumph and return to the kitchen with the dirty dishes. Since it's slow out there I grab a leftover croissant and count inventory as I eat, and when I eventually make my way back to the front, I see Nate say something to Marcela, his expression stern, and the tight set of her mouth as she stands at his side. She looks like a reprimanded child who's being made to apologize.

"What's going on?" A quick look around the shop shows we're down to three customers, all of whom are sufficiently absorbed in their own activities.

"I have to leave early tonight," Nate says. "You two need to close and do the bank deposit. Together."

"There are like, eight people in this whole town right now," Marcela argues, clearly not for the first time. "And this place is dead. One of us can do it."

"You'll stay and do it together," he says, his voice remarkably firm. "I'm leaving at six, you'll lock the doors at nine-thirty and be out of here by ten. Together."

Marcela rolls her eyes but drops the argument. Once he's got our unspoken agreement, Marcela heads off for her break, Nate disappears into his small office to work on payroll, and I tend to the random customers who stroll in over the next couple of hours. Marcela keeps herself busy in the back and I don't even think about her again until Nate comes up with his jacket on, car keys in hand.

"Think you two can be civil for a few hours?"

"We're always civil."

"Like the Civil War," he replies dryly. "Don't burn this place down."

"Me? Never."

"And keep all your clothes on."

"I told you. I turned over a new leaf."

"A new leaf that's living with Kellan McVey?"

"How did you—" I break off when I spot Marcela over his shoulder, halfway out the kitchen doors and most definitely having overheard that last bit about Kellan if her stunned expression is any indication.

Nate winks at me. "There are no secrets in this town."

I shoot him a warning look. "Are too."

He points between Marcela and me as he backs away. "Best behavior."

"Aye aye," Marcela replies, sounding bored.

I give him a thumbs up and watch Marcela retreat into the kitchen, a festering feeling of guilt growing in my stomach. I know it's not fair of me to be the one to end our friendship and then resent the fact that we're not friends, but I do. It wasn't like she had to work to convince me to do any of the stuff we did, but she's a gateway drug. A super fun, loyal, sensitive gateway drug in a black sweater dress, fishnets, and red platform heels.

I didn't come to the decision to call things off easily. But my scolding visit to the Dean's office was followed up with half a dozen irate phone calls from my parents and a very stern talking-to from the judge when I got called in to be reprimanded for my drunk, naked sprint through town. There's only so much a girl can take. If only to get everyone off my back, I swore up and down I'd make things right, and "make things right" involved giving my friendship with Marcela the ax. It's not like she's Miss Perfect—the streaking was her idea, after all. She's just a faster runner. And better at hiding. Because while I got caught crouched naked behind a compost bin, she never got found at all, even though I knew where she was hiding. I also refused to supply her name, which resulted in an additional fifty hours of community service for me.

Marcela was a lot of fun, but staying friends with her and *not* going to parties is like a recovering addict saying they'll just go to the movies with their former dealer—nobody's watching a movie. If I fail another class, my scholarship is over and I'm out of here. My parents can't afford another year of tuition, and my income from the coffee shop is barely enough to cover minimal rent and groceries. This is it for me, and that, more than anything, is what has me picking up a dishtowel and heading off to wipe down tables instead of following Marcela into the kitchen to clear the air.

* * *

By eight, things in the shop are pretty much dead. I'm working on the Sudoku puzzle in yesterday's *Portland Press Herald*, and Marcela's sitting at one of the tables doing some sort of glitter polish thing on her fingernails. Nate doesn't care so much about the Sudoku, but the nail polish is strictly off limits and I know Marcela's just doing it to get back at him for sticking her with me tonight. Oh well—if her fury is directed at someone else, hopefully she'll forget to aim it at me for once.

I've finally figured out which number goes in the upper right corner of the puzzle when the door swings open and Kellan and Crosbie stroll in. Despite the chilly night air, they're wearing T-shirts, shorts and sneakers, and both are drenched in sweat.

"Hey," Kellan says, grinning as they approach.

Crosbie follows at his shoulder, and is it wrong if I notice that Crosbie's shirt strains across his chest just a little more than Kellan's? That his biceps look like they could snap the seams of his sleeves if he flexed, just a little?

Focus, Nora.

"Hi," I say. My eyes flicker to Crosbie and he gives me a little nod. Between him and Marcela, I have officially pissed off half the people in this room. "What are you guys doing here?"

Kellan links his fingers behind his back and stretches. "We figured we should get in a few runs while we could, so here we are. I've gotta step up my game. I came in third in nationals last year—I can't let that happen again."

"Third in the country sounds pretty good."

"It's not."

Er… "It's better than fourth?"

Kellan jerks a thumb over his shoulder. "Crosbie came fourth."

Crosbie nods at me. "'Sup."

Frick. "Are you guys hungry?"

Fortunately the subject of food is an easy way to distract Kellan. "Maybe a bit."

"We don't have any mac and cheese," I warn, and hear Crosbie snicker.

"Ha ha," Kellan says. "I'm here for the brownies."

"Anything for you?" I ask Crosbie.

"Yeah," he says, looking at the Sudoku puzzle. "Same."

I open the display case. "We've got triple chocolate or chocolate banana. What's your preference?"

"Triple chocolate," Kellan says. "For both of us."

I look at Crosbie for confirmation and he nods. Seeing the look, Kellan explains that Crosbie hates bananas.

I try not to laugh. "What? Who hates bananas?"

"They're awful," Crosbie replies seriously. "They taste like dirt and they're impossible to peel. It's a sign."

I'm pretty sure I'll just laugh if I respond so instead I bite my tongue and plate up two inoffensive triple chocolate brownies. I'm entirely aware that Marcela has stopped painting her nails and is openly watching us, and a little thrill goes through me when I realize that neither Kellan nor Crosbie has gawked at her, as so many guys do. They're only talking to me.

"How often do you work here?" Kellan asks, scarfing half the brownie in a single bite.

"Three shifts a week, now that school's starting."

"Is this the sign up sheet?" Crosbie speaks through a mouthful of brownie, and licks off his finger before flicking open the binder labeled "Open Mic Night."

"Yeah," I say, still feeling guilty about offending him earlier, even if every bit of it was true. "Do you want to sign up? We only do four each year and it's coming up in a few weeks—"

"Dude, no," Kellan interrupts. "For the love of all that is holy, do not."

Crosbie smirks at him. "Why not? I've got magic fingers, man. All the girls say so."

Both Kellan and I roll our eyes. "I say this as your friend," Kellan adds. "Spare yourself the embarrassment."

Crosbie just laughs and elbows him in the side, but I swear a flicker of hurt crosses his face before he smoothes it away. He'd opened to the page for the next show, which at present is only half full, though we're always booked solid when the night rolls around.

"It fills up pretty fast. You can put your name down now," I suggest, "and if you change your mind just let me know and I'll cross it out. You might not be able to get in, otherwise."

He finally meets my eyes, and a strange sort of energy passes between us. Like he knows I know he wants to do this, just like I know he doesn't want Kellan to know how much he does. "It's fine," he says, shaking his head. "Another time."

I offer a conciliatory smile and close the book. "Whenever you're ready."

"Hey." Kellan leans in and lowers his voice. "That's Marcela Lopes, right?" He nods his head in Marcela's direction, where she's finished with her nails and is now straightening a display of hand painted wooden spoons.

"Ah…" A sick kind of disappointment spreads through me, but I can't very well pretend it's not her. "Yeah," I say. "That's her."

"I didn't know she worked here."

I force another smile. "Yep."

"I saw her around a lot last year." He looks contemplative and I want to shove him. *You saw her?* I want to yell. *I was right beside her! You didn't see me! Apparently not even when we were the only two people in the closet, you fucker.*

"Well, she goes to school here." I pick at a thread on my apron, and when I finally glance up, it's not Kellan watching me, it's Crosbie. And there's that energy again. But this time he's the one learning my secret.

"Let's head out," Crosbie says. The words are for Kellan, but he's looking at me. "Three more miles."

Kellan shoots one more look at Marcela, then tugs out his wallet and puts five dollars on the counter. "Keep the change," he says. "See you at home." He smiles and waves, and I stare at the money as they leave. The brownies are actually three dollars each, so I sigh and fish out a dollar from the tip jar.

* * *

What is just a light drizzle at the start of my bike ride home quickly turns into a downpour, and I'm drenched and cranky when I push through the front door, my jeans chafing painfully against my inner thighs with each step.

Kellan and Crosbie are on the couch playing video games, a bucket of fried chicken between them. It's quarter past ten, my first class is at nine tomorrow, and all I want to do is take a shower and go to sleep, not listen to shoot 'em up sounds through the paper thin walls.

"Hey." Kellan glances over when I enter, taking in my bare feet, wet socks in hand.

"Hey."

Crosbie and I look at each other but say nothing, and I head into my room to exchange my sopping wet clothes for a robe and a towel. I don't like the idea of cutting between the guys and the TV to get to the bathroom, but I don't have a choice, so I duck past, self-consciously clutching the robe against my breasts. I climb into the shower and turn on the hot water, shuddering when it pounds my shoulders.

I shampoo my hair, finger combing out tangles as I work in conditioner, then washing my face and willing the hot water to carry away my bad mood. I shouldn't even care if Kellan thinks Marcela's hot—everyone thinks she is. Hell, even I think she is. It just…stings. I'll get over it.

Eventually I climb out and towel off, scrubbing a hole in the foggy mirror and watching as I brush my teeth. I smear on moisturizer, then tighten the tie on the robe before darting back into my room as the guys continue to play their game. I usually shower in the morning so typically there wouldn't be an issue with having an audience on my way back from the bathroom. Today, however, I swear I can feel a hot gaze on my bare legs, tracking my return.

When I close the door behind me I feel strangely exposed, and I suppose I am. Who really wants Kellan McVey—or Crosbie Lucas—to see them straight out of the shower, hair wet and makeup-free, wearing a ratty old robe printed with a bizarre owl pattern? Then I laugh. Until now I've been sulking about Kellan not noticing me, and suddenly I'm worried that he will.

I swap the robe for shorts and a sweatshirt, then sit on the yoga mat that'll serve as my bed for one more night. I have two classes tomorrow, both in the morning, so I'll be around for the bed and desk delivery scheduled for mid-afternoon.

I kill a couple of hours on my laptop and eventually the faint explosions coming through the wall fade to background noise. It's only when they stop shortly after midnight that I remember them at all.

I yawn into the crook of my elbow and shut off the computer, then lie down and try to get comfortable, which isn't the easiest task, given the mat's all of a quarter inch thick. The second my eyes close, there's a soft knock on the door. I sit up and switch on the desk lamp—currently a floor lamp—and shove the comforter to the side. I'm expecting Kellan, but when I open the door, it's Crosbie.

"Hey," he whispers, taking in my hair, still damp and tumbled over my shoulders.

"What's up?"

"Can I talk to you for a sec?"

"Um, yeah." I half-expect him to ask me to secretly sign him up for open mic night.

He nods over my shoulder at my room. "In there?"

I hesitate. "Wh—"

"Relax." He makes a face. "Kellan's not going to spread

rumors about you."

"That's not what I—" I blow out a breath. "Fine. Come in."

I step back and he enters, closing the door. His expression is equal parts horrified and amused when he takes in my shoddy set-up: the closet is half-full, every item of clothing I own either hanging inside or still stashed in an open duffel bag on the floor, since I don't have a dresser. My laptop sits on one of the overturned milk crates, the other still holds all my books, and the yoga mat is unrolled in the corner, my crumpled comforter and pillow crushed against the wall.

"What the fuck?" he whispers.

"The furniture's coming tomorrow." I scratch my elbow, embarrassed. "I lived in residence, remember? I didn't need a desk."

"Or a bed."

I cross my arms. "What can I help you with?"

"Nice artwork."

I follow his gaze over my shoulder to the framed paper with "Steve Holt!" written on it in Marcela's best handwriting. It's a character/quote from *Arrested Development*, and no one ever knows what it means. It probably took her five minutes to make, but I love it.

"Thanks. So…?"

He grows serious. "Right. So. I don't know if you know this, but it's Kellan's twenty-first birthday on Friday, and some of us want to have a party for him."

"Uh-huh." After the countless "you're forgettable" references, no part of me thinks I'm about to be invited, even though I—and everyone else on campus—know about Kellan McVey's birthday. Not that I could go, anyway, since I'm on the straight and narrow now.

"But…" He looks at me from under his lashes, probably trying to be cute, and only sort of succeeding. "Not everybody's twenty-one, so they can't get into the bars…or strip clubs."

I feel my eye twitch. "Uh-huh…"

"And since Burnham polices the Frat Farm pretty seriously during September, we were hoping we could have the party here."

"Here? In this apartment?"

"Yeah," he says quickly. "It would just be this one time, ever. I promise."

"You want to have a bunch of drunk frat guys and strippers here, in my apartment? The one I moved into with the express understanding it was for studious homebodies only?"

He's trying not to laugh. "Yes."

"Crosbie, no. Get out."

"It'll just be this once, Nora. I swear. I'll never ask you for anything again."

"Stop looking at me like that. It's not working." I think about how awkward I felt hurrying past Crosbie and Kellan on my way to the bathroom; what would I do with a bunch of drunk guys and strippers? Hunker down in my bedroom and hope I didn't have to pee all night?

"What's the problem?" he asks. "I'm sorry we can't invite you, but it's guys only, unless you're there to strip."

"That's sweet."

"I promise to keep everyone out of your room," he says. "All this..." He gestures to my meager belongings, "will be safe."

"What am I supposed to do during this party, Crosbie? I don't—" I stop myself before I can blurt out that I don't have any friends or anywhere else to stay. I could go to work or hang out at the library until it closes at eleven, but after that I'd be wandering around on my own, and I don't imagine the party will wind down early.

I see realization dawn. "You can...you can stay in my room," he announces, sounding pleased with himself. "The door locks, I'll stay here all night, most of the guys will be here, and no one will know you're there. I'll even change the sheets for you."

I shake my head. "This isn't—"

"One night," he says. "And I'll owe you."

How the hell did my plan to stay away from the Frat Farm fall to pieces so quickly? Now I'm about to agree to not only spend the night there, but spend the night in Crosbie Lucas's room.

"If it's the Crosbabes thing, I swear to God I'll kill anyone who talks about you. No one will think we…whatever."

I run a hand across my brow. "It's not that."

"Then—"

"Show me a magic trick."

His grin freezes. "What?"

"Right now. Show me a magic trick."

He stares at me for a long moment. "Why?"

"Because I want to see one."

"And then what?"

"Then I'll let you throw your party here."

He scrutinizes my face, and I really wish I wasn't standing here with messy hair and no makeup, ready for bed, with Crosbie Lucas eight inches away, peering at me with so much doubt that I know no one has ever asked to see his tricks without fully intending to mock him afterward.

"I won't laugh," I promise.

His chest puffs up a bit. "I don't care if you laugh."

"Then I—"

"You need cash for this one. Two bills."

I hear the stubborn note in his voice, the unwillingness to back down from a challenge. This is the guy who studies for a class that hasn't even begun, then spends an hour on the elliptical and runs ten miles that same night. I don't even care if the trick is stupid or disastrous; I'm not going to laugh at him when he's trying. Instead I crouch next to my "bed" and dig in my purse, glancing over when Crosbie sits on the mat facing me.

"Are a five and a one okay?"

"Yeah. Perfect."

I pass him the bills then sit down too, cross-legged, so I can watch. He sets the five on his knee then folds the one lengthwise and shows it to me. "A normal one dollar bill, folded in half. Any questions?"

"No."

"All right. Do the same with the five." He hands me the bill and I carefully fold it lengthwise. When I finish he's waiting patiently, still holding the first bill between his fingers. "Good. Fold it in half again, the other way."

I do, and he takes the folded five back and places the one behind it. He flips the bills back and forth so I can see that it's the folded one pressed to the back of the folded five like a lowercase *t*. "Pretty straight forward," he says. "Now count to three."

I know there has to be something shady going on here, but whatever it is, I can't see it. "One…two…three."

As I count he jerks his hand slightly, and on the third count the one dollar bill suddenly slips through the folded halves of the five so it's scissored in between. "How did—"

"Shh. I'm not done. See how it's in there?" He tugs the one so it bumps against the edge of the five, trapped inside.

"Crosbie, seriously, how—"

He ignores me. "Now watch." I stare closely as he tugs the one against the solid folded edge. "One," he says. "Two. Three." On the count of three the one dollar bill pops through the five and comes free in his hand.

I've only just managed to shut my mouth when it falls open again. My eyes fly to his. "Tell me how you did that."

He looks decidedly pleased with my reaction. "You wanted a trick, and you got one. I'll give you the key to my place on Friday and you can spend the night. I'll protect your trusty yoga mat while you're gone."

"I don't even do yoga."

"No?" He glances down at my bare legs, pale against the dark blue of my shorts. "Could have fooled me."

He returns the money and stands, and I do too. If he were any taller, he'd be too big, but I'm five-five, and he's not even six feet. I like his height. He's so broad that any taller would be too tall; he'd be enormous. Right now he just feels like he takes up a lot of space. Suddenly I'm too warm in my sweatshirt; I'm wide awake when I should be falling asleep.

He's about to say something when a sharp rap on the door startles us, and we both turn to see Kellan peering in. "Cros?" he says, looking between us. "What are you…?"

"Just showing Nora a trick," he says.

Kellan looks suspicious. "What kind of trick? I promised you wouldn't bother her."

"He wasn't bothering me," I say quickly. "And it was a pretty good trick. You should see it sometime."

The suspicion fades to surprise. "Oh yeah?"

I try to sound casual. "If you want."

"Maybe I will."

He steps back as Crosbie exits. "Good night, Nora," he says, before Kellan closes the door on him.

"Good night, Crosbie," I say to no one.

chapter five

My full class load and shifts at Beans keep me busy, but the real reason I haven't opened the boxes containing the pieces of my bed frame and desk is because I don't want to. I've set up the box spring and mattress in a corner of the room, dutifully covered them in a fitted sheet and comforter, and now inch out of my room whenever Kellan's around so he doesn't see that I have neither the inclination nor the know-how to build things.

It's Friday evening, the night of Kellan's twenty-first birthday, and I have to be at work for five. I met Crosbie on campus earlier and he gave me his house key and promised every guy in the frat would be gone by ten. This suits me just fine, since that's when I finish work and the last thing I need is to be the lone girl in a house full of horny frat guys on a Friday night.

At least, not this year.

Anyway, Crosbie told Kellan his parents were coming to take them out for dinner and they'd head back to the frat afterward to party, so Kellan's sitting on the couch in a suit and tie, a textbook open on his lap, video game controller in his hand, trying to straddle the line between college kid and dutiful son.

"Hey," I say, slipping on my jacket. I close my bedroom door behind me and wish not for the first time that it had a lock. As it stands, I'll have to trust Crosbie that he'll keep everyone out. Not that I have anything worth stealing—I've got my laptop in my bag, and nothing else I own is valuable. Or built.

Kellan pauses the game. "Off to work?"

"As always."

"You know, for roommates, we don't see very much of each other."

It's true. Most of my classes are in the morning so I can work in the afternoons and evenings, and Kellan picked afternoon classes so he could sleep in or run in the morning. If I'm not working I spend my evenings in the library studying— I really didn't think "applying myself" would be this difficult, but it is—and when I get home Kellan's either out or asleep.

To his credit, he's been keeping up his end of the bargain about not bringing people home. With the exception of Crosbie, he's done all his socializing away from the apartment. I pretend I'm doing the same, though I mostly just spend time by myself. Even though I know it has to be killing her, Marcela has not brought up the "roommates with Kellan McVey" thing, and Nate's too nice to really tease me about it.

Strangely enough, the person I talk to most…is Crosbie.

I'm not going to think about that.

I shoot him a smile. "Happy birthday. Enjoy your dinner." What I really mean is, "Coat this place in spray bleach after the strippers are gone," but when he grins back and says thanks, I do nothing more than wave goodbye and head downstairs to grab my bike.

Beans is bustling when I arrive. From five until eight we're pretty much run off our feet. We could use more staff, but the place is small enough that there wouldn't actually be room for more people behind the counter. As it stands Nate, Marcela and I bump hips and elbows and stomp on each other's feet with such regularity that we no longer bother with "ouches" and "sorrys."

When we finally catch a lull we slump against the counter as Nate makes us each an espresso. The silence has more to do with our tiredness than any lingering awkwardness, but Nate changes that when he says, "So. Kellan McVey's birthday."

I glance over at him. "Uh-huh."

"Big plans?"

I gesture to the shop. "This is my plan."

"It's his twenty-first birthday and he's not doing anything?"

"I didn't say he wasn't doing anything. *I'm* not doing anything. New leaf, remember?"

Marcela snorts into her espresso but manages to bite her tongue. After all these weeks I imagine she has a lot to say, but she's been remarkably composed. Or maybe she's just bottling it up, ready to explode at any moment.

"I saw this…" Nate starts, tugging his phone from his back pocket and pulling up his Facebook page. Somehow Nate manages to be invited to absolutely everything, though he never goes. I think it's a combination of him seeming older than us and therefore cooler, but not actually being older than us, and therefore not creepy. Even though I shouldn't look, both Marcela and I edge closer so we're standing on either side of Nate and peering down at his phone.

It's a group-only invite to a party at Kellan's apartment—our apartment—to celebrate TWENTY-ONE ROCKIN' GOOD YEARS. It promises strippers, beer, and oh yeah, strippers. It actually says strippers seven times.

Marcela and Nate look at me, their expressions accusatory. "What?" I protest. "Look at the contact list—I'm not even invited."

"It's at your home," Marcela points out.

"Guys only, unless you're a stripper."

Nate frowns. "So what are you doing tonight?"

I shrug awkwardly. "Just…going somewhere else."

Marcela forgets she's mad at me for a second. "Where somewhere else?"

"Just a friend's house."

Her eyes flash. "You were able to make some 'decent' new friends?" She uses air quotes around "decent," even though I never used that word when I broke things off.

"I didn't say I needed 'decent' friends, I said I needed *different* friends."

"Better friends."

I try to take a calming breath. "Friends who don't like to party. Who didn't hide in backseats while I got arrested."

She recoils slightly, and I see the flash of pain on her face before it smoothes back into that perfect, angry mask. "You shouldn't have hidden behind a fucking compost bin."

"No kidding!"

"Who's this 'friend?'"

"It's no one."

"Is it Kellan McVey?"

"No!"

Her eyes narrow. "It's Crosbie Lucas."

"No," I say too quickly. "It isn't."

"Are you fucking him?"

"Keep your voices down!" Nate finally snaps.

"Who my friends are is none of your business."

"It's hard to make 'nobody' my business," Marcela retorts.

"Then don't."

"Girls—" Nate tries to interject.

"I'm going to do inventory," Marcela says, whirling on a black leather heel and stomping into the kitchen.

I feel hot and dizzy with anger, the espresso forgotten in my hand. I set it on the counter with a clatter and try to compose myself.

"I'm sorry," Nate says after a moment. "I just thought—"

"It's not your fault," I say stiffly. A customer has bravely approached the register and orders a skim latte. I plaster on a smile as I make the drink and slide it over.

"Are you okay?" Nate asks, lingering uncomfortably.

"Just fine."

"I don't mean the fight. I mean, living there. And whatever you're doing tonight."

"Everything's fine." But the words are less than convincing when I have to blink back tears afterward.

* * *

I wake up confused and disoriented. Warm orange light filters through the window, and when I reach for my phone to check the time, it's sitting on a desk, not an overturned milk crate.

Too many mornings last year I woke up much the same way, but this time when I warily turn my head to look beside me, the strange bed is empty.

Crosbie Lucas's bed.

True to his word, the house was empty when I arrived last night, and I'd dragged myself up the stairs, swapped out my work clothes for pajamas, and crawled right into bed. He'd washed the sheets as promised, and they're soft and lemony, the mattress the right balance between firm and giving.

Getting comfortable in Crosbie Lucas's bed is not a thing I am going to do. If the rumors are to be believed, a lot of girls have been in here, but very few have been invited back. And he's never had a girlfriend. He's committed to school and track, and while he makes time for fun, it's never serious. That's totally fine, it's just not a road I'm about to go down. Not that that's an option, anyway.

I change into jeans and a T-shirt, hurry across the hall to splash water on my face and brush my teeth, put on some mascara and lip gloss, then gather my things. I hesitate at the top of the stairs, listening for voices, but the house is still silent at this hour. I tiptoe down the steps as fast as I can, heart pounding when I make it outside without being spotted. The combination of a hastily packed overnight bag and my normally riotous hair has the two other girls creeping out of frat houses in last night's party clothes nodding at me as though we're partners in crime. I nod back even as I cringe inwardly. Because last year, that was me. A bunch of times.

I start to bike home, then detour, pretty sure whatever mess they made last night is still on full display. Instead I turn around and bike into town, parking my bike in front of a small café and heading inside to order an omelet. The combination of a good night's sleep and a full load of self pity has made me hungry. I pull out my laptop and bury myself in an English Lit assignment, coming up for air only when the server asks if I want a fourth cup of coffee. It's nearly noon and I promised myself I'd tackle building the desk and bed frame today. I turn down the coffee. It's time to face whatever horrors await me at the apartment.

I settle the bill and bike home, the late summer air crisp and clean. Burnham's campus is normally deserted on weekend mornings, the students sleeping off last night's overindulgence, and I pass just a handful of people as I wind my way along leafy side streets.

The apartment is quiet when I arrive, chaining my bike to the handrail along the steps before trudging up and sliding my key in the lock. The front entrance is tidy, Kellan's abundance of running shoes lined up neatly along one wall, my two pairs on the other. I add my boots to the group and climb the steps to the living room, expecting to find a dozen strangers sleeping on the floor, but there's only Crosbie, a dust rag in one hand, wiping down the coffee table.

"Hey," I say. No response. I realize he's got earbuds in and say it again, louder. Still nothing. I walk up and tap him on the shoulder. He leaps up and spins around so quickly we both yelp and stumble back. I catch myself on the entertainment console, shoulder blade smacking the TV, and he grabs the couch for balance.

"Fuck, Nora!" he exclaims, laughing, embarrassed, as he turns off the mp3 player and sticks it in his pocket. He's wearing jeans and a white dress shirt, unbuttoned over a wife beater. His feet are bare, short hair tousled, cheeks pink from the near heart attack. "You scared me."

"Sorry." I try not to laugh, but one sneaks out. "I said hi."

He pinches his brow. "I didn't hear you."

I glance around the empty space. Both bedroom doors are closed. "Is everyone gone?"

"Yeah. They left a little while ago."

"How was the party?"

"Pretty epic."

I turn slowly to take in the apartment. With the exception of two full trash bags waiting at the top of the stairs, a recycling bin overflowing with bottles, and a blown up photo of Pamela Anderson from one of her Playboy spreads taped to the wall, the place looks the same as usual. And it smells like Lysol.

"What'd you do to get stuck with cleaning duty?"

He shrugs. "Luck of the draw." Then he spots Pam. "Shit." He hurries to the wall and yanks down the life-size picture.

"Were you responsible for the décor, too?"

He blushes. "Sorta."

I pass him his keys. "Thanks. I took pictures of all your things and posted them on eBay."

"That's great. And I kept my promise—nobody went into your room but me and a couple of strippers." I glare at him and he smiles sweetly. "You're going to need some new sheets."

I head for my door. "I know you're kidding, but I'm still going to check." I take a breath and turn the knob. The room is exactly how I left it.

"About this."

I jump. Crosbie's right behind me. So close I can feel his breath on my hair when he speaks. I don't move a muscle, every traitorous part of me unwilling to step away even though I know I have to. "About what?" I hear myself say, motionless.

"This." He pushes open the door farther and gestures at my lame set up. "Why haven't you built your stuff yet?"

I wilt a bit, disappointed. I don't know what I expected him to say. *"About this strange chemistry we seem to have, Nora. About the fact that I'm the only one left in your apartment, and you slept in my bed last night. What are we going to do about this?"*

I clear my throat. "It's on my to-do list."

"You need a hand with anything?"

A strange tingling starts in my feet and shoots straight up my legs, converging between my thighs. *There is something I could use a hand with, Crosbie...*

And last year, maybe I would have said those words. But this year? Nora Bora 2.0? Even with a three-month sexual hiatus? She's going to say no.

"If you don't mind."

He slaps his hands against his thighs. "I don't mind. I like this sort of thing."

I stomp all over the strange warm feelings that are trying to bloom, like they're a patch of weeds that needs to be destroyed. It's not easy, and maybe one or two twisted tendrils remain, but I do a pretty decent job. Especially when Crosbie takes off the button-up so he's just in jeans and the wife beater, muscles flexing as he grabs the box holding the pieces of my soon-to-be desk and lays it on the floor.

"Do you have a box cutter?"

"Sure. I sleep with one under my pillow."

It takes him a second to realize I'm being sarcastic. "Jerk." He makes a face at me. "Kellan's got a toolbox under the sink. Want to grab it?"

I come back with the toolbox, then join Crosbie on the floor as he cuts open the box and finds the instructions. To my surprise, he reads them. Or, rather, looks at the pictures, since there are no words. In any case, he doesn't try to pretend he knows everything, like he's a desk building master. Once he's done with the paper he sets it aside and starts assembling pieces, telling me what to hold, what to look for, what to do. I should be annoyed, but I really didn't want to do this so I don't mind at all. And after an entire summer of solitude, it's kind of nice to have someone to hang out with.

"What'd you get up to last night?" he asks. He's got his lips pursed around two screws he's holding in his mouth as he twists a third one into the wood.

"Not much." I concentrate on holding the boards at a ninety degree angle so my desk isn't tilted. "I just worked then went to bed."

"On a Friday?"

"I'm not very exciting."

He glances at me. "I'm sure you're very exciting, Nora."

I laugh and he smiles around the screws, fishing one out of his mouth and sliding it into the next hole.

"How'd you do on your quiz?"

"What? Oh, Bio? Aced it."

"Good for you."

He shrugs and moves onto the last screw. "You know what's weird?"

This whole situation? "What's weird?"

"I fucking hate school."

"You do? I thought you wanted to teach."

"Yeah. I want to be a teacher. Stupid, right?"

"Not really."

"No? Why not?"

"If it's what you want to do, I don't see why it's stupid."

"Because I hate school," he repeats. "And I suck at it. Why do you think I have to study for hours to learn what other people can learn in five minutes?"

I watch him assemble a drawer like he's buttering a piece of bread. There's nothing stupid about him. "Because you know how to work hard?" I offer. "There's nothing wrong with trying."

He's focused on his task, but I see his mouth quirk. "I guess you'd know."

"What do you mean?"

"I mean, how you're always at the library. You've got five classes and a job. You work hard, too."

I think about last year, how I did just the opposite and landed myself in this position. "Well, I have to."

"Yeah? Why?"

"To have a good life. Isn't that what everybody wants?"

"I guess so."

"You want to have a bad life, Crosbie?"

Now he grins. "Yeah, Nora. I want to have a terrible life."

I laugh and hand him the piece of wood he points to. "What do you want to teach?"

He blows out a breath and begins work on the second

drawer. "Maybe history."

"I thought you'd say Phys Ed."

"Why?"

I roll my eyes. "Oh, I don't know, Crosbie. Just a guess."

"Is it this?" he asks, flexing his biceps. And though I do my very best to look unimpressed, a little frisson of sexual awareness trips down my spine. He's very...big.

"I have no idea what you're talking about."

He laughs and gestures for me to move aside so he can work on the other desk leg. "What about you? What's going to make your life so great?"

"I don't know. But a degree seems like the first step."

"A degree in what?"

"I'm still undecided."

"Really? I'd think a girl who spent her whole summer at school would be working toward a very specific goal."

My goal was to raise my average to a C+ from a D- and complete my two and a half months of community service without attracting too much attention. "Just trying to keep on top of things."

"What'd you do when the campus was so empty?"

I swallow. I don't want to lie, but I'm not ready for another person to know how badly I messed up. "Just worked, mostly. Studied and worked. Went for...walks." Where I picked up trash along the highway.

"Alone?"

"There were four people on my floor," I say. Eight in my clean-up crew. "Two didn't speak English, and the other girl spent twenty hours a day practicing piano. Her fingers actually bled."

He grimaces. "That's gross."

"Tell me about the party."

He grunts. "You don't want to know."

"Why not?" If I can't actually attend parties, maybe I can live vicariously through Crosbie. But even as I think the words, I find myself hoping he doesn't tell me about hooking up with strippers—or any other girls.

"You ever been to a frat party, Nora?"

I avoid his stare. He probably thinks I'm too timid, but I just find it hard to meet his eye when I'm lying. "No."

"Well, stay far away. They can get pretty out of control."

"But you can handle it?"

Another laugh. "I kind of love it. It makes all the other shit worth it. It's the only thing that comes easy to me."

"Partying?"

"Yeah."

I think about last year. How I'd thrown myself headfirst into that world. How great it had been. Until it wasn't anymore.

"What do you do for fun?" he asks. I realize he's trying to be kind. To make my assumed hobbies of knitting and star gazing sound interesting.

"Ghost hunting," I say.

"You're a fucking liar, Nora."

I can't keep a straight face. "I don't do anything fun," I tell him. And this time it's easy to meet his stare. "I kind of...can't."

"You can't have fun?"

"I can't balance it," I clarify. "How you study and run and party—I can't. It's all or nothing for me. Always has been. I don't know why."

"So you just study? You never have fun?"

"Studying's not the worst thing in the world."

"Well, that's a ringing endorsement. Okay, stand up." The desk assembled, we both rise as he arranges it upright and positions it against the wall. He rattles it a bit, one big hand wrapped around the edge, and I want so badly to do something "fun" right now. To feel that hand on me. "Look good to you?" he asks.

"Yes," I say too quickly. A bit breathlessly.

He gives me a weird look. "Are you okay?"

"Totally fine."

"Did anyone bother you last night?"

"No. I didn't even see anyone."

His brow is wrinkled, and slowly it relaxes. "Good."

Because my bed takes up too much room, we assemble the wooden frame in the living room, where there's just barely enough space. As before, Crosbie does all the work. I mostly watch and pass him pieces. I don't know if he senses that things were getting weird in my room or he just wants to change the subject, but he asks again about my "Steve Holt!" artwork and from there we just talk about TV.

When the frame is assembled he carefully edges it through the doorway and back into my room. I stand at the end closest to the door and hoist up the frame, then he lifts the mattress as I push the frame under. It sounded better in theory, but we eventually get it in place, and when I start to smooth the rumpled blankets, Crosbie stops me.

"What?"

"You've gotta make sure it's sturdy," he says.

"I beg your pardon?"

"Up you go." He grips my arm and herds me onto the bed so I'm standing in the center. "Jump," he says.

"I'm not going to—" I feel absolutely ridiculous.

"Jump, Nora. For my peace of mind."

"I'm not planning to do a lot of jumping on this bed, Crosbie. If the frame collapses, it's a six-inch fall. I'll survive."

He folds his arms. "Jump."

"Screw off." I try to climb down but he blocks me. "Crosbie—"

"Have fun," he says. "Just for a minute. I want to know that you can."

"All right, you know what?" Now I'm just annoyed. "I appreciate your help, but you're making me feel really stupid. I know how to have fun, I'm just choosing not to right now. I don't need to perform for you to be fun."

He looks surprised. "It's not a performance." Then he glances at the bed. "Though I can see how it might be misconstrued."

He doesn't stop me when I step down, and I feel a little bit bereft. Like maybe that was my chance and I missed it. And later tonight by myself, if I jump on the bed alone, it won't be nearly as fun as if Crosbie were here.

"Okay," he says, stepping up onto the bed. "I gave you a shot. But if the frame breaks, you're on the hook for it."

"What are you—"

He starts to jump. The mattress squeaks, the pillows bounce, but nothing breaks. And still he jumps. "This is the most fun ever, Nora!" he mock squeals.

"Shut up. Get down."

"I can't believe you're missing out on all this fun!"

"Knock it off."

"One jump."

"You're going to break something."

"Who cares? You're paying for it."

"Crosbie—" It's impossible to keep a straight face. This may have started as a joke, but I think he's really enjoying himself. And when he holds out a hand, I take it and climb on.

"Just once," I say.

"Totally," he agrees.

I jump and the frame breaks.

The bottom left corner gives out, sending the mattress skidding to the end. Crosbie and I collapse, banging our foreheads together, squawking our surprise and alarm. When we finally come to a halt I'm halfway off the edge of the bed, held up only by Crosbie's big arm around my waist. His eyes are wide with shock and then they crinkle at the corners as he starts to laugh. I worm my way out of his grasp and flop onto the floor and start to laugh too.

"Shit," he gasps. "Nora, I'm so sorry."

"This is what happens when people have fun!" I say, sticking a stern finger in the air. "Never again."

He swats my hand. "It's your fault," he says. "I know I'm not supposed to say this to a woman, but I think you're too heavy. Your heaviness is what broke the bed."

I'm a hundred pounds soaking wet, and, as Marcela liked to say, I carry my weight in my boobs. I know I'm not fat, and Crosbie knows it, and that's why I'm not really angry when I snatch up a fallen pillow and smack him with it.

"Sorry." He laughs and rolls away, face red. "Should I have said 'big boned?'"

"You're going to hell, Crosbie. Fix my bed frame." I feel hot and happy, despite the mess. Despite the fact that the wood is snapped and splintered and I don't think it can be fixed.

He slides down the angled mattress and joins me on the floor to inspect the damage. "I have to go."

"Crosbie Lucas."

"Bye, Nora. Take care." He stands but doesn't actually go anywhere, staring at the ruined frame.

I stand, too. "Product defect?" I try.

"Definitely."

"I guess it'll have to be taken apart now."

He glances at his watch. "Wow. Is that the time?"

I smile a little. "Thank you, Crosbie."

"For breaking your bed? No problem. Wherever, whenever."

I laugh. "For the first part. This…not so much."

"I'll help you pack it back up and drive it to the store. You don't have to wait for the delivery. We can do it today."

"I'm sure you have better things to do."

"I do, but I'm trying to be a gentleman."

"You nailed it."

"Who nailed who now?"

We whirl around to see Kellan standing in the doorway, arms crossed, one dark brow raised suspiciously. And I suppose an off-kilter bed, scattered pillows and beddings, and Crosbie's discarded shirt might suggest someone had gotten nailed, but…they hadn't. Unfortunately.

"I bought a defective bed frame," I say, pointing to the mangled corner.

"Oh." He frowns and comes inside for a better view. "What were you doing to break your bed?"

It's so hard to keep a straight face. "I was jumping on it."

"You were jumping on your bed?"

Crosbie coughs into the crook of his elbow, trying to mask his laughter.

"Yes."

"I'm surprised, Nora. That doesn't seem like you."

"I thought it sounded fun."

"Well, they might not give you a refund if they know you were just jumping around on it like that. It's irresponsible."

Crosbie coughs again and hustles out of the room. After a second we hear the tap in the kitchen sink turn on and I picture him drowning out the noise of his laughter.

"I'll just tell them it came that way."

Kellan stares at me like he can't decide if I'm serious or not, then his face relaxes and he smiles. "They'll believe you. Who wouldn't?"

He returns to the living room and I hear him ask Crosbie what he's still doing here.

"I was cleaning up," Crosbie replies.

"Why is your shirt in her room?"

"It's not."

"It's the one you were wearing last night."

"Dude, then I don't know how it got in there. You know what I did last night. Nora was not it."

Their voices grow muffled as they enter Kellan's room, so I hang Crosbie's shirt on the out-facing doorknob and gently close the door on their conversation.

chapter six

I don't see Crosbie much in the week after the bed incident. We don't end up going to Ikea together, though a couple of days later they do take away the "defective" frame and swap it out for a new one. The delivery comes when Kellan is home, and he surprises me by putting it together before I return from class, saying he's concerned about my building skills and making me promise not to jump anymore. Otherwise, he's not really around all that often. He's been hanging out at Alpha Sigma Phi, so Crosbie doesn't have a reason to turn up, either. I try to pretend I don't notice, but I do.

"Earth to Nora. This is Earth, asking Nora to report to home base."

"You're a huge loser."

Nate laughs, unoffended. It's Tuesday evening, ten days since the bed hopping debacle, and we're at the Burnham library near the center of campus. We have Intro to French together, and have to put together a cheesy dialogue about a French person teaching an English speaker how to order a cup of coffee.

"How's this for a first line?" Nate asks. "*Bonjour.*"

"*Bonjour?* We've been here for thirty minutes and you came up with one word?"

"That word says a lot!"

"It says you're going to fail."

He snorts. "You're one to talk. You've been doodling

'Mrs. Kellan McVey' all over the assignment worksheet."

I gasp. "I have not! I'm brainstorming."

"Yeah? What'd you come up with?"

"*Je veux boire le café.*" *I want to drink coffee.* I think.

"What does that mean?"

"Are you even listening to the CDs?" I've been putting in close to two hours a week, and I'm pretty sure I'd be screwed if I unexpectedly wound up in France. Or Québec.

"No." Nate shakes his head. "What do they say?"

I laugh and toss my pen across the table. It bounces off his shoulder and he snickers and snatches it up. We're on the fourth floor, which is relatively quiet at eight o'clock at night, so there's no one to glare or shush us. It's this very silence that makes the low male chuckle filtering through the bookshelves loud enough to jolt us in our seats.

"*Whaaaat?*" Nate mouths, looking delighted.

I'm about to tell him it's probably nothing when a female voice joins in the laughter, ending abruptly on a heated moan.

How annoying.

I'm trying to study.

I'm trying to concentrate.

I'm trying not to be terribly jealous.

I mean, I went from high school where I had zero relationships, to college, where the only way I met guys was when Marcela and I were partying. The combination of a high volume of alcohol, lowered inhibitions, and Marcela's expert wingwoman skills led to a lot of introductions—and a few that went beyond mere introducing.

But I haven't been drunk since the night I got arrested, and I haven't had sex since then either, which puts me firmly at the four-month mark of my sexual hiatus and I have to say…I miss it. Especially when every time I see Kellan he's shirtless or sweaty or eating or playing video games—whatever the guy does, it's sexy. What's worse, of course, is knowing that every time I close my eyes, the guy I picture leaning in to kiss me isn't Kellan at all.

I know I'm lonely. And with the exception of Nate, who's

among the legions of men lusting after Marcela, Crosbie's the only guy I've really talked to or hung out with in eons. And as weird as it is, I've kind of missed him this past week. I'd gotten used to coming home from work and finding him camped out on the couch, eyes glazed as he blows up cars and robs banks with Kellan, tearing his gaze away long enough to spare a smile, switching that intense focus from the TV to me, just for a second. Which is all it takes to kick my hormones into gear and wish he'd do so much more.

The moans are increasing, mostly from the female half of the equation, and they're muffled now, like he's covering her mouth. Nate and I are tucked back in the corner near the balcony, so unless they'd scoped out the floor or spotted us from the ground level, they have every reason to think they're alone.

Nate scribbles something on a piece of paper. *Ten bucks says it's Kellan and a blonde.*

That's kind of like putting your money on Meryl Streep being nominated for an Oscar.

He writes again. *Go look.*

I swallow a laugh. *No.* Two emphatic underlines.

Chicken.

I'm boring now, remember?

I certainly do. Zzz.

I kick him under the table and he yelps.

I dare you, he writes. *Triple double dog dare you.*

"How old are you?" I hiss.

He leans in. "Not a hundred and five like you've been acting."

I recoil, offended. "I have not—"

"You're killing yourself. If you're not going to do anything fun, the least you can do is spy on the people who are and report back to me."

"I think you have some kind of once-removed voyeur fetish."

He grins. "Guilty."

But I really don't need any more prompting. You can't get

arrested for accidentally noticing a couple getting it on in the library. It'll only take a minute, my grades won't suffer. No phone calls to my parents, the Dean, or the police. What's the harm?

Plus I'm so bored.

I inch back my chair and stand, my sneakers making no sound on the worn old carpet. The moans increase as I approach the aisle stuffed with books on capitalism, and I glance over my shoulder at Nate. He gives me the thumbs up as I turn one aisle before the lovebirds and crouch as I creep along. Halfway down I spot two pairs of legs—one in denim, one barely covered by a miniskirt—and I ease closer, their heavy breathing more than masking any noise my approach might make. Hell, I could topple over a shelf and I'm pretty sure it wouldn't interrupt the makeout.

I'm about twenty books away when the female half of the equation moans, "Oh, Crosbie."

His low chuckle, the one I've been missing all week, is immediately, terribly, unwelcome. My skin prickles with nauseating goose bumps and I feel a strange, achy clench in my chest.

"I got you," he murmurs.

Any fleeting hope I'd held that it was a *different* Crosbie shatters. It's him.

And it's certainly his reputation.

Somehow, when I thought it was Kellan, I didn't really care what I'd find.

But this hurts.

Instead of wisely returning to my table and telling Nate we have to go, I retrace my steps to the end of the aisle, snatch a book off the shelf, and take a breath before turning into the occupied aisle as though searching for an interesting book on capitalism.

And there they are.

Ten feet away, grinding against the shelf, his hips pinning hers to the row of books I'm never going to touch. They're fully clothed, at least, only their lips involved in the encounter, and even though they look like they're glued together, Crosbie jerks away the second he spots me.

His partner in library crime looks dazed and confused until she follows his gaze to discover the problem, and even though I knew what I'd find before I rounded that corner, I still hear myself stammer a pretty convincing, "Sorry, I didn't know—" before I race back to the table where Nate waits.

"Pay up," he says, holding out his hand.

"Joke's on you," I say, trying to act like I find the whole thing amusing and not appallingly, horribly painful. "It wasn't Kellan."

"It was too."

"It wasn't. I swear."

He frowns as he realizes I'm jamming my books in my bag like there's a fire and they're the only thing I need to rescue.

"What are you—"

"I just remembered I have to do something," I lie, utterly unconvincing.

"Nora, what—" His eyes focus on something over my shoulder and I know that Crosbie and his Crosbabe have fixed their clothing and emerged from the aisle.

"Don't," I say tightly, when the look on his face changes from confusion to concern. "Don't say anything."

"Nora, I—"

"Please." I think I might cry. And it's so stupid—I don't care about Crosbie, I don't *want* to care about Crosbie, and I never thought he cared about me.

I grab my bag and stride toward the stairs at the far end of the floor, my route keeping me parallel to Crosbie and his friend. But their pace is no match for mine and I reach the top of the stairs just in time to hear her demand to know why they can't take the elevator.

I jog down the stairs and maneuver my way through the main level and out the front doors to my bike, locked up in the rack on the sidewalk. My fingers tremble as I fumble for the combination, and the tumblers align just as I hear the front doors open and Crosbie's date's shrill inquiry about why they have to walk so fast.

I sling my leg over the seat and don't look back as I pedal home as fast as I can. The sidewalk is damp and edged in the first fallen leaves of the season, but not even the welcome signs of fall improve my mood.

I know I'm being stupid.

Just like I knew streaking down Main Street was a bad idea.

Just like I knew blowing off Art History—five weeks in a row—was not smart.

How I knew partying the night before my Linguistics midterm was a mistake.

I know things are bad for me, but I do them anyway. And letting those stray shoots of feelings for Crosbie stay when I should have gotten down on my hands and knees and torn them up before they could take root—that was a mistake.

And I am done making mistakes.

I usually chain my bike to the handrail, but tonight I drag it up the front steps and ditch it in the foyer of our apartment. I stomp upstairs but there's no one to impress with my bad mood because Kellan's not home—as usual. I turn off all the lights to make it look like I'm not home, either, like I have plenty of interesting places to be while some people are getting off in the library.

I flop onto my bed and stare at the dark ceiling. My heart is pounding and my temples are damp with sweat.

I mean, what the fuck.

* * *

"Sorry about last night."

I glance up at Nate as I tie on my apron in the kitchen at Beans. "It's no big deal."

Marcela's there too, not pretending not to eavesdrop. Not pretending Nate didn't fill her in on the whole humiliating debacle.

"I tried calling you a couple of times—you didn't pick up."

"I was listening to the French lessons." Technically true, but my phone was on my milk crate nightstand and I heard it vibrate, I just refused to look at the display. Just as I heard a tentative knock at the front door but didn't dare get up to answer. I didn't know what I'd say if it were Crosbie, and if it wasn't him, that would have somehow been worse. So I did what I always do: I chose one end of the spectrum and I stayed there. Confront my demons or ignore them? Hello, denial. I'm Nora.

"I thought you had a thing for Kellan," Marcela remarks. She sticks a tray of muffins in the convection oven, a wave of heat wafting over me as I walk toward the swinging door to the shop.

"Me too," I say.

They follow me out front, and I sigh when there's just one customer in the shop, an old man who always comes to browse the artwork but never buys anything.

"I was just surprised," I say. "That's all. I barely know Crosbie. I'm worried things might be awkward at home. He's there all the time."

Nate and Marcela share a look.

"What?"

"He came here last night," Marcela says.

I grow very still. "What?"

"Around nine. He came in asking for you. He looked stressed."

I take a breath. "He was probably trying to find Kellan."

"I don't think so."

"Well, maybe he just wanted another brownie."

"He didn't flirt with me at all."

"Huh." That *is* weird. Though it's hardly placating to know that after he dropped off his date he came looking for me, his second choice. It doesn't mean anything, and I can't let it. I'm barely a month into my new life and despite my best efforts, I'm failing. Again.

And I really can't afford to. It's not like I come from nothing. My parents worked hard, saved their money, and instilled in me the importance of doing the same. And I did— all through high school. I never got into trouble, never rebelled, never so much as dyed my hair. And it's not like I had dreams of robbing banks or getting a dozen tattoos, I just wanted to have *fun* last year. Just for a little bit, I wanted to let loose.

Nate clears his throat and wanders over to chat up the old man, and for a second Marcela and I just stand side-by-side at the counter and watch. She uses one fingernail, painted black, to pick at a sticker someone stuck on the counter, and I don't know what to do. This is where I want to be, even though I shouldn't.

Story of my life.

"I'm sorry you got arrested," she says eventually, watching the corners of the sticker peel up. "And I'm sorry I didn't say anything."

I keep watching her fingernail. "It's not your fault."

"Well, it was my idea."

"Okay, so it was mostly your fault."

She laughs a little. "And if I made you fail your classes last year, I'm sorry for that too. I know you have a scholarship and you need to keep your grades up."

I glance at her. I'm terrible at confrontation, if last night's events weren't proof enough. "You didn't make me fail. I failed all by myself. I was just embarrassed."

"Do you really never go out anymore?"

"Never."

"Where'd you stay the night of Kellan's birthday?"

I sigh. "Don't laugh."

"Did you hide in the closet and spy?"

I smile. "No. I stayed in Crosbie's room at the frat house."

Her mouth opens.

"He wasn't there," I say hastily. "He stayed at my place." I assume he did, anyway. Perhaps he'd been in the library all night.

"Do you like him?"

I shrug. "I thought I did. A little bit. But…no. I can't. I need to focus on getting my grades up and staying out of trouble."

"Last year was fun."

"It was awesome."

"And this year has been terrible. I hang out with Nate, like, all the time."

"Outside of work?"

"Yes. He makes me go to vegan restaurants and buy candles and watch foreign films. He's a hipster stereotype and it's killing me."

"He's in love with you."

"It doesn't change anything."

I watch Nate show the old man the newest set of nesting dolls. We all know the guy's never going to buy anything; he comes in three days a week and doesn't order so much as a coffee. But still Nate holds out hope.

"What do I do?" I ask. Marcela has stopped picking at the sticker and now I take over. I've been dying to ask her that very question all month, and now I feel like I can barely breathe as I wait for her answer.

"You just get on with your life," she says, eyes on Nate. "And you forget all about the other person."

"Sounds simple."

Her red lips curve. "Nate," she calls. "We're closing shop early. Lock it up."

Nate looks surprised but doesn't argue, and fifteen minutes later we're out the door, the three of us bundled up against a chilly fall wind as we hustle down the street in the direction of the bank and the nearest bar. Marcela and I stand guard as Nate drops off the small deposit, then we dart across the street into Marvin's, a crowded pub that's popular with Burnham's older students.

The music is muted, the air is warm, and everyone's wearing cords and cardigans. In her silver sequined top, black tights, and thigh-high white pleather boots, Marcela makes a statement. As usual, all eyes are on her as she picks her way through the crowd and finds us a tall table in the corner. Nate heads up to the bar to grab a round of shots, and I take a deep breath. I know I shouldn't be here, but I miss this. Not the alcohol, but the atmosphere. The people. Not being home alone by myself. Again.

Nate returns a few minutes later with six shot glasses precariously clustered in his hand and Marcela helps arrange them on the table. "What are you going to drink?" she asks, blinking at him, deadpan.

He makes a face and she grins and I do too, then we all take a glass. "What are we toasting?" Nate asks. "The end of the Cold War?"

"Yeah," Marcela says. "And bygones being bygones, and fuck Crosbie Lucas."

Nate shrugs, not fully comprehending, but gamely echoes, "Fuck Crosbie Lucas."

I didn't think I'd laugh again for a long time, but I'm laughing when I say, "Fuck Crosbie Lucas," and we all toast to it.

* * *

It's shortly after midnight when I stumble in the front door. The stumbling has more to do with the fact that my legs and fingers are numb from the bike ride home than the alcohol. I mean, don't get me wrong—I'm a little bit drunk, but nothing crazy. Not out of control.

"Middle ground drunk," Marcela called it, when I lamented my inability to hang out in the center of the spectrum. "You will only be middle ground drunk this evening, I will see to it."

She did a pretty good job. We'd laughed and danced and flirted and made up, and it's a surprise and a relief to learn that she missed me too. Actually, it's an enormous relief, even if hanging out with Marcela did involve ditching work early and drinking on a school night. But what the hell—I had fun. Finally.

Kellan and Crosbie are watching something on TV when I come up the stairs, and I spot the DVD box for the first season of *Arrested Development* sitting on the dining table as I enter. I squint at the screen and recognize the familiar characters, and when I look at Kellan he's got the same "I don't get it" look Marcela had when I made her watch it.

"Steve Holt," I say.

Kellan scratches his chin and glances over at me. "Who?"

I can practically feel Crosbie's stare, but I refuse to make eye contact as I head into the kitchen and pour myself a glass of water. I'm a bit woozy and I brace myself against the counter as I drink.

"Are you drunk?" Kellan calls, muting the show. It sounds like he's trying not to laugh.

"Just a little bit," I reply. "I'll be okay."

"Where were you?"

"Marvin's. Near work."

"With who?"

"With whom," I correct, putting my glass in the sink and heading for my room. "And that's none of your business."

He raises an eyebrow. "I might like drunk Nora."

"You did," I say, without meaning to. "Good night." I enter my bedroom and close the door.

When I first realized Kellan didn't remember our hookup, I was mortified. But now I think I was just naïve. My "relationships" last year were fleeting and shallow, and because I was only doing it to convince myself I was somebody exciting, I wasn't even remotely invested in them, emotionally. The longest one lasted a month, and that's just because it was the guy who took my virginity during frosh week and we felt obligated to keep seeing each other.

Kellan is the crush everybody has. Crosbie is the sidekick.

He's the Nora to Kellan's Marcela.

He's the one you forget.

chapter seven

I have a ten o'clock class on Thursday mornings, so I sleep in until nine then stumble bleary-eyed out of my room to hunt down some frozen waffles for breakfast. It's chilly in the apartment and I shift from foot to foot as I shiver in my sweatshirt and shorts waiting for the toaster to finish its job.

"Hey."

I jolt and turn around to find Kellan on the living room floor, dressed in his running clothes and touching his toes. "What are you doing here?" I never see Kellan in the mornings and I've kind of gotten used to having the place to myself. He's either sleeping in—or sleeping out—when I leave for class, and this is unusual.

"Group run," he says, switching legs. "In ten minutes."

I glance out the window. The sun is up, glinting off the yellowing leaves of the trees that line the street. It's already shaping up to be a much better day than yesterday. In fact, now that I've made the decision to forget Crosbie Lucas, everything is looking up.

"Have fun," I say, stacking the waffles on a plate, dousing them in syrup, and preparing to retreat to my room. I know Kellan's running group slowly picks up members as they begin their route, and Crosbie normally comes inside when they reach our place. My new plan does not involve seeing Crosbie nine hours after the plan went into effect.

"Hey," Kellan says, standing and cracking his back.

71

I pause at the door to my room, waffle halfway to my mouth. "What's up?"

"Thank you."

"You're welcome?" I have no idea what he's thanking me for.

"I suppose I should have realized this on my own, but Crosbie told me last night that you let them host my birthday party here, and I appreciate it. I know that's not what we agreed, so…thank you."

"Ah. You're welcome."

"And…" he adds, again halting my return to my bedroom. "I think we should go out."

I'm already stopped, but now I freeze completely, half an unchewed waffle in my mouth. "What?"

He grins and reaches back to grab his foot to stretch. "As a thank-you. Let's go out to dinner tomorrow. You know Verre Plein, the French place on the edge of town? What about there?"

I'm so stunned I can barely speak. I'm pretty sure I have maple syrup on my face and my hair is a mess and I haven't brushed my teeth and this—*this*—is when Kellan McVey asks me out?

"Are you serious?" I try to swallow the enormous bite of waffle without chewing.

"Yeah," he says, smile widening. He's the hottest guy I've ever seen. Confidence practically radiates off of him, never quite edging into obnoxious territory, unlike somebody whose name I will have forgotten by lunchtime. "It's really nice," he continues, when I don't answer. "I went once with my parents—you have to wear a tie and everything. I mean, not you—just I'll wear—I mean, you can wear—Fuck." He groans. "I haven't had coffee yet."

"You don't drink coffee."

He laughs, embarrassed. "Right."

"Sure," I say. "I'll go." I don't want to read too much into this. Plus I feel…odd. Not like anything about his offer is untoward, it's just that something is missing. That spark. The excitement that should accompany an invitation to have dinner with the hottest guy on campus. I'm flattered, but that's all. Probably because it's early, I tell myself. I'm only half awake. Maybe once I've eaten these waffles and had a shower, the momentousness of this occasion will sink in.

"Awesome," he says, just as there's a knock at the door. "I'll make a reservation for eight."

My heart starts beating double time, and I step into my room. "Tomorrow," I say.

He shoots me one last smile as he jogs toward the stairs. "It's a date."

* * *

I'm supposed to work from five until closing on Friday, but when I tell Marcela and Nate I have a date with Kellan McVey, they agree to cover my shift. Coffee shops in Burnham aren't exactly booming on Friday nights, so they'll be okay. They tell me so half a dozen times as they sit on my bed and mull over the outfits I'm considering.

Verre Plein is a tiny French restaurant with a lengthy wine list, a pricey menu, and servers with long white aprons. It's a far cry from mac and cheese and the fast food that's available on campus, and my regular uniform of jeans and a T-shirt isn't going to cut it. I rustled up a few dresses I'd buried in the back of my closet, and I have a whopping three pairs of heels— black, gold, and red—to pair them with.

"Too prim," Nate says when I hold up a retro blue dress with a Peter Pan collar. "It's a date with Kellan McVey, not an Amish man."

"Hold onto that one, though," Marcela adds, "in case you *do* get a date with an Amish man."

I put it on a hanger and return it to the closet. "Here's hoping."

My next option is a strapless white dress with black leather straps crisscrossing the waist and black trim at the hem, which stops a good six inches above my knees.

"No," we all say at the same time. Is it sexy as hell? Yes. Is it appropriate? Absolutely not. Am I a little bit mortified that I once—maybe seven times—wore it out in public? Er, yeah.

They quickly veto my four remaining dresses, calling them dowdy, boring, scandalous and offensive, respectively. My all or nothing problem summed up in one piddly wardrobe.

"So I've got heels and nothing else." I slump on the bed beside them.

"On the bright side," Marcela says, "that might be all you need."

"Get him to buy you dinner first," Nate interjects. "At least pretend to play hard to get by putting on clothes."

I laugh. "Thanks, Dad."

"Okay, fine," Marcela says. "I thought it might come to this, so I brought something for you."

She had her backpack with her when she came, but I assumed it was full of books. Now, however, she digs around until she comes out with a little black dress with tasteful lace cutouts. I know from last year's clothing swaps that we're the same size, so at her urging I take the dress into the bathroom, try it on, and return for their perusal.

"Yes," Marcela announces.

"Try it with the red shoes," Nate urges.

I do, pirouetting in front of them so quickly I have to grab the wall before I fall down.

"Gorgeous," they say. "Perfect."

And, looking in the full-length mirror—propped against the desk, since I can't be bothered to hang it—I have to agree. The dress is sleeveless and stops just above my knees, so it shows plenty of skin but not so much as to be inappropriate for an upscale French restaurant. The red heels make it youthful, and when Marcela comes up and twists my hair into a loose bun, it looks pretty and romantic.

"I love it," I say.

Nate glances at his watch, then rises. "Text us and tell us how it goes. We have to get out of here."

"Spoilsport." Marcela tucks another piece of hair behind

my ear and nods, satisfied. "Do everything I would do," she orders.

I grin. "Promise."

No panties, she mouths as Nate drags her out of the room.

"Oh my God," Nate groans. "Wear panties, Nora."

I laugh and wave goodbye, then study my reflection some more once they're gone. Kellan has class until seven, leaving me with a few hours to kill before our eight o'clock reservation. The dress doesn't have a zipper so it has to come up over my head, and since I don't want to ruin my hair, I decide to leave the dress on while I wait. I kick off the heels and grab my anthropology textbook to get in some reading.

I doze off a bit when anthropology is no more exciting than I thought it would be, and wake up slouched on the couch. I check the time: ten after seven. Kellan's class will be wrapping up, then he'll walk home, which takes about twenty minutes. I hurry to the bathroom to wipe up my smudged mascara, then add another coat. A swipe of red lipstick and I'm doing my best approximation of effortlessly glamorous.

I consider pouring myself a glass of wine while we wait, thinking I'll look sexy and sophisticated if I'm sitting at the breakfast bar in my dress and heels, but we don't have any wine and it's hard to boost myself onto the stool in this dress.

My hesitation from yesterday is nowhere to be found. All I needed was a little time to let the whole "Kellan McVey just asked me out!" news to sink in, and now that it has, I'm excited. Tiny butterflies flit about my stomach, and I pace around the living room, trying to calm myself.

I didn't exactly go on a lot of dates last year. I went *out* a lot, but always with Marcela. Parties, bars, raves—I never said no. And in my effort to make up for my lonely high school years, I said yes to a lot of things I shouldn't have. Maybe that's why tonight feels special—I've said no so long, saying yes actually means something.

Saying yes to Kellan McVey—technically not my first time, but the first time he'll remember—means something.

I check the time. Ten to eight. He should be here any

minute. I drop back onto the couch and switch on the TV, watching a bit of the news. We don't see each other a lot at home so I'm really not sure what we'll talk about. Maybe an update on current events is in order.

When the news wraps up at the top of the hour, Kellan still isn't home.

No big deal. He has a car and it's a ten-minute trip to the restaurant—who cares if we're a few minutes late?

Fifteen minutes later, I'm definitely starting to care. And I'm really hungry. My stomach is growling its displeasure, and finally I give in and eat a cracker. I don't want to spoil my appetite.

By 8:40 p.m. it's dread and disappointment that have my stomach twisting, not hunger. He wouldn't stand me up, would he? I mean, I could text him, but what's the point? If he was held up somewhere—or remembered at all—he would have texted me. Or called. Or made some effort to tell me I hadn't been forgotten. Again.

At ten to nine my phone beeps and I snatch it up like a lifeline, but it's just Nate asking for an update. I blow out a heavy breath and don't respond. I'm not in the mood to report my second romantic disappointment of the week.

At five after nine I hunt around the fridge for something to eat, but it's the weekend and I'm always out of groceries by Friday. All we have are cupboards full of Kellan's stupid mac and cheese, a few containers of protein powder, and half a box of cereal, no milk.

I eat a handful of dry cereal and try not to cry, the only thing that could possibly make me feel even more pathetic. I imagine Kellan walking in as I stand, mascara-stained tear tracks on my cheeks, a handful of dry cereal in my palm, my hair done, my dress borrowed, my pretty red heels pinching my toes.

It's that image that has me tossing the remaining cereal into the sink and kicking off the shoes. I stomp into my room and wrench the dress over my head as though it somehow played a part in this disappointment. My hair gets a little more tousled but I leave it, even as I grab a tissue to wipe off the lipstick, hurling it violently into the trash. As violently as one can hurl a tissue, in any case.

My lower lip trembles as I pull on a pair of sweatpants and a tank top. My whole body feels hot, flush from head to toe with humiliation and frustration. I return to the kitchen and pour myself a glass of water, trying to calm down and think rationally. What should I say when Kellan comes home? Should I pretend that I also forgot about our date? Play it off like it was a casual "maybe we will, maybe we won't" invitation? Or should I tell him how righteously pissed I am that he couldn't even be bothered to text his roommate to tell her he wasn't coming? I know his parents pay for his phone— all he has to do is use it.

A knock at the front door has me lurching in surprise, and I choke on the mouthful of water I'd just consumed. A brief coughing fit later, I yank open the door expecting to find a shame-faced Kellan saying he'd been robbed, losing his phone and his house keys in the process, but it's not him.

It's Crosbie.

Of-fucking-course.

"What?" I snap. I cross my arms, both because I'm angry and because there's a sharp chill in the air. And because dressed in a gray T-shirt, jeans, and an open brown corduroy jacket, a satchel slung over his shoulder, Crosbie looks far more appealing than he should.

"Ah…" His tentative smile disappears when confronted with my stone-faced scowl, and he darts a glance over my shoulder. "Is Kellan here?"

I arch a brow. "No."

He shivers a little. "Can I come in?"

"Why?"

"Because we were supposed to play *Fire of Vengeance* and he has the game."

"Well, he's not here."

Now he sounds annoyed. "I heard you. Let me come in and grab the game."

I don't care enough right now to try to hold the game hostage. "Fine. Whatever."

I step aside and he comes in, kicking off his shoes. "Why are you so angry?" he asks as I follow him up into the living room.

"I'm busy." I'm the polar opposite of busy, but I'm not about to admit I got stood up. Especially when I'm pretty sure Crosbie Lucas never gets stood up.

"What are you doing?"

"Studying." It's the first thing that comes to mind, and the most believable. Even if it is Friday night.

"Huh." He hunts through the stack of games on the console, finding the one he's looking for. "It's quiet here."

"It's supposed to be."

"Right." He hesitates. "Do you mind if I hang out for a bit?"

"I don't feel like listening to you blow things up right now."

"Not to play. To study. It's pretty crazy at my place, and I'm behind on my reading."

I snort. "Try the library." I did *not* mean to say that. Saying "library" in my most snide tone of voice only gives more weight to Tuesday's incident, and I'm supposed to be pretending not to care. Hell—I'm supposed to be forgetting not just the encounter, but Crosbie Lucas altogether, and here he is in my living room. As always.

Crosbie winces. "I wanted to apol—"

Oh fuck. I cannot handle an apology right now. Not when I'm hanging onto my composure by the very edge of my fingernails. "You know what?" I interrupt. "Do whatever you want. Just don't bother me."

I turn and stalk back into my room, slamming the door. I'm not doing a great job of keeping my feelings under wraps, but at least I've put some distance between us.

I'm sorely tempted to hide under the covers until this whole dreadful night passes, but I'm wide awake, my empty stomach won't stop grumbling at me, and every word I write for my English essay is garbage. I feel like a tiger pacing in its cage, desperate to get out, not quite sure where I should go, and pretty confident I'd like to rip off someone's head.

A soft tap on my bedroom door has my head whipping around like the girl in *The Exorcist*, and even though I planned to ignore him, I still call out, "What?"

"I ordered pizza." His voice is muffled by the door, but he doesn't turn the knob.

My stomach jumps joyfully at the news. Food! Sustenance! And then it sinks, because Crosbie and Kellan order in their fair share of pizza, and they load it up with ground beef, anchovies and olives, all of which I find revolting.

"I don't want your disgusting pizza," I mutter. "Thanks anyway."

"It's only half disgusting," he replies. "The other half is boring."

My stomach perks up again. We've had this discussion before: I like pepperoni and extra cheese, which Crosbie and Kellan unanimously declared the dullest pizza on earth.

I get up and pull open the door, making Crosbie jump back like he's been zapped. I look around suspiciously. "Is there really pizza?"

"Yeah." He points at the coffee table where a closed box awaits.

"Are you lying about the boring half?"

"I wish." Even as he speaks I see his eyes flicker over my shoulder, and I know he sees the crumpled dress at the foot of the bed, the forgotten red heels toppled over beside it. Let him think whatever he wants.

I shut the door and trudge out of the bedroom, grabbing a plate from the cupboard in the kitchen. There's a two-liter bottle of Pepsi sitting next to the pizza and that looks good, too. I grab a glass and handful of napkins from some of Kellan's leftover takeout, and head to the couch to take a couple of slices.

I open the box and confirm Crosbie was telling the truth: one half is blissfully untarnished by his horrible toppings. I grab two pieces and stick them on my plate. He approaches, almost shyly, and sits on the couch with his own plate and takes a piece for himself.

"Are you going to stay?" he asks when I pour a glass of Pepsi without sitting down. "Take a break and watch TV with me."

I glance at him from the corner of my eye. He's got a smudge of tomato sauce on his upper lip and licks it away as he reaches for the remote.

"There's nothing on," I say, if only to be disagreeable.

"There's always something."

Though this is the very opposite of my "avoid and forget Crosbie Lucas" plan, I'm not exactly eager to return to my room, so I take a seat on the far end of the couch and curl up my legs, tucking my bare toes between the cushions. My first bite of pizza makes my eyes roll back in my head a little bit.

Crosbie flips through the channels until he finds an old true crime show, one that reenacts a decade-old mystery and its eventual conclusion. I tell myself I'm only going to stay until I finish the pizza, but the story of a young wife and mother murdered in her home on a sunny Sunday afternoon keeps me glued to my seat, my morbid side unwilling to leave without answers.

"Totally the husband," Crosbie says at the first commercial break. "He was having an affair and didn't want to pay child support, so he killed her."

"It's the helpful neighbor," I counter. "The way he started that volunteer search party—he totally knew she was in the attic. Murderers always try to be involved."

"You know a lot about killers, huh?"

I give him a look. "You'd be surprised."

He laughs and grimaces. "Jesus, Nora."

I don't want to, but I smile. By the time the show ends, I've eaten three and a half pieces of pizza and I feel like a bloated, satisfied whale.

"I can't believe it was the kindergarten teacher," Crosbie says, turning off the TV and looking at me. "What a psychopath." She'd developed a dangerous infatuation with the oblivious husband and viewed the wife as unnecessary competition.

"Yeah." We fall silent, staring at the dark television screen. I pick at a loose thread on the hem of my pants and Crosbie drums his fingers on his knees.

"Nora," he says eventually.

I don't look at him. "What?"

"I'm really sorry about the library."

Even though I half-expected him to bring it up, I still feel an uncomfortable tightening in my chest, all the stinging memories of that night surging to the surface. "Forget about it," I say, though the instructions are more for me than him.

"That was the guy from the coffee shop, right?"

"So?" I make a move to stand, which seems to prompt him to ask, "Is he your boyfriend?"

I try not to look to disdainful. "Nate? No. He's in love with Marcela, like every guy who sees her." I think of Kellan asking about her that night at the coffee shop. How every head turns when she walks by. How even though I live here and we had plans, Kellan still managed to forget about me. And how I suddenly care less about his absence than Crosbie's unexpected company. How this keeps happening.

"Oh. I thought maybe you were together."

"Not in the way you and your…friend were together."

"We're not together."

"Whatever." This time I do stand up, snagging my glass and plate from the table and bringing them to the kitchen. After a second, Crosbie follows with his plate, standing next to me as I rinse mine and stick it in the tiny dishwasher. Kellan didn't lie about this—he really does do dishes and take out the trash. He's a decent roommate, just a terrible date.

"I feel like a jerk about it," Crosbie blurts out. "I saw the look on your face and I just—"

The hurt I'm feeling about Kellan's rejection twines with the burn of the reminder of Crosbie's makeout session and when he doesn't finish the sentence I snap, "You just what?"

It's possible I'm jealous and a little sexually frustrated.

He blinks, startled. "I just wanted to say I'm sorry," he says awkwardly. "I'd had a bad day and she was a friend of a friend and…I don't know. I thought I'd forget things for a bit. But I made them worse."

"It didn't seem like you felt 'worse' when I saw you."

"Not then," he says, meeting my eyes. "But after."

I realize I'm clenching my hand around the dishwasher door and I force my fingers to uncurl. "You don't owe me any explanations."

Neither one of us moves, and the kitchen is small enough that it feels crowded with two people. "I think I do," he says, scuffing his foot on the floor. For a long moment, we both watch our feet, his gray wool socks, my nails painted red in anticipation of tonight's date. As much as I want to close the short distance between us and feel something—anything—besides this rejection and frustration and sadness, I don't move a muscle. Because maybe my "forget Crosbie Lucas" plan has failed, but my "don't fuck up, Nora" plan hasn't, and messing around with someone who *only* knows how to mess around isn't on the agenda.

He's about to say something else when we hear the front door open, a car horn honk, and Kellan's slightly drunk laugh from the entryway. Crosbie shoots me one last, meaningful look before retreating to the living room and grabbing his bag from the floor, putting plenty of space between us before Kellan comes up.

"Hey, guys," he says with a grin. The smile falters a little as he looks between us. "What are you two doing here? Together? Alone?"

"Together alone's not a thing," Crosbie says, hefting the satchel over his shoulder and snagging his jacket from the back of a chair. "And I came over to get *Target Ops: Fury.*"

That is most definitely not the game he mentioned when he first arrived, and if I had any doubts about my memory, *Fire of Vengeance* is still sitting on the coffee table. I'm contemplating this when Kellan says, "You should have come to the game,

Cros. It was epic. Huge brawl on center ice."

At the mention of "ice" I remember seeing posters around campus touting a pre-season game between Burnham's top-ranked hockey team and some other college. And that's when it finally dawns on me: Crosbie didn't come here looking for Kellan.

As though he knows I'm piecing this together, I see Crosbie's ears turn red and he jogs down the stairs. I hear the rustle of clothing as he puts on his shoes and shrugs into his jacket, then the creak of the door as it opens.

"Dude," Kellan calls. "We can play right now if you want. Don't be mad."

The only response is the front door slamming shut, an ominous chill wafting up the steps.

"Wow." Kellan runs his hands over his hair. "Can you believe this? That guy has not been himself lately. I'm getting kind of worried."

His eyes are glazed, his shirt is buttoned incorrectly, and suddenly I'm exhausted. Whatever heat had been brewing in this kitchen was extinguished by Kellan's untimely arrival, and I don't know if I'm relieved or disappointed. When I look at him, however, I feel nothing but tired.

"I'm going to bed," I mutter, rounding the breakfast bar and heading for my room.

"Do *you* want to play *Target Ops: Fury*?" he calls. In all the countless hours he's spent playing that stupid game, he's never once asked me, and no part of me wants to join him now. Plus I'm pretty sure that if I agreed he'd find some way to disappear, anyway.

"No," I say, tugging my bedroom door closed. "I don't."

chapter eight

The next morning I emerge from my room to find Kellan sitting on the couch, studying. "Hey," he says.

I frown and swipe a self-conscious hand over my tangled hair. "What are you doing here?" Kellan never comes home on Friday night—or Saturday, for that matter—so even though I'd seen him, I'd somehow assumed he would vanish again before sunrise.

I shuffle into the kitchen, rubbing my bleary eyes and wishing my hair didn't look like it had exploded over night. My plan was to grab a glass of water and some crackers—prison fare, or a perfectly normal breakfast if you're a college student who doesn't know how to meal plan—then trek to the grocery store before heading to work at three.

"Nora."

I close the fridge door and turn to see Kellan standing at the entrance to the kitchen, clutching a small bouquet of flowers wrapped in pink cellophane. "What's happening?"

"I'm so sorry," he says earnestly, my second kitchen apology in twelve hours. "I totally fucked up last night. I absolutely forgot we had plans—I made the reservation and everything—and I feel like such an asshole. I'm so, so sorry. Please forgive me."

I stare at the flowers like they might be covered in anthrax. How many girls would die to get flowers from Kellan McVey? Okay, fine—a tiny part of me still wants to raise her hand. But standing here holding my crackers, the position is a stark reminder of last night's disappointment and a few flowers aren't going to fix it.

"That was really rude," I say.

"I know. I'm so—"

"I waited for you."

"I—"

"And I felt like an idiot."

"Please—"

"And I was starving." Because I wasn't expecting to see Kellan for a while, I really hadn't decided how to handle this confrontation. It looks like I'm going with the direct approach.

He rubs his free hand over his face. "I was drunk when I got home and I didn't even remember. I turned off my phone at the game and this morning I saw the call from the restaurant asking about the reservation and it all came back to me and— I'm sorry, Nora. Really. Truly. Please forgive me. I like you and you're a good roommate and I'd never hurt your feelings on purpose. Or make you hungry, for any reason."

I try to hold onto my anger, but even though I'm offended to have been forgotten—again—the truth is, Crosbie's visit took away a lot of the sting of Kellan's disappearing act. I let out the breath I didn't know I was holding. "Forget about it," I tell him. Unlike my "whatever" to Crosbie last night, this time I mean it. Those two events hurt on two wholly different levels, and I'm not about to risk taking the time to figure out why.

Kellan looks relieved. "Thank you," he says, stepping in and folding me in an awkward hug. Apart from our initial handshake and one high five he insisted on after achieving a top score in *Fire of Vengeance*, I'm not sure we've ever actually touched. Except for that time we had sex and he forgot about it.

"No problem," I say when we step back. "Now if you'll excuse me…" I hold up the crackers. "I'm going to have breakfast, then take a shower."

He eyeballs the crackers. "That's breakfast?"

"It's grocery day."

"Do you want some mac and cheese instead? I have lots."

My stomach roils. "I'm all set."

Suddenly he points at me. "That's it," he announces, like he's just solved all the world's problems. "I'll take you to the grocery store. I have a car, so we can go to Carters, not the place on campus."

As much as I don't want to rely on Kellan for anything right now—even something as simple as a trip to the grocery store—the campus shop is tiny and overpriced, which might account for my meager food supply. Carters is a huge chain store and a much better bet, but it takes three buses to get there and is too much of a pain to manage. "Are you sure?" I ask, narrowing my eyes doubtfully. "I'm not going to get out of the shower and find you missing?"

"Cross my heart," he says, tracing an X on his chest with his index finger. And for once I don't find myself admiring what a beautifully muscled chest it is—I'm wondering how much weight his words hold.

I guess we'll find out. "Okay," I say. "Give me twenty minutes."

"I won't move a muscle."

My mind instantly fills with images of a sexy, muscled torso—but it's not Kellan I'm picturing. "Make it ten," I say, hightailing it out of the kitchen. No way I'll be able to withstand a cold shower for longer.

* * *

Going to the grocery store with Kellan McVey is a lot like what I imagine it's like to go to the grocery store with Zac Efron: it's crazy. Everybody stares. It's like no one has seen a handsome college kid before. And don't get me wrong—Kellan's super hot. But he's wearing a ratty old T-shirt, sweatpants, sandals, and a baseball hat. He's not trying whatsoever and yet every pair of eyes seems to follow him through the parking lot, into the store and down each aisle.

I can't help but wish I'd dressed a little better for the outing. Because we were only coming to the grocery store, I'd opted for skinny jeans, ballet flats, and a baggy white button-up shirt. My hair is tied back and the only makeup I'd bothered with is mascara and tinted lip gloss. None of my clothes have holes in them, but you'd swear I was wearing garbage bags from some of the disapproving looks I get.

We're in the cereal aisle when Kellan's phone rings. He tugs it out of his pocket and glances at the display. "It's Crosbie," he says, then answers. "Yo."

I can't make out the words, just the muffled sound of Crosbie's voice.

"Yeah," Kellan says, scratching his ass and adding a box of granola to the cart. "I'm just at the grocery store with Nora. She was eating crackers for breakfast."

A mumbled answer, then Kellan looks me over from head to toe. "I know," he says. "I'm going to fatten her up."

I make a face and he makes one back, and I can't help but laugh.

"Actually," he continues, "I'm trying to win my way back into her good graces. Remember how I told you I was taking her to dinner last night? I totally forgot about it and went to the game instead, so—"

I hear Crosbie's frantic tone as he tries to interrupt. But it's too late—I'd started to suspect as much last night, but now it's confirmed: Crosbie knew Kellan stood me up. He knew we had dinner plans, he knew Kellan decided to go to the game—and he came over with some lame excuse about a video game then stuck around to "read" and order pizza. He saw the abandoned dress and heels in my room; he saw everything.

Maybe I should feel outraged or embarrassed. Maybe I should feel manipulated or fooled. But I don't. Because despite how much I wish I could be invisible at this very moment, I've been complaining about how easily overlooked I am all the time, and last night Crosbie did his very best to make sure I wasn't.

I'm horrified when my sinuses tingle and my eyes start to

sting; it must be my period. There's no way I'm about to cry in the middle of Carters because someone made up a reason to hang out with me.

"Okay, man," I hear Kellan saying as I struggle to compose myself. "I know, I know. Want me to pick up anything for the bus ride? Yeah? What flavor? Okay, will do. Bye."

He hangs up and though my heart is still galloping around my chest, I've managed to head off the embarrassing crying jag. "What, uh, what bus ride is this?" I ask, trying to act like I didn't just connect the dots about what I overheard.

"Huh?" Kellan tosses in another box of cereal and resumes pushing the cart. "Oh, we're heading out tomorrow for a week of 'mock meets.'" We round the corner where two girls in dresses and heels—at the grocery store! In the morning!—giggle and wave, and Kellan smiles and nods back. Before my mind can start coming up with its own definition of "mock meets," Kellan explains. "It's for track. Like, we'll travel around to different colleges just to square off against their teams. It's not official; it's more like practice. And motivation. We see what they've got; they see our stuff. Then we all know what to work for."

I think of Crosbie. "*We* means the track team?"

"Yep."

An absolutely gorgeous blonde strolls down the baking aisle, shooting Kellan a dazzling smile. "Hey," she says.

"Hey," he replies.

They smile at each other, just two beautiful people being beautiful.

I sigh.

And that's when it hits me: I'm not jealous. And I don't really care that Kellan's leaving for a week. It's Crosbie I'm going to miss. Which is totally contrary to my plan. I should be ecstatic that the track team's schedule is lining up with my agenda to forget him, but I'm not.

"You all right?" Kellan peers at me with concern.

"Totally fine," I lie. I smile at him, but I feel like a dim bulb compared to the blonde.

"I thought you'd be stoked." He considers a bag of flour, then, for some reason, puts it in the cart. "You get the place to yourself all week."

"You're not there that much as it is."

"No way!" He laughs. "I'm there. You're the one who's always gone. You go to class, you go to work, you go to the library. You're go-go-go. When do you just kick back and have fun?"

"I have fun."

"Yeah?" He looks interested. "When?"

I bite my lip. "Okay, fine. I *had* fun."

He shakes his head. And I have to give the guy credit—half a dozen other women have walked past, and now that we're talking, his attention is undivided. "Had fun? Like, in the distant past?"

I laugh a little, feeling like a moron. "It feels that way." I study the back of a box of cake mix, hoping he'll drop the subject, but when I next look up he's just staring at me with a look that says, "I can wait all day."

I sigh and put the box back on the shelf. "I don't study so much because I love school," I admit, tugging the cart around the corner into the dairy aisle. "I study because I have a scholarship and last year I didn't study—like, at all—and nearly lost it. In fact, I lost half of it. So this year I have to buckle down and do better. A lot better."

He looks surprised. "Me too."

I grab yogurt and add it to the cart, then follow that up with some eggs. Plenty of breakfast options now. "And I don't go out to party or whatever because I did too much of that last year, and I don't really seem to have an off switch. It's just all or nothing. All partying, no studying." I'm not going to mention getting arrested. "And if I didn't stop, it would be 'all living with my parents, no job prospects.'"

"I totally hear you," Kellan says, nodding. "That's why this arrangement is perfect." He gestures between us. "You're like this awesome role model. I come home and see your door closed, and I know you're in there studying so I'm like, 'Better study, Kellan, if you want to graduate.' And then you go to work and I think, 'Time to work out.'"

I squint at him. "Seriously?"

"Yeah. That's why I posted the ad that I did. I wanted somebody like you; I just never thought I'd find it."

You found me at the May Madness frat party, I think. But what I say is, "I'm glad it worked out. For both of us."

He grins. "I'll keep up my end of the bargain from now on, too," he says. "Now that I know why studying is so important to you. And I'll tell Crosbie to stop dropping by unannounced—he totally could have played one of his own games last night. He didn't need to bother you."

Wrong game, Kellan.

"Crosbie's not a problem."

"You don't have to be nice about it. He's my best friend, but we can hang out at his place."

Another slice of disappointment at the thought of seeing less of Crosbie. Who could have predicted this?

"Really," I say. "He's fine."

And that's the understatement of the year.

* * *

Unfortunately, Kellan is true to his word. I don't see Crosbie before they leave for the road trip, and when they get back it's mid-October, and I don't see him then, either. He's around—I hear Kellan talking to him on the phone, or sometimes he'll tell me about something Crosbie said or did when they were hanging out that day, but he doesn't come to the apartment. Not when I'm there, anyway. He doesn't come to Beans, either, and though I try not to, I start to obsess. What did Kellan say to him? *Stay away from Nora, she needs her education?* Or does it have nothing at all to do with Kellan and everything to do with what didn't happen in the kitchen that night? Is he embarrassed? Does he regret it? Does he hate me?

Okay, I really don't think I've done anything to be hated

for, but after exhausting all other avenues, that's where my mind goes.

"Hey," I say abruptly. I'm eating a plate of spaghetti at the dining table and Kellan's watching one of the *Die Hard* movies.

"What's up?" he asks, pausing the show.

"Do you know if Crosbie's still interested in doing open mic night at Beans?"

Kellan frowns and rubs a finger between his eyebrows. "Has he been badgering you with his 'magic' again?" he asks with a heavy sigh. "I'm sorry. I'll talk to him about it."

"No," I say hastily. "I haven't even seen him, that's why I'm asking you. I thought he was interested, but he hasn't signed up and all the slots are almost taken." That's technically true, though I haven't actually given open mic night or Crosbie's "magic" much thought recently. I just don't know how else to ask Kellan what the hell his best friend has been up to without fielding certain questions in return.

"Oh," he says. "He hasn't mentioned it. I can check with him if you want."

I swallow. "Sure. That would be great." I don't have Crosbie's number, and I've never given him mine. I don't know his class schedule, either, so short of skulking around outside the frat house, I have no way to run into him. I know I'm being contrary. It was my plan to forget him, but now that he's the one who seems to have forgotten me, I can't seem to think about much else besides getting him to notice me again.

"Want to watch this with me?" Kellan asks, nodding at the TV. "It just started. I can rewind it if you want."

"No." I shake my head. "Thanks, but I have to—"

"Study," he finishes for me, giving me a big thumbs up. "Got it."

I take my plate to the kitchen. I'm glad I ate most of the spaghetti before our conversation, because my appetite seems to have fled. I rinse the plate and stick it in the dishwasher, then head into my room to grab my jacket and bag.

"See you later," I call, heading outside.

"Have fun at the library."

I don't respond, shivering as the foggy night air greets me. It's dark and quiet, the air so dense it's impossible to see more than ten feet in front. I climb on my bike and pedal in the direction of the library, though for once that's not my destination. Despite my determination to be smarter this year, it has taken me way too long to figure out how to learn what Crosbie Lucas has been up to: I will quite literally read the writing on the wall.

It's an antiquated and distasteful tradition and the school puts up a token protest and paints them every couple of years, but the fourth floor bathrooms in the Student Union building are notorious for listing frat house hookups. The more popular the guy, the longer the list. The lists appear in both the men and women's bathrooms, and for some it's about the bragging rights, while for others it's just plain embarrassing. Last year I'd come up here daily in the week after my hookup with Kellan to see if my name appeared on his very lengthy list, but it never had. At the time I'd been a confusing mix of relieved and disappointed; now I'm just relieved.

At six o'clock on a Wednesday, the building is relatively quiet. I pass a few people as I approach the elevator, but ride up to the fourth floor alone. There's a girl coming out of the bathroom as I enter, and then it's just me. I take a breath and study the long row of stalls. If I recall correctly, the third one is dedicated to the Alpha Sigma Phi guys. I'd seen Crosbie's name on there last year when I checked Kellan's list, but I hadn't paid it any attention. Now it's the only one I'm interested in.

The stalls are the standard cramped metal affairs with chipped gray paint. The lists are written mostly in black marker, with the guy's name at the top and his conquests scrawled beneath. A lot of them are dated, too, like a time stamp. It's a mix of handwriting, some neat, some sloppy, updated by random people with random intel. Out of curiosity, I check out Kellan's list. There's a whopping sixty-two names listed on it, dating back to last September when he first started at Burnham. I can't help it: my jaw drops. I know he's...prolific, but that's more than I expected. I had sex with five guys last year and I thought that was a lot.

I frown as I scan his list. It's numbered, and there are a couple of gaps on it: numbers four, nine, twenty-two, forty-one, forty-two, and fifty are blank. I don't know where I fall in, but I take sick satisfaction in learning I'm not the only girl he forgot.

I tuck my hair behind my ears and study the rest of the stall. There are about twelve guys' purported hookups documented in here, and the lists range in length from six to sixty-two, which I guess makes Kellan the "winner."

I spot Crosbie on the opposite side of the stall. His list has twenty-five names on it, and I feel each one like a jealous little kick to the heart. I know it's stupid, but I read the names in case I recognize them, so I can see what kind of girls Crosbie Lucas likes. What kind he suddenly starts avoiding. But I don't recognize any of the "Crosbabes," and when I get to the bottom of the list, I frown. The final entry is dated June second of this year. He wasn't on campus all summer, but if he's the Crosbie Lucas I thought I knew—the one with twenty-five Crosbabes notched into his bedpost—surely he's messed around with someone since the new school year started. What about the girl in the library? Just to be sure, I check the other lists, and most have entries for September and October. Kellan alone has ten since Labor Day.

My eyes drift back to Crosbie's list. I have no more information than I came in here with—or do I? I'm scared to hope what I'm hoping, that he hasn't had sex with any girls since we met, but that's ridiculous. I know his reputation. I've seen him in action. I see his history scrawled right here on the bathroom wall. He's not a monk, and he certainly doesn't suffer from a lack of female attention.

I leave and grab my bicycle, but I don't go to the library. Instead I just pedal around, my feelings as murky as the thick fog. I can't afford to care about Crosbie Lucas, but I can't seem to stop, either.

* * *

On Friday I have a two o'clock progress meeting with Dean Ripley. He and my father had been roommates thirty years ago, so he has an unfortunately vested interest in my progress.

I have two classes on Fridays and normally hang out at the library in between instead of biking home. Today, however, I want to change out of my standard uniform of jeans and a T-shirt so I look upstanding and presentable when I meet with Dean Ripley. The last time we met was after my arrest, and I'm pretty sure I was wearing that white dress with the leather straps and a pair of Marcela's platform boots. This time when he calls my father with an update, I want "leather" to have no role in the conversation.

I groan and fish around in my closet until I find the blue dress with the Peter Pan collar. I pull it over my head, pair it with some flats, and twist my hair into a high bun. Stray strands flutter out, but I think I look kind of wholesome and sweet—not easy to do when big boobs and a tiny waist make everything I put on look anything but wholesome.

I pace back and forth as I imagine the upcoming discussion, and I'm halfway through my mumbled declaration about learning from my mistakes and channeling them into a newer, better version of myself when I hear the front door open and the raucous laughter of approximately half the track team. I freeze. I have to leave in ten minutes and I'd really rather not explain why I'm home in the middle of the day, or where I'm going. Or why I'm dressed like this.

Shit shit shit.

Maybe they'll leave. Maybe Kellan just dropped by to pick up a game or something.

But ten minutes later, they're still here. I can hear the telltale explosions of *Fire of Vengeance* and non-stop shouts and curses. When I can't wait anymore, I take a breath, plaster on what I hope is a pleasant and not at all irritated expression, and step out of my room.

Absolutely everyone falls silent. Even the game takes the

hint and things stop exploding.

"Nora," Kellan says, standing abruptly. He looks guilty. "I—You're—"

"Going out," I say. "Stay. Play your games. Have fun." That's when I notice Crosbie straddling one of the dining chairs. Everyone else is clustered in the living room, sitting on either the couch or the floor, but he's slightly apart. I'll have to walk within six inches of him to get to the stairs.

Kellan glances at his friends as though he's worried what they might think if he cares too much about what I think, but I don't care about any of them. It's been two and a half weeks since I last saw Crosbie and he looks good. He's wearing a pair of faded jeans and a long-sleeve black shirt that strains against his biceps. His hair needs a trim and sticks up like he'd just run his fingers through it, but it's the look on his face that gets me. Just for a second, I'd swear I see something that looks a lot like...longing in his eyes. Then it's quickly replaced by his usual cocky grin and a full-body once over.

I hear whispers of, "Dude, who is that?" and "That's your roommate?" and then, even though I know I should just call out, "Sorry, gotta run!" I stop when Kellan says my name.

My face stretches with a polite smile and I turn to greet the room. There are ten guys piled onto the couch and the floor around it, and maybe half look familiar. "Hi," I say.

"Nora." Kellan comes to stand at my side and gestures to the group, rattling off names as he points, finishing with, "And you know Crosbie. Everyone, this is my roommate, Nora."

"Hey, Nora," they chorus.

Kellan points a stern finger in their direction. "Nora's a very good student and a very good influence," he says. "No one try to corrupt her." To me he adds, "If any of them tries to corrupt you, tell me right away."

I'm not entirely sure he's kidding.

"Nice to meet you," I say, even though I instantly forgot everyone's names.

"Are you coming to the Halloween party?" one guys asks.

"Ah...what?" I want to take the words back as soon as I

say them. Who doesn't understand the words "Halloween" or "party?"

"Alpha Sigma Phi," another guy clarifies. "We host a Halloween party every year. It's invite only, but for Kellan's roommate, we'll make an exception."

Marcela got an invite last year and I actually went to this party dressed as a slutty mermaid, and it was pretty amazing. They turn the place into a haunted house—complete with spiked punch with fake eyeballs and rubber spiders frozen in ice cubes—and only "real" costumes are allowed to enter, no writing "book" on your forehead and trying to convince people you're Facebook.

"Oh, thanks," I say, trying to hide my interest the way a junkie, three days clean, might pretend she's not craving meth. "But I have to work that night." That's not true at all; Beans closes early on Halloween to prevent drunk college kids from coming in and wreaking havoc, which has happened in the past. Costumes make people daring; I should know. After my sorta-boyfriend and I broke up last year, the Halloween party was where I had my first one night stand with a guy dressed as a plastic army man. I had green paint in too many crevices to count for a full week afterward. Lesson learned. Sort of.

"Call in sick," Crosbie suggests, and for a moment, it feels like the whole room falls silent, the simple suggestion hanging in the air like a challenge.

One of the guys pipes up before I can respond. "He'll make it worth your while," he adds, jerking a thumb in Crosbie's direction. "Last year he went as an underwear model."

Because he's an obnoxious attention whore, I'd noticed Crosbie last year but immediately dismissed him. Now that it's pointed out, however, I recall him wearing a pair of Calvin Klein underwear and strutting around, drunkenly shouting, "Where are you *now*, Mark Wahlberg? *Huh?*"

I smile as I recall it. "What about this year?" I ask him.

"I'm going as Clark Kent," Kellan interrupts. "Crosbie's going to be Superman." He grins at me, his eyes lighting up.

"You should be Lois Lane!"

The room explodes in approving cheers and applause, and I laugh dryly. A woman torn between two men? Not part of the "better Nora" agenda. "We'll see," I say, though we most definitely will not be seeing this.

"She's in!" someone cries.

I wave and head down the stairs. "I have to go."

Kellan leans over the rail to watch me put on my coat. "You look hot," he says, nodding at my dress. "Big date?"

"Something like that," I tell him. At the last second I spot Crosbie behind Kellan, listening.

"Have fun," Crosbie says, holding my stare just a little too long.

chapter nine

Nothing about enduring a forty-five minute sex talk—with Dean Ripley's ninety-year-old secretary called in to "witness" the lecture—is fun. I stop reliving that horror, however, the moment I hurry into Beans for my evening shift and feel like I've walked right into a freezer.

I toss my coat into the storage closet and pull on an apron over my prim blue dress, but the second I step foot behind the counter I can almost see my breath fog in the air. "What the...?" I look around, perplexed. It doesn't take long to find the source: the shop's large front window is missing, several sheets of wood resting against the wall. Despite the damage and the cold, the business is still open, patrons sitting at tables with jackets on, steaming cups in hand. When people want coffee, they want coffee.

"What's going on?" I exclaim when Nate hustles through the front door, coat zipped to his chin, wool hat tugged low over his ears.

"Freak accident. They had a couple of guys working on the power lines out front when one of their ladders fell over and smashed through the window."

"Was anybody hurt?"

"Nope. It was just Marcela and I at the time, and we were both in the back."

"That's lucky."

"Yeah." But his face is grim and his jaw is set, and Nate's

just not a guy who really looks angry a lot. It's worrisome.

"Isn't it?" I try. "I mean, despite the damage."

He sighs. "It's fine. It'll be fine."

"Where's Marcela?"

"I sent her to the hardware store to pick up a couple of space heaters."

I glance around. The ladder's gone and the glass has already been swept up. "How long ago did this happen?"

"Almost two hours."

"And she's still gone?"

A curt nod.

"Did you look for her?"

"I don't need to look for her."

I frown. "Are you sure? The hardware store is three blocks down. I know Marcela likes to shop, but two hours is a lot, even for her."

Nate sighs and runs a hand over his head, knocking the hat askew. "We had a...disagreement."

"About what?"

"I'm dating someone."

I do a double-take. He could have admitted to smashing out the window in a drug-fueled rage and I wouldn't have been so surprised. "Come again?"

"You heard me."

"You—I—But—Who?"

"Thanks, Nora. That's really great."

"Well, I'm sorry, I'm just surprised. I thought you..."

The look he gives me warns me not to say "loved Marcela," so I bite my tongue. "I don't," he says tersely. "Not anymore. I'm dating Celestia, and it's going well. And how Marcela feels about it doesn't factor in."

"Celestia?"

"Yeah. You know her, actually. She comes in from time to time. Blond hair, really pretty...fur coat." He mumbles the last words into the crook of his arm, pretending to fix his hat.

I gape. "Did you just say *fur coat*?"

He clears his throat. "Maybe?"

"As in mink?"

"I don't know what animal it is."

"You're dating Mink Coat."

"I'm not sure it's mink."

"No wonder Marcela's annoyed! Her drink orders are dreadful."

"They're...specific."

"She wears mink year-round!"

"What's wrong with—Okay, fine. The fur's a little odd, but on days like today, you have to admit, it's perfect."

I roll my eyes. "Okay, Nate. You got me."

He smiles a little. "Sometimes you have to accept what's right in front of you." He gestures to the window. "And what's not."

"I really don't think that analogy works."

At least, it doesn't, until Marcela strides up, a boxed space heater tucked under each arm. She shoulders her way through the front door and dumps the heaters on the counter. "Voila," she says without stopping. We watch her disappear into the kitchen in a rush of particularly frosty air.

We're quiet for a moment. "Wow," I say finally.

"Yeah."

"What'd she say when you told her?"

He blows out a breath. "I didn't exactly 'tell' her. We bumped into her last night when we were walking home from dinner and she looked startled, but not angry. Then when she came in this morning I tried to tell her I'd been seeing Celestia for the past month—"

"*Month?*"

"And she just froze me out." A pause. "That was before the window broke."

"Life imitating art."

"Or just shitty luck mirroring shitty luck."

"Well, for what it's worth, if you like Mink Coat, I'm happy for you."

"I like Celestia, I do not like mink coats."

"It's too cold for mink, anyway. Fox, maybe."

He glares at me and tries not to laugh. "Go do some work. I have to call these glass guys and ask what's taking so long."

I head into the back and find Marcela smearing frosting on a tray of cooled cinnamon buns. "Smells good."

"They're warm, that's all that matters."

"Fair enough." Because of the ovens and the sanitizer, the kitchen is always hotter than the front. Normally we complain about it, but today it's a blessing. When Marcela doesn't say anything else I add, "Nate told me about Celestia."

She snorts. "Me too."

"And you're…angry?"

"That she's dating him to get half-price drinks? Of course I'm bothered."

I watch her massacre a cinnamon bun in the name of caring. "You look more than a little bothered."

She sighs and tosses down the spatula. "I was just surprised."

"So was I." I watch her closely. "Are you jealous?"

"What? No! Look, you should be bothered, too. She's going to come in here even more now, with her fur coats and her ridiculous drink orders. We're all affected."

"It's not—"

She holds up a hand. "I don't want to talk about this anymore. It's not important. Tell me something good."

I rack my brain, filtering past the Dean-Ripley-gave-me-a-sex-talk horror until I come to something I know she'll like. "I got invited to the Alpha Sigma Phi Halloween party."

Her eyes light up. "You're kidding!"

"It's true."

"We have to go. I've been trying to think of ways to get in, but my best guess was tracking down that army man you hooked up with, except I don't think we ever saw his face when it wasn't painted green."

I groan. "Don't remind me."

"Right. Sorry. Now let's talk about our costumes. Slutty cat? Slutty aliens? Slutty nurses? No, what am I saying? We're modern women. Slutty doctors!"

I laugh too. "No slutty anything. How about you go and tell me about it later?"

She gasps in offense. "Absolutely not. We're a team. Where you go, I go— Actually, never mind. You spend a lot of time at the library. But where I say we'll go, we go. And we're going to this party. We can be the Black Swan and...the white one."

"What?"

"Or the two broke girls from TV."

I gesture to my apron. "Perfect. I won't need to change."

She claps her hands, bits of cream cheese frosting flying from the tips of her fingers. "Thelma and Louise!"

"We—"

But she's on a roll. "It's perfect. They're classic, they're best friends, they're gorgeous, and—"

"They die at the end?"

"And Thelma bangs Brad Pitt. In the name of friendship, you can be Thelma. I think you could use a Brad Pitt."

"You realize he robs her, right?"

"Your belongings fit in a milk crate. You're safe."

"I don't think—"

She presses her frosted fingers over my lips. "You need to stop thinking and take the night off. Halloween is the Saturday after midterms. You can bury your nose in a book until then, but on October thirty-first, you're mine. And we're hitting the road."

"They drive off a cliff."

She winks at me. "That's the spirit."

* * *

The sensible part of my brain tells me to steer clear of all Alpha Sigma Phi parties, but when Nate closes shop early so the window guys can do their job, I detour one block over to Duds, Burnham's only second-store. I can't stop thinking about driving off a cliff, so to speak. It's been a long time since

I've "driven" anywhere with anyone, and though I have good reason for hunkering down to atone for last year's mistakes, it hasn't exactly been easy. Or interesting. Or satisfying.

It's on exactly that unsatisfying note that I step into the musty-smelling store and bump into Kellan. The front row is lined with all manner of Halloween costumes and paraphernalia, and Kellan is, for some reason, pushing a shopping cart.

"Nora!" he exclaims. "I thought you were working."

"I was. We closed up early, so I figured I'd come get some costume inspiration."

His face lights up. "Me too. Clark Kent needs a good suit, and where better to find one than Duds?"

"Don't you already own a suit?"

"Yeah, but I don't want to get...bodily fluids on it."

"Thank you for that imagery."

"Are you going as Lois Lane, then? Because this is perfect. We can coordinate our outfits. My tie, your shoes—"

"I'm not going as Lois."

His face falls, then immediately lights up when he spots a French maid outfit, still in its vacuum-sealed bag. "Slutty maid?" he tries, holding it up.

"No slutty anything."

"Who's slutty? I'm interested." Crosbie skids onto the scene, sneakers squeaking across the tiled floor. Duds is a big store for Burnham, full of countless racks of clothing and walls lined with shelves of shoes and housewares. It's mostly empty at this time of day, so the noise attracts nothing more than a single disapproving stare from an employee hanging up jackets nearby.

Kellan sighs and replaces the French maid outfit. "Not Nora."

Crosbie scoffs. "Obviously. I thought we were talking about someone cool."

I shoulder my way past the duo. "This has been fun."

"Aw," Kellan calls to my back. "Come on, Nora. Now that you're here you can help me choose a costume."

"Your costume is just a suit."

"But when I model for Crosbie he tells me I'm fat."

Crosbie shrugs. "You are."

Kellan socks him in the shoulder. "Dick. I'm going to look at ties. I'll let you know when I'm ready to begin modeling."

"Remember blue is slimming!"

Kellan flips him off and wanders away, leaving Crosbie and I next to the costume display. For a second we just stare at each other, Crosbie rubbing his newly injured shoulder, me trying to come up with something to say that doesn't reveal just how much I noticed his absence these past few weeks. Or how hot he looks. His hair is damp, like he'd just taken a shower, and he's wearing jeans and a puffy black jacket that makes his brown eyes look darker than usual as they take me in.

"What's it going to be?" he finally asks.

"Pardon me?"

"Your costume. What is it?" He nods at the options. "Witch? Scarecrow? Viking?"

"Ah, Thelma."

"Who?"

"Thelma. From *Thelma & Louise*? Marcela's going to be Louise."

"Which one was Thelma, Geena Davis or Susan Sarandon?"

"Geena Davis. I came to shop for some high-waisted jeans and sunglasses."

He looks me over. "I can see it."

"What about you? Browsing for a cape? Maybe some new tights?"

"I've already got my Superman costume at home. I sleep in it every night."

"I don't doubt it." I make my way over to the women's clothing and Crosbie comes with me, thumbing through the long rack of jeans for a suitably tight, acid-washed pair. After a minute I get warm and unzip my coat, realizing my mistake the second Crosbie's eyes lock on my chest, then slide up to the prim Peter Pan collar of my dress.

His brows tug together and he gestures at me with one finger. "Let's talk about this," he says. "Did you have a big date today? Or perhaps a...very pleasant date?"

I smile thinly, remembering the afternoon's unpleasantness. "I had a meeting with...someone."

He leans in conspiratorially. "Was it a boy?"

I snort and push him away. "Why? Are you jealous?"

For a second he doesn't react. Our eyes lock and my hand feels like it's stuck to his chest, my fingertips digging into his pecs. And then he shakes his head and smirks and I take away my hand. "You see right through me, Nora."

"Ha. I haven't seen you much at all since pizza night." The night he pretended to be looking for Kellan, but really came looking for me.

He turns his attention back to the jeans. "I've been busy."

"I see."

"With school."

"Right. Me too."

A pause. "And Kellan told me you had some trouble last year and really need to study, so you can't afford any distractions."

"You don't distract me." The words come out a little too quickly.

"He said maybe the video games were a problem."

"I just tune them out, like I do with most of your comments. It's kind of like white noise now."

He glances at me. "So what you're saying is...I help you."

"That's exactly it."

"I make you better."

"Shut up, Crosbie."

"You've missed me."

Our eyes meet again, and even though he'd said the words in jest, I think we both know they're a little bit true. Maybe a lot true.

"Kellan's right that I have to keep my grades up, but it's

not terrible, having company sometimes."

"Oh yeah?" He looks decidedly pleased and more than a little smug.

"Occasionally."

"I'm your best friend, aren't I?"

"I've changed my mind. The video games are a real problem."

"Is that why you're coming to the Halloween party?"

"Is what why? The video games?"

"To talk to someone. To meet people. To do what people do at parties." He waggles his eyebrows and leans in a little, close enough I can smell the faint scent of shampoo on his still-damp hair.

Even though I know exactly what he's referring to, I pretend I'm not sniffing him and ask, "What do you mean?"

"Have you ever been to a party, Nora?"

"Of course."

"I don't mean birthday parties when you were a kid."

I roll my eyes. "Oh. In that case, no."

"Yeah? What are you like at parties? Do you stand in the corner? Hide in the bathroom? Take a couple of pictures to show you were there, post them on Facebook, then run home to read?"

I stick out my tongue. "I'll have you know I'm great at parties." Or rather, Marcela was great at parties; I was okay after two drinks had loosened my inhibitions.

"Tell me."

"Well, first I like to head right to the snack table."

"Ooh."

"I really go to town on the free chips."

"This is a wild story, Nora."

"Then I study all the family pictures on the wall, and ask the host questions about them."

Crosbie grins. "I know you're trying to sound like you're joking, but I think this is true."

"And then I go home. In bed by nine."

He laughs. "What I always suspected."

undecided

I find a couple of pairs of jeans and drape them over my forearm. "Okay, tell me your party strategy."

"All right. Listen closely. Not a lot of girls get this type of intel. Mostly they're too amazed by me to appreciate the process."

"I don't doubt it for a minute."

"First I put on a T-shirt."

"Whoa."

"Then I add a pair of jeans."

"I don't think I can take much more."

"Then I show up. Bam. Game over." He brushes his hands together, mission accomplished.

"You make it sound so easy."

He shrugs, exaggeratedly cocky. "For some of us, it is."

"Yo! Gossip queens!"

We turn to see Kellan waving from the changing rooms in the corner. "I'm about to get dressed. Prepare yourselves for the thrill of a lifetime."

I snag another pair of jeans before following Crosbie to the back of the store to see Kellan's show. He grabs two cheap wooden chairs from a dining room display and arranges them side-by-side, and when we sit down it's like we're the only people at a strange discount theater.

"So what have you been up to these past couple of weeks?" he asks, taking one pair of jeans and holding them up to study.

"Why?" I ask, echoing his earlier joke. "Did you miss me?"

He looks at me from the corner of his eye. "Desperately."

I laugh. "Well—"

"Hey, Crosbie."

We turn as two girls stroll by, arms laden with costume options. While I don't appreciate them interrupting the conversation, I do appreciate that they have at least steered clear of the slutty French maid outfit.

"Hey," Crosbie responds, stretching one arm along the back of my chair as he grins at them. If I were an idiot I might

107

think the gesture was a possessive one, an action meant to say, *Hey, I'm busy here.* But because I have two eyes, I know the gesture has more to do with allowing his coat to gape open, revealing a well-defined chest beneath his thin white T-shirt.

I sigh inwardly as the trio makes small talk. My gaze shifts around the store, landing on a display of sunglasses. I need a pair anyway, and now suddenly seems like the perfect time to check them out. When I stand, however, Crosbie circles my wrist with his calloused fingers and keeps me in my seat.

"Don't go," he says in a low voice. To the girls he adds, "See you at the Halloween party, ladies."

They take the cue and say goodbye, but I don't miss the way their eyes flit to the still-closed door of the change room before they leave.

"I need to look at the sunglasses," I say before Crosbie can accuse me of being jealous or anything equally ridiculous and untrue. But this time it's not his fingers that stop me from standing, it's his words.

"They're only talking to me to get close to Kellan."

I freeze. "What?"

He strums his fingers on the back of my chair and focuses on something over my shoulder, avoiding eye contact. Which is probably for the best, because there are only about ten inches separating us, and I'm all too aware of the warm length of his arm along my shoulders, the way his big knee presses into the outside of my thigh.

"You heard me."

"And that's...a problem?" The Crosbie I know—thought I knew—wouldn't have cared why he was getting the attention, as long as he was getting it.

His nostrils flare slightly as he exhales. "I wasn't complaining about it last year. I met a lot of girls I wouldn't have met otherwise. But this year...the girls Kellan attracts just don't do it for me."

I recoil, stung. "I see." My chest suddenly feels tight and I blink to clear my vision.

"I didn't mean—"

The change room door bangs open to reveal Kellan propped against the cheap plywood wall, hands tucked into his pockets, one foot crossed over the other at the ankle. He's wearing a navy suit with a red and white striped tie, shiny loafers, and a pair of black-framed glasses. He looks more like a fashion model than a journalist, but who's complaining?

"Thoughts?" he asks, strutting out of the stall and taking ten steps down the nearest aisle before executing an exaggerated turn and strolling back. He poses, jutting out his jaw, then tipping down the glasses to fix me with a laughably intense stare.

I snicker, my hurt feelings subsiding for just a second. "Very nice."

He studies the price tags stapled to the jacket sleeve and the tie. "All for a grand total of...twenty-two dollars."

"You make it look like an even forty."

He winks at me. "I know." Then he turns to Crosbie, who's looking more than a little uneasy. "Don't tell me I look fat, bro. This is navy. You said it was slimming."

Crosbie clears his throat. "Ten out of ten. Good call with the tie."

Kellan fingers it thoughtfully. "I like it." He disappears back into the change room and I stand.

"Nora," Crosbie says.

"Good night." I hang the jeans on the closest rack, no longer interested in playing dress up or any other games. The burning humiliation I'd felt at his words is welling right back up, threatening to bubble over. I just want to go home.

"Nora." He follows me down an aisle of children's clothes, fingers folding around the hem of my coat. "Would you stop?"

"No," I say, even as I stop. "Fuck off. I was just being nice—"

"I didn't mean you," he interrupts. "You're not the kind of girl he likes—"

"Oh, Jesus Christ." I yank my coat out of his grasp. "I mean it, Crosbie. Shut up."

"Come on. You know what I meant."

"No," I bite out. "Obviously I don't."

"He likes you," he says, running a hand over the side of his face, frazzled. "And so do I. You know I do."

I glance away, more angry than I should be. No, not angry. Sad. Because I missed Crosbie, for reasons I don't want to dwell on, and he hurt my feelings.

"Come on," he says again. "Thelma is super hot. I want to see you in those jeans. Don't go home empty handed."

I scowl. "If you noticed me at a party, it would be the first time."

"What? There will be a lot of people, but—" He shakes his head. "Fine, I'll set a trap. I'll put family photos on the wall and wait until you approach."

"I don't want to see your photos."

"And I'll buy all the best chips."

I blow out a breath. "I have to go, Crosbie."

He shuffles closer. "Wait until Kellan's ready and I'll drive you back."

"I rode my bike." I turn to go.

"I'm sorry I hurt your feelings."

The words make me pause. Maybe it's just because he's had a lot of experience issuing apologies, but he's good at this. I'm already calming down and starting to feel a little embarrassed by my reaction. "Maybe I overreacted," I mutter.

He nudges my foot with his. "Yeah, you're a fucking psychopath."

I meet his eye. "I live with Kellan, Crosbie. I don't need to be nice to you to get close to him."

He frowns. "I know."

I watch him for a moment. "I really don't think you do."

chapter ten

At eight o'clock on Halloween night, I'm sitting on one of the stools at the breakfast bar in my Thelma get-up, a half-finished bottle of beer in one hand as the other hovers over my phone, ready to type a furious "How dare you do this, Louise!" message to Marcela.

"Hey," Kellan says, coming out of his room.

"Hey," I mutter, too disappointed and frustrated to manage many more words than that. I'm reading Marcela's text— *"Sorry, babe, but I'm dying—like for real dying, vomit everywhere dying—and I cannot be your Louise tonight. Find Brad Pitt and bang his brains out for me"*—and trying not to cry.

Kellan eyes me warily. "Everything okay?"

I sigh. "Marcela can't make it," I mutter. "There's no Thelma and Louise without Louise." And there's no way I'm about to show up to Alpha Sigma Phi solo—Marcela's more than a wingman, she's the tour guide, and I hate to admit it, but I still want her to hold my hand until I get warmed up for the evening.

Kellan sets his briefcase down on the dining room table. It takes me a full five seconds of staring before I realize he's in costume—and he looks *good*. Imagine the sexiest Clark Kent in the history of the world, and transplant him to my living room. He's wearing the navy suit, polished black wingtips, and the red and white striped tie. Paired with gelled back hair and horn-rimmed glasses, he is the epitome of smart and sexy.

111

"Wow," I manage. "I know I've seen it before, but you look great."

"You too, Thelma," he returns, gesturing to my dated ensemble. "Don't even think about letting all this go to waste."

I'm wearing the tight, high-waisted jeans and a denim shirt Marcela transformed with a pair of scissors and a spool of thread so it's sleeveless and ties in the front just below my belly button. We'd found a curly orange wig at the drugstore and topped off everything with red lipstick, sunglasses, and a plastic pistol. I thought I looked pretty good, but without Louise, I just look like a trashy criminal. The reason the movie's so awesome is because they're a team. And now I'm flying solo. As always.

I force a smile and take another sip of beer. "I won't," I lie. As soon as Kellan leaves I'm shucking this denim and pouting in bed.

"Nuh-huh." He sets his jaw and stubbornly shakes his head. "The second I leave you're going to take off that costume and cry yourself to sleep."

My mouth falls open. "That is so far from true—"

"Fine," he says. "You don't go, I don't go." He starts to undo his tie.

"You have to go," I protest. "Every girl on campus will bawl her head off if you don't. And half the guys, too."

"I'm not going to leave you home alone on the one night you're supposed to have fun. I know you aced those assignments, now get your ass out the door."

"I can't go as Thelma—"

"Where's Louise's outfit? I'll go as Louise if you need a partner."

I laugh at the idea of Kellan squeezing into Marcela's size four jeans. "The outfit is at her place. There's nothing here."

"Fine. Do you have a business suit? I need a Lois Lane."

I think we both know there will be at least a dozen Lois Lanes at tonight's party. As soon as word got out that Kellan was going as Clark Kent—and maybe a few people knew Crosbie would be Superman—Lois became the campus's most popular costume idea.

"Of course I don't have a business suit. I work at a coffee shop."

Kellan crosses his arms and manages to look terribly sexy doing so. "Then figure something out. Because we're spending this night together, Nora—whether it's here or there is up to you."

I run an exasperated hand through my fake hair. "Kellan, just go, please. I'll come later."

"Liar."

I totally am. "I don't have—"

"You have a white sheet? Be a ghost."

"I—"

"Or put on that outfit you wore the day we first met. We'll stick a book in your hand and call you a librarian. Wait— that's too close to the truth."

"Har har."

He sticks out his tongue, refastens his tie, and tosses me my coat from the back of the chair. "Get your ass out the door, Thelma. You don't need Louise to have fun."

I suck in a breath, then slowly exhale as I shrug into my coat. Okay, maybe I am overreacting a little bit. I'm just not someone who knows how to show up to a party alone and not stand around awkwardly. But if I'm showing up with Kellan McVey, I won't be alone, will I? And if things go south, I can just head home early—we've already established I'm virtually invisible at frat houses, anyway.

"When was the last time you went to a party?" Kellan asks as we trudge through the cold night. Leaves crunch under our feet and our breath puffs out in white clouds as we make the fifteen minute trek.

"Last year," I say, stuffing my hands in my pocket.

"Last year?"

"I mean, last school year," I amend. "Late spring."
Specifically the Alpha Sigma Phi May Madness party where we screwed in a coat closet and you followed it up by getting a blowjob from some girl while a crowd looked on. Remember? No?

"Did you have fun?"

I hedge. "Mmm."

"Crosbie said you almost flunked out."

"Yeah." I shoot him a smile. "I had a little too much fun."

He smiles back. "I hear you. So did I."

"You're still having fun," I point out. He's been more than true to our promise not to bring dates home—I never hear him having sex, never see anyone sneaking out in the mornings. I know he sleeps out fairly frequently, but I also see him studying regularly and last week he boasted about the B+ he got on an English essay.

"Why not?" he asks, shivering and picking up the pace, forcing me to speed walk to keep up. "I mean, if there's no one tying you down, why not?"

I frown. That seems like an odd thing for Kellan McVey to say. "Was there?" I ask. "Someone?"

He's quiet for a second. "Nah," he says finally. "There've been a lot of someones, but no one special."

Ouch. "I see."

"What about you?"

I force a smile. "No one special."

"And tonight? You have anyone in mind? Want me to introduce you? Because honestly, Nora? You're super hot. And in that outfit, you could have anyone you want."

I laugh because I can't help it. "I'm steering clear of green paint," I say, "otherwise, I'm keeping my options open."

He gives me a weird look. "Green paint, huh? I'm making a mental note to ask about that in the morning."

"I'm sure I won't know what you're talking about."

"McVey!"

Ten feet from the front door of the Alpha Sigma Phi house, it's like a starting whistle has been blown. Every guy and girl in the vicinity start to cry Kellan's name, and he grins and waves and greets them like the world's best politician. Almost immediately I feel myself fading into the background.

The walkway leading up to the front door is lined with

modified tiki torches, each boasting a severed head with flames licking out the eyes. There are jack-o-lanterns and stuffed black cats, ghosts dangling from bare tree branches, and the entire front lawn is covered in tombstones, many of which appear to have been recently disturbed.

The front door is open, crime scene tape fluttering on either side, chalk outlines of broken bodies etched on the steps and floor. Dance music fights to be heard over shrill screams and ghostly howls, and the laughter of the living is barely audible over the sounds of the dead.

Kellan shoots me an apologetic look over his shoulder as he's quickly whisked away, some sort of beverage in a plastic skull shoved into his hand. I shiver a little in my coat, wishing I'd come up with an outfit that didn't bare my midriff and show more than a hint of cleavage. I try not to look uncomfortable as I climb the steps and enter the dim house, every light swapped for either red bulbs or flickering black lights, casting everyone in an eerie glow.

I shrug out of my jacket as I make my way through the throng of writhing bodies, barely miss walking through an enormous web, and finally find a table full of bowls of spiked red punch, tiny spiders and eyeballs peeking out between bubbles.

"It's not bad," comes a voice from over my shoulder. "If you don't mind blood and guts."

I glance back to see a zombie smiling at me, part of his skull missing, his overalls and plaid shirt covered in blood and gore as his innards spill out. "If it's got spiders, I'm drinking it," I say.

He takes in my costume. "Did you come with somebody?"

"Louise got a bad case of food poisoning."

He ladles punch into my skull cup and pours himself a glass. "Lucky me." He touches his cup to mine. "Cheers."

"Cheers."

We sip the sickly sweet liquid, dosed heavily with vodka. I try not to wince as it burns on the way down, telling myself it'll soon wash away all this awkwardness. I came here to have fun, dammit—and I'm going to.

"I'm Max," the zombie says, extending a hand.

"Nora." We shake and he smiles and under the gruesome makeup, I think he's probably quite handsome. "Do you live here?"

He shakes his head. "I did two years ago, but I moved off campus. I come back for the parties, though. Are you in a sorority?"

"No. My, uh, roommate has friends here."

"Cool."

"Thelma!" someone bellows.

I jump back as a bright blue blur cuts between Max and I, zipping around in a circle before coming back to stand beside us, hands on hips, chest proudly thrust out to reveal the iconic S on his skin-tight suit. It's Crosbie, clad head to toe in spandex, a red cape hanging down his back. Even in the darkness I can see his clearly defined muscles, and just as quickly as I notice, I chastise myself for noticing.

"Hey, Cros," Max says dryly.

Crosbie spares him a formal nod. "Maxwell."

Max rolls his eyes.

Then Crosbie takes my arm. "Let me borrow Thelma for a minute, would you? I need her help with something."

"I didn't think Superman had a sidekick," I say as he drags me through the crowd to the staircase. I grab the banister before he can pull me up. "What's going on?"

"Kellan told me your friend bailed," Crosbie explains. He stopped when I stopped, so now he's one step up, looking down at me. "And he said you wanted to meet somebody. Well, I'm here to help."

"I'm pretty sure Superman's skills can be put to better use. Plus, if you didn't notice, I was talking to someone."

"You do not want to hook up with Max Folsom," he says seriously. "Trust me. Now come on." He reaches around my shoulder to draw me up the stairs.

"How am I going to meet somebody upstairs when the

party's downstairs?" I ask, trailing him down the hall toward his room.

He pulls a single key from a nearly invisible pocket and unlocks his door. "Vantage point."

I'm not sure what he means until I follow him inside, watching as he goes to the window and shoves it open. Frosty air rolls in, and when Crosbie gestures for me to crawl through, I peer out cautiously. The window opens onto a small eave that overlooks the front lawn. We're high enough up that someone would have to crane their neck to see us, but from here we can easily spy on everyone who comes and goes.

"See?" he says, tapping my back to indicate I should start moving, which I carefully do, shivering while I put my coat back on. Crosbie follows, and when I hear glass clink I look over to see two bottles of beer have materialized in his hand.

I accept one after he twists off the cap. "Where'd you get this?"

"Personal stash." It's the same local craft brew Kellan drinks. I'd never heard of it until I found it in the fridge one day, and while I don't drink it often, I'd mentioned once that I liked it.

"This is good," I say. "Kellan buys it."

"I know." Crosbie sips his beer and studies the mass of people below us. Like me, his knees are drawn up to his chest for warmth. There's about a foot of space between us and the cold shingles chill my ass through my jeans.

"Do you come out here a lot?" I ask when he doesn't say anything.

He shakes his head. "No. What for?"

I shrug. "I don't know." I scan the crowd. I don't see Kellan or Max or anyone else I recognize. Not that I'm likely to recognize many people given my determined homebody status. "What was wrong with Max?"

"The Walking Douche?" Crosbie asks, angling an unimpressed look my way. "We call him that even without the zombie getup."

"He seemed nice."

"You can do better." He tips his bottle at a guy dressed as a lumberjack. He's even carrying a fire log. "How about him?"

"Who is he?"

"I don't know. He's probably getting a degree in forestry. Smart and environmentally friendly—doesn't get much better than that."

The guy drops the log and promptly pukes behind one of the tombstones.

"Not him," I say at the same moment Crosbie says, "Moving right along." He scans the crowd and points at someone dressed in chef whites. Even from here we can hear him cursing viciously at people in a British accent.

"Seriously?"

"What? It's Gordon Ramsay. He can cook you breakfast in the morning."

"After calling me names all night."

"Some girls are into that."

I drink my beer. "I'm not."

Crosbie smirks. "I didn't think so. Okay—what about him?" I swat his hand when he points to a guy dressed in a long blond wig and red bathing suit, *Lifeguard* stenciled across the chest, pubes poking out at his crotch.

"Pamela Anderson?"

"Bet he's good at mouth to mouth."

"You're terrible," I accuse. "I think you brought me out here because you need assistance finding somebody."

He grins. "I don't need your help, Nora."

I think of his abruptly-ending list. "Really? I think you might." I tap my chin and study the selection. "Let's see. How about…her?" I point to a pretty brunette in a predictable cat costume. It's mean, but Crosbie probably prefers things simple.

"Been there," he replies. "Done that."

I mock gag. "Fine. What about her?" I point to a cute ballerina, her blond hair twisted into a high bun, pink satin toe shoes laced up her calves.

"Ugh," he says. "Too much work getting under that tutu."

"Good grief."

He laughs. "I mean, first you've gotta get the tutu off, then the body suit, then the leggings… I'm looking for something with a little easier access."

I hit him in the leg with my empty bottle. "You're disgusting." I sit up straighter when I spot a guy dressed as a baseball player. There's nothing especially creative about the outfit, but I have a thing for athletes, and he's the definition of tall, dark and handsome.

Crosbie sits up, too. "What are we looking at?"

"Number nine," I whisper, though he couldn't possibly hear us. "Do you know him?"

"Ah…" Crosbie scratches his chin. I hear the faint rasp of his five o'clock shadow, and when I glance over he's closer than before, leaning in to see the guy I'm pointing out. "Yeah," he says eventually. "His name is Phil. But you don't want him."

"I don't? Why not?"

"Because Thelma hooks up with Brad Pitt," he answers. "And he's no Brad Pitt."

"I'm keeping him on the list," I say, just as a petite girl dressed in a skimpy schoolgirl costume minces up the walkway. "There," I say, nodding at her. "That's the one."

"You want to hook up with a chick?" Crosbie asks. "I'm all over it. You can use my room. I'll just sit quietly in the corner and watch. You won't even know I'm there."

"For you, jerk. Short skirt, no tights—easy access."

He watches her progress. "All right. She's in."

I shiver as I study the partygoers.

"You okay?" he asks, shifting closer. "Want some cape?" He flings the tail end over my shoulders before I can answer.

"Thanks," I say, fingering the flimsy fabric. "All better."

"They don't call me a superhero for nothing."

We fall silent as a familiar laugh rings out from below, then Kellan jogs through the cemetery to greet the two beauty queens who have just stepped out of a cab curb side. They're dressed in floor-length gowns, one red, one silver, with sashes and tiaras. One even has a bouquet of roses. We watch him

sling an arm around each of their shoulders, grinning as he
leads them toward the house.

I recognize them from parties last year—and if I'm not
mistaken, the one in red appears on Crosbie's bathroom list.
"Don't you, um…know her?" I ask, wincing as the girl in
question giggles and tugs on Kellan's tie.

"Not really," Crosbie says, unconcerned.

They squeal in mock-terror as a chainsaw-wielding maniac
charges the trio, and Kellan roars with laughter before pulling
out his cell phone and trying to call someone. He frowns,
hangs up, and quickly sends a text, waiting a moment for a
reply that doesn't come. Because I'd planned on walking home
and wasn't worried about getting separated from Marcela, I
hadn't even brought my phone. If Kellan's texting to find out
if I've bailed, he's not going to get an answer.

"It doesn't bother you?" I ask, when I notice Crosbie
looking a little more tense than he had a minute earlier.

"Me?" he echoes. "No. Does it bother you?"

I think it'd bother me if my name appeared on the
bathroom wall, but I don't especially care that the girls are
here. "No."

He studies me for a second, then nods. "Good."

A group of coeds arrives, clambering out of a limo, all but
one dressed in a tight business suit, heels, and carrying a
briefcase. A couple even clutch a newspaper. I toss back my
head and laugh. "I've been wondering where they were."

Crosbie frowns. "The businesswomen?"

I gesture to his costume. "The Lois Lanes."

"Why didn't you come as Lois?"

For a second my mind goes blank. Somehow I'd managed
to forget I was sitting up on a tiny eave with Crosbie Lucas
while he wore only spandex. Somehow I'd managed to forget I
was awkward and uncomfortable. I'd even managed to forget
that I'd promised myself one guilt-free night of anything goes.
And now I'm remembering.

"I…" I try. "I don't have a business suit."

He blinks. He's got very long eyelashes. For such a big

guy, it's an oddly endearing trait.

"But you had a red wig?"

"Well…no."

He smiles faintly. "I prefer Thelma to Lois any day, anyway."

"You do?"

"Yo! Cros!"

The sudden shout sends us scattering, as far as the eave will allow, anyway. We both whip our heads around to see a guy dressed as the Cat in the Hat peering out the window.

"What the fuck, Alex?" Crosbie mutters, running a hand over his face.

"Kellan's looking for you. He's got a couple of Miss Americas that want to say hi."

My scalp itches under the cheap wig. "You should go," I say. Now that whatever weird spell had been brewing is broken, I'm cold and my butt hurts. "I'm freezing, anyway." I flash him a fake smile, then gesture for the Cat in the Hat to move aside as I clamber back through the window, my frozen limbs screeching as they unfold.

"Nora," Crosbie says.

"Thanks for your help," I tell him. "I can take it from here." I step back as he comes through the window, pulling it closed.

"Get out," he says to the Cat in the Hat.

"There you are!" comes a familiar voice. Crosbie looks pained and closes his eyes for a second, but when they reopen, he's looking over my shoulder—at Clark Kent.

"We're not supposed to be seen together," Crosbie says. "We're the same person, remember?"

"I thought you'd be happy to make an exception," Kellan replies. "For Miss Maryland or Miss Louisiana?" Upon hearing their cue, the slightly tipsy beauty queens enter the room, doing their best formal waves and collapsing into each other as they giggle.

The Cat in the Hat and I share a look, then murmur our excuses as we leave the room.

"You doing okay, Nora?" Kellan asks.

"Just great," I assure him.

Crosbie says something, but it's drowned out in more laughter, and I'm moving too fast to make it out, even if I wanted to. It's only nine-thirty when I get downstairs, so I grab another drink and make a half-hearted lap around the room, checking out the décor, the costumes, the couples. I see Max—The Walking Douche—and all of a sudden I just want to go home. Phil strolls by with Dorothy from the *Wizard of Oz*, his hand squarely glued to her ass, and I sigh and set my drink on a table. Maybe the reason I was so good at this last year is because practice makes perfect—and I am now sorely out of practice.

I zip up my jacket and make my way to the front, wincing when a group of vampire football players rush by, knocking me into the wall. Their apologies are lost in the throbbing music and I rub my sore tailbone, turning to scowl at the doorknob that bruised me. And then I freeze, because I know this doorknob. I know this closet.

When Kellan first spoke to me that ill-fated May night, I'd been equal parts stunned, thrilled, and terrified. We were already drunk when we started talking, and two drinks later we were blitzed. The alcohol may have loosened my inhibitions but it had done nothing to calm my nerves, and as he'd led me through the house looking for an empty room, I'd rambled on inanely about every dull thing I could think of, from our unseasonably warm weather to the periodic table. I think we were both grateful when he found the closet, kissed me, and put an end to the impromptu science lesson.

Now I turn my head slightly to see what would have once been the house's formal dining room, but is now just a room filled with couches and cheesy posters. Forty-five minutes after our less-than-memorable sex, I'd walked by here to see Kellan standing in the center of the room, a blonde girl on her knees in front, blowing him while his frat brothers cheered him on.

My face floods with heat and remembered humiliation and I shoulder my way through the crowd and out the front door, the icy air more than welcome. For all accounts and purposes, this is a great party. Lots of people, free booze, loud music—but the best part was when I was away from it all, drinking a single beer with a guy I shouldn't even like.

But I do.

chapter eleven

I keep my head down and hurry along the sidewalk. I dart over to the next block to avoid the groups of people arriving for the party, encountering only a couple of hardcore kids approaching houses, most of which have gone dark. Street lamps and flickering jack-o-lanterns offer a little light, but I welcome the darkness. Rather, I welcome it until I hear footsteps thudding along behind me, coming too fast to be anything other than running. I risk a terrified look over my shoulder, prepared to sprint—and very grateful Thelma favored practical shoes—then come to an abrupt halt when I find Superman bearing down on me.

"Crosbie?" Seeing someone I know should encourage my heartbeat to slow to normal levels, but instead it keeps pounding. He's still wearing his costume, but now he's added sneakers and a heavy jacket, the red cape bunched up around his neck, like he got dressed too fast to think it through.

"Hey," he says, stopping a few feet away. I don't know if it's because he's breathing heavily, but he's having a hard time meeting my eye, so for a second I just watch the white puffs of his breath dissipate in the air.

"What are you doing out here?" I think of the house, the beauty queens, the everything I'm not.

"You can't walk home alone." He rakes his fingers through his hair, leaving pieces sticking out every which way. "People do crazy things on Halloween."

"I'm pretty sure all those people are at your house."

He smiles briefly. "Maybe. Anyway. Come on."

Even though it's a thirty-minute round trip and he'll be back at the party with plenty of time left for fun, I feel obligated to tell him to go home. "This isn't necessary."

"Let me do it anyway." He's got his hands crammed in his pockets and I realize he must be freezing in that costume. Hell—I'm freezing in mine, no spandex in sight.

We walk a block in silence. "How'd you do with your French paper?" he asks finally.

"Pretty good." I'm surprised he remembers my classes. "These past couple of weeks have been hell, but I think I'm on top of everything. How about you? How'd midterms go?"

"I feel good about Bio and Art History, but Econ is kicking my ass."

"Two out of three ain't bad?"

He smirks and kicks a piece of smashed pumpkin off the sidewalk. "Two out of three is sixty-six percent. It ain't great."

"Who says you aren't good with numbers?"

"Hey," he says suddenly. "I'm sorry."

I look at him. "For what?"

"For messing up your night back there. If you're leaving because of Max or whatever, I didn't mean—"

I wave him off. "Don't worry about it. Maybe tonight just wasn't meant to be."

"It was your one night to blow off steam."

"There'll be other nights. Like, between Christmas and New Years, or spring break…"

He laughs at the depressing timeline. "You don't think you'll regret it?"

We pass a quiet block that's a dedicated dog park, mulch running paths and stands of bare trees marking the grass.

"Not flunking out?"

"Missing out on the things you want because you're trying so hard to be good."

"I am good."

"I know you are."

"Well, what about you?" I counter.

"What about me?"

"I saw the bathrooms in the student building a couple of weeks ago. Your 'list' doesn't have any new names on it."

He's quiet for a second. I expect him to say something cocky, like maybe he just hasn't updated it yet, but he surprises me when he says, "I got tired of that."

"What? Being popular?"

"Being a dick."

The second surprise in as many seconds. "You—"

"Look, Nora." He stops at the corner, a tall cluster of trees blocking the street lamps and houses so we're folded in darkness, only the faintest slashes of light making it through. I stop, my back to the trees, and when he steps into me, I feel the cold bark through my coat and my jeans. "I'm just going to do this," he says, lifting a hand to rest on the trunk beside my head. "And if you don't want me to, say no."

He's so close. With his head dipped his mouth is only a couple of inches away from mine, and though we've been in close proximity before, this is the first time there's ever been any intention in his gaze. The only time he's ever shown it, at least. He lowers his head another inch, then another, until his lips are only millimeters from mine, giving me every opportunity to push him back, run away, not do something ridiculous.

But my hands remain fisted squarely in the sleeves of my jacket, my feet planted on the soft grass, my head tipped up to his. Waiting for something I'm finally ready to admit I want.

I see his eyes drift closed and then his mouth brushes over mine. I'd never allowed myself to give kissing Crosbie Lucas much thought, but if I had I'd have predicted it to be hard or invasive, grabby hands and lewdly thrusting hips. But it's nothing like that at all. The hand on the tree stays where it is while his other finds the dip of my waist and rests there on top of my coat. I feel the chill of his nose bumping mine, the contrasting warmth of his lips, and though shock and awe are currently duking it out for top billing in the feelings department, I'm starting to feel some very unexpected other things, too.

A tiny sigh escapes and Crosbie seizes the opportunity to slip his tongue into my mouth, very gently finding mine. My fingers uncurl themselves long enough to fist in the front of his coat, and the permissive action has him stepping into me even more, so I'm caught squarely between him and the tree. The hand resting on my side slides up to tangle in my silly wig, and when he tries to tug my head back the wig falls off.

"What the—" he mutters, frowning at the mop of hair in his hand.

This isn't really the time for laughing but I do, my forehead bumping his shoulder as my body shakes from the force of it. I'd hoped to do some new things tonight, but at no point was Crosbie Lucas on the list.

"I forgot," he explains. "I'm sorry."

I laugh harder.

"Nora."

I feel his fingers under my chin, tilting my face back up to his, and even in the darkness I can feel the intensity in his gaze, the seriousness there, and I stop laughing when he kisses me again, this time a little harder, a little more sure. He's not waiting for me to take him up on his offer to stop, and he shouldn't. I rise onto my tiptoes and kiss him back, teeth and tongues and lips, feeling his raspy breath, hearing the hungry sounds he makes as he winds his fingers through my real hair and—

"Shit," he whispers, jerking back. "Fuck."

Then I hear it too. Raucous mixed laughter, male and female, approaching from the next block. They're heading toward the Frat Farm and there's really no way for me to step out of a copse of trees with Crosbie Lucas without starting rumors. As though he's thinking the same thing, Crosbie nudges me backward into the trees, and then we just stand there, hot and cold, waiting for the group to pass. They stumble by a minute later, not even glancing our way.

We stare at each other for a long time. I don't know quite

how this happened, but parts of me that have been quashed beneath my responsible new veneer have whirred back to life and they're not ready to end whatever this is just yet.

"Tell me what you want," he says, his voice slightly hoarse.

I swallow. He seems sincere and a little on edge, and I understand—certain parts of me are howling at the mere prospect of doing the responsible thing and sending Crosbie Lucas back to the frat house to bang Miss Maryland. So instead I do as he asks, and tell him the truth. "Walk me home."

He nods. "Fine."

"And promise that no matter what happens, my name will never end up on any lists."

He flinches, so fast I'd have missed it if I blinked. "I promise, Nora."

We start walking, our brisk pace due only in part to the cold. We don't touch and we don't speak, and when we reach my block I look up and down the street to make sure we're alone. Crosbie glances around too. "Want me to go around back?" he offers. "Come in through your window?"

"Oh. Would you—"

He growls and snatches the keys from my palm, hauling me up the steps to the front door. "I'm not crawling through the fucking window. That was a joke."

"I thought maybe with the Superman thing—"

"He leaps over buildings. He doesn't break into places."

"Well, I really don't know a lot about Superman, Crosbie."

He shoves open the door and nudges me in first. "I don't want to talk about this right now." And then the tentative kisses from the tree are gone, replaced by hot and wet and dirty. Soon my coat is on the floor and I'm kicking off second-hand cowboy boots, not caring where they land. Crosbie scoops me up like I weigh nothing and I wrap my legs around his broad waist, hard muscles pressed against the tender insides of my knees.

He carries me into my bedroom, flipping on the light and

closing the door. When he sees my gaze catch on the knob he must realize I'm worried about the lack of a lock because he says, "He won't be home tonight. I'll be gone before he comes back."

I nod and swallow as Crosbie toes off his sneakers and drops his coat on top. Now he's waiting there in that ridiculous costume, a very conspicuous bulge in front making it clear where we stand. "I really wish I wasn't wearing this," he says, reaching behind his neck to fumble with the zipper.

"Let me help," I say, stepping close. He turns to face the door and I slide the zipper down, watching the fabric separate to reveal the very broad, very muscled plane of his back, dotted with freckles. Impulsively I lean in and press a kiss to the warm skin, goose bumps popping up on contact. The muscles ripple as he reaches up and shoves the sleeves down his arms, the attached cape catching and tearing slightly, though he doesn't seem to care. When he turns around he's naked to the waist, the shiny fabric bunched around his stomach.

My mouth goes dry. Crosbie is almost accidentally perfect. Too broad, too big, too hot. He looks like the guy who can lift a tractor with his bare hands, hands that are now reaching for me and slowly, intently, undoing the myriad buttons on this two-dollar shirt.

"You can just tear it," I murmur, fighting the temptation to do it myself. I want this. It's been too long and I want it all right now. "I'm never going to wear this again."

"Nora," he says seriously. "I'm going to need you to wear this outfit on many, many occasions."

I fail to stop the unladylike snort of laughter that escapes, and Crosbie laughs too, though he never falters in his task. Finally he pushes the cheap denim over my shoulders and lets it fall to the floor so I'm left in a white lace bra and Thelma's high-waisted jeans.

He sighs and steps back, blatantly eying my chest. "Can I tell you something?" he asks, never lifting his gaze.

"Ah, okay?"

"I have wanted to touch these for a long time."

I laugh, surprised. "What?" I suppose I shouldn't be so shocked: he's a guy, these are boobs. It's like peanut butter and jelly.

He reaches around and I feel his fingers slide under the bra's lace band, undoing the hooks. "That first day," he whispers against my hair, "when you showed up with that tight little sweater with the buttons on the front? I think about that a lot."

My whole body floods with desire at the words. Because the grittiness in his tone, the feel of his erection bumping my belly as he stands so close and guides the straps down my arms—I know he's talking about jerking off as he thinks about that cardigan.

I want to laugh but I don't think I can anymore. When he finally bares my breasts for the first time, the sound of his sharp breath steals my own. Very slowly he trails his hands up my hips, over my stomach, until he's lifting a breast in each calloused palm, his touch as reverent as his skin is rough and scratchy. And while his fingers stroking back and forth over my nipples feels great, it's the look on his face that's really turning me on. He's completely absorbed. Like he's memorizing this moment. Like he'll never forget it.

"Crosbie." I slip my hands up over his big biceps, his wide shoulders, his neck, his ears, before finally tangling in his hair.

"Nora," he replies, shifting forward so I have to step back, my calves hitting the bed frame. He releases my breasts long enough to skate a hand between my shoulder blades, anchoring the other on my ass and lowering me onto the mattress before kneeling between my parted legs. His big hands go to the button on my jeans and he looks me in the eye. "Okay?"

I nod, not sure I can speak. My heart bounces around my chest as he carefully peels the denim down my legs, leaving me in only a purple thong. I see his throat bob as he swallows, then he reaches down to the floor for his jacket and pulls out his wallet, retrieving a condom and tossing it onto my milk crate night table. He smiles at me before pushing the spandex over his hips, past mouth-wateringly muscular thighs and strong calves. When he catches me looking he shyly fists his erection, the fingers of his other hand playing with the lace edge of my thong.

"Lift your hips."

I can barely breathe. Just looking at him makes me want to squirm in anticipation. Never in my admittedly short sexual lifespan have I wanted someone so badly that just looking at them made me wet. But I am wet, and I know Crosbie sees it because he makes a pained little groan when I lift my hips so he can slide the silky fabric down my legs, then gently nudges my thighs apart to look between them.

He lowers himself over me, elbows digging into the mattress on either side of my head, and pushes a stray hair behind my ear, sliding his lips back and forth across mine, in absolutely no hurry at all. I turn my head to look at the full-length mirror propped against the desk, angled just enough that I can see Crosbie's perfect ass positioned over me, so tempting I have to resist the urge to flip him over to look at it up close.

Not that I could budge him, even if I wanted to. Though he's being very conscientious about not crushing me, just the weight of one of his legs between my thighs is enough to remind me how big he is. How strong.

"Hey," he says softly, lifting his head to look at me.

"What?"

"Have you done this before?"

The question startles me, but eventually I nod. "Yes," I manage. It reminds me of how little we know about each other. How last year if you'd asked me how Crosbie Lucas fucked I'd have said he did it like a porn star, all ass slapping and hair pulling, boasting to his friends afterward. All style and no substance. But the guy over me now isn't the obnoxious jock I thought I knew, just like I'm not the responsible bookworm he thinks he knows. And when he nods and glides a hand between my legs, the relief on his face when he finds me wet and ready is almost palpable. I moan when he pushes one finger inside, then spread my legs wider when he stretches me with two, fucking gently as he kisses my mouth, eyes open, gauging my response.

I had a couple of orgasms with my partners last year, nothing mind-blowing or exceptional, just perfunctory, okay-we're-on-the-right-track orgasms, but they never felt half as good as Crosbie Lucas's fingers and the promises they're making right now.

"Crosbie—" I gasp as he rubs the heel of his hand over my clit.

"You okay?"

"It feels—"

"Say whatever you want," he says when I forget the rest of the sentence. "I'll do whatever you want."

"I think I might—" I don't know if I should be embarrassed that I'm going to come this easily, but Crosbie's cocky grin and intensified fingering tells me he's not bothered by it at all. He kisses me rough and wet, his hand rubbing in all the right ways, and before I'm fully ready I come, deep waves of desire radiating from my center, through my legs, curling my toes.

I moan into his mouth and he strokes my cheek as though he's encouraging me, egging me on. And I don't care anymore about anything, only how good this feels. How if every name on that stupid bathroom wall was practice that led to this moment, I'm absolutely okay with it.

I turn my face away and struggle to control my breathing as Crosbie slowly eases his hand from between my legs. He gives me a minute, busying himself with my breasts, his tongue circling my tight nipples, mouth sucking lightly. I feel his knuckles bump against my inner thigh and lift my head to see him slowly jacking himself with the hand that was just inside me, using my juices as lubrication.

"Crosbie," I whisper, reaching for the condom.

"You need a sec?" He searches my face as he uses his teeth to open the packet. I shake my head and he rests back on his heels as he rolls on the condom, propping my legs wide apart and gazing intently at my pussy.

Okay, that's embarrassing. I'm wet and exposed and he—

"Hey," he says.

I realize I'm staring determinedly at the wall. "What?"

"What's wrong?"

"Nothing."

"What are you thinking about?" Despite the fact that he's got a raging hard-on and a willing vagina ten inches away, he's not making any move to put it in.

"It's just a little embarrassing," I mutter, scrubbing a hand over my face.

"What is?"

I wave a hand toward my vagina. "Having someone stare at it!"

He wrinkles his nose and laughs. "Nora, you're hilarious."

"I'm not trying to be funny."

"You want to look at mine?"

"I did look."

"You want to look closer?" He's stroking the insides of my calves, his fingers tickling the soft skin behind my knees.

"Are you asking me to blow you?"

He smiles. "No. Not this time." He hooks his hands under my legs and lifts them high and wide, but before I can be mortified he comes down over me, one arm on the pillow beside my head, the other guiding his cock between my legs. "Can I?"

"Do you really have to ask?"

"I just want to be sure."

I look into his eyes, molten brown I now know darkens to nearly black when he's turned on, the flush in his cheeks belying the utter control in his voice. I think he'd stop if I asked him to. I think he'd put on that Superman costume and do a jig if I requested it. I think Crosbie Lucas is not quite the cocky, smug ass hat he pretends to be.

"I'm positive," I say.

Something soft passes across his features and he smiles as

he kisses me, sweet and sure, then he presses inside slowly, carefully, and very welcome. His cock is as big as his build would suggest, but after the initial pang of discomfort it only feels good, and he groans into my neck, his damp breath making me shudder. It takes him a minute, then he lifts his head and watches my face as he slowly starts to fuck me, taking his time, focused and intent.

I like it, but I don't think I'm going to come again so soon. And I don't really care—I just had the best orgasm I've ever had with a partner, I'm not complaining. After a while I wrap my legs around his hips, my fingers seeking purchase in that beautiful ass, feeling it shift and bunch as he moves.

"Can you come like this?" he whispers, trailing his fingers over my damp temples.

"I don't think so," I reply, feeling strangely comfortable with this kind of honesty. "But it doesn't matter. I just did. You come."

He arches a brow. "Oh, I'm going to. No question. But not without you." He stops thrusting and reaches back, fingers encircling my ankle. I prepare myself for some sort of inane sex contortion showcase, but he merely bends my left leg up against my chest and shifts his body to the side a little more. This time he hits my clit when he thrusts, and a few moments later, I'm forced to reconsider my stance on a second orgasm.

"How about this?" he murmurs. He nips my earlobe and I focus on the newly building sensation between my legs.

"I think I might…"

"Tell me what'll get you there."

"Let's try this for a minute."

"Got it." He grinds his forehead into the pillow beside me, his damp hair brushing my cheek, showing me just how difficult this is for him. How hard he's working to make it good for me. His faint dusting of chest hair rasps over my nipples, and when I urge him to move faster he does, and I know I'm going to come again.

"I'm close," I whisper.

"Nora." He groans and threads his fingers through mine

on either side of my head, holding me down and holding on, all at once.

"Just a little…"

"Oh fuck…fuck…"

"I'm—I'm—*ohhhh*…." I come and Crosbie's right behind me. I feel him pump into me harder, a few rough thrusts, a litany of mumbled curse words in my ear, the almost painfully tight squeeze of his fingers on mine. But I couldn't possibly care less about any of that, because my pussy is spasming so tightly, so good, just endless waves of pleasure I never knew I could feel.

Crosbie may be exactly the type of guy to boast about knowing how to do this, and I'm the type of girl who would roll my eyes and blow him off. Until now. This is no laughing matter. This is *incredible*.

Eventually he lifts his head and I turn so we're eye to eye, and it's a tiny relief to see the same stunned and satiated expression on his face that I know is on mine. "Wow," I mumble.

He laughs, a tired sound, and wipes his hand over his forehead. "Jesus, Nora. You're so fucking beautiful. I don't think I've ever come like that."

"Is it the blue eye shadow?" I ask, belatedly remembering that not only did I wear Thelma's hair and clothing, I wore the makeup, too.

"No," he says, pressing a kiss to the corner of my mouth as he slowly pulls out. "It's you."

He gets up and pads out of the room, bare-assed, to dispose of the condom and clean up, and I slide under the comforter and stretch out like a very satisfied cat. I don't know what the hell I'm going to feel like tomorrow, but right now I feel amazing, all the stress and tension of the past couple of months forgotten.

Crosbie comes back in with two glasses of water, then sets them on the milk crate and flicks on the lamp before turning off the ceiling light. "So," he says, crawling under the covers before passing me a glass.

"So," I say.

We drink in silence and stare at the ceiling. I'm aware of every inch of his body that's touching mine, the sound of his throat working as he swallows, the hum of his breath when he puts the empty glasses on the floor and turns out the light. And then I'm not aware of anything else, because somehow, impossibly, I fall asleep next to Crosbie Lucas.

chapter twelve

I wake up alone. It's just before eight the next morning, the bright November sun spilling in through curtains I forgot to close during last night's activities.

Speaking of which. I arch my back and flex my fingers and gently feel between my legs—a little sore, but in a good way. Hell, in an amazing way. So amazing I'm not even especially worried about the fact that I had sex with Crosbie Lucas. That I moved into this apartment on the understanding that it was a place to be studious and responsible, and then banged my roommate's best friend. Because it was so worth it.

I yawn and climb out of bed, buck naked, smiling foolishly as I fish out a pair of panties, shorts, and a sweatshirt, then head into the bathroom to wash my face and brush my teeth. Jeez. I'm glad Crosbie's gone. Thelma's blue shadow and extra thick mascara now ring my eyes, making me look like a crazed nineties raccoon.

I spit toothpaste into the sink, rinse my mouth, and tell myself not to be a Crosbabe. I'd seen plenty of girls trailing after him last year, girls who wanted to be with him or who had already been and wanted another round. I won't be one of those girls, though I now understand where they're coming from.

Tidied up and half-awake—there's not much I can do about my hair except tie it back—I shuffle into the kitchen, squawking in terror when Kellan rises up from the far side of the kitchen island.

He jumps when I screech, a spoon flying out of his hand to crash into the cupboard behind him. "Nora!" he exclaims. "Shit!"

I cover my face with my hands and try not to have a heart attack. "What are you doing here?" I mumble through my fingers.

"I live here."

"This early! This quiet!"

"I was being quiet because you were sleeping," he says. "And then I thought you heard me." He tosses the spoon in the sink and gets a new one from the drawer, then indicates the bowl of cereal on the counter. "I made breakfast while you were in the bathroom."

I shake my head, guilt making me antsy. "Sorry." I squeeze past him to grab a carton of orange juice from the fridge. "I was just surprised." I pour a glass and join him at the island, my forgotten cell phone sitting on the counter. I check my missed messages and find five from Marcela, each more self-pitying than the last, promising to bequeath me all her belongings if she should die, and asking me to come find her corpse the next day so she's not already half-decomposed at her funeral.

I smile and put down the phone, and it's only when I notice Kellan's smirk that I realize I'm still smiling, more than a few morbid texts can justify. I try my best to act casual. "What?"

"What'd you get up to last night?" He shoots a deliberate glance toward my half-open bedroom door. "You disappeared fast."

Now he notices what I do? "I got tired."

"If you don't want to tell me, you don't have to," he says. "I just hope you had fun."

"I did," I assure him, desperate to change the subject. "Did you?"

"Actually, no." He's spooning cereal into his mouth with his right hand and checking his phone with his left. "I'm a little worried."

I think about Miss Maryland and Miss Louisiana—is he worried about which beauty queen's name to add to his list first? North-south or south-north? Alphabetical or chronological?

"What about?" I ask politely.

"Crosbie," he says, thumb flicking over the keys. "He's been acting weird lately, and last night I brought him two girls to choose from and he just took off. Said he'd be right back, then disappeared."

"Oh?"

Kellan looks at me seriously. "I think he might be having problems at the frat house. He's been spending a lot time here. That doesn't bother you, does it?"

I stare into my glass and shake my head. "No. He's okay."

Kellan sighs and hits send. "I hope so."

A muffled beep has us both twisting in our seats to locate the sound. A quick glance at our phones shows the screens are dark.

"Did you hear that?" Kellan asks, frowning and peering around the apartment.

I try not to let my mouth fall open as my gaze lands on the closet next to the dining table. Oh fuck.

"It's another text from Marcela," I say, snatching up my phone and pretending to read. "She's very sick."

"It beeped right after I sent Crosbie a text." Kellan looks unconvinced as he punches in another message. This one's short: *Where r u?*

I hold my breath, but there's no telltale notification. Crosbie must have turned off his phone.

Kellan exhales heavily. "Maybe I'm losing it," he admits. "I had my pick of two very beautiful state representatives last night, and all I could think about was Crosbie."

I don't know whether to laugh or cry. "I'm sure he's fine."

"I spent the night in his room, waiting for him to show up."

"Maybe he met somebody," I offer. Then clarify: "A stranger."

Kellan gives me a dry look. "I know everybody," he says. "And everybody knows Crosbie. I asked if anyone had seen Superman and they hadn't. The guy's not easy to miss."

"Hmm."

"Do you think he's depressed?"

"Depressed? I—no. I don't think so, Kellan."

"We talk about everything," he frets, squeezing his hands together. "And I know I haven't been very encouraging about his magic tricks, but if that's getting him down—"

I'm going to die. "That's probably it," I say, barely succeeding at keeping a straight face. "Just support his magic a bit more."

Kellan nods sagely. "You're right. I will. I've been an ass."

The two most sensitive boys on the planet, right here in this apartment.

"I'm sure he'll text you in a few minutes," I say a little too loudly, making Kellan flinch. "He's probably back on the Frat Farm, ready to tell you about the hot girl he hooked up with."

"God." Kellan runs his hands through his hair. "I hope so."

We stare at his empty cereal bowl for an increasingly awkward moment. "You know," I say, "why don't you take a shower and try to get some sleep? It'll make you feel better."

Kellan sniffs his armpit. "Do I smell?"

"I— " He doesn't, but if it gets him out of the room so Crosbie can come out of the closet, I'm willing to fib. "A little."

"Dammit. That suit was wool. I always sweat when I wear wool."

I nod sympathetically as he rinses his bowl and puts it in the dishwasher, then glances hopefully at his dark phone display.

"It'll be okay," I say. "Just give him some time to wake up. It's only eight o'clock."

"You're right." Kellan pats my hand. "I'm not going to

worry anymore until lunch."

The awkwardness is killing me.

"Actually," he says, pausing en route to the bathroom. "That's a lie. I'm not going to worry about Crosbie until lunch. You're another story."

"Me?"

"There's a condom wrapper on your floor, Nora Kincaid. And we had a deal about not bringing people back here."

"We—I—" Oh my God.

"And I know Crosbie comes over a lot, but he doesn't count."

I shake my head fervently. "I'm so sor—"

Kellan grins and laughs uproariously. "Are you kidding? Don't apologize, Nora! You finally got some and I'm happy for you. And a little jealous of the lucky bastard. Did you have a good time?"

I don't need to see Crosbie to know he's got his ear pressed to the closet door. "Yes," I mutter.

"Did he make you scream?"

"Kellan, go take a shower."

He laughs some more and extends his hand for a fist bump I reluctantly return. He's chuckling as he disappears into the bathroom, and I sit very still on the stool, listening to the water turn on, then the muffled sound of his singing.

"Crosbie!" I hiss, leaping to my feet.

The closet doors bang open and he topples out, hair tousled, wearing a pair of Kellan's running shorts and a T-shirt that's two sizes too small and clings to every one of his thousand muscles. He's got his jacket in one hand and his costume and phone in the other.

"He sent me forty-one texts last night!"

"He thinks you're depressed!"

He covers his face when he laughs. "You really want me to tell him about the hot chick I hooked up with?"

"Make something up," I say, herding him toward the stairs.

"Maybe I'll say I got with Miss Washington," he says,

pulling on his coat. "Not quite a lie."

"As long as Miss Washington remains nameless, I really don't care."

"Hey." Crosbie catches my arm before I can yank open the front door.

"What?"

"You really think he's going to be more supportive of my magic?" He manages to keep a straight face for three whole seconds.

"Text him to say you're alive," I order, twisting the deadbolt.

"I will." He catches my hand and backs me into the wall, holding my gaze as he lowers his head to kiss me, a couple soft swipes and the briefest touch of his tongue. And just like that, all my responsible composure threatens to crumble, ready to beg him to fuck me again, right here.

The shower shutting off puts an abrupt end to those thoughts, for both of us.

"I had a good time, Nora," Crosbie says, opening the door.

"Me too."

"And I want to do it again."

If his reputation is true, Crosbie Lucas *never* wants to do anyone again.

"You do?"

"Yeah. Soon. After I have a fucking heart-to-heart with Mr. Sensitive up there."

"Just text him."

"I already did."

I can hear Kellan moving around in the bathroom. "Crosbie, you have to go."

"Give me your number."

I rattle it off quickly, knowing he won't remember.

"Got it," he says. "Now c'mere. One more." He taps his lips.

"Crosbie—"

But I don't resist when he grips the front of my shirt and

pulls me in for another kiss, even as the frigid air chills my legs and steals my breath.

"That's just the warm up," he says, finally releasing me. "I didn't make you scream last night." Oh God. Of course he'd focus on that.

I shove him out the door. "That's because I'm not a porn star."

He grins. "I bet I can get you to scream."

"I'm very close to it right now."

He laughs and jogs down the steps. "See you soon, Nora."

* * *

Classes are sparsely populated on Monday, post-Halloween weekend hangovers being what they are. Last year, after downing half my body weight in shots and hooking up with the army man, I'd spent three solid days scrubbing off green paint and regretting my life choices.

This year, however, I feel fine. Better than fine, actually. Maybe even a little...optimistic.

Which is stupid, I know. Crosbie's got a reputation for one night stands, and it's far easier to say "See you later" than "Goodbye forever," even if that's what you mean. Still, this is the first time since Nate started bringing Celestia to the shop that I haven't watched them with a little bit of longing. Now that some of my more basic needs have been met, I've gained some perspective.

That perspective shifts quickly when Marcela strolls in. She's dressed modestly for Marcela, in tight dark jeans and an equally tight sparkly white sweater, red lipstick and black velvet heels. The shop is half-full when she enters, and everyone watches as she strides through, including Nate and Celestia.

"Hey," I say, when she squeezes behind the counter and reaches for an apron. "Feeling better?"

"That's what drugs are for," she replies, filling a mug with hot water and dumping in an enormous amount of honey. "I figure I've got three good hours before I collapse. I just had to get out of that apartment."

"I offered to visit you yesterday."

"I know," she says, patting my arm. "And that was sweet of you. But that place is a germ market and I wanted to spare you."

"You're very kind."

"I am, aren't I?"

Truth be told, I was glad she turned me down, and not just because I didn't want to catch her cold. Marcela has a sixth sense about sex, and I needed to put some distance between my…thing…with Crosbie and Marcela's innate ability to recognize when anyone has done the deed.

Maybe I'm a great actor or maybe it's just the cold that prevents her from catching on. Or perhaps it's the fact that though she's trying hard to pretend she doesn't notice them, she's got one eye on Nate and Celestia, who sit in a corner working on a crossword puzzle together.

"Want to go in the back and make donuts?" I ask, hoping to stop her tirade against Celestia before it begins.

"I'll come in the back and *eat* donuts," she replies, reluctantly pulling her gaze away from the adoring couple. "We—" She breaks off and stares over my shoulder as the door opens, the faint sounds of light traffic filtering in along with the new customer. "Well, this is interesting," she murmurs, a coy smile curving her lips.

My heart immediately starts beating overtime as I slowly turn, expecting Crosbie.

But it's not Crosbie. It's Kellan.

"Hey," he says, shooting me a grin. He's wearing a sweatshirt, shorts and sneakers, dark hair damp at the temples.

"Hey," I respond, hoping I don't look as disappointed as I feel.

"Hey," Marcela says.

It doesn't take a genius to see where this is going.

"Hey," Kellan replies.

They smile at each other, no other words needed.

"Did you want a drink?" I ask loudly. "It's on me. Marcela, why don't you go into the back and start on the donuts?"

"Donuts?" Kellan echoes with great interest.

"Come on," Marcela says, lifting the panel on the counter so he can step behind. "I'll show you how we make them."

"You're sick!" I accuse. "You can't make donuts." I turn my attention to Kellan. "And you don't work here, so you can't make donuts, either." I herd them both out from behind the counter and follow, effectively locking us all out.

Kellan holds up his hands defensively. "Simmer down, Thelma. I thought you'd be more relaxed after—"

I widen my eyes in a warning Kellan actually heeds, cutting himself off before he announces my mysterious sexual escapade to Marcela. Marcela scowls as she grabs a lemon from the basket on the counter, turning her back to us as she slices a piece for her drink. With her attention averted, Kellan makes a face like, *Why doesn't she know?*

"I'm shy," I mouth back. It's not the best response, but it's all I can come up with. Fortunately, Kellan buys it, nodding his understanding.

The sound of a throat clearing gets our attention, and the three of us look over to see Nate standing a few feet away, next to a customer waiting for a refill.

"Sorry," I mutter, hastily reaching around to grab the coffee pot and pouring him a new cup. "My apologies."

Nate crosses his arms and looks at Kellan. "If you're not going to buy anything—"

Marcela looks ready to argue, but Kellan answers before she can, pulling a wallet from his pocket. "No problem," he says with an easy smile. "I came for the brownies." But the way he's looking at Marcela says his focus may have shifted.

"Here," Marcela says, using tongs to select a brownie from the plate in the display case. "This is the biggest one."

Kellan's smile widens. "Lucky me."

I look at Nate and he looks at me. We both look like we want to gag.

"What's the hold up?"

The four of us turn at the sound of the door and the wash of crisp fall air that sweeps in alongside Crosbie. Like Kellan he's wearing shorts and sneakers, but instead of a sweatshirt he's got a black T-shirt that clings to his broad chest.

Our eyes meet for a split second, then he turns his attention to Kellan. "You said you were getting a snack," he accuses, joining our awkward little group. "Not robbing the place."

"I *am* getting a snack," Kellan replies. Then he shoots Marcela a charming little smile. "And maybe a phone number?"

I cannot believe he just did that. The same disbelief is stamped all over Nate's face, and this no doubt spurs on Marcela as she grins and writes her number on a nearby order pad. She rips off the top page with a flourish and slips it into Kellan's waiting hand, their fingers lingering about twenty-eight seconds longer than necessary.

I feel bad for Nate and annoyed with Marcela and exasperated by Kellan. But they're all just background noise when Crosbie shifts a little bit closer, near enough that I can feel the heat radiating from his skin, smell the faint tang of his sweat.

"Um..." I say when the silence lingers awkwardly. "Do you want a brownie?"

Crosbie grins at me, but there's nothing special in the gesture, nothing to suggest anything happened between us, nothing to suggest it will ever happen again. "A brownie?" he asks. "Or a phone number?"

Everyone laughs and I grit my teeth, annoyed.

"Dude," Kellan says, still laughing. "As if!"

Another customer comes in and Nate looks at us all sternly. "Let's break this up, shall we? You two have work to do."

"And you?" Marcela snaps. "You have to figure out the answer to thirty-three across?"

Nate narrows his eyes. "Get back to work."

"Sorry," Kellan says, polishing off his brownie and putting a five dollar bill on the counter. "We're out of here. See you at home, Nora." He smiles at Marcela. "And see you later. I hope."

Ugh.

I turn to go back to work, halting when a firm swat on my ass makes me jump. I whip around, stunned, to see Crosbie casually strolling out the door after his friend. He doesn't look at me until they're outside, but when he turns his head to catch my gaze through the glass, the slight arch of his brow says everything I'd hoped to hear.

chapter thirteen

"I'm sorry," Marcela says immediately. Ten seconds later we've hustled into the kitchen, away from Nate's evil eye and any actual work.

I look at her blankly. "For what?"

She gestures toward the front. "For that! I know you're into Kellan and—" She lowers her voice as though there's someone around to eavesdrop, "and you two hooked up. This isn't me trying to hurt your feelings or steal him—"

I stand frozen as she rambles on. Somehow, over the course of moving in with Kellan McVey, sleeping twelve feet away from him, and sharing the occasional bowl of cereal, I've absolutely gotten over whatever lingering remnants of attraction I'd had. If I looked annoyed out front it was because Marcela was putting on a show for Nate's benefit and Kellan was, well, being Kellan.

"Stop," I say, holding up a hand when she shows no signs of tiring. "It's fine."

"It's not fine," she replies, looking pained. "That was a terrible thing to do—"

I hesitate, hoping to walk the fine line between girl-who-used-to-be-into-Kellan and girl-who-is-now-into-his-best-friend. "I'm over him," I say firmly. "I'm just…over it."

"But you—"

"You know that saying, absence makes the heart grow fonder? Well, living together has had the opposite effect. He's a nice guy and a surprisingly tidy roommate, but that's it. I'm not into him."

She looks like she wants to believe me but can't. "Are you sure?"

"A hundred percent. Honest."

She lets out a breath. "I wasn't actually going to go out with him," she says anyway. "It was just—"

"To make Nate jealous?"

"No!" she protests, too loudly. "To show Nate I'm fine with him and what's her name. I'm less fine with the discount she gets on her shitty drinks, but…"

I don't believe her for a second but I'm feeling guilty about keeping the Crosbie thing in the dark, even though not for one second do I consider coming clean about it. "Her drinks are so shitty," I agree instead.

Marcela grabs the tray of uncooked donuts from the oven where they've been rising. "And can we talk about the fur coats?"

"Of course—" I break off when my phone buzzes in the front pocket of my apron. "One sec," I say, frowning at the screen. The number is local but the caller is unknown. I open the message anyway.

Sorry, it reads. *Shouldn't have slapped your ass.*

Crosbie. Did he really memorize my number when I rattled it off two mornings ago? More likely he stole it from Kellan's phone. Not that I'm complaining.

As for the apology, it's completely unnecessary. I'm not interested in being tossed over his lap and having my ass spanked, but the faint sting of his hand is a pretty heady reminder of the other things those hands can do.

No prob—I start to type, stopping when another message arrives.

I'm hard just thinking about it, it says. *Makes running a bitch.*

I delete my response and stare at the screen, feeling my chest and stomach tighten. I want more. I want more texts and more hands and more, more, more. More Crosbie Lucas, if it can be believed.

149

Another text. *When do you get off tonight?*

I write back immediately. *Eight.*

I'll pick you up.

Aware of Marcela watching me, I keep my expression neutral as I type "Okay" and hit send.

"What was that?" she asks when I put away my phone.

"My mother," I lie, too easily. "She wants to know if I'm going home for Thanksgiving."

"Are you?"

I shake my head. "No. I'll save that special brand of torture for Christmas."

"Good. We can cook a turkey."

"Do you know how to cook a turkey?"

She's quiet for a second. "No. Do you think Kellan does?"

I look at her sharply, then follow her gaze through the glass windows on the doors, where Nate and Celestia huddle behind the counter while Nate makes one of her specialty drinks.

I sigh.

* * *

My bike is parked in the alley behind the shop, so when we close up for the night I wave good night to Nate and Marcela, who head to their respective cars with goodbyes so cold I shiver in my winter coat. Because Burnham is tiny, the town shuts down fairly early and the streets are dark and quiet, making it easy to spot Crosbie parked half a block away, his car shut off. He lifts a hand in greeting and I nod back, then round the building to the alley. A second later the growl of an engine turning over cuts through the night.

We'd texted back and forth a bit more throughout the evening, agreeing to meet back here after Nate and Marcela were gone. Now I watch headlights illuminate the dumpsters as Crosbie turns into the alley and drives toward me at a crawl.

I'm not going to lie. I'm totally willing to shuck my jeans

and hustle into the backseat and do everything people do when they meet each other in dark alleys at night. Though our texts were relatively tame, I'm burning with anticipation. I've never really felt like this before. Truly, seriously…horny. A crude, lame word to describe what's going on in my belly and the places below, but there you have it.

Crosbie seems to be on a different page, however, because he stops the car and simply reaches over to push open the passenger side door. No lunging out for a passionate, forbidden embrace. I squash my silly disappointment and get in, and the overhead light immediately blinks off, leaving us in the dim glow of the tiny dashboard lights. The car is old but clean, with roll down windows and seats that sag slightly in the middle. There's a gear shift between us and an air freshener in the shape of a candy cane dangles from the mirror, making the car smell like toothpaste.

"Hey," I say, suddenly shy.

He glances over and smiles as he puts the car in drive. "Hey." He's wearing a puffy black jacket and jeans, and even in silhouette, he's sexy.

This seems like a good "Your place or mine?" moment, except neither of those places is an option. I live with Kellan, and Crosbie lives in a frat house. I peer surreptitiously over my shoulder at the small backseat.

"Don't worry," he says, steering us out of the alley and turning onto the street. "I cleaned up."

"I wasn't worried about that." Though I am disappointed—clean or not, there's no way the two of us could fit back there. In fact, now that we're here, I'm not sure where it is we are, exactly. Or where we're going. Crosbie heads for the freeway, taking the exit south and merging neatly with the sparse traffic. I clear my throat and look around. "What, uh… What's going on?"

He looks over. "You all right?" He drives with just his left hand, his elbow propped up against the window. His free hand rests on top of the gear shift, fingers tapping in time with the song playing on the radio, the volume so low it's almost impossible to hear.

"I'm fine. Just...what are we doing?"

"Getting out of Burnham for a bit," he replies. Then he takes a second look at me, concerned. "Is that not okay?"

Two exits away is a slightly larger town called Gatsby. No buses come this way, so I've only been a handful of times when Nate or Marcela drove. It's a nice enough place, with box stores and movie theaters. Things to do that don't revolve around coffee, alcohol, or school.

"It's fine."

"You want to go back? We can, no problem. But I didn't know where we could go, you know? Kellan twisted his ankle and wanted to stay in to ice it, and my place is always busy."

"I don't want to go back," I tell him. "I just wanted to know where we were going."

"We can go wherever you want," he answers. "Do whatever you want."

Crosbie flips on his blinker and pulls into the right hand lane to exit into Gatsby. From here I can see the large signboard for the theater, the marquee too distant to read.

"Want to see a movie?" he asks as we drive closer.

I squint at the list of shows. It's an enormous multiplex and the parking lot is packed. Crosbie inches past the front so we can see what's playing.

"*Kill Glory 3* is out? I thought it wasn't coming until December."

Crosbie laughs uncomfortably when I name the latest installment of the popular horror franchise. "What else is playing?"

I look at him. "You don't like scary movies?"

He purses his lips. "I like them fine."

My jaw drops. "You're afraid."

"Am not."

"Maybe *Toy Story 6* is playing."

"The *Toy Story* franchise is classic."

"Okay, fine." I crane my neck to try to see some more names. "There's *Tanker Race 2, Soda Shoppe Gals, Operation*—I think that's based on the board game—and that documentary about seals. Anything you're dying to see?"

He finds parking at the end of a row and unbuckles his seatbelt. "Lady's choice."

"*Kill Glory 3.*"

"Never mind, you can't choose."

"Have you seen the first two? They're excellent. It's about this death angel named Glory who keeps returning to earth to try to get revenge—"

"I saw five minutes of the first one, and that was enough."

"So…*Soda Shoppe Gals*?"

He tips his head to peer out the windshield at the start times. We've got half an hour until the next showings. "We can see *Kill Glory 3*," he says reluctantly, reaching over to tug me in by the collar. "But let's make out for a bit first."

"Make out?" I feign offense. "You haven't even bought me popcorn."

"Can I just give you the ten dollars?"

We're laughing when our lips meet, teeth bumping until we get serious. Crosbie displays none of the urgency I'm feeling, kissing me leisurely, exploring, learning. Again, it's a surprise. He's got one hand curled against my neck while the other rests against the back of the seat. If I'd ever given any thought to making out in a car with Crosbie Lucas, I'd have pictured him sticking his hand up my shirt—or down my pants—in the first thirty seconds. But that doesn't appear to be the plan for tonight, and I quash the tiny part of me that's disappointed and tell myself to just enjoy the moment. I've actually never done this before. I had zero boyfriends in high school, and I don't think any of the guys I kissed last year even had a car. At least, I never bothered to learn enough about them to find out if they did.

Teenagers walk by and holler "Get a room!" breaking us apart. We're both breathing hard, the windows only starting to steam up, advertising our activities without actually obscuring them.

"Hi," Crosbie says, smiling.

I can't help but smile back. "Hi."

He reaches over to tuck a piece of hair behind my ear. "Did you get in trouble at work after we left?"

It takes me a second to remember what he's talking about. "Oh, Nate?" I shake my head. "Nah. He's all bark and no bite. And there's very little bark to begin with."

"He seemed pretty upset."

I think about Marcela giving Kellan her number. "It was nothing. He was just trying to seem authoritative because his girlfriend was there."

"Ah." He's quiet for a second. "What do you think about Kellan hooking up with your friend?"

I roll my eyes. "They're not going to hook up. She was just..." I wonder how much I can say before I'm a bad friend. "Things are weird between Marcela and Nate and she was just doing that to show him she'd...moved on."

Crosbie's brows raise. "They're hooking up."

"How do you know?"

"How do you think I know?"

"They just met this afternoon! She got off work twenty minutes ago."

"And Kellan's got the apartment to himself."

"You said he needed to ice his foot. And he promised not to bring people home."

He shrugs. "So you're not okay with it."

"I'm—" I stop myself. Crosbie's studying the steering wheel with far too much focus. Belatedly I realize he wasn't just gossiping, he was testing me. I think back to that first conversation we had, right after I'd gone by to view the apartment. How he told me not to expect happily ever after with Kellan McVey, assuming I'd be like every other girl on campus, desperate for his attention. He hadn't been entirely wrong then, but he's wrong now. "Crosbie," I say seriously. I repeat his name when he doesn't look at me, and finally he turns his head. "I don't have a thing for Kellan. Honest."

"Sure."

"He's a good roommate," I add. "He cleans up after himself and so far he's upheld his end of the bargain about only using the apartment to sleep and study."

"Uh-huh."

"But he eats way too much mac and cheese."

Crosbie huffs out a laugh.

"And I think he steals my shampoo."

"He loves that stuff."

"He should love it. It's expensive. The point is—we're just roommates."

"You seemed pretty annoyed when he got your friend's number."

"That's because she's just doing this to hurt Nate, and I'm going to be stuck in the middle and work will be awkward. That's it."

"You're sure?"

"Positive. Can we see *Kill Glory 3* now?"

"Will I be able to follow along if I haven't seen the first two?"

"Probably not. But I expect you'll have your eyes covered most of the time anyway, so it won't matter."

He pushes open his door. "You're buying your own popcorn."

* * *

Two and a half hours later, we're sitting in the adjacent chain restaurant, sharing a plate of nachos. "For the hundredth time," Crosbie is saying, "that wasn't a yelp. I stubbed my toe. It was a manly grunt of pain."

I stare at him earnestly. "You know you can tell me anything, right? I absolutely won't re-enact it for Kellan."

"You're a monster."

I twist a chip until the string of cheese connecting it to the plate gives up the fight and snaps in half. I'm on a *date* with Crosbie Lucas. I'd met him tonight expecting some frenzied, cramped sex in the backseat of his car, but here we are, movie,

155

dinner, the works. I know I'd vowed to do this year completely differently, but this isn't exactly the "different" I'd envisioned.

"Have you given any more thought to open mic night?" I ask, steering the subject away from his fear of scary movies.

He sips his orange soda. "That hasn't passed already?"

"It's in two weeks."

"Huh."

"You should do it. I liked that trick you showed me."

He smiles. "It was an illusion."

"Do you know any more *illusions*?"

"Of course I do."

"Let's see one."

He stares at me for a second. "Do you have any change?"

"Are all these illusions going to cost me money?"

"This way you know there's no shady business going on, Nora. Two pennies or two dimes, whatever you have will do."

I fish around in my purse until I find two dimes, then place them in his outstretched hand. He moves the plate of nachos to the side so the center of the table is clear, then holds out both his hands, palms up, a dime in the center of each.

"Two coins, one in each hand," he says. "Got it?"

"Got it."

He flips his hands over and I hear the clack of the coins hitting the table, hidden from view. "Pick a hand," he says.

I hesitate, then tap the right.

"Good choice. You know why?"

"Tell me."

"Because that's where the money is." Slowly, dramatically, he lifts his right hand to reveal two dimes. I gape as he lifts the left, which has nothing underneath.

"How did you do that?"

"Magic."

"Crosbie, seriously. Tell me."

"Never."

"Do it again."

He slides the dimes across the table and eats another nacho. "Don't be greedy. There are other things I want to do to you instead."

I'd really like to say that those other things won't be happening if he doesn't tell me how he did that trick, but I've told enough lies for one day. I really want to know the secret, but even more than that, I want Crosbie.

Still.

"Just give me a hint."

He laughs and scoops up guacamole with his chip. "Forget it."

"How about—" The words fade as the doors open and a group of guys wearing Burnham hockey team jackets struts in, the standard cluster of fans trailing in their wake. Crosbie has his back to the door but turns to follow my horrified stare. Slowly, he shifts back to face me, eyes narrowed.

"Problem?"

I swallow and watch with relief as the hostess leads the rowdy group to the opposite side of the restaurant. I don't personally know any of them, but their names occupy more than a few bathroom stalls, and I know at least two of those girls have black markers ready and waiting. If I'm spotted eating nachos with Crosbie Lucas, the rumors will start. And even if they don't care enough to learn my name, I'll be another blank space next to a double-digit number on another guy's list, which is quite possibly even worse.

"No," I say, as my plan to quit lying dies a quick death. My appetite has fled so I push the nachos in his direction and finish the last of my drink. "Are you ready to go?"

He arches a brow. "Do you know them?"

"No."

"Then what's the problem?"

There's obviously a problem so I exhale and study my fingernails. "I don't want to be a Crosbabe." I glance up through my lashes to see his jaw tense as he watches me.

"You know I'm not in there updating that list, right? Your name's not even on it."

"I don't want it to be."

"Then—"

I shoot a pointed look across the room and he finally clues in. "You're being paranoid," he says. "What do you want me to do? Put a bag over your head and lead you out of here through the kitchen?"

"Shut up."

"Look—I promise you won't wind up on the list, okay? Like you said the other night, there aren't even any new names on it. People aren't paying attention to what I do anymore. I'm boring. So are you."

My face is hot and I feel stupid and embarrassed. I know it's not fair to blame Crosbie for being himself, especially when the only thing he's done tonight is pick me up from work and take me to dinner and a movie. I just can't stomach the thought of sitting across from Dean Ripley as he gives me another stern sex talk.

"Who was it?" he asks.

I snap out of my reverie. "Who was what?"

"That did this to you? Made you so worried?"

"What are you talking about?"

"When we hooked up, that wasn't your first time. So who was it? A bad experience last year? Tell me and I'll deal with it."

My eyes bulge. "There's nothing for you to deal with!" I snap. And I'm definitely not telling him about my ill-fated Kellan hookup. "There wasn't—I didn't…" I sigh. "Look, I know you think I'm boring."

"I didn't mean—"

"No, you're right. I'm trying to be. I *want* to be boring. Do you know what my nickname was in high school? Nora Bora. You know what I did? Graduated. Then last year I partied a lot, trying to make up for being such an invisible loser in high school, and nearly got kicked out. I lost half my scholarship and now I have to have these meetings with the Dean and…"

"And turning up on my list will make you look bad."

"It will make it look like I'm not taking all their threats to expel me seriously. And I am." It's half the truth, but it's the only half I'm willing to share.

"I get it."

"It's not you, Crosbie."

"I know that, Nora."

We stare at each other, hurt and confusion roiling between us.

"Free refill?" The server's shrill voice pierces the tension and we both jump.

"No," Crosbie says, eyes on me. "I've had enough. You?"

"I'm fine," I tell her. "Just the bill."

"Sure thing. You want the rest of these wrapped up?" She gestures to the half-eaten plate of nachos. Seconds earlier it was a platter of cheesy goodness, and now it's just a soggy mess. I shake my head.

We sit in unhappy silence as we wait. After a strained minute Crosbie reaches across the table to take back the two dimes I'd forgotten.

"Watch," he says, placing a coin on each of his upturned palms. I pay close attention as he flips his hands, the coins pinging as they connect with the table. "See that?" he asks.

I frown. "I don't think so."

"Like this."

He does it again, slower. This time I see him toss one dime into his left hand, so that hand has two coins and the other has none. It's so fast I'd miss it if I blinked. Or even if I was watching very, very closely, apparently.

"That's the whole trick," Crosbie says, sliding the dimes back in my direction. "You see what I want you to see. And sometimes you see what you want to see."

"I'm sorry."

"Look. I don't want to get you in trouble with the Dean. I just thought you were a nerd. A hot one, but still a nerd."

"Thanks."

"And if you want to keep things quiet because you and Kellan have some 'no fun' policy in place, and you don't want the Dean breathing down your neck and you want to keep your name off that fucking list, then that's fine. But I'm not doing this if you're embarrassed to be seen with me."

"I'm not embarrassed—"

"If your name shows up on that wall, I'll head up there with a bottle of whiteout and get rid of it, okay?"

"Okay, Crosbie."

His shoulders are hunched, his cheeks pink. He's trying. The good-time party boy who has women flocking and makes it look like everything comes easy to him, works harder than anyone I've ever known. And anyone I'm pretending to be.

The server brings the bill and Crosbie sticks some money underneath and pins it in place with a salt shaker. "I can pay," I offer, but he shakes his head and stands.

"Let's just get out of here."

We shrug into our coats and head for the door. Crosbie holds it open and from behind us I hear a few voices call his name. He returns the greeting but doesn't stop, and I hurry out into the cold night, my breath condensing in the air. We'd walked here from the theater, and now we make the quiet trek back to his car, the parking lot mostly empty.

The car door locks aren't automatic so I linger as he unlocks mine and pulls it open, waiting until I'm seated before closing it. His manners, his unexpected honesty—it unnerves me and my hands are shaking a little as I reach over to pull up the plastic lock on his side. He drops into the seat, sticking the key in the ignition and turning up the heat to high. Chilly air bursts out of the vents and I stick my hands between my knees for warmth. Crosbie rubs his palms together, and when the thin film of fog on the glass has cleared, he puts his hands on the wheel.

"You good to go?" he asks.

"I'm good."

"Anything else you need in Gatsby?"

"I'm all set."

We drive in silence until we reach the freeway, more of an uncomfortable I-don't-know-what-to-say quiet than an angry one, and Crosbie finally reaches over to turn up the volume on the radio. An old pop song fills the air and I think about one time last winter when a freak snow storm blew through and Marcela, Nate and I were trapped in the coffee shop over night. Marcela played this song on her phone and showed us the dance she'd done to it in her third grade talent show, where she'd come in second. I remember watching Nate hand her a star-shaped cookie and telling her she would have gotten first place if he'd been the judge. He'd done so many sweet things for her and she'd been entirely oblivious.

"I'm sorry I hurt your feelings," I blurt out when Crosbie turns onto my street.

He's quiet as he parks beneath a tree a couple of doors down. The streetlights are blocked out and we're cocooned in darkness. He flexes his fingers on the steering wheel. "It's fine. You didn't."

"I think I did."

He glances at me. "You didn't."

"Thanks for the movie. And the nachos."

"You're welcome."

"And the illusion."

He laughs roughly. "Any time."

I unbuckle my belt. I should get out of the car and let this strange thing between us melt away, but I don't. Instead I shift onto my knees and lean over the gear shift to kiss him. I hold his face in my hands and press our lips together, waiting for him to stop me like he'd waited for me that first time, but he doesn't. I stroke his ears and his hair and the stiff muscles in his neck, all the things I've been wondering about. His hair is a cropped mess of unruly curls but it's surprisingly soft, and when I trace my nails along the back of his ear I feel him inhale. I sink my teeth lightly into his lower lip and he groans deep in his throat and parts his lips. I slip my tongue into his mouth and he finally lifts one hand to cup the back of my head, the solid pressure of his fingers the only indication he needs this as much as I do.

But I *want* so much more than this, and if the increasingly frenzied intensity of our kisses is any indication, so does he. My heart is pounding as I unzip my jacket and shove it over my shoulders. Crosbie opens his eyes, the whites just visible in the darkness. "You want—" He doesn't finish the sentence before I'm kissing him again, undoing his jacket and unbuttoning his shirt. I scrape my nails across his chest and he unbuckles his seatbelt and turns as best he can in the close quarters. I want to straddle him, fuck him, ride him, but there's no room for both of us in the driver's seat.

"Nora," he gasps.

"I want," I breathe against his lips.

"You…" He looks around quickly, assessing the situation. "All right. Hang on." He lifts my hips so he can raise himself over the gear stick and slide into my seat instead. He reclines the back and I come down over him, hands and lips and heat everywhere.

"You've gotta get these off," he mutters, fingers tangling in the waistband of my jeans. I mumble incoherently as I try to kick off my sneakers without kneeing Crosbie in the crotch, then we both work my jeans and panties down my legs until I get one foot free to properly straddle him.

He keeps his eyes open, locked on mine, as he unbuttons his own jeans and frees his erection. It's too dark for me to fully appreciate it, but I see his arm move and know he's stroking himself. He'd done this last time, too, and I never even got to touch.

"Let me," I whisper against his lips. My hand replaces his and we both groan. He's thick and hot and hard, everything I want and need. Even before he slips his hand between my legs I'm moaning, and the stretch of his fingers inside me, teasing, preparing, makes me want to seize up and explode. It's freezing outside but I feel sweat on my back, see it beading on Crosbie's temple, reflecting in the tiny bit of moonlight that filters in.

"Let me get a condom," he grunts, straightening up to reach into the glove box. He gets one open and rolled on in record time and moments later I'm slowly easing him in. My breath catches at the feel, perfect and satisfying. An enormous relief after the tension at dinner. My muscles go weak and my thighs shake as I try not to impale myself too quickly, shuddering when he's finally buried and I can catch my breath.

"Nora," he murmurs, cupping my face and kissing me. Our chests press together and even through my shirt I can feel the heat of his skin, the rapid thud of his heart. He kisses me deeply, wetly, like it means something, and though I wanted to fuck him, my body has other ideas. Instead I shift and slide slowly, the movement slick with friction and heady arousal, reaching places I didn't even know existed.

Crosbie strokes the side of my face, my ribs, my back, my ass. He guides me gently, the pace increasing, the sound of skin on skin soon filling the car, drowning out our gasping breaths.

I come first, thighs locking as I grind against him, dragging out every ounce of pleasure. His fingers dig into my ass and I see him gritting his teeth, trying not to move. I sag against his chest and he correctly interprets it to mean I'm done, then lifts me slightly and slams his hips up, driving into me a dozen more times before he cries out, the sound smothered in my throat.

Eventually I blink, breathe, move. I'm collapsed over Crosbie Lucas, in the front seat of his car, on a public street, my bare ass on full display for whomever should walk by. And I really don't care.

"Fuck, Nora," he groans.

"I don't think my legs work."

"That was better than the last time, and I thought last time was the best thing to ever happen to me."

I smile, exhausted, thrilled, flattered. "Same here."

He meets my eye. "Oh yeah?"

"Oh yeah."

He grins. I lift myself off and we spend the next couple of minutes trying to get dressed and repositioned in the cramped front seat. Eventually I'm back in place with my pants and shoes on, my jacket half zipped, and my hair retied in what I hope is an I-didn't-just-have-sex ponytail.

Crosbie, on the other hand, has an incorrectly buttoned shirt, even more tousled hair, and what might be a hickey on the side of his neck. With the heated part of the night over, the cold air quickly creeps back in and I shiver. Crosbie reaches over to zip up my jacket to my chin. "Good night, Nora."

"Good night, Crosbie."

He leans over to kiss me, then pauses, touching his neck. "Did you give me a hickey?"

"I'm very sorry."

He laughs and presses his lips to mine. "Classy."

I gesture to our surroundings. "Couldn't you tell?"

"I'll see you soon."

I clamber out of the car, hurrying up the sidewalk to the apartment. I climb the stairs and unlock the door, turning to wave as Crosbie pulls away from the curb and watches until I'm inside. I toe off my sneakers and head up to the living room where Kellan sits on the couch, one leg propped up on the coffee table, a bag of melting ice draped over his ankle. He's alone.

"Hey."

"Hey." He doesn't look away from the game. I think he's trying to blow up a sewer.

I'm nearly in my room when I hear a loud bang, then silence, then my name. I turn slowly to see Kellan setting down the controller, his game paused. "Can I ask you a question?"

I try not to look guilty. "Sure. What's up?"

"Don't take this the wrong way, but your friend Marcela…is there any chance she's crazy?"

I nod somberly. "Yes."

He purses his lips. "Figures." A pause. "Is she good in the sack?"

"Kellan, that is not a thing I would know."

"Worth a shot."

"What makes you ask?" I say. "About the crazy thing?"

He scratches his chin. "We were texting for a bit, and I thought things were going pretty good, then she asked if I had a turkey recipe."

I cough out a laugh. "Do you?"

"Of course I do. I'm the youngest of four boys. Who do

you think got stuck helping in the kitchen?"

I cover my mouth. "You didn't tell her that."

"Why not? It's the truth."

"But you thought she was crazy!"

"She's hot, Nora. That makes up for a lot of things."

I shake my head. "This is a mistake, Kellan. And if you end up with a broken heart, I don't want to hear about it."

He draws a cross on his chest. "I promise I won't say a word. And speaking of broken hearts, where were you tonight?"

"The library."

Kellan's not fooled. "Your bag's in your room. So are your books."

"Well, I was just…reading."

"Yeah. Somebody's dick."

"Kellan!" I snatch a stray ketchup packet from the breakfast bar and hurl it at his head. It smacks into the wall and falls behind the couch as he roars with laughter.

chapter fourteen

When Open Mic Night at Beans rolls around a couple weeks later, Kellan is still focused on the subject of my "reading partner."

"It's him, isn't it?" Kellan nudges me hard enough I lose my balance and have to catch myself on the back of a chair before I fall over. He's referring to a middle-aged man in a blue suit with an anchor embroidered on the breast. I'm pretty sure he's the father of one of the performers. And a ship's captain.

"No!" I snap, shoving him away. "He's not here."

"He's definitely here." He folds his arms across his chest and surveys the dim room dramatically. "And I'm going to find him."

I roll my eyes. "If you say so." To date he's considered all of my professors, our eighty-year-old neighbor Ted, and three of the line cooks at the Chinese place on campus, but he's never once contemplated Crosbie.

Speaking of which. "Have you seen Crosbie?" I ask, frowning as I peer around the crowded space. "He's not up for a bit, but…"

Kellan pulls his phone out of his pocket and squints at the display. No missed calls or texts.

"Do you not have any friends?" I inquire politely.

He makes a face at me. "Shut up. You know who I'm 'friendly' with at the moment."

Now I make a face. "Spare me."

Kellan and Marcela have some sort of painfully immature sixth grade-style relationship going on. They text, talk on the phone late at night and go on group dates, but they never actually seem to…do anything. I know why Marcela's reluctant to get physical—she's into Nate and this thing with Kellan is simply to make him jealous. But while she's relieved not to have to pry his hands out of her pants at every turn, she's equally perplexed as to why she doesn't have to.

"And here comes my 'friend' now," Kellan murmurs, putting away his phone and grinning over my head. He's so handsome when he smiles. Hell, he's handsome all the time. And now, in the muted lighting, wearing a white button-up shirt and fitted dark trousers, he looks like the world's most handsome waiter. But when he slings an arm around Marcela's shoulder and kisses her cheek, I feel nothing. Not an ounce of envy. Because this secret, unexpected, and extraordinarily hot thing Crosbie and I have going leaves no room for jealousy. It's that good.

It's not good enough to block the death rays Nate's shooting from behind the counter, however. I peer over my shoulder and widen my eyes in warning. Celestia is here, after all, fur coat draped in her lap, pretentious drink in hand, ready to watch the show in the prime front row seat Nate reserved for her. The second the track team filed in and filled the remaining seats you could see him kicking himself, but there wasn't much he could do save drag her chair to the back row and pretend it offered a better view.

As much as I'd love to remain immersed in their petty dramas, I'm working tonight—so is Marcela, though it's hard to tell the way she's running her fingers through Kellan's hair and gazing up at him adoringly, doing a pretty great job convincing anyone who's looking that they're hooking up left, right, and center, when in fact they've only kissed twice, and neither time "with tongue." This is Marcela's recounting; Crosbie confirmed the details when he spoke to Kellan, and we both agreed we didn't want to know anything more.

My phone buzzes against my leg and I know it's Crosbie.

"I'm going to grab more supplies," I say to absolutely no one, since they're all fixated on each other. The low murmur of voices is amplified in the acoustic space, and though we're at the maximum number of occupants allowed by the fire code, a hundred and thirty people manage to sound like a thousand.

I grab my phone out of my apron pocket and shoulder my way through the swinging door into the kitchen. We're busy enough that Nate asked our part-time dishwasher to come in for the night, and two other staff members are hurriedly filling trays with freshly made donuts and brownies. The air is warm and smells like coffee and sugar, but I won't find privacy or quiet in the kitchen, so I head into the dark, narrow hall that leads to the fire exit.

It's colder and quieter here, and I shiver as I rest against the wall and pull up Crosbie's text. *Come out back*, it reads. Assuming he's actually here, "out back" means the alley, which is currently coated in a thin layer of snow.

I march to the end of the hall and push open the door, the rush of cold November air making me shiver. Fat snowflakes fall, gleaming in the yellow glare of emergency lights that showcase our stuffed trash cans and recycling bins. "Crosbie?" I whisper.

"What took you so long?"

I jump. He's standing behind the door, so I have to step outside and close it to see him. "What are you doing out here?" I fold my arms around my middle. Beneath my polka dot apron I'm wearing dark skinny jeans and a long-sleeve top, neither of which are warm enough for this.

He rubs his hands over his face and I frown. He looks pale and sick. "Crosbie?" I put a hand on his arm. "Are you okay?" He's wearing a black dress shirt and pants; no magician's hat and cape, despite my pleas. He's trembling a little bit, and I don't think it's because of the cold. I press the back of my hand to his forehead—his skin is hot and clammy.

"Do you have the flu?"

He shakes his head miserably. "Stage fright."

Huh. For a guy who's very much at home in the spotlight,

be it at parties, on the track team, or just strolling around campus, this is very unexpected. But instead of offering an unhelpful *"Whaaat?"* I say, "Everybody gets nervous. It's normal."

"I haven't been able to concentrate all day. I just keep picturing this whole thing...failing."

"You're not going to fail." He'd shown me a few of the tricks he planned for tonight, and they were great. "You're good at this, Crosbie. And everyone's going to love you."

"Everyone?" He looks terrified. "How many people is 'everyone?'"

I hesitate. "Um...a few."

"More than twenty?"

"How long have you been back here?" The shop has been full for close to an hour as everyone showed up early to claim seats and snacks.

His head falls back and he groans unhappily. "A while."

A muted buzzing sound interrupts and we both pull out our phones. Crosbie's is lit up with a new message.

"Oh, Jesus," he mutters.

"What is it?"

He shows me the screen. It's a picture of a bunch of hands gripping wrists, forming a solid circle. "Kellan," he explains. "He's been sending me supportive messages all day." He glares at the screen. "This one says, 'We've got you, brother.'"

I try not to laugh, but fail completely. "It's sweet," I protest when he glowers at me.

"It's horrifying. How many of them are here?"

I don't pretend not to know he's referring to his track teammates. "I'm not sure," I hedge. "A couple. The front row."

"Oh my God."

"They want to see you succeed! It's nice."

"I can't do it."

"You can."

"Why did I let you talk me into this?"

169

"For the same reason you showed me the tri—the illusions. Because deep down you want to do this, you just needed a reason."

"And you're that reason?"

I arch a brow. "Is that not enough?"

He opens his mouth and closes it. "Of course you're enough," he says finally.

Now *my* phone buzzes with a text from Kellan. *I can't find Crosbie.*

I show Crosbie. "What do you want me to tell him?" My frozen finger hovers over the reply button and I shiver.

"Shit," Crosbie says, yanking open the door and grabbing my shoulder to steer me inside. "Why didn't you say you were cold?"

"Why wasn't it obvious? It's snowing!"

The door slams shut, cocooning us in marginally warmer air and even less light.

"Look," I say, "if you don't want to do this, you don't have to. People bail all the time. Just go home and say you fell asleep. Or you got the date wrong. Or you have the flu. I'll back you up."

He stares at me for a long time. "Thank you, Nora."

"You're really going to bail?"

"No, I'm going to do this. And if it goes epically wrong, I'm blaming you."

"That sounds totally mature and reasonable."

"Where are you going to be?"

"When? When you're performing?"

"Yeah."

"On the floor. Serving, watching, whatever. I'm working, remember?"

He nods. "Right."

"Do you want me to watch? I could not watch, if you prefer. I'll duck down behind the counter and cover my ears."

"No," he says. "Be there."

I lean in to kiss his cheek. "Promise."

"Hey." He catches my chin and backs me into the wall.

"Don't be a tease."

"I was being encouraging."

"Be *more* encouraging," he suggests, before he kisses me. Really kisses me. So intense and thorough I have to wonder if this whole "stage fright" thing was just a set up to get me back here, hand inching its way under my shirt, a shameless grope in the name of consolation.

"Hey!" I finally pull away, snagging his inquisitive hand. "I'm working. And you're up soon."

He nudges me with his hips. "I'm kind of up right now."

"Good luck out there. Not that you'll need it."

He smirks and reaches behind my ear, pulling out a quarter. "Of course I don't need it."

* * *

He really doesn't, as it turns out. He does the handful of tricks—illusions—I've already seen, plus a few more that are totally new to me. After forty-five minutes of slam poetry, acoustic song covers, and two Salt-N-Pepa dance tributes, he's a welcome change of pace.

I hover next to Kellan at the end of the second row and smile over his shoulder when I see him recording the whole performance on his phone. Crosbie glances at me from time to time, but as he settles into the show you can see his nervousness abate and his confidence grow. The audience eats it up, laughing when they're supposed to, oohing and ahhing appropriately. At the end of the set he gets a standing ovation and blushes beet red as he gathers his things, offers an awkward bow, and rushes off the stage.

"That was great!" Kellan exclaims. Marcela's seated to his left and he nudges her. "Wasn't that great?"

Marcela's watching Nate and Celestia in the front row. "So great," she echoes distractedly. But when Nate takes the stage to introduce the next act, she suddenly turns to beam up at Kellan, knowing they now have an audience of one. "You must be so proud."

I try not to gag and maneuver through the crowd. I saw Crosbie disappear down the short hall that leads to the bathrooms, and I shoulder my way through the throng in the same direction just as a blonde in a tasseled vest takes the stage to do her best Jewel impression.

The hallway is empty when I get there, both doors closed. I knock cautiously on the men's room door, figuring I can just say I need to refill the soap if there's anyone other than Crosbie inside. After a second the door opens and his head pokes through, brow furrowed.

"Did you knock?" he asks, looking confused.

"I wasn't sure if you were alone."

"Sure am." He pulls open the door and gestures me inside. I've been in here before, of course, but it's not exactly my favorite place to be. It's a typical coffee shop bathroom, with two stalls, two urinals, and two sinks. It's clean and cramped and smells like bleach.

"Feeling better?" I ask. Now that I'm in here I can see his face and hairline are wet, like he'd just splashed them with water. I watch as he grabs a couple of paper towels from the dispenser and dries off as best he can.

"Yeah," he answers after a second. "I'm glad it's over."

"Are you glad you did it? Because I'm glad. You were great."

He meets my eye in the mirror, then smiles. He's so hot when he smiles, all white teeth and tiny creases around his eyes. He looks like a mischievous little kid who knows he's never going to stop being bad. "I'm glad," he says, tossing the paper towel in the trash and turning to stalk toward me. "And I'm really fucking amped."

"Amped?" I echo, reading his intentions clearly. And quite eagerly.

"Amped," he repeats. He backs me into the door and reaches down to flip the lock. His lips are a millimeter away from mine when someone rattles the knob, finds it locked, then knocks loudly.

"Hello? Cros?"

It's Kellan.

"Oh my God," Crosbie mumbles into my hair. *"Whyyy?"*

More knocking. "Crosbie? Are you in there? Are you okay? Where's the manager? I need a key."

Crosbie backs away, takes a deep breath and looks at me, adorably exasperated. "Hide in the stall," he says with a sigh. "I'll get him out of here."

I can't help but laugh, covering my mouth so Kellan, who's probably got his ear glued to the door in a misguided show of friendship, doesn't hear. "He's your number one fan."

Crosbie rolls his eyes and pushes me toward the stall. "He's my number one cock blocker."

I shuffle into the stall and twist the lock. A second later I hear Crosbie pull open the door to the bathroom, the outside noise rushing in along with his best friend.

"Dude!" Kellan exclaims. "Are you okay? I've been knocking."

"Sorry," Crosbie answers. "I didn't hear. How was the show? Did everyone think it was stupid?"

"No way. It was awesome. How'd you bend that quarter?"

"I told you. Mind meld. Let's get back out there."

"Why was the door locked? There's someone in that stall, man."

"Is there? I hadn't noticed."

"You probably freaked him out!"

The accusation fades as Crosbie hustles him away. I count to twenty and hurry out of the men's room, lucky not to encounter anyone coming in. The show lasts another half hour and though Crosbie's sitting with the track team in row two, we're so swamped with last minute food and drink orders that we don't get another chance to talk.

The open mic wraps up at ten-thirty and once everybody's gone, it takes another forty-five minutes for us to get the shop restored. We refold a hundred folding chairs, mop a thousand muddy footprints from the floor, and drag tables and art displays back into place. Celestia sits in the corner reading a book, and Marcela's only slightly more helpful as she works with one hand while texting constantly with the other.

"We're going out," she announces at one point.

Everyone looks at her. "You're all welcome," she says after a second, but points to me. "But you're definitely coming."

"Coming where?"

"Marvin's." She names the popular nearby pub. "That's where Kellan and the other track guys are, celebrating Crosbie's big night. He wants us to join them."

She's obviously expecting me to turn her down, and though I'm tired, I really want to see Crosbie. I'll just be mindful of keeping my clothes on, enforcing a two-drink maximum, and steering clear of any camera phones so Dean Ripley doesn't wind up with a digital track record of tonight's festivities to show my dad.

"Sure," I say with a shrug that's far more casual than I feel. "I can come for a bit." As soon as I agree my phone buzzes with a text from Kellan bearing the same instructions.

Be there soon, I type back.

He responds with a smiley face, and fifteen minutes later he's beaming at me in person and pressing a bottle of beer into my hand. "We're going to party, Nora!" he sings. "And it's going to be so fun!"

I glance around at the sea of blue and orange Burnham athletics jackets. The crowd is so thick I can barely tell them apart, never mind find Crosbie in the throng.

"Is he here?" Kellan whispers, dipping his head so his lips brush my ear. "Who is it? You can tell me." He looks at the bartender, a guy in his late twenties with five facial piercings. "*That* guy? Interesting."

"Wrong," I reply. "As always."

"I'll figure it out soon enough."

"I'll bet."

His attention is stolen by something over my shoulder, and I don't need to look to know it's Marcela. She's stripped off the sweater she wore at the shop to reveal a sheer black

174

camisole with lace trim and twisted her bleached hair into a sloppy bun on top of her head. Add a fresh coat of red lipstick and she looks like every guy's fantasy of a naughty librarian.

Nate's fantasy, in particular, never mind the fact that his date is also blond and has an actual book in her hand. He looks agitated as he watches Kellan and Marcela hug and kiss chastely on the lips, though to be honest, the gesture looks more like estranged cousins coming together at a funeral. For two people I know to have fairly extensive sexual track records, their libidos really don't seem to be very much in sync.

"Hey," comes a breathless voice from over my shoulder.

I turn around to see Crosbie holding two bottles of the beer we'd had on Halloween. He's unbuttoned his shirt to reveal a tight wife beater underneath, and I want so badly to run my hands under that shirt, feel the contrast of smooth warm skin and hard muscle and know that it's mine to explore. But I can't.

"Hey." I return the smile even as his falters when he sees the beer in my hand. "Kellan," I explain. "He just gave it to me."

"Crosbie!" Two guys from the track team approach, arms slung around each other's shoulders. "We figured it out, the way you tore that card in half and then repaired it." A dramatic pause. "You had *another* card somewhere."

Crosbie shakes his head. "A good magician never reveals his secrets."

The guys nod in unison, though they're obviously disappointed. "Right, man. You have a code. That's cool."

The pair leaves, but before Crosbie and I can speak, Marcela and Kellan take their place. "Let's dance!" Marcela exclaims, bouncing on her toes to eye the writhing dance floor that makes up half the pub.

"C'mon!" Kellan grips Crosbie's wrist. "You remember Miss Maryland from Halloween? She's here and she still wants to meet you. Don't blow this!"

Crosbie shoots me a helpless look before Kellan steals both bottles of beer and sticks them in my free hand. "For safe keeping!" he shouts, then the trio disappears into the crowd.

I watch them go, chastising myself for being disappointed. *I'm* the one who wants to keep Crosbie and me a secret. *I'm* the one making it so we can't hold each other's hands and drag each other onto the dance floor. I'm also the one standing here alone, feeling like an idiot.

"I've heard of double fisting," says a voice from over my shoulder, "but triple fisting? I guess you're on a mission."

I glance up to see Max—the Walking Douche—grinning down at me. He's already got a drink of his own and I hold up my three. "Think you can keep up?"

He laughs. "With you? I'm not sure."

"Were you at the coffee shop? I didn't see you."

"I was," he says. "It was great. I didn't know you worked there."

"Yeah, a few nights a week. I—"

The song changes to something fast and popular, and everyone cheers, crowding onto the floor. "Come on," Max says, clinking one of my bottles with his. "Drink up and let's dance."

What am I going to do? Insist on lingering on the perimeter and safeguarding the drinks? "Sounds good," I say. I down half a bottle, then stick the trio on a nearby table and let Max lead me onto the dance floor. It's been far too long since I've just let go, and it's fun. It's not hard to gravitate toward the track team since half of them are still wearing their jackets, and soon we're part of a big, writhing circle of bodies, all moving to the same up tempo beat.

I didn't have anything to change into so I'm still in my skinny jeans and long-sleeve top from work. I feel sweat beading along my nape and gathering in the small of my back, but I don't stop, not when one song turns into two which turns into five. Because even though Max is beside me, his hand occasionally grazing my hip or my shoulder, it's Crosbie I'm watching, and he's watching me. On the opposite side of the circle, Miss Maryland doing her best to steal his focus, he's dancing too. This is as near as we can get, thanks to my whole secretiveness kick, the reasons for which I'm having a lot of trouble remembering at the moment. Because he looks so hot, six feet away, his eyes searing me all over, stopping on parts of my body that so desperately want to feel more than his gaze.

But this is as close as we come for the rest of the night, just two casual acquaintances in a group that gradually dwindles until it's one o'clock and time for last call. Soon the four of us—Kellan, Crosbie, Marcela and I—are huddled on the sidewalk, shivering in the cold as Kellan confirms that everybody's okay to drive.

Crosbie looks at me in frustration, but there's not a whole lot we can do about it. Kellan and I live together—it would be weird if I insisted on getting a ride with someone else. We all hug goodnight, and Crosbie squeezes my hip harder than necessary, a promise or a warning or something in between. I shoot him an apologetic look he returns with a look of his own, one that clearly says, "It doesn't have to be this way."

But if I invite him over I'm breaking my promise to Kellan, and if I go to the frat house I'm a Crosbabe. There's a clear lesser-of-two-evils option here, but I'm not ready to pick it.

"Bye, guys." Kellan and I wave and trudge down the slippery sidewalk to his car, parked a block over.

"Do you want me to drive?" I offer when we round the corner. "I only had one drink."

"Nah," he says. "I'm good. I didn't have anything."

I look up at him in surprise, belatedly realizing I never saw him drink anything other than water the whole night. "Why not?"

He shrugs, leaving his shoulders hunched up to ward against the cold. "Just not in the mood."

I think about his strangely asexual relationship with Marcela. Just how many things is he not "in the mood" for? I wonder but don't dare ask, not sure what I'd do with the answer.

Ten minutes later we're back in our apartment, still shivering as we head into our separate rooms to get ready for bed. I'm finally tucked in and reaching up to turn off the light when my phone buzzes. Even as I reach for it, I know who it is. What I can't predict is what he'll say.

I tap the message and stare at the three little words that fill the screen.

I miss you.

chapter fifteen

The next afternoon I return home from the library, shivering from the below freezing weather outside. Kellan's normally never around at this hour, so it's a surprise to find him lying on the couch with a damp face cloth covering his eyes, a notebook clutched to his chest. If you picture a male model trying to look both stressed and reflective and doing a terrible job of both, Kellan is exactly that guy. Except he's utterly sincere.

I unwind my thick wool scarf and hang it and my jacket on the back of one of the dining chairs before dropping my backpack and heading into the living room.

"Hey," I say softly. "Are you sick?"

He's completely still for a moment, then slowly shakes his head.

"Are you...pondering something?"

His lips quirk and he shakes his head again. He doesn't move much, but I notice his fingers tightening their grip on the notebook as though there's any reason I might be tempted to steal it.

"Do you want to be left alone?"

A longer pause, then another head shake. Eventually he reaches up to remove the cloth. His eyes are slightly red, otherwise he looks fine, as always.

I perch on the edge of the coffee table. "What's going on?"

He inhales heavily and tries to meet my eye but can't, so

instead focuses on the ceiling. "Have you ever…" He trails off, inhales again, and reattempts. "Have you ever thought about your life and realized you were just really stupid?"

I flash back to the whole of last year. "Yes."

He looks surprised. "Really?"

"Yeah. Why do you think I'm spending all this time at the library? Studying my ass off? Choosing to spend Friday night at home instead of out with friends?"

"I thought you didn't have any friends."

I punch his knee. "Ass."

He grins and slowly sits up. "I just thought you were a bookworm. Not that that's a bad thing," he's quick to add. "That's why I asked you to move in. So your good behavior would rub off on me." He winces briefly, then tries to hide it.

"And did it?" I ask. "Are you failing a class? Is that what this is about?" I nod at the notebook and he clenches it more tightly.

"Not exactly."

"Then what?"

"Were you happy?"

"When? Last year?" I shrug. "Yeah. I had a good time."

But he's shaking his head. "No, this year. When you were 'being good.' Before you met this mystery guy. Were you happy not…doing things?"

I feel like a contestant on one of those game shows where you have to match up the pictures to slowly reveal a riddle underneath. I'm turning over panels but none of the clues are making sense. Not sleeping with Marcela. Not drinking last night. Protecting that notebook. Still, I play along and furrow my brow, recalling the Crosbie-free days between moving in and Halloween night. "I was happy," I answer, trying to be honest. "But I was also bored."

He swallows and nods, like he's trying to convince himself. "There are worse things, right? Than being bored?"

"Of course there are. Kellan, what's going on?"

He groans and runs a hand through his hair. "Nora, I fucked up."

"Is it your grades?"

"No."

"Marcela?"

"What? No."

I rack my brain. "Problems with the track team?"

"No."

"Kellan, I'm really not—"

"Don't judge me," he interrupts. "Please." He looks so legitimately panicked that *I* start to panic. Kellan's living the college dream: every girl wants him, every guy wants to be him. If something's wrong in his world, we're all screwed.

"I won't," I promise, hoping it's true.

"I have…" He takes a deep breath. "I mean, I don't have, but I *did* have… I *had*…gonorrhea." He looks like he's about to pass out.

"You have an STI?" I echo, startled.

"*Had*," he's quick to clarify. "I started feeling weird so I went to the doctor and got some antibiotics and now it's gone. I had it. Now I don't." His eyes are so wide, his words so rushed, he could easily be talking about a government conspiracy while wearing a tin foil hat.

Slowly more puzzle pieces turn over, the unexpected mystery becoming clear. "That's why you and Marcela aren't…"

He waves a hand vaguely, as though that's only part of the issue. "Eh."

"And why you didn't drink last night?"

A nod.

"Does Crosbie know?"

He pinches his brow. "No. At first I was embarrassed and then he was so anxious about the open mic night that I didn't want to add to his problems."

"So what's the notebook for?"

He sighs and stares at it. "It's a list."

"Of?" I'm wondering how many STIs he may have had.

"Girls," he answers, putting an end to that theory. "The doctor said symptoms normally show up within a few weeks, but sometimes they can take months. And since I've had a few…partners, I don't know where or when I got it. I'm supposed to contact every girl I've been with and let them know they need to get tested."

I think about the very lengthy lists on the bathroom walls in the Student Union building. "That's awkward."

He turns the notebook around so I can see. The list is two columns long and there are approximately fifty names. And four blank spaces.

Now I'm the one who needs a hot compress.

"A few months," I say, trying to sound casual. "You've been with all those girls since September?"

"I'm going back to January," he says soberly. "Just to be on the safe side."

"Don't you think that's a little excessive?" I'm desperately trying not to sound, well, desperate. Because even though we'd used a condom during our poorly thought-out closet session, my name—or rather, my *blank space*—is on that list. I'm pretty sure I don't have anything, but I'm most definitely feverish. And nauseous. What are the symptoms of gonorrhea?

"Nora?"

I blink and realize he's said my name a few times.

"Sorry." I shake my head. "I'm just…glad you're okay."

"Me too. Though I'm going to have a lot of awkward phone calls to make. And some intense Facebook stalking. I mean, I don't even remember a lot of these girls. That's terrible, isn't it?"

Speaking from experience, it certainly is. Until it works in your favor. I squint at the list and realize some of the entries aren't names at all, but notes. *Kitchen at Beta Theta Pi house party. Pool at community center. Redhead from science lab.*

Kellan rubs his hands over his face and stares at me beseechingly. "When the doctor asked how many girls I'd been with and I took a minute to count, he gave me a *look*."

"A look?"

"Yeah. A disapproving *look*." He gives me just such a look now, as an example. It's mostly funny, but also disapproving.

"Ooh."

"He was *shaming* me!"

I try not to laugh. I mean, he's free to do whatever and whomever he pleases, but that list isn't exactly bolstering his self-righteous case at the moment. Instead of responding I slump onto the floor, wrapping my arms around my bent legs. I'm feeling too many things right now. I'm surprised Kellan confided in me; not surprised he caught something over the course of fifty-plus random hookups. I'm worried I might have something; relieved he'll never be able to figure out I'm one of those blank spaces. Nervous he might try to figure it out; confident he never will.

"I'm glad you told me," I say, when I realize he's waiting for me to say something. "And you have nothing to be ashamed of." I'm not a great actress and it takes everything I have to utter those words with a straight face. "If there's anything I can do to help, just let me know."

"Don't tell anyone," he says quickly. "That's the only thing. I'm going to work on figuring out how to find these girls, then…it'll be over."

"Over," I repeat. "Excellent." I don't point out that somehow, over the course of fifty-plus notifications, the likelihood of this secret slipping out grows exponentially.

The confession seems to have lifted a serious weight from his shoulders because he finally grins at me, a big, unburdened smile. "Thanks, Nora," he says. "I'm glad you're here. Too bad we didn't meet sooner, huh? Maybe then I wouldn't be in this mess."

* * *

I normally work on Tuesday afternoons, but I have an archaeology paper due on Friday so I'd booked the day off to give myself time to prepare. Instead of heading straight home after my morning class, however, I bike over to the student health center for a hastily-made appointment. Even though I know that the odds of having an STI are slim—I've been with six guys and always used condoms—I'm still shaking when I pee in a cup and hand it to a nurse who promises to call with the results in a few days.

By the time I get home I'm only slightly calmer than I was, and the last thing I want to find is Kellan and Crosbie huddled at the dining table poring over Kellan's sex-partner notebook. Fuck. Another thing I shouldn't really worry about, but most definitely will. Because with the exception of a positive test result, the last thing I want is for Crosbie to help Kellan cross names off his long list of sexcapades, knowing that mine is supposed to be on there.

"Still working on that, huh?" I hope I sound casual and not shrill as I dump my things in my room before joining them at the table. I'd overheard Kellan calling Crosbie last night and correctly assumed he'd told him everything, and now here he is, like a good best friend, comparing the names/descriptions Kellan had jotted down with something on his phone. "What are you doing, exactly?"

Kellan and I are at either end of the table, Crosbie seated in between, and now he turns his phone so I can see the display: it's a close up shot of the bathroom wall in the Student Union building. Kellan's list.

I try to keep my expression neutral, but Crosbie's watching me, no doubt waiting for some sort of Crosbabe rant. Instead I say, "Have you made any calls?"

Kellan nods. "It went about as uncomfortably as you'd expect."

"He's working his way back," Crosbie explains. "Starting with the most recent girls and asking them to call if they get a positive result."

"I use condoms," Kellan interrupts. "I swear. So however this happened, it wasn't like I was spreading it around after."

I nod like I'm in total agreement. When I'd gone for the test the nurse asked if I'd had either oral or anal sex with the infected person, since that would require a swab. Kellan and I had done neither, but since I'd witnessed him getting a condom-free blowjob—forty-five minutes after we'd screwed in a closet—I know there's one opportunity for him to have picked it up. And if it happened once, it could have happened twice. Or—I squint at the notebook—sixty-two times. Well, sixty-one, since I can eliminate myself from the possible oral gonorrhea givers.

I frown and pick up the notebook. The bathroom wall gives actual names, since it's not Kellan who updates it. Kellan's notes, however, are quite different. There are entries like: *starts with a C or K, blonde in blue dress, hostess from that tapas place, girl from bus stop,* and *girl who looked like Kate Middleton.*

"Did you never ask them their names?" I ask. "Even once?" It's not much of a consolation prize, but at least I'm not the only nameless entity in this mess. Though I don't appear to warrant much of a description, either.

"Hey," Crosbie says, shooting me a sharp look when Kellan winces. "No judgment."

I roll my eyes. He's on that bathroom wall too, and we all know it. It's not only Kellan's honor he's trying to defend.

"No judgment," I say, holding up my hands in surrender. "It would just make things a bit...easier."

Kellan sighs. "I know. Lesson learned."

I tap the top of the list. "So these are the most recent girls?" There are about ten candidates spanning October and November.

"Yeah. I spoke with three of them today, since they're in my science lab and we have a class contact list." Oh dear. "And these two work at that bar near the library, so I can probably find them pretty easily. This one—" He points to number six, known as *Pink shorts with stripe.* "She runs the same route as me on Thursdays, so I can talk to her then. Number seven is Dane's sister, and eight is his cousin—"

"Dane?" Crosbie interrupts, looking alarmed. "Dane who lives down the hall from me? Dane who thinks his sister's going to become a nun?"

Kellan whistles. "She's definitely *not* going to be a nun."

"Oh Jesus."

"Can you ask Dane for their numbers? Um, and their

185

names?"

"Kill me." Crosbie looks at me. "Please, Nora. Just put me out of my misery before Dane does." He turns to Kellan. "How did you meet them? They don't even go to Burnham."

"They were at the Halloween party."

"You said you didn't hook up that night!"

"I didn't say I didn't get a few numbers and call them the next week!"

"What about Miss Louisiana?"

"I got her number, too." He holds up a hand proudly. "And her name is Dana." A pause. "Or Darla."

"You're making everything worse."

"Guys!" I exclaim. "Let's focus." The sooner we find the girl, the sooner we end the hunt. Given the timeline, I'm probably either blank space forty-one or forty-two, which gives me twenty chances to end this search before they start trying to track me down. "What about number eight? *Super hot kinkster?*"

Crosbie looks intrigued. "Kinkster, huh? How kinky are we talking?"

I forget about wincing and kick him in the shin. He curses and scowls at me, but Kellan doesn't even notice.

"Very," he assures us dreamily. "Remember when we went to that club earlier this year on the track team trip?" This is directed at Crosbie.

"The one with the foam or the snakes?"

"The foam."

"Yep."

"She was a waitress, and she was wearing this white leather dress—the tiniest thing I'd ever seen, despite her massive—" Kellan breaks off as he remembers I'm sitting three feet away. "Ah, she had a great body. Anyway, we were dancing and the foam was piling up, and she kept grinding back against me, inching up her dress until her whole ass was on display, just split in half with this little red G-string. So I'm like, 'Your dress is riding up,' and she's like, 'I know,' and I'm like, 'Want to go someplace?' and she's like, 'Right here's good.' And next thing I know we're fucking, right there on the dance floor. It was hot." He rests his chin on his hand. "I miss her."

I know I'm supposed to be outraged or offended or somehow off-put by this story, but those last three words—*I miss her*—only make me think of Crosbie. His text. His fingers. His body. And how much I want him. I dart a glance at his face and he's looking at me, the same thoughts mirrored in his eyes.

Crosbie clears his throat. "Okay," he says, shifting in his seat. "So you know where she works. You can probably call the club and leave your contact information. Hopefully she calls you back."

Kellan nods. "Good one. Will do."

I take a breath. "Number nine? *Lin from stairwell at gym?* You meet girls in stairwells?" Is there any place he can't meet women?

"We didn't exactly 'meet' there, if you know what I mean." Kellan grins thoughtfully. "Or rather, we met there, but for the express purpose of—"

"I think I get it."

"She's a volleyball player," he supplies, though I hadn't asked. "And we'd been eye fucking for a while, then after one of her matches we bumped into each other and decided to just go for it. She kept the kneepads on, if you know what I mean."

I rub a hand over my hot face. *Be indignant,* I tell myself. *Be righteous!* But all I'm doing is picturing myself on my hands and knees, Crosbie behind me, in front of me, under me, doing so many dirty things.

I've lost track of how many times we've had sex since that night in the front seat of his car. He picks me up after work regularly and we drive some place to mess around as best we can. Because it's cold out and I'm not willing to get arrested for public indecency—again—we've had to be creative. Hand jobs in the back row of a mostly-empty movie theater, a quickie against the wall in the supply closet at Beans after I let him in the back door, one painful attempt to squeeze into the backseat of his car that left us both with seatbelt-shaped bruises and vows never to try again.

We'd finally gotten so frustrated that I'd pulled up the hood of my jacket and hidden my face as we ran up the stairs to his room at the frat house, so desperate to just have fully-naked, proper sex, that I'd been willing to ignore the consequences. Unfortunately we weren't the only ones with sex on the brain, and his next-door neighbor and his very vocal partner were doing their best to bring the house down with their sex sounds. When the wall shook so hard it rattled Crosbie's bed, he'd thrown on jeans and a shirt and stormed out of the room to threaten the guy with castration if he didn't keep it down. When he got back neither one of us were in the mood.

By the time Kellan's walked us through the details of his romp with number ten (*either Tiffani or Brittani, but it definitely ends in an i*), I'm ready to combust. I can barely sit still, my thighs clenching with need, and I'm familiar enough with Crosbie's flushed cheeks and darkened gaze to know he's on the same dirty page. The problem is, we have nowhere to go to *read* this page.

Kellan's phone rings suddenly, jarring us all out of this strange sexual haze. "It's Dane," he whispers, before picking up and saying hello. "Good," he says. "You?" He nods and listens, nods and listens, then for some reason, gives us a thumbs up. "He's right here," he says. "I'll tell him, absolutely. Cool. See you soon." He hangs up and gapes at us as though he can't believe his good luck. "This is perfect!"

Crosbie and I exchange wary looks. "Is it?"

He turns to Crosbie. "Dane said they're going over to prank the Kappa Deltas tonight, and we need to be there. In fact, we need to go right now, to help prepare. Come on. You walked over, right? I'll drive you back."

Crosbie's flush is deepening and I see his chest rise and fall as he takes a calming breath. "Right now?"

"Yeah, right now. You can talk to Dane and get those numbers for me. Let's go." He snatches up the notebook and tosses it into his room, where it flutters to the floor like a bird dying of sexual frustration.

I stare miserably at my hands, twisted on the table to stop myself from lunging at Crosbie and dragging him into my room, shouting at Kellan that the deal's off, feel free to bring any girl he wants back to the apartment.

"Actually…" Crosbie says tentatively. "I'll follow you over in a bit. I wanted to ask Nora to look over my English paper. She said she wouldn't mind proofing it before I turned it in. It's just a few pages."

I've never agreed to proofread this paper, because it doesn't exist. But Kellan doesn't know that and I'm more than willing to play along. "You finished it?" I say. "That's great. Of course I'll take a look."

Kellan's frowning. "Can't you just email it?"

"I brought a hard copy," Crosbie says. He reaches into his bag and passes me a stapled sheaf of papers. It's a bunch of recipes for protein shakes to help build muscle faster.

Kellan grabs his jacket from the couch and pulls it on. "Okay, whatever. Will it take more than fifteen minutes? I have to get gas, so we'll just run over, fill it up, and come back to pick up the paper—is that enough time? I know you're both trying to keep your grades up, but tonight is really important. Last year the Kappa Deltas covered the Alpha Sigma Phi house in toilet paper. *Dirty* toilet paper. Remember that?"

"Er…" Crosbie and I exchange tortured looks.

"Why don't you get gas and stop here on your way back?" Crosbie suggests. "I don't want to come to the gas station."

"Why not?"

"The, uh…fumes. They make me sick."

"They do? Since when?"

"Since always."

"Geez, man. I never knew." Kellan looks a bit incredulous, but then just shakes his head. "Fine. I'll get the gas and swing back here to get you. Think you'll be finished in time?"

We both freeze. I speak first. "If I work fast."

"I don't think it'll take that long," Crosbie adds. "The

paper is really ready to go."

Kellan stares at us like we're morons, then shrugs. "Okay, fine. Whatever. I'll text you when I'm back." Finally he puts on his sneakers, grabs his keys, and leaves.

The door's been closed for exactly one half-second before Crosbie's on me. "Oh, thank God," he mutters. He snatches the papers out of my hand and hurls them onto the floor before hauling me in for a frantic kiss.

"Finally," I mumble against his lips. "I'm dying."

"*You're* dying? I've been dying for days."

"I bet I died more."

"I bet I died harder."

We fumble to our feet and I feel his erection against my belly. Hard is the perfect adjective. "You win."

"If we do this right, we'll both win."

I moan into his mouth as his fingers carefully unbutton my shirt. He doesn't even bother to unhook my bra, just shoves down the cups and fills his hands. "Crosbie," I pant. "Faster."

"I want this all the time," he says, pulling back long enough to look at me, his fingers tugging lightly on my nipples. "I think about you every day."

He's wearing an old concert tee over a long-sleeve shirt and I pull off the top layer and throw it on the floor. "Me too." I stand on my toes to kiss him again. "It's not enough."

"No," he groans. "It's not."

The rattle of keys has us lurching apart. I clutch the front of my shirt together and dash into my room, trying to fix my bra. I hear Crosbie curse, then his T-shirt sails past me and lands on my bed, a very weak stab at hiding the evidence.

I keep my back to the room as I hear the thud of Kellan's feet climbing the stairs. "I forgot my phone."

"Oh. Right." Crosbie sounds hoarse and annoyed.

"Are you guys done already?"

My body spasms unhappily at the possibility of this being over before it even begins.

I turn around to find Kellan looking at the floor where

Crosbie's "essay" sits, discarded. Hastily I pick up random papers from my desk and wave them to distract him. "I thought it'd be easier to read in here," I lie. "So Crosbie wouldn't be breathing down my neck the whole time."

Crosbie crosses his arms, making his biceps bulge. "I just want to make sure you do a good job."

"Nora always does a good job," Kellan replies, oblivious. "And she's fast, too."

Oh God. "I'm going to get back to work."

"Right. I'll be back soon. Don't give her a hard time," Kellan adds, pointing at Crosbie. "She's doing you a favor."

"I'm very grateful," Crosbie replies, straight-faced.

"You should be. Back soon." Kellan jogs down the stairs and disappears outside. This time we scurry over to the front window and hide behind the curtains as we watch him climb into his car and drive down the block.

"Fuck me," Crosbie mutters, grabbing me by the waist and backing me into the wall.

"That's the plan," I say.

He laughs. "C'mon. I'll show you how grateful I really am."

We strip down to our underwear in record time and Crosbie squeezes my ass and boosts me up so I'm pinned between his chest and the wall. I wrap my legs around his waist and feel his cock against the cotton of my panties, grinding into me. I gasp for breath and rotate my hips, desperate for more friction. Just desperate, generally.

"I wish we had more time," he mutters, tongue trailing over my neck, teeth nipping lightly. "And a door with a lock he didn't have the keys to."

"I know. I know." I can't think much beyond the hand he's sliding under my panties, coasting over the skin of my ass and lower, down between my legs, finding the wetness that waits.

"Oh fuck."

I echo the sentiment when one of his thick fingers pushes inside. It feels like only seconds before I'm clinging to his neck, my short nails digging into the muscles of his back as I switch between begging for more and swearing I can't wait any longer.

"Nora, I'm gonna—Oh, fuck, Nora, I think—" He lowers me so I'm standing, then hurries to his pants to retrieve a condom. He's shaking as he rolls it on and I know there's no way he's going to be able to hold me up again. Truth be told, as long as he fucks me, I don't care how he does it.

There's no time to debate, so I just pull off my panties and bend over the arm of the couch. "Like this," I tell him.

His brows raise. "Are you sure?"

"Yeah." Our previous encounters haven't really given us the opportunity to do much more than face to face, a few hands sliding into pants whenever possible. We've never done it from behind or so much as tried oral, and when he eases into me I'm thinking about how much more time we need to do everything we haven't done. Everything we want to do. Just everything, really.

In record time I'm thrusting back and biting my lip to stifle my cries. His fingers squeeze my hips too hard and my flesh burns, but I don't try to stop him. Next thing I know I'm coming, fingers clawing the couch, muscles straining, clasping, squeezing. Crosbie's grunting behind me, powering through my body's contractions, and soon I hear him come, too, hunching over me, one hand tangled in my hair as though anchoring himself.

"Nora," he groans on a ragged breath, his hips bumping mine artlessly as he forgets finesse and just gives in to his body's demands. "Nora, Nora, Nora."

I reach up weakly and cup the back of his neck, the only thing I have the strength for. "Crosbie."

chapter sixteen

Two nights later I'm trudging down the sidewalk toward my apartment. It's quarter to eight and Kellan had texted mid-afternoon to ask if I wouldn't mind coming home until after seven. I figured he'd put enough time between the gonorrhea news and treatment that he's ready to get back in the game, and if I'm not mistaken, he'd planned some sort of date night for Marcela. Nate's still bringing Celestia by the shop and Marcela is still bitter, so even though *I* can think of a million better things—and people—for them to do, this is their mistake to make. And everybody makes mistakes. I should know.

I squint up at our living room window. There's a faint glow shining through, as though a light has been left on in one of the bedrooms. I'm really not looking forward to the prospect of walking in on my roommate and my best friend, but I'm cold and I'm hungry and I just spent two hours memorizing irregular French verbs and I want to go home. If need be I'll creep quietly into my bedroom with my eyes closed and my ears covered, and sleep with headphones.

I make as much noise as I reasonably can as I let myself in, but I'm not greeted by the sight of naked, writhing bodies. Instead I inhale the stomach-pleasing scent of garlic and tomatoes and warm bread. I eagerly tug off my boots and hang my jacket on the rail, then climb the stairs, praying there's some food left.

On the top step, I come to an abrupt halt.

There's Kellan. There's candlelight. There's a table set for two.

And there's no Marcela.

My eyes skip around the room, taking in the strangely romantic set up. "Er…what's going on?"

He's standing in the kitchen in dark pants and a white shirt, the sleeves rolled up to expose his strong forearms. His feet are bare and if I'm not mistaken, the apron he's wearing was "borrowed" from Beans. He's stirring a pot of what smells like tomato sauce and appears to have been waiting. For me.

I hope not. "Are you expecting someone?"

He grins, the devilishly handsome guy in every romantic comedy, the one you know doesn't exist in real life. Except he does. And he's *right here*. "I was," he says. "Have a seat. I hope you're hungry."

I stare at the table like it's a bomb. "What's going on?"

He tastes his sauce, nodding appreciatively. "I've been thinking about how great you are," he says. "How nice you've been about this whole situation lately, and just what a good roommate you've been. Then I remembered we were supposed to go out to dinner that time and I totally flaked so I thought I'd plan something special."

I can't convince my feet to move. The vibe in here is not special, it's weird. He's moved the dining table into the living room so there's more space, and it's covered in what looks like a white bed sheet folded in half. It's set with plates and wine glasses and candles. There are even half a dozen votives spaced around the room, making for a very cozy—and confusing—ambiance.

The oven timer dings and Kellan pulls out a loaf of garlic bread, so hot and perfect the butter is still sizzling when he sets it on a cutting board. My stomach urges me to get my ass in a chair. My heart tells me this is going to send someone the very wrong message. And my head is telling me this will only end badly.

"Come on," Kellan says, garlic bread in hand. I feel the

gentle press of his fingers in the small of my back as he guides me to the table, then sets down the bread and pulls out my chair, resting his hands on my shoulder to urge me into the seat. This, of course, is the moment Crosbie walks through the front door.

The three of us freeze, a complicated, decidedly unromantic, garlicky tableau. Crosbie's still wearing his jacket and holds a video game, mouth open in surprise. He stares at us, his gaze locked on Kellan's hands on my shoulders, before shifting to take in the candles, the wine glasses, every damning detail.

"Crosbie—" I begin.

"Hey," Kellan says.

Crosbie's mouth moves, but for a second no words come out. "I wanted to drop off your game," he says finally. Very stiffly he reaches out to place the game on the counter, and even Kellan—delightfully obtuse Kellan—realizes something is wrong.

"Are you okay?" he asks, dropping his hands and stepping toward his friend. "Cros?"

But Crosbie's only looking at me now, his brown eyes hurt and bewildered all at once. I know he's never had a girlfriend before—not that I *am* his girlfriend—and he's definitely never been in a position to be cheated on. But I also know he's the sidekick in Kellan's story; Kellan gets Miss Louisiana, Crosbie gets the runner up. All those questions about whether or not I was into Kellan—I'd finally convinced him, and now this.

"Crosbie," I say again, but he just shakes his head and disappears back down the stairs. A second later the door slams shut, the icy wind making the candles flutter.

"What the hell was that?" Kellan asks, running a hand through his hair. "I said he could keep the game until tomorrow if he really wanted to."

I shake my head and blink away the guilty tears stinging my eyes. I should probably let him go. I should probably not follow him into freezing temperatures and beg him to hear me out. I should never have started this in the first place.

But I did.

I run down the stairs, pause long enough to shove my feet into my boots, and yank open the door. The cold air steals my breath but I can see him half a block down. I don't even think about it, I just start running. The air is so crisp it feels like something might shatter. The faint dusting of frost on bare tree branches flitters down, glinting in the light from the streetlamps before melting into my hair.

"Crosbie!" I shout.

There's no one else around, no sounds, no cars, no anything. I know he hears me, but he doesn't stop. If anything he hunches up his shoulders and walks even faster.

"Crosbie!" I pick up the pace. My lungs hurt because it's cold and I'm not in shape, and I shiver in my thin shirt and leggings, feeling my hair slip out of its bun and flop against my neck

"Crosbie!" I shout. "*Stop!*" I'm three car lengths away when he finally halts, though he doesn't turn around. His hands are crammed in the pockets of his jeans and I can see his breath coming out in fast white pants. I'm gasping when I finally reach him, putting my hand on his arm for balance and nearly falling when he jerks it away.

I'm prepared for his hurt, but not the raw anger on his face.

"Crosbie." My voice cracks on the word. "It's not—"

"Don't bother, Nora." He stares past me up the street, at nothing.

"I've been home for two minutes," I say. "I didn't know he was planning this."

"Right."

"I thought he had a date with Marcela."

"You said you knew they weren't into each other."

"They're not. They—I don't know. I don't know, Crosbie. But I'm not into him. I never will be. This is just really bad timing."

He shakes his head but doesn't move. "You wanted to

keep us a secret for a reason. It never had anything to do with me or that stupid fucking list."

"It did, but it doesn't now."

His jaw flexes and his nostrils flare as he inhales. He's angry, but he's still here. He's listening. He wants to believe me.

"I swear," I add. "I swear. Please don't…" I break off to catch my breath so I don't start crying, like that's the one thing that could make this situation worse. "Please come back with me."

"Why?"

"So there are no more secrets. So we all have to eat spaghetti together. It's going to be terrible, but let's just do it."

He finally looks at me. "I won't tell anyone," he says.

"What?"

"If you're doing this because you think I'll tell everyone we slept together, I won't. If you want to be with him—if you are with him—I'm not going to spread rumors. I'll get the fuck over it. Don't lie to me."

"I've never lied to you." I swallow past the guilty lump in my throat. A lie of omission isn't really a lie, is it? "And I'm not afraid of you. I like you. Only you."

He scrubs a hand over his face and finally notices that I'm freezing my ass off. My arms are wrapped around my still-growling stomach and I'm bouncing on my toes for warmth.

"Where's your coat?"

"I didn't stop to get it."

"Well, you should have. It's freezing."

"Well, if it's the coat or you, I choose you."

It's super lame, but his face softens, mouth quirking reluctantly. He looks down at me and believes whatever he sees. "All right, Nora. Let's go."

* * *

Five minutes later we're sitting at the dining table to partake in the world's most awful dinner party. I brought out my desk chair for Crosbie while Kellan wordlessly blew out every candle and set a third place. Now we sit in front of three untouched plates of spaghetti and garlic bread, unwilling or unable to meet each other's eyes.

Kellan's first to speak. "Seriously?" he mutters, shaking his head. He snatches up his garlic bread and takes a big bite. "You two?"

Crosbie and I look at each other. "Yeah," Crosbie finally answers.

"How long?"

I nibble at my garlic bread like a guilty rabbit. "Halloween."

"*Hallo*—" Kellan's eyes widen. He gapes at me but points at Crosbie. "That's who—?"

I know he's talking about the condom, so I cut him off. "Yes."

He glares at Crosbie. "You said you banged Miss Washington!"

"Well, she's *from* Washington."

"I cannot believe this. Under my nose."

I can't believe it either. And finally I start to laugh. I laugh so hard my shoulders heave and my eyes water and I even snort a little bit. I slump in my chair and toss back my head and just really fucking *laugh*.

"Are you just banging or is this for real? Boyfriend-girlfriend real?"

The question sobers me up pretty quickly. I straighten in my seat and Crosbie and I exchange a look.

"It's for real," he says quietly, picking up his fork and twirling it in his spaghetti. My heart lurches at the words, because I know he's never said them about anyone before. Neither have I.

Kellan takes another bite of his bread and chews while he surveys us. "I knew it."

"You knew?" Crosbie echoes, sounding doubtful.

"Yep. You've been different this year. I knew there was something going on." He tilts his head, conceding. "I didn't know it was Nora, but I knew there was something."

Crosbie's jaw twitches. "I see."

"First you started noticing chicks with glasses after Nora came over to see the apartment that first time. I just thought you'd developed some new fetish, but it was that outfit she had on. She made you like nerds." He nods at me. "No offense."

I roll my eyes.

"I didn't—"

"And how you kept changing our runs so they would go past Beans, then talking about brownies so I'd suggest we go in."

"I'm not—"

Kellan looks at me. "It was his idea to invite you to the Halloween party. I mean, I was on board with it, but it wasn't my idea."

Crosbie glares at him. "What are you—"

Kellan shrugs innocently, though I think we all know he's far from it. And while Crosbie's looking a little embarrassed to have his eighth-grade seduction strategy exposed, my heart's beating a mile a minute. I don't know anyone who works as hard as he does, for anything. Especially not for me.

"Thank you," I say.

It appears to take some effort, but he pulls his attention away from Kellan and focuses it on me. "Thank you?"

"Yeah." I nudge his leg under the table. "If what he's saying is true, then thank you."

He blushes when he smiles. "Any time."

The rest of the meal is only slightly less awkward, though it's admittedly more than a little weird when Kellan tidies the kitchen while Crosbie plays video games and I work on my archaeology paper. No one really speaks, and eventually Kellan joins Crosbie and they blow things up for a while. Around eleven I'm sick of analyzing cave finds in the fictional region of Malaruhu, and I shut down my laptop and head into the bathroom to brush my teeth and wash up. When I come out the explosions abruptly stop, and Crosbie looks from me to Kellan and back, then slowly stands.

He wipes his hands on his thighs, hesitant, and I realize we're at a turning point. If he stays the night, the entire pretense of my arrangement with Kellan is shot to hell. If he goes home, the entire pretense of our relationship is undermined. We're standing in a room with the most popular guy on campus, and we're choosing each other.

"There's an extra toothbrush in the bathroom," I offer. "If you want to brush your teeth before you come to bed."

I see heat flare in his eyes and very slowly, he nods. "Will do."

"Fuck," Kellan groans. "Is this what it's going to be like from now on?"

"I know this isn't what we agreed," I say, balancing on the arm of the couch when Crosbie leaves to clean up. "I'm sorry to flip the script on you."

He shakes his head. "I lived in a frat house last year," he says. "You really think I didn't hear Crosbie banging—" He cuts himself off way too late.

I cross my arms. "Huh."

"Dude!" Crosbie exclaims from behind me.

Kellan hesitates, then unpauses the game, turning the volume way, way up, and studiously ignores us. Slowly I look at Crosbie.

"That was last year," he says quickly. "I'm different now."

I glare at him, then relent. "Me too."

His relief is palpable as he follows me into the bedroom, closing the door and waiting until I've turned on the bedside lamp before shutting off the ceiling light. "Don't be pissed," he says.

"I'm not." I slip out of my jeans and sweater and pull on a tank top, stopping as I reach for a pair of shorts. I glance over my shoulder to find him staring at my ass. "Should I bother putting these on?"

He yanks off his shirt and undoes his pants so fast he almost falls. "No," he says, tackling me onto the bed. "You're not going to need them."

* * *

Crosbie Lucas is my boyfriend.

I'm not the only one who's stunned by the news, but I really don't care what other people say. Well, except for Marcela, who gave me an earful about keeping secrets.

Two days after the spaghetti debacle-turned relationship reveal, I'm sitting across from Crosbie at one of the tiny tables at Beans and splitting a cinnamon bun during my fifteen minute break. Nate attributes my excellent mood to all the orgasms I must be enjoying—and I do enjoy them—but my buoyed spirits are due in no small part to the phone call I'd gotten from the campus clinic this morning, informing me that my test results had come back all clear. It's what I expected, but it's still nice to have it confirmed.

I'm wearing a turtleneck under my apron, but I still shiver when a customer strolls in, the late November winds following. "Grr," I say, trailing my finger through a smear of cream cheese frosting left on the plate. "I hate the cold."

"Seriously?" Crosbie pops the last bit of cinnamon bun into his mouth. "I love winter. You get snow, Thanksgiving, Christmas and New Years—it's awesome."

"Thanksgiving's in the fall."

"Close enough. The point is, winter is great and you're wrong."

"Bah humbug."

He smirks. "Are you going home for Thanksgiving?"

Thanksgiving is on Thursday, and my plan is to work overtime to save up money for Christmas presents. My reasoning is if I buy expensive gifts, no one will complain too loudly when I show up late on Christmas Eve and bail around noon on Christmas Day. I love my family, but I do not love the Kincaid family Christmas tradition of non-stop fighting, one small fire, and overpriced pizza delivery when the turkey inevitably winds up either burned or missing.

"No," I say, when I realize Crosbie's waiting for an answer. "Are you?"

"Yeah. I'm going to drive down, then join the guys for the mock meet right after."

"That's next week?"

"I told you about it."

And he had, explaining it was a pre-Christmas thing they did every year to test their progress and also remind themselves not to overindulge during the holidays. Apparently they never learn and everyone returns in January ten pounds heavier and still hungover, but it's a three-day visit of nearby colleges that brings them back to Burnham on Friday.

"I remember."

"I'd invite you for dinner if I was coming back," he says, misinterpreting my distraction. "I mean, if you really want, you can still come. I'll drive you back to campus, then turn around again. It's only an hour, so—"

"Crosbie." I press my fingers to his lips. "It's not a problem. I'm just thinking how nice it'll be to have the apartment to myself. What will it be like to not smell powdered cheese every day?"

He grins, relieved. "I'll bring you back some leftovers."

"Leftovers that have survived the mock meet? Thank you, but I'll pass."

"What's wrong with Thanksgiving? If you hate winter and Thanksgiving's in the fall, it should be a safe holiday."

I roll my eyes. "Nothing with my family is safe." My parents are what they like to call "functional, friendly, and former." Basically they're a divorced couple, each of whom resides in one half of a duplex, and they tell everyone they get along, but really they hate each other. They divorced when I was ten and neither one has remarried, and they bring a different date to every holiday in a desperate attempt to show how mature they are. As the only child marching in this dysfunctional parade, I'd much rather hide in the woodshed and eat worms than sit down to dinner with whichever unsuspecting date is unlucky enough to show up that day.

I relay this information to Crosbie, whose eyes widen as I talk. "It's torture," I say. "And nine times out of ten, there's not even any turkey. If it's not—"

"Hi, Crosbie."

We glance over to see a trio of girls who look like they just stepped out of a winter catalogue. They wave at Crosbie over cups of steaming hot lattes as they take a seat nearby. I'm instantly transported back to the day we met, when Crosbie invited himself to join me for dinner then promptly abandoned me when something better came along.

Now, however, he just lifts a hand in a vague semblance of greeting and sips his water, gaze trained on me. "If it's not what?" he prompts.

I shake my head. "If what's not what?"

"You were saying there's never any turkey. If it's not...?"

"Oh. Um...if it's not burned to a crisp it's completely raw. They've actually sent three people to the hospital."

"You're kidding."

"Nope. And once my mom got so angry at my dad that she threw the turkey into the street and it got run over by a bus."

"Tell me you filmed it."

"I wish. My favorite is the two times the turkey just disappeared."

"*Disappeared?*"

"Yep. There was just an empty roasting pan in the oven and a wishbone sitting on the counter. I wished for a turkey."

"Twice?"

I lift a shoulder. "Point is, it's not worth the trip."

"What about Christmas?"

"I'll take the bus on Christmas Eve and make up some excuse about why I have to come back on Christmas Day. They know I work—they're usually pretty willing to believe me. That way they don't have to keep up the 'functional, friendly, former' charade any longer than necessary."

"That's really sad, Nora."

"The distance helps."

"I couldn't help but overhear your turkey sob story," Marcela says, flitting over and collecting the empty plate.

"You've heard it before," I say, recognizing the glint in her eye and hoping to end whatever it is she's plotting before it can get underway.

She barrels ahead. "Since I'll be in Mexico for Thanksgiving, why don't we make our own post-Thanksgiving turkey dinner? You and Crosbie, me and Kellan. A double date."

She says "double date" unnecessarily loudly, and entirely for Nate's benefit. Not that the raised voice is required, since he's clearly hanging onto every word she says, anyway.

I shake my head and start to stand. Break's over. "I don't—"

"The more turkey, the merrier," Crosbie says, oblivious of my murderous stare. "Why don't we do it right before the Christmas break? That way everybody gets some turkey." He glances at me and must interpret my glare as more turkey terrors, because he just pats my hand reassuringly. "Don't worry, Nora. I'll keep an eye on it the whole time. That turkey won't go anywhere."

Since he's immune, I turn my glower to Marcela, who smiles smugly.

It's time for this little emotional tug-of-war she and Nate have going on to come to an end. "You know," I say, tapping my chin thoughtfully. "A whole turkey is a lot of food for just four people. Why don't we invite someone else?"

Her eyebrows shoot up when she realizes where I'm going with this. "No—" she begins.

"Nate!" I call. "Turkey dinner at my place. You and Celestia are invited."

He's polishing silverware, and I see his mouth quirk up. "Wouldn't miss it for the world," he says.

I beam at Marcela. "That settles it." I do my best to pretend her fulminous glare isn't legitimately frightening. "And would you look at that? My shift's over."

She hustles after me into the kitchen when I retrieve my coat. "Why would you do that?" she demands. "Are you trying to be the queen of terrible dinners?"

"Maybe I'm trying to be a grown up," I counter, swapping my flats for rain boots. The weather has finally eased up a few degrees, the snow rapidly transforming into slushy puddles and soggy grass. "If you can't fake a relationship with Kellan for a few hours three weeks from now, why don't you just call it off?"

"It's not a fake relationship!"

"It's incredibly fake. If he was the one dating Celestia, you wouldn't bat an eye."

She makes a face. "He would never date her."

"Yeah, because he learned her name."

"What?"

I shake my head. "Never mind. Take notes while you're in Mexico—you're going to need to stuff a turkey soon."

She rolls her eyes and huffs as I leave, meeting Crosbie up front and calling goodbye to Nate before heading outside. The morning's rain has let up, though the clouds are still gray and heavy overhead, making three o'clock in the afternoon look and feel much later.

"Ready for your chem lab tomorrow?" I ask Crosbie, stepping over an especially large puddle. He'd walked over straight from class so he doesn't have his car.

"A couple more hours should do it."

"Seriously? That much?"

He shrugs. "I want to do well." He'd been studying at Beans for the past three hours while I worked, getting Nate, Marcela and I to quiz him on each section he reviewed.

"You'll do fine," I assure him. "I feel like even *I* know everything there is to know about cell division by now."

"Yes," he says, elbowing me. "But you're a nerd."

"Better than being the girl who lost her scholarship and had to return home to work at a gas station for the rest of her life."

"There's no way you were that bad."

"It wasn't good."

"Tell me."

I exhale. "I guess it's a matter of perspective. For me,

pretty bad." I think of the moment the flashlight beam cut across my bare knees while I squatted naked behind the compost bin. The moment of unbearable shame as I slowly lifted my eyes to face the cop who had found me.

"What's bad, though?" he presses. "B minus? Because I'd take that, any day."

"Ha." I scoff. "B minus was something to aspire to. I skipped a lot of classes, drank too much, did stupid stuff."

"Yeah?" He looks intrigued. "Like what?"

I try to hide my flinch. We were at the same parties.

"Just…" I don't want to talk about frat parties. I don't want to talk about the mistakes I made there, one in particular. "I got arrested," I blurt out. If I sound guilty he'll think it's because I'm embarrassed about the arrest—which I am. But I'm only telling him this to throw him off the trail of the real source of my guilty conscience.

Crosbie stops in his tracks. "Come again?"

I scrub a mittened hand over my chin. "You heard me."

"Nora Kincaid got arrested? For what? Wait." He holds up a hand when I start to reply. "I want to guess. Hmm. Shoplifting?"

"No."

We resume walking as he ponders. "Vandalism?"

"Nope."

"Dognapping."

"Is this really what you think of me?"

"I'll be honest, Nora. I don't care what you did—the thought of you in an orange jumpsuit is totally turning me on."

I laugh in spite of myself. "Shut up."

"Fine. What'd you do?"

I sigh and hold up two fingers.

He gasps. "You got arrested twice?"

"Once. Two charges."

He covers his face. "Nora!" He's practically squealing with joy.

"Don't tell Kellan," I say sternly. "Don't tell anyone."

"Who knows?"

"My parents. The Dean. The probation officer who monitored my community service."

"This keeps getting better."

"One night in May…" I try not to laugh at Crosbie's enthusiasm. As many times as I've replayed that dreadful night, I've never once found it funny. But now I suppose I can sort of see it from where he's standing. I clear my throat. "It was the morning I learned I'd failed two of my five classes and was borderline failing the other three. To cheer me up Marcela suggested we go to this party she'd heard about. The point, of course, wasn't the party, but the free booze. We drank everything we could get our hands on, danced around, and acted like idiots."

"Or college students."

I smile ruefully. My parents certainly hadn't seen it that way. "Anyway, we decided we simply had to have donuts and left the party to go to Beans. Marcela had keys and we knew Nate would have already locked up, so we walked into town. Then we realized Main Street was completely deserted. It wasn't quite eleven, but the street was empty. So we decided to go streaking."

Crosbie's mouth falls open. "Naked?"

"Yeah. We dropped all our clothes right there—" I point behind us to the barber shop on the corner, "and sprinted as fast as we could toward the other end."

"And you were naked? Together?"

"Well, we were together for the first few blocks. Then Marcela stepped on a rock and stopped and I ran ahead." I pause. "Then the police came. We both hid, but they only found me. I was hiding behind a compost bin near the hardware store—"

Crosbie's laughing so hard I'm not sure he can hear me.

"The policeman had to get a blanket from the trunk so I could sit on it in the backseat. They'd found our clothes so they knew there were two of us and he kept asking where my 'friend' was. I said I didn't know and eventually he drove me to the police station."

"And they charged you?"

"I was the only person in the holding cell! They had nothing else to do."

He gives up the pretense of walking and bends over to hold his thighs as he roars with laughter, tears gathering at the corner of his eyes. My parents had had a very different response.

"Anyway," I continue primly, "they charged me with two misdemeanors: public intoxication and indecent exposure."

Now he just kneels on the wet sidewalk and laughs his ass off.

"I got three hundred hours of community service and had to collect trash on the side of the highway all summer. That's why I stayed at Burnham."

I kick him when he doesn't stop laughing, and eventually he sobers up and gazes at me, almost worshipfully.

"I like you so much more now," he says, slowly getting to his feet.

"Funny. I'm liking you much less."

"I mean, don't get me wrong—I really like the cardigan-wearing, library-obsessed Nora who doesn't jump on beds, but this... Well, I like the criminal side of you. It's hot."

"Stop."

"I mean, the Burnham Police Department also saw it..."

"Crosbie!"

He teases me the rest of the way back to the apartment, even though it means passing the Frat Farm so he'll have to double back later. We're not at the point where we spend every night together, and I'm definitely not ready for a sleepover at the frat house, anyway.

"Remember," I say, sticking my key in the lock. "Not a word to Kellan. This is a secret."

"Got it." He mimes zipping his lips. "Top secret."

Suddenly the door is wrenched open and Kellan's standing there. "What's a secret?"

"How long have you been waiting?" I exclaim.

"I saw you through the window. Come in here—I want to

show you guys something."

Crosbie and I exchange bemused looks but follow him inside, stepping out of our boots and climbing the stairs to the living room…where Kellan has erected a giant easel with a huge sheet of paper with the numbers forty through fifty printed on it. There are eleven spots for entries: seven have actual names, four have descriptors. That bathroom wall is burned onto the back of my eyelids: the last time I saw it, forty-one and forty-two were blank. Now forty-two reads "BJ at May Madness party" and forty-one reads "Red Corset."

Fuck. Me. Aka "Red Corset."

"What's this?" I ask, trying to hide my terror.

"I've eliminated sixty-two through fifty-one," Kellan answers. "They're all clean. This is the next batch."

"Good job," Crosbie says, studying the list. "You're making progress." He taps the blowjob entry. "I'd forgotten about this."

"Me too," Kellan replies, as though that's totally normal. As though getting a blowjob while a bunch of your friends look on is par for the course. "Except then I remembered that she—" number forty-three, *Karina (brunette)*, "mentioned it when we hooked up the next week. Which made me remember that right before the BJ there was a chick in a closet."

I want to die.

"A closet or a corset?" Crosbie asks, squinting at the writing.

"Both. I banged her in a closet, and she was wearing a red corset. I remember watching her tits bounce as we fucked."

"That's hot."

"It'd be hotter if I could remember her face. I was so drunk, man. I'd messed up at finals, coach put me on probation for the team… I was just doing everything I could to forget."

Crosbie looks wholly unconcerned with this reasoning. "Looks like it worked."

I try not to gag. It's absolutely nauseating to have your roommate and your boyfriend discuss your most regrettable sexual encounter like it's nothing. Like *you're* nothing. Which, if "Red Corset" is anything to go by, is entirely accurate.

Crosbie pulls out his phone and scrolls through, muttering, "Do you have contact info for any of them? I might have Karina in here somewhere."

I look at him sharply.

"Dude," Kellan whispers.

"What?" He finally clues in. "She's in my chem lab," he says hastily. "That's it."

"Uh-huh."

Kellan tries to change the subject. "I'm pretty sure Susanna still works at The Sling. I can drop by there tomorrow."

Susanna has been written in alongside her scratched out descriptor, *Smells like French Fries*. The Sling is a campus greasy spoon, known for serving late night breakfast to drunken revelers. And possibly STIs. This sounds bad, but I hope it's her. Then the search is over and "Red Corset" stays in the closet, both literally and figuratively, because now that I think about it, I know exactly where that tacky thing is.

"And Purple Hair still has purple hair and sits in the front row of my English Lit class, so I can talk to her on Friday." Kellan thinks. "Assuming it's not another girl with purple hair. I never really looked at her face."

"Oh my God," I mumble, running my hands over my heated cheeks. "Oh my God, Kellan. Did you *ever* look at their faces? Ever ask their names? Even once? Did that not matter? Did they really matter so little that you can't remember more than the color of their hair or that they smell like grease or they blew you at a party? Is it really that easy for you?"

He looks startled.

"Nora." Crosbie puts a hand on my arm. "Calm down. It's—"

I jerk away. "Why don't you see how many of their numbers are in your phone, Crosbie? Do you have an entry for *Sparkly Green Shirt* or *Parking Lot at Grocery Store* or *Walks with Slight Limp?*"

"I don't—"

"I mean, they're people, you jackasses! *Blowjob at May Madness*? That's a person! *Red Corset*? That's a person too! And they have names and they have feelings and it's so fucking infuriating to hear you talk about them like they don't matter."

"It's—"

I swipe angry tears from my eyes. "Maybe it's a big deal for them. Maybe they loved it. Maybe they hated it. Maybe they regret it. But maybe it's more than some stupid game or some bathroom wall or some list in my living room."

"Nora, we—"

"I can't," I say. "I can't look at this. I can't look at you." I storm into my room and close the door, slumping against the wall before sliding down onto the carpet. So much for playing it cool. So much for putting last year behind me. I'd tried my very best to not be the non-entity I'd been in high school, the invisible girl hiding behind baggy clothes and tangled hair. And now here I am, hiding behind cardigans and library books and nowhere closer to knowing who the hell I am. "Red Corset" is the most exciting girl I'd even been, and all that got me was a bi-monthly meeting with the Dean, three hundred hours of community service, and not-so-prime placement on Kellan McVey's "Did she give me gonorrhea?" sex list.

I grind the heels of my hands into my eyes, willing myself to get a grip. I'm just barely hanging on when there's a tentative knock on the door. It slowly eases open and Crosbie sticks in his head, spotting me on the floor.

"Hey," he says softly.

"Sorry," I mumble, twisting my fingers. Sorry you think "watched her tits bounce as we fucked" is hot. Sorry I'm *Red Corset*. Sorry, sorry, sorry.

He joins me on the floor. "You don't have to apologize. All that stuff you told me outside—I mean, I thought it was funny, but if it really upsets you, I won't make any more jokes about it. I mean, you obviously beat yourself up for stuff, and maybe you're right. Maybe all the girls on that list regret being on it. I know one does, for sure."

My breath snags in my throat until he clarifies: "The gonorrhea girl."

The heart attack I was about to have subsides. "Oh. Right. Her."

"And I'm going to ask them to paint over my name in the Student Union building. All that meaningless shit isn't worth boasting about. The best girl I've ever known is sitting right here, and I'd die before I saw her name on some list like that."

I'm about to start crying again.

"On *my* list," he adds, making it all so much worse. "How bad would that be?"

I can't speak, so I just shake my head.

"Are we okay?" he asks. "I don't want to go if we're not okay."

"We're okay," I mumble. "I'm just tired."

"Sure. All this gray weather makes people depressed. I saw a thing about it. Did you know they sell lamps specifically designed to give you vitamin D?"

"I did know that."

"Should we get you one?"

I laugh helplessly. "I'll be fine tomorrow. I just need to sleep."

"Of course." He leans forward and kisses my forehead. "Feel better."

"Thanks."

He stands to go, putting his hand on the knob. "And please don't kill Kellan in his sleep. He's a jerk sometimes, but he's my best friend. I'd hate to have to help bury him."

"I can hear you," Kellan calls from the living room. "And I keep mace under my pillow. Just FYI."

* * *

At two-thirty in the morning, I'm still wide awake. At some point I'd ventured out of my room and apologized to Kellan, who promised to keep the easel turned facing away in the corner of the living room, as though it were being punished.

Now, however, it's an entirely different kind of guilt keeping me awake.

Try as I might, every time I close my eyes I see that stupid red satin corset, the one that cinched up so tight I couldn't take a full breath. Paired with a leather mini-skirt and a pair of Marcela's stilettos, I'd thought I was the pinnacle of high fashion. Certainly not the invisible girl whose high school yearbook photo is a large question mark, since the school accidentally misplaced my picture and only realized it an hour before the book was set to be printed.

It didn't matter, I vowed. I would reinvent myself at college, be somebody people remembered. Because if I'm being honest, I'm pretty sure only a handful of my high school classmates would recognize my photo even if it *had* appeared in the yearbook.

Turns out, being memorable is not that easy.

I roll onto my side and stare into my darkened closet. I know I'm imagining things, but I swear I can see that red corset winking out at me, reflecting in the slivers of moonlight easing through the gap in the curtains. The wind howls outside, the promise of yet another storm, and even as I shiver, I sit up and swing my feet to the floor. I flip on the bedside lamp and hurry to the closet. When I moved in I'd tossed all my...less tasteful clothes into the back corner, buried safely behind my boring new wardrobe of jeans, T-shirts, and cardigans. Now I rummage through the pile, finding mini-skirts and sequined halter tops, dangerously tiny cut-off shorts and the neon pink bikini I'd paired with them for a pool party probably no one remembers I attended.

And there, in the deepest recesses of the closet, is the corset. The bright red beacon of guilt that neither Crosbie nor Kellan can ever be allowed to find. I contemplate leaving it right where it is, since there's no earthly way anyone will ever root through my closet. Then I consider grabbing a pair of scissors and hacking it into such tiny pieces that even should someone find it, they wouldn't be able to guess what it was. But in the end I settle for the far more ridiculous option and stuff the corset in a grocery bag, toss on boots and a jacket, and run two blocks up and two blocks over to a completely random street until I come across a garbage can. I wrench out a bag and stuff the corset underneath, securing it with the first bag of trash and replacing the lid.

I'm breathing hard as I stare at the can, wondering if this is how people feel when they hide a body. A bit relieved, a bit gross, and a whole lot guilty.

chapter seventeen

Thanksgiving is remarkably uneventful. I pick up a turkey burger from The Hedgehog and eat it while watching reality TV, reveling in the knowledge that I'll have the whole apartment to myself for the next few days. Me and that stupid easel. From time to time I glance over at it, wondering if there's something I can do to…help. Maybe change "red corset" to "red hair," or cut the bottom of the pages so there is no forty-one and therefore no one to identify. Or maybe burn the whole thing to ashes and say we were vandalized.

We're down to five names in the current group. Kellan has identified everyone from forty to fifty except the mysterious and entirely forgettable "Red Corset," and is working on figuring out how to get in touch with the remaining lucky ladies. Two are Canadian backpackers he met during the summer. He thinks he got one of their email addresses while giving them a "tour" of southern California, and now that he's home for Thanksgiving, he's going to dig through his things and see if he can't find a few more clues.

As nice as the quiet is, I'm lonely. I don't miss the smell of cheese or the non-stop explosions emanating from the television, but I miss having a roommate and I miss having a boyfriend. My *first* boyfriend. Kellan and I are Facebook friends and I smile as I see photos from the track team trip, mostly the guys goofing off on the bus, running bare-assed into the freezing ocean, or doing inappropriate things with whipped cream. Crosbie doesn't have an account of his own but he's pictured there too, looking as handsome as ever.

By the time I get home from work on Friday night, I'm more than ready for the boys to be back. I smile when I bike up the street and see lights on in the living room, dragging my bike up the stairs and thudding inside to find Crosbie sitting on the couch, alone.

"Hey," I say, looking around. Kellan's room is dark. "Where's Kellan?"

Crosbie stands and stalks toward me. "Does it matter?"

"Is he—Oomph!" I forget my question as Crosbie backs me into the wall and kisses me like I'm not the only one who missed somebody this week.

"You were saying?" he asks when we break apart to breathe.

I'm fumbling with the zipper on my coat, trying to get it off. Trying to get *all* my clothes off. "Are we going…to be…interrupted?"

Crosbie crouches and digs his shoulder into my stomach, hoisting me up and carting me into my bedroom as I squeal. I'm no match for him in any position, and this one certainly doesn't make it easy. Fortunately I'm not upside down for long, because he tosses me on the bed and quickly covers me with his body.

"That's all you want to say?" he asks, shoving my leggings down and helping me kick my feet free. "I've been gone all week and you want to ask about Kellan and interruptions?"

"Um…" I work on undoing the buttons of his shirt as I rack my brain, trying to come up with the right answer. Finally I settle on, "Did you win?"

He drops his head into the crook of my neck and laughs. I feel his torso shaking above me. "You're supposed to say, 'Crosbie, I miss you. Life hasn't been the same without you. I feel such…need, Crosbie.'"

Now I'm laughing. "I feel such *need*?"

He pulls off his shirt. "Okay, Kincaid, you don't deserve it, but I've been thinking about this all week, and now I'm going to show you a trick."

All the hormones racing through me come to a screeching halt. I support Crosbie's interest in magic and even enjoy his illusions, but I really don't want to see one right this minute. "Er...now?"

"Yes, now."

I sigh. "Does it involve your penis?"

"Like how I'm going to make it disappear inside you?"

I smile even as I roll my eyes. "Yeah."

"No, Nora," he says sternly. "That's biology, not magic. This might explain why you almost flunked out last year."

I laugh. "Shut up."

He kneels between my legs and strips off his boxers, leaving us both completely naked. We've done this more times than I can count now, but seeing his broad shoulders, the delineated muscles of his chest and stomach, and yes, his cock...it gets better every time.

His eyes trace over every exposed inch of my body, leaving behind a laser line of goose bumps in their wake. "Come here," I say, tugging on his hand. "I want you."

"I was serious about that trick," he murmurs. He lets me draw him down for a kiss, but only lingers at my mouth for a moment before he twines his fingers through mine and lifts my hands over my head. "Keep them there," he orders, slowly kissing his way down my neck, over my collarbone, and lower. I swear he can feel the hard kick of my heart as I realize what he means to do, and I squirm with nerves and excitement. I'd had two lackluster experiences with this last year, both over in what felt like ten very unsatisfying seconds.

"You know," Crosbie says conversationally, dipping his tongue into my belly button before sliding down farther, "the first time we did this, you said it was weird."

"We've never done this," I answer breathlessly, my legs parting at the urging of his big hands.

"Sex-this," he clarifies. "The first time I looked at you right...here." He trails a finger straight through my folds, then presses inside.

I remember now. It's still a little embarrassing, but it's different when it's someone you know. Someone you care about and who cares about you.

"Still weird?" he asks. I feel his breath brush over my sensitive skin, hot and damp and clenching around his gently thrusting finger.

"Hurry up."

He laughs. "Tell me."

"I just did. Hurry up."

"What do you like?"

I groan. "Crosbie."

"What?"

"I don't know. Just do something."

There's a second as he clues in. "Have you done *this* before?"

I swallow and stare at the ceiling, wondering how best to phrase it. I hardly want to talk about other guys when Crosbie's got his head between my legs. "Not successfully," I finally say.

"Ah. Well, Nora, let's see if I can't succeed where all others have failed, all right?"

I laugh so hard I bump his chin with my pelvis. "You're such a dork."

He answers by pulling out his finger, separating my folds, dragging his tongue right up the middle and swirling over my clit. I immediately stop laughing.

"What was it you said?" he asks casually. "Hurry?" He licks me hard and fast and I squirm until I can't take it and push away his head.

"Slower," I gasp. "Slower…for now."

"Hmm…" He licks me again, agonizingly slow. And he licks everywhere. Inside, outside and all around.

I lift my head to see him crouched down there, my legs splayed around his shoulders, his auburn hair dark against the pale skin of my stomach.

"Crosbie," I whisper.

His head comes up, mouth damp, eyes blazing when they meet mine. "Any more requests?"

My head thunks back into the pillow. "Please don't ever stop."

He chuckles and kisses me, drawing my most delicate flesh against his teeth. "I want you to say something," he says.

I give an exaggerated sigh and reach down to pat his shoulder. "Thank you for showing me your 'trick,'" I say obediently.

He laughs again and pushes two fingers inside me, feeling around until he finds what he's looking for. My hips buck up but he's ready for it, his free hand pressing into my stomach and holding me down.

I squeak. "What do you want me to say?" I plead, writhing against his devious fingers.

"Say, 'Crosbie, eat my pussy.'"

My head jerks up. "I can't say that!"

"Why not?" He holds my stare as he slowly licks my clit.

I beg with my eyes. "It's… I'm not…"

"That's not what you want?" He stops, blinking in faux concern.

"You know that's what I want!"

He glances down at my pussy, his fingers still twisting inside. "Yeah, I do. And I want to hear you say it. Come on, Nora. It makes me hot."

I lift a foot to weakly kick at his arm. "You're already hot."

"Nice try."

"Crosbie. Please…"

"Three more words," he says, punctuating each of his words with another torturous kiss. "You're very close." I'm so close that if he said six words, I'd probably be able to come.

I cover my eyes with my hands, feeling my burning skin against my palms. "Eat my pussy," I say hastily.

"Nora," he groans, putting his talented mouth back to work. "I'd love to."

* * *

"So, is it serious?" Marcela asks as we make donuts on Wednesday. "Are you two in love?"

"What?" I concentrate on dropping dough into the fryer without splashing myself. "No, we're not in love. It's been a month."

"You seem happy."

"I am."

"So does he."

"Of course he is. He's with me."

I set the timer and turn to Marcela, who's perched against the sanitizer, slurping on an iced coffee. "How about you?" I ask.

"What about me?"

"How's Kellan?"

She shrugs. "Fine."

"How's Nate?"

She scowls and bites her straw. "He and Celestia are off to cut down a Christmas tree for her apartment. That's why he's not working."

"They picked the right day. I don't know the last time we saw sunshine."

Her expression darkens even further. "You know what Kellan and I did last night?"

"Please don't tell me."

"Facebook stalked strangers for two hours, trying to find the backpackers he hooked up with over the summer."

"That's…romantic?"

"I don't want romance."

"Then you're with the right guy."

"You didn't want it either, last year. You just wanted to have fun and not worry about things."

"Yeah. That all came to a crashing halt when I got arrested."

She tries not to laugh but comes up short. "I knew," she says after a second.

I start fishing out donuts, resting them on a metal rack. "That I would get arrested?"

"That it was Nate."

"What are we talking about?"

"Last year. The secret admirer. I knew right away it was him."

I stop what I'm doing and look at her in surprise. "You did?"

"Yeah. I just didn't...want it. I mean, it was sweet, but nobody thinks about coming to college and settling down, you know? And Nate's that guy. He's the guy who cuts his own Christmas tree."

"You said you *didn't* want it," I say after a moment. "Past tense. What about now?"

She sighs and slurps up the last of her drink, sticking the glass in the rack to be cleaned. "Now it's too late."

"What's too late?"

We both whirl to see Nate standing at the back entrance, dressed for tree chopping in a fitted plaid lumberjack coat, heavy boots, and skinny jeans. Well, sort of dressed for tree chopping. He strides to the sink and starts washing his hands, completely oblivious.

Marcela and I exchange looks and I slowly shake my head. He didn't overhear.

"The donuts," Marcela says eventually. "We forgot two and now they're burnt."

"Aw." Nate dries his hands on a paper towel and walks over to check in the fryer, where I have indeed left two donuts to die. "Come on, Nora," he chides me. "Food costs."

"Sorry, boss. What are you doing here?"

"We got the tree. I'm just coming in to grab Celestia a drink."

Both Marcela and I roll our eyes.

"It's not that bad," he protests as we trail him out front. The shop is empty so we sit on the counter as he starts foaming low-fat milk.

"Why didn't she come in?" I ask. "Afraid someone will steal your tree?"

His mouth quirks. "Hardly."

"Then what's the problem?"

He glances pointedly at Marcela. "You really have to ask?"

Marcela clutches her chest, offended. "Me? I'm nice to her!"

"No one anywhere, ever, would describe you as being 'nice' to Celestia," he replies. "*Barely contained seething resentment* would be more accurate."

"She wears fur year-round! It's suspicious."

"Or maybe…" He watches his hands as he pours the drink into a to-go cup. "Maybe she wants to wear fur, so she just wears fur."

"That doesn't even make sense."

Nate doesn't respond as he strides through the swinging door back into the kitchen, lifting a hand in acknowledgment.

Marcela turns to me. "He totally heard."

"What are you talking about?"

"'She just wears fur?' That's obviously a dig at me because I don't 'wear fur!'"

"Don't you think you're stretching things, just a little bit?"

The front door bangs open and the same group of catalogue models that have been frequenting the shop since Crosbie started spending time here filters in. They're dressed in adorable pastel-colored pea coats and tiny hats with pompoms, and their convoluted drink orders put Celestia to shame. Even Marcela grumbles as she gets to work.

"It's quiet in here," one of the girls remarks. She's got pin straight white-blond hair that gleams against her lemon yellow jacket.

"Slow day," I agree, sliding her a half-sweet almond milk mocha.

"Where's Crosbie?"

I pass her the change and she sticks a dollar in the tip jar. "I'm not sure."

"Hmm." She studies me for a moment, then turns to rejoin her group at the table in the corner.

"What was that about?" Marcela asks under her breath.

"It happens," I say, trying not to sound bothered.

"What happens?"

"People. Ever since Crosbie and I started dating openly, it seems like people are watching, gossiping, whatever."

"Does the Dean know?"

"We have a meeting next week. If my grades are good and I'm not arrested for anything, it shouldn't be a problem."

"Right. Until he shows you a picture of your name on the bathroom wall in the Student Union building and asks which part of the sex talk you misunderstood."

My heart stops beating. "What are you talking about? My name—"

"Hey." She holds up her hands in surrender. "That was a joke. I'm sorry."

I take a deep breath. "It doesn't matter," I say firmly. "Because it's different. *We're* different. I'm not a Crosbabe."

She pats my arm. "I know."

But my protest sounds lame even to me, and the words are still ringing in my ears when we close up the shop at eight and I swear to myself I'm going to bike straight home, even as I take the route that will get me to the Student Union building in half the time.

I lock up my bike and speed walk through the mostly empty lobby, trying to appear casual. As I ride up in the elevator my pulse is throbbing in my temples and all I can think about is seeing my name on a list I would have been stupidly proud of last year and horrified by now. Because that statement was true: I am different. *We're* different.

The bathroom is empty when I push through the door, striding right to the stall that houses the track team lists. My fervent prayers that the walls have been painted are not answered, and the stall is as I remember it.

I exhale as I force my eyes to Crosbie's list, trailing down the names until I reach the bottom. No Nora Kincaid.

Then I look again.

My name may not be on there, but the last time I visited Crosbie's list ended at twenty-five. Now it ends at twenty-eight. And all of the dates are during the week of the mock meet road trip.

I stumble back, staring at the list in shock. Part of me thinks there's no way he would do this, and part of me thinks he most definitely would. Especially after my emotional explosion two days before he'd left. I think back to the night he'd returned, showing me that "trick"—was it an apology?

My lower lip trembles and I fight back tears. *He wouldn't do this*, I tell myself as I storm out of the bathroom and stomp my way down the steps, too angry and confused to wait for an elevator. I think about how he reacted the night he walked in on Kellan and I sitting down to dinner—he wouldn't do something to make me feel that way. He wouldn't. We're not in love, but we're not casual, either.

We are—or we were—on the road to something better.

Once again my brain tries to direct me toward home, but my heart and my feet steer me straight to the Frat Farm. I drop my bike on the front lawn and jog up the steps, knocking loudly. Without the sun to moderate, the night is dark and cold and I shiver as I wait, shifting from foot to foot. Finally Dane opens the door, smiling when he sees me. I've never spent the night here but I've been back a few times since Crosbie and I got together, and the guys seem more amused by our relationship than bothered by it.

"Hey, Nora," he says.

"Hi, Dane. Is he here?"

"Yeah. Go on up."

"Thanks." The welcome mat is predictably absent, so I wipe my feet as best I can before hurrying up the stairs, trying to calm myself. I will be rational. I will be patient. And if he didn't cheat on me with three girls last week, I will be totally fine. Because if he did...

Then I don't understand.

All the doors on the upper level are closed, and when I try Crosbie's it's locked. I can hear the familiar thud-whir of the elliptical and I knock hard enough for him to hear me even if he's got earbuds in. After a second the thud-whir stops and he pulls open the door, looking surprised to see me. He's wearing an old T-shirt that's wet with perspiration, green basketball shorts, and nothing on his feet. His hair sticks out helplessly, as though he'd run his fingers through it before answering.

Like an idiot, I feel my eyes start to sting with the threat of tears, and for a second I stare at him, too many thoughts rattling around my brain for just one to come out. Finally I cut to the chase. "Why?"

He wipes his mouth with the back of his arm. "Why what?"

"Why…" I step into his room when he shifts back and gestures for me to enter. I shut the door and take a breath. "Why did—Why is—" I look around frantically, for words or proof or something I don't have a name for. "There are three new names on your list," I say, struggling to keep my voice level. It comes out cold, but that's better than shrill and desperate. "And they're all from last week. When you went on that trip."

It takes him a full ten seconds, then finally his expression turns from confusion to shock. "Are you talking about the Student Union bathroom?"

"Of course I am."

"And *my* list has been updated?"

"Yes."

"Whose name is on it? Yours?"

"No, Crosbie, not mine. Girls I don't know. Three of them."

He raises an eyebrow. "What are you asking me?"

"I'm asking *why*."

He finishes the water and casually sets the bottle on the desk behind him. "Why the list got updated? I don't know. I told you I don't sneak up there with a marker and add names to it."

"Then who did?"

"I don't know."

"Why would they?"

"I don't know that either."

"Is it…accurate?" I swipe my hand across my eyes,

refusing to let any tears fall.

His cheeks are flushed now, and it has nothing to do with the interrupted exercise. He's gripping the edge of the desk so tightly his knuckles are white, refusing to show his anger. "Are you honestly asking me if I banged three girls on the road trip? No, Nora, I didn't. I was busy, and I thought I had a girlfriend."

I shake my head. He's got the window propped open with a textbook, but it's still too hot in here. My skin is prickling and I feel like I'm smothering. Like my only goal for this year—*don't fuck up*—has just backfired in spectacularly painful fashion.

"Tell me the truth."

"That *is* the truth."

He holds my stare but it's hard for me to return, so my gaze flickers around the room. The elliptical machine, a calendar with sports statistics for each month, the neatly organized desk, the eternally unmade bed. And the man in the middle of it all, who last year seemed so untouchable, but is just a guy. Flawed and functional like the rest of us.

He sighs and flexes his fingers. "I don't know how to prove it, Nora. You heard what Kellan said that night—I've wanted you since the first day I saw you. I wouldn't fuck this up when I finally got it."

"What about…" I feel so stupid. Stupid if I'm wrong, stupid if I'm right. "What about when I freaked out that night about Kellan's list?"

He shrugs. "So what?"

"So maybe you reconsidered this."

"Because a girl got upset about her roommate's sex list, where the girls on it have names like *Purple Hair* and *Smells Like French Fries*? No, I get it. I get where Kellan's coming from, too. Sometimes you mess around and it doesn't mean anything more than an hour or two, then you forget all about it. And sometimes…" He steps closer, though not close enough to touch. "Sometimes you mess around and you can't stop thinking about it. And then you're not messing around at all."

He catches my chin between his fingers and makes me look at him. "We're not just messing around, Nora. At least I'm not. And I'm not sleeping around. From the day I saw you until now, there hasn't been anybody else. I can't say it any better."

I suppose he doesn't have to say it at all. He could just open the door and usher me out with a swat on the ass and a "Thanks for the memories." But he's not. He's not flipping out about me showing up and accusing him, he's not protesting too much and sealing his fate, he's not doing anything other than being the guy I've gotten to know these past months. He's real. And he's trying.

"I'm sorry," I mumble miserably. "I just…"

He waits, but when I don't finish he asks, "Why were you up there, anyway? What were you looking for?"

I squint at the ceiling, embarrassed. "My name."

"And?"

"It wasn't there. But sometimes people stare at me or they whisper and I just started worrying about the Dean giving me another sex talk or just…" I take a breath. "I think last year I wouldn't have cared if I were on that list, I'd just be happy to have been noticed. And now I would care. I said I was going to be different this year, and I really didn't think I was making much progress, but I have."

"You don't want to be a Crosbabe, I know. I don't want you to be one either. I didn't come up with that nickname, and I don't use it, and I wish it didn't exist. But I can't erase last year and neither can you, no matter how hard you keep trying. I'm just focusing on doing things better this year. And I thought I was."

I meet his stare. "You are. I'm sorry."

He's silent for a second, then nods. "Fine. Hang around for a bit. I have to take a shower, then I need you to quiz me for my chemistry exam."

"I thought that wasn't for another two weeks."

"It's not, but it's the worst fucking class I've ever taken, and I need a head start." He grabs a towel and a change of clothes, then opens the door. "Don't go anywhere. I'll be five minutes."

"Okay."

I take a breath and slowly exhale, forcing myself to relax. That could have gone better, but it could also have gone much, much worse. Though it's kind of mortifying to realize I could take lessons in maturity from a guy whose idea of hiding his well-read copy of *Hustler* is sticking it inside his pillowcase.

I make the bed and take a seat against the wall, playing a game on my phone while I wait. When Crosbie returns a few minutes later, his hair is freshly wet and he's changed into sweats and a T-shirt. He smells like soap.

"Are you cold with this open?" he asks, tossing the towel in the general direction of his hamper while nodding at the window.

"No, I'm all right."

"Okay." He grabs his chemistry textbook from the elliptical and joins me, shunting his newly fluffed pillows to the side and sitting at the head of the bed.

"Where do you want to start?" I ask, flipping through the pages he's marked with neon green tabs. "Anywhere?"

"Sure."

"Okay… Let's start with an easy one. What are the ten most abundant elements in the universe?"

"Ah, helium, hydrogen, oxygen…nitrogen…carbon…" He picks at a hangnail. "Calcium?"

"No."

"Did I already say helium?"

"Mm hmm."

"Help me out."

I gesture to the weight stack in the corner. "You like to pump…"

"Iron."

I flick one of the tabs in the book. "What color is this?"

"Green?"

"More specifically."

His brows tug together. "Bright green."

"I was going for neon."

"Remind me what the hell neon is?"

"A noble gas." I don't take the course now, but I actually really liked chemistry in high school, opting for the advanced class just for the hell of it. "Did you know that the guy who organized the periodic table denied that the noble gases existed—"

I break off when I see Crosbie pinching the bridge of his nose as though he's in pain. "Are you okay?" I ask, reaching over to touch his leg. "Chemistry's not that bad. And this story is pretty interesting."

"You know what I can't believe?" He bends his leg so I'm no longer able to reach it, and for a second I just stare at the now-empty spot on the comforter.

"What?"

"The first day you came up here and I got you to quiz me, I swore the next time you were here, we'd do a lot more than 'quiz.' And now here you are, my girlfriend, on my bed, and I'm just…"

I bite my lip. "Mad?"

"Yes, Nora!" He thumps his hand against the pillow and we both pretend not to hear the magazine rustle inside. "What the fuck?"

I tug on a loose thread at the hem of my shirt. "I said I was sorry."

"Well, you should be. Opening the door to see you standing there is like waking up Christmas morning and finding this huge gift under the tree, then you open it and it's just…a banana."

I do my very best not to laugh. "A banana?"

"Yes, a banana. A disappointment."

I gasp. I'm sure me accusing him of sleeping around on the road trip wasn't his favorite part of the day, but calling me a disappointment? I'd heard that term enough last spring to last me a lifetime.

"Crosbie," I say tightly, "I'm sorry. I tried to sound…civil when I came here, but what was I supposed to do? The writing was quite literally on the wall, and whether or not you like your

229

reputation, it's not like you didn't earn it."

"Are you kidding me?" He shifts so he's sitting on his knees, like the wall couldn't possibly support the weight of his irritation. "First of all, I don't even know what names are on that list, but none of them were my girlfriend. You know how I know? Because I didn't *have* a girlfriend. The writing might be 'quite literally' on the wall, but I didn't do anything wrong. I never lied to anybody, and I haven't lied to you."

"I said I was sorry!"

"Who was it?" he asks abruptly.

I freeze, confused. "Who was what?"

"The guy. You said there was a guy last year. He obviously did something to make you...like this."

I gape at him. "*Like this?* Like, *what*, exactly? Like, sees that her boyfriend supposedly slept with three girls and dares ask him about it? Like that?" I toss the book at him and swing my feet to the floor, halted by his grip on my arm.

"Seriously?" he demands. "You're going to storm out? After you stormed in here in the first place? You're the only one who can ask personal questions?"

"No one 'made me' like this," I snap, jerking away my arm and standing. "I *chose* this. I chose to ask if you cheated on me. I chose to believe you when you said you didn't."

He's breathing hard, his chest rising and falling beneath the thin T-shirt, and finally he pushes to his feet. "You know what?" he says irritably. "Fine. Let's go."

"Go where?"

"To get rid of the list, once and for all. We've got some paint around here somewhere. Maybe Kellan's list came in handy, but mine sure as fuck hasn't."

I watch as he stuffs his feet into sneakers and grabs his jacket from his desk chair, tossing me mine. Unable to believe we're really doing this, I trail him down the stairs and wait as he confers with Dane in the living room to determine where they keep the paint. Why this is something they would have, I don't know, but he disappears into the basement for a minute and comes back up with an old can of blue paint and two brushes. "All right," he says tersely, grabbing a wool hat with a hockey logo and sticking it on his head. "Let's go."

"Let's go," I echo. "To the Student Union building."

"Uh-huh."

He starts to stomp down the path to the street, but reconsiders when he spots my bike on the grass. Instead he snatches it up and gestures for me to get on the back.

"Crosbie—"

"Are you coming or not, Nora?"

I sigh and swing my leg over the seat. It's not even remotely comfortable, and for the first minute I expect us to topple over in an uncoordinated tangle of angry limbs. Eventually Crosbie finds the right balance and pedals us toward campus, the paint can hanging from the handlebars and thumping against his knee.

"We don't have to do this," I say when we park at the building and clamber off awkwardly. Painting school property seems like a pretty solid way to get in trouble again, and Crosbie's making no effort to hide the evidence of our poorly thought-out plan. Fortunately the lobby is even emptier now than when I first visited, and the security guard is nowhere in sight. Crosbie's breathing hard from the exertion but I'm shivering from the cold and the warmth of the indoors is no match for my common sense.

Still, I'm supposed to be behaving better. "Crosbie," I hiss, yanking my hand from his while he jabs the button for the elevator. "This seems like something that is most definitely against the rules."

"It's my name," he says stubbornly, nudging me into the elevator when it arrives. "And I want it gone. If they won't paint it, I will."

We don't speak for the rest of the ride, nor when we enter the women's bathroom. Crosbie shucks his jacket so he doesn't get paint on it, and after a reluctant second I do the same. "You seem pretty comfortable in here," I comment, earning myself a cutting look and a brush slapped into my hand none too gently.

He shakes up the can then wedges off the lid, sticking it in one of the sinks. "Which stall?" he asks.

I sigh and point to the correct one, trailing him inside like the world's most aggrieved accomplice. He scans the wall until he sees his name, and I believe him when he says he's never seen it before. From the way his eyes widen, I don't think he's seen any of this.

"You've never been up here?" I confirm. I know the lists are copied in the men's bathroom as well, so he could have seen it.

He shakes his head distractedly, trailing a finger down his list to find the three most recent entries. They seem legit, first and last names, carefully dated. "I don't know them," he says, glancing at me. "And I know Kellan hasn't exactly been a good example, but I learn names."

"Okay, Crosbie."

He sticks his brush in the paint and swirls it around, then carefully swipes it across his own name at the top. Watching it disappear is unexpectedly sad and satisfying.

I'm envious. I wish erasing my own mistakes were this easy. Failed a bunch of classes? Nope. Got arrested? Never happened. Slept with your future boyfriend's best friend? Definitely not.

I'm already addressing those mistakes the best I can, so I bend down and stick my brush in the can and help Crosbie cover up his. It only takes a few minutes but it's unexpectedly rewarding, and soon we're marching into the men's bathroom and doing the same. It's worth noting that the list in here still ends at twenty-five; the three mystery women are absent. He doesn't comment on it, though, and we paint in silence until the list is gone, a pale blue void on the graffiti-covered wall.

For a long moment we just stare at the empty space, and I wonder if he regrets it. If that list was the most tangible type of bragging right, proof positive that he's a stud. "What do you think?" I ask eventually.

He's quiet for a second. "I like it."

"Yeah?"

He glances at me. "Yeah."

We shuffle out of the stall and rinse off the brushes, then put on our jackets and retrace our steps back to the lobby. With some of his anger burned away, Crosbie makes more of an effort to hide the paint can, though of course now the security guard is back at his post, watching us suspiciously.

"Evening," he says.

"Evening," we call back, hustling away. One of the paintbrushes falls out of Crosbie's pocket, leaving a wet mark on the polished floor, and I quickly snatch it up.

"What're you all getting up to?" the guard asks, standing. He's a heavyset guy, armed with nothing more than a flashlight and a walkie-talkie, no threat to us when we sprint through the doors and jump on my bike.

The guard doesn't give chase but Crosbie pedals like a madman anyway. I grip his waist, feeling the paint can pressed against his stomach, his rib cage expanding with each breath. The cold air is biting and I bury my face in the back of his puffy jacket and close my eyes. Before I even know I'm going to do it, I start to laugh. I laugh so hard the whole bike shakes and Crosbie throws a look over his shoulder, trying to figure out what's going on.

"Nora!" he shouts, the word whipped away in the icy wind. "What are you doing?"

"Nothing," I mumble into the fabric, knowing he can't hear me. "Don't stop."

Even though he couldn't possibly understand, he doesn't stop until we're back at the Frat Farm, parking on the lawn again.

"Are you laughing or crying?" he demands, letting the paint can fall out of his coat to bounce on the frozen ground. "I can't tell."

"Laughing," I admit. "I don't know why."

It's too dark for me to recognize the glint that normally appears in his eye when he gets this way, but I don't stop him when he backs me into the trunk of the ancient oak tree and covers my mouth with his. His fingers tangle in my hair, pulling almost painfully, but I don't stop him then, either. I just kiss him back, angry and relieved and exhilarated, and suddenly much more hot than cold.

"Inside," I gasp, breaking away to breathe.

"Here?" he asks. "You sure?"

I shove him toward the house. "Yeah."

He grabs my hand and tugs me up the stairs. I hear a couple of catcalls from the living room but ignore them, unzipping my coat and following Crosbie into his room. We kiss and grope and strip, but when we're halfway undressed he suddenly stops, pushing me back a step. "Fuck," he mutters. "Nora, I don't have any condoms."

For a second my mouth just opens and closes wordlessly. "Can't you...borrow some?"

"I will, but do you really want me to go down there and ask? I mean, they're probably filling in the blanks already, but I know how you feel about your name getting tossed around..."

It shouldn't, but the words do throw a wet blanket on the whole idea. My shirt is gaping open to my waist and I slowly button it to hide my lacy pink bra. Crosbie groans and scoops his T-shirt off the ground.

My stomach clenches when I see the erection tenting the front of his sweats. He follows my gaze and waves away my proffered apology. "It's not your fault," he says. "I kept sticking them in my wallet to bring to your place, and forgot to get more."

"I should have gotten some more for my room so you didn't always have to be the one bringing them."

"You're right. This is all your fault."

I smile at his attempt to alleviate some of the tension simmering between us. It's not quite angry any more, but it doesn't feel finished, either.

"You know..." I begin, planting my fingers in the center of his chest and bumping him back toward the bed. "Last time you showed me your 'trick,' but I didn't show you mine."

His brows raise almost comically high. I've never gone down on him, and even though that first night together I'd asked about it and he'd said "not this time," he's never once tried to get me to do it. But now I want to. My experience with blowjobs is rather limited and unenjoyable, but so was my experience being on the receiving end of oral, and that turned out to be pretty excellent.

He stops when the back of his knees hit the bed, but doesn't sit down. He exhales heavily when I drop my hand and stroke him through the cotton fabric, hot and hard. "I haven't done much of this either," I whisper against his ear, keeping my face turned so he can't see that the confession embarrasses me. "So tell me what you like."

"Nora." The word is raspy and pained and such a turn on.

I start to kneel, but he stops me.

"You don't have to," he says, closing his eyes briefly. "If you're just thinking you should because you're sorry, don't be. It's okay."

"I'm not trying to apologize."

"Only do this if you really, really want to."

I hold his stare and we both break at the same time, smirks turning into full-blown grins. "I want to, Crosbie. I feel such *need*."

"Okay, I'm convinced," he says quickly.

I tug his sweatpants and briefs down as I kneel, urging him to sit, then slowly press his knees apart, hoping I don't look as nervous as I feel. I'm excited too, but having just come from painting over the names of twenty-five girls who might have excelled at this very thing, I can't help but fret.

"You all right?" he asks, tucking a piece of hair behind my ear.

"Yes," I say softly, leaning forward to take him in my mouth. I'm instantly rewarded with a sharp groan and the tensing of his thighs against my shoulders. He strokes my hair and mutters my name and a bunch of other incoherent things, and though I know it's not perfect, he seems to like it. He murmurs praise and pleas in equal amounts, and before he comes he pulls out and grabs a tissue from a box conveniently located nearby, finishing in his hand.

His head falls forward and he sighs, then weakly reaches down to tug up his pants. I sit beside him on the bed, quiet, and look over when I feel him turn. He smiles faintly and reaches over to brush my cheek, pulling back to reveal a quarter pinched between his thumb and forefinger. "Ta da."

"You're a master magician."

He leans in to kiss me. "Thank you."

"I'm never saying it again, so enjoy it."

He laughs. "Not for the compliment, Nora."

I bite my lip, pleased and still slightly embarrassed. "No problem."

He smiles and bears me back onto the bed, deftly opening the buttons on my top. "What are you doing?" I ask, stilling his hand.

"You said it yourself," he says, working his hand free and resuming his task. "I'm a master. And now I'm going to show you some of my other tricks."

"I said you were a master magician."

"You also said you wouldn't say it again, so you can't be trusted."

I laugh until he slides his rough hand over my stomach and under the waistband of my jeans, right into my panties. "Crosbie," I breathe.

"Master," he corrects.

I snort with laughter. "Fuck off."

He kisses me again. "All in good time."

chapter eighteen

On Saturday afternoon I'm at home, studying on the couch with Crosbie to make up for our lack of studying the other night. Kellan's in the kitchen cooking up a storm—a potentially dangerous one—as he tests recipes for next Sunday's post-Thanksgiving pre-Christmas dinner party. A venture I have been unsuccessful in derailing.

"All right," he says, holding up a spoon, steam rising from its contents. "Whose turn is it to try?"

Crosbie slants a look at me. "Yours," he says in a low voice.

"I went last time!"

"My tongue is still burnt!"

"All the more reason for you to test it!"

"Just go over there, Nora!"

"No! You go."

"This is hurting my feelings," Kellan calls. "I can hear you. I'm not that far away."

"How many variations on gravy can there possibly be?" I moan, shoving to my feet. "I can't believe I'm saying this, but I don't think I ever want any more gravy."

"Relax." Kellan holds out the spoon for me to taste. "This is the last batch."

"Thank God."

"Next up: stuffing."

Crosbie groans from the couch. "I can't believe you came

237

up with this dinner party idea, Nora."

"Marcela came up with it," I point out, "and you seconded it."

He closes his textbook and joins us in the kitchen. "Speaking of Marcela, why isn't she here suffering? I mean, sharing in the fun?"

Kellan glares at him. "She has plans."

"For a girlfriend, she seems to have an awful lot of plans that don't involve you."

"You both know she's not my girlfriend. She's like, my beard, except I'm not gay."

There's a moment of startled silence, then Crosbie and I both burst out laughing. "What?" I exclaim.

Kellan scowls. "Look. I started feeling weird in October, but I put off going to the doctor. I knew the news wouldn't be good, so I stopped hooking up."

"That's why you didn't sleep with Miss Louisiana on Halloween!" Crosbie crows. "I knew it wasn't out of concern for me."

"It was out of concern for you," Kellan snaps. "And also Miss Louisiana."

"You're a gentleman."

"Anyway, I have a reputation to keep up and I didn't want people to talk and Marcela wanted to make that guy you work with jealous—"

"Nate."

"The point is, we're helping each other."

Crosbie's face is red with glee. "So she's your gonorrhea beard?"

Kellan smacks him in the arm. "It sounds gross when you say it out loud."

I gag a little bit. "Trust me, it's gross even if you just think it."

"Both of you shut up and try the gravy."

Crosbie and I both sigh, then carefully taste. If I'm being honest, Kellan's had more hits than misses today, I'm just really tired of being a guinea pig.

"Not bad," I say, wiping a drop from the corner of my mouth. "But it might be missing something."

"Yeah," Crosbie agrees. "It's the best one yet, though."

Kellan thoughtfully licks a spoon. "You're right. I think I know what will fix it. This Chrisgiving is going to feature the best gravy any of you have ever tasted."

"Chrisgiving?"

"Christmas plus Thanksgiving," he explains.

Crosbie's shaking his head. "Everyone is going to be confused by that."

"They will not, it's crystal clear." He's already ignoring us, grabbing spices from the shelf.

Crosbie and I exchange helpless looks and retreat to the couch. "Speaking of girlfriend duties," he says, tossing the chemistry textbook in my lap. "Stop trying to jump my bones and help me study."

"I tried to help you study," I remind him, "and you thought 'green' was an element."

Kellan snorts in the kitchen and Crosbie shifts to glower at him.

"That's because chemistry is the worst," he says, turning the evil eye on me.

"Then why did you take it?"

"I don't know. To appear well-rounded?"

I laugh and open the book. "You're very round, Cros."

"Are you calling me fat? I knew that was too much gravy. Dammit, Kell!"

"Stop stalling and focus," I say, kicking him in the knee. "Now, where were we? Oh, that's right. Still on question one. What are the ten most abundant elements in the universe?"

He sighs, aggrieved. "Hydrogen, oxygen, neon, helium, nitrogen…um…iron, carbon, silicon, magnesium, and…green."

I give him a high five. "You're ready."

He laughs. "Sulfur."

"Even better. Look, this doesn't have to be so hard. Chemistry is cool. And the periodic table is actually really interesting."

"It's a bunch of gibberish."

"The elements are arranged according to their atomic number, which is determined by how many protons they have. All of the elements on this side…" I tap the right side of the table, "are stable, while the elements on the left are unstable. What's another word for stable?"

"Please kill me."

"The answer is 'inert.'"

"Is there such a word as 'ert?'"

"There's such a word as 'fail,' is that what you were looking for?"

"I'm looking for a new tutor. Kellan?"

"Busy."

I warm to the topic. "When the periodic table was first created, they only knew sixty-something elements. But based on the way it was arranged, they were able to predict the existence of yet-unknown elements and their properties. If you think about it, it's kind of like magic. And if you fold it in half—"

Kellan suddenly starts coughing, the nose-running, eyes-streaming kind of coughing. "Are you all right?" I call.

"Too much pepper," he gasps, running the faucet and shoveling water into his mouth with his hand. "Definitely too much pepper."

The oven timer dings and he snatches out a muffin pan, each cup filled with various versions of his stuffing recipe.

Crosbie whimpers. "Do you need a guinea pig? I mean, a willing victim?"

"No." Kellan wipes his eyes. He won't even look at us anymore, just yanks off his apron and stuffs it on the counter. "I have to…nap."

Crosbie frowns. "At three o'clock?"

"Cooking's exhausting, man. Not that you'd know." Without another look back, he strides into his room and shuts the door. Firmly.

* * *

Normally when my phone rings it's Crosbie or Marcela, so my only excuse for answering without checking the display is that I dangerously assumed it was either of them. But it's not. It's much worse.

"Hi, Dad." I try not to yawn directly into the phone. It's seven o'clock on Thursday morning and my alarm went off four minutes ago. This is what I get for not jumping out of bed immediately.

"Hi, sweetie. How are you?"

"Just fine. Really busy. I have work in—"

"Great, that's great. Listen, I'm calling to talk to you about Christmas."

I perk up. "Oh? Are you…going somewhere?"

"What? No. I wanted to make sure you were still coming."

My heart sinks. "Oh. Yeah. I'm coming." My parents did this last year, too. Each trying to one up the other, calling earlier and earlier, trying to ascertain whose side of the house I would be staying on, where I would wake up on Christmas morning. It's telephone tug of war and if it weren't so cold, I'd just camp out in the neutral front yard.

"Well, your room's ready for you. Remember that quilt you saw last year? The one with the stars? I bought it!"

I have no recollection of this quilt. Or any quilts. "Thanks," I say, hoping I sound grateful. "Listen, I—"

He interrupts. "And honey, I wanted to let you know I spoke with Phil—Dean Ripley—and he assured me you were doing great. I'm so glad you got that wild behavior out of your system last year."

I flop back onto my bed and twist a piece of hair around my finger. "All gone."

"Now," he says, finally noting the fact that I'm maybe not quite as enthused about this conversation as he is, "that's not to say you can't have any fun. Are you…enjoying your life?"

Ugh. "Yeah, it's fine. Really busy, with work and classes. I actually have to go to work—"

"Any new friends? Boyfriends?"

He makes this same inquiry on each of his once-monthly phone calls, and every time I've answered no. As far as my parents are aware, I live with an equally studious roommate and we have no other friends. In fact, we're barely friends with each other. Since Crosbie now most definitely falls into the category of "boyfriend," this is a pretty open window for me to explain that I'm seeing someone and it's going well and please can I hang up the phone. But when I open my mouth to answer in the affirmative, all that comes out is a simple and rather convincing, "Nope."

I close my eyes and try not to picture the easel in the living room. One more lie to add to my own list. But is it really wrong if I'm just trying to avoid unnecessary grief?

"Okay," he says. "Well, listen. We can't wait to see you. We're hosting one of those murder mystery parties for New Years, and I've already selected your role. You'll be Lucy Loo—"

I frown, thinking of the actress.

"...owner of a high-end plumbing store, who's a little behind on her bills, giving her the perfect motive for—"

"Dad?"

He finally stops talking.

"I'm sorry to interrupt, but I really have to get to work."

"Oh, of course, honey. You're still at that coffee shop?"

"I am. Thanks for calling."

"Okay. We'll see you soon."

I hang up and exhale. That part wasn't a lie—I actually do start work in forty-five minutes, and I'm still in my pajamas. I roll out of bed and drag on jeans and a fitted sweater, then head for the bathroom to wash up.

The front door opens and closes, and I hear feet on the steps. I stick out my head and wave at Kellan, who's returning from a run. "Hey."

He nods at me. "Hey."

I quickly wash and dry my face, and when I lower the

cloth, I'm startled to see Kellan standing in the doorway. "Jesus!" I stick the towel on the rack and reach for the moisturizer. "You scared me."

"Sorry." He studies his socked toes, looking uncomfortable, and in the process, making me uncomfortable.

"What's going on?" I ask, rubbing lotion on my skin. "Please don't tell me there's more gravy."

He smiles politely at my lame joke, and finally lifts his head to meet my eye in the mirror. "It's you," he says.

I study my reflection. "So it is."

He holds my stare for a long moment. "Red Corset." The words are so quiet that for a second I actually convince myself I didn't hear them.

"I—Wh—What?" I stammer. The hand holding the mascara wand is suddenly shaking so hard I have to set it on the counter or risk losing an eye.

"The party," he says. "The closet. The corset. It was you."

"How do you—"

"You talked about the periodic table, Nora. I'm pretty sure no one else has ever used that as foreplay before."

Oh my God. Why didn't I think about that before prattling on yesterday like the world's stupidest know-it-all?

"Kellan, I—"

"Did you know?" he asks, cocking his head. "I know we had a lot to drink that night, but did you remember any of it?"

I can barely stand up. My knees have turned to mush and I'm bracing myself on the counter like it can teleport me out of here. I'd like to lie and assure him he's mistaken—hell, I'd love for it to be true—but I can't do it. My voice, when it comes, is a whisper. "I knew."

His face crumples, just for a second. "*Nora.*"

"I'm sorry."

"You're sorry? I'm the one who didn't remember. Who put your name on that fucking easel and said...said whatever."

I shrug weakly. "You didn't know."

"When you showed up here that first day, did you know then?"

"I didn't know it would be you. You said your name was Matthew."

"But you remembered me? From before?"

I nod, guilty. "I swear I had no intention of moving in when I realized it was you, but you had obviously forgotten what happened and then the whole break on the rent thing and I... I just..."

"Jesus."

"Please don't..." I blink rapidly and try not to cry like an idiot. "Please don't—"

"Tell Crosbie?"

I nod, knowing how heartbroken he would be. How horrible it would be to learn he's still coming in second, even in this.

"Of course I won't. I'm not going to tell anybody."

I exhale so heavily I almost fall over. "Thank you."

"I'll just say I figured out who Red Corset was and she's not the one." He pauses. "You're not the one, are you?"

"No. I promise. I checked."

He sighs. "Yeah. I think I know who it is, anyway. I finally got in touch with one of the backpackers and she said she's pretty sure her friend realized she had something when they got home, so..."

"So the search is over."

"Almost."

"That's good."

He shakes his head. "It's not good at all. It's so fucking ridiculous, this whole thing. I mean, have you ever dug yourself a hole so deep you thought you'd never get out? Because last year that's what I did. I partied so much, slacked off, thought I was above it all, and I almost got cut from the track team. That's why I was so drunk the night we...I... Well, you know."

"We both had our reasons for being there."

A terribly awkward moment of silence drags on. And on.

"I'm sorry," we blurt out at the same time.

He laughs sadly and shakes his head. "It'll never happen

again."

I frown. "I wasn't expecting it—"

"I mean, screwing around like I did all of last year. I had this idea of what college was supposed to be like, and I totally fucked it up."

"I know what you mean."

We look at each other for a long moment. "Okay," he says finally. "Okay."

I lick my dry lips. "Okay."

"So we're...okay?"

I'm still trembling, the shock of being found out almost worse than the fear of it. "We're okay."

"And this stays between us, forever?"

"Absolutely."

"Maybe we should blood swear."

"Get out of the bathroom."

He grins. "I know what's even better than a blood oath."

"I can't imagine that's true."

He retreats and returns a second later with an armful of easel paper, a lighter caught between his teeth. Then I'm pretty sure he says, "Let's burn it."

"Let's burn down our whole apartment? Sure, that sounds reasonable."

"Ha ha. We'll burn the list in the tub."

"That's a terrible idea." But even as I say it I'm wrapping the shower curtain over the rod and helping him tear up the large piece of paper bearing the first batch of names.

"I can't destroy the second one yet," he says. "But once I confirm that *Backpacker Two*—sorry, Janna—is the one, we'll burn it, too."

"Can't wait."

I hold the showerhead and prepare to put out an inferno as he carefully touches the flame to one of the crumpled pieces. After a second it catches and starts to crinkle and darken, folding in on itself, consuming all his sins, our shared secret.

It never gets out of control, just spreads to the next piece and the next, burning itself into a tidy pile of ashes I simply wash down the drain. It's as easy as painting over Crosbie's name on the bathroom wall; everything erased, swiftly and surely. It's over.

We're safe.

chapter nineteen

Chrisgiving falls on Sunday, December seventeenth, smack in the middle of finals. The last day of school is officially this Wednesday, but some people, like Crosbie, have already finished their exams and are ready to celebrate. People like me, however, have tests both tomorrow and Wednesday, and really wish their apartment wasn't hosting the inaugural Chrisgiving dinner.

"Smells good!" Crosbie says when he arrives. He shucks his coat and heads straight to the kitchen where Kellan and Marcela wear matching aprons and do things like peer in the oven and drink wine. I'm on the sofa, frantically reading through my most recently revised set of English Lit notes and wondering why my brain has turned into a sieve.

Crosbie's pained shout has me looking up in time to see him clutch his hand, Kellan wielding a wooden spoon and a stern expression. "Do not touch the potatoes!" he orders. "Out of the kitchen!"

"Aren't there hors d'oeuvres at this party? Chrisgiving sucks."

"Chrisgiving is amazing, dipstick."

"Merry fucking Christmas."

They grin as they flip each other off, and Marcela and I exchange eye rolls. Crosbie snags Kellan's wine glass before strolling over to join me on the couch. As per the evening's strict dress code, he's wearing a white button down with a pale

247

green tie and dark brown pants. I'm wearing a fitted gray knit dress and kitten heels, and beneath their aprons, Marcela and Kellan are similarly attired.

"You look nice," Crosbie says, closing my laptop and setting it on the coffee table. "And study time's over. Have some wine."

"I was reading that."

"Read my lips instead: it's Chrisgiving. Time to par-tay like it's a fake holiday."

I smile in spite of myself. My stomach's been in knots for days. Last year at this time I'd been partying my face off, not bothering to crack a book, figuring I'd retained enough information from the few lectures I'd actually attended to earn a passing grade. I'd been wrong. But not nearly as wrong as I'd been a few months later, when I employed the same study strategy and came out with two failing grades to show for my non-efforts.

Crosbie kisses my cheek. "You okay?"

"Just nervous about exams."

"You're going to be fine. If I can pass, you can pass."

"You don't know that you passed."

"There's that supportive spirit I know and love."

I laugh and take a sip of his wine. "Sorry."

"No problem. It looks great in here. Who decorated?"

"Guess."

"Mr. Chrisgiving?"

"Mm hmm."

To be fair, it does look nice. A little over the top, maybe, but nice. We've got everything minus a Christmas tree, though Kellan drew one on the easel, strung lights and garland around the frame, and stuck presents underneath. There's fake snow sprayed on the window, fairy lights line the perimeter of the entire apartment, and evergreen boughs hang along the television console. He's added a leaf to the dining table so it'll now seat six, we'd borrowed chairs from our neighbor so everyone can sit down without taking turns, and the white sheet is back to serve as a tablecloth, though the votive candles are thankfully absent.

Old Christmas carols play on a low volume, and with the scents of turkey and pine in the air, it really does feel like Chrisgiving.

"Are you looking forward to going home tomorrow?"

Crosbie shrugs. "Yeah. It'll be nice to see my family. Not so nice not to see you until the New Year."

"That's what Skype is for."

"I thought that's what porn was for."

I laugh and drink more wine. "Whatever works, pal."

The doorbell rings and Marcela and I immediately lock eyes. "I'll get it," I announce, standing and hurrying down the stairs.

Despite her fur coat, Celestia is shivering on the front stoop. Nate's not faring much better, clutching an umbrella overhead to protect them from the not-quite-rain but not-quite-snow that's been spitting down all day, making the streets a slippery, treacherous mess.

"Come in, come in," I urge, stepping back. "Welcome."

Nate passes me a bottle of wine. "Burnham's finest."

"Thank you. Hi, Celestia."

"Hi, Nora. It smells good in here."

"It's going to taste good in about ten minutes," Kellan says from the top of the stairs, looking like a movie star. "Glad you guys could make it."

Nate's jaw twitches. "Glad to be here."

"A triple date," Kellan muses. "How rare."

I make a face at him and he retreats as I lead Nate and Celestia to the living room. "Something to drink?" I offer. "There's a bottle of white already open, or we could open this. And we've got beer."

"What kind of white is it?" Celestia asks.

I draw a blank and turn around to read the bottle Marcela hands me. "Tell her it's a no-fat, half-decaf nectar blend from the wilds of Papua New Guinea," she whispers.

"Chardonnay," I say instead, extending the bottle.

Celestia studies it and purses her lips. "Maybe I'll just

have Perrier."

We all pause.

"We have tap water," Kellan offers tentatively. "And ice?"

Marcela is glaring daggers at Nate, as though it's his fault his girlfriend likes the finer things in life. Nate, in response, is glaring right back, seeing through the matching aprons for the charade this whole thing is.

"Maybe beer," Celestia says. "Any type is fine."

"I'll have the same," Nate adds.

I grab two bottles from the fridge and hand them over.

"Very festive," Nate offers, nodding at the easel. "Your work, Nora?"

I choke a little on my wine. "Ah, no. Kellan drew it. And collected the branches." I point at the greenery decorating the television console, desperate to draw attention away from the easel, despite the fact that it is quite literally lit up like a Christmas tree. Because beneath the drawing on the top page is the remaining page of the sex list. Kellan crossed out *Red Corset* like he'd done with the others, leaving only the remaining backpacker behind, but refuses to toss the list until her identity is officially confirmed.

"They're pine boughs," Kellan says, straddling one of the dining chairs and pointing at the console. "I like the scent."

"It does smell great in here," Celestia agrees.

Marcela pulls up a chair and crosses her legs, exposing miles of skin beneath her mini-skirt. "You said that already."

"Did I?"

"Are those real gifts or did you just wrap up cereal boxes?" Crosbie asks, changing the subject and earning himself a very grateful hand squeeze.

"Fake," Kellan says. "It's too early to start shopping."

"Christmas is a week away."

Nate looks intrigued. "Surely you two have exchanged gifts," he says, looking between Marcela and Kellan. "What did you get each other?"

"You heard him," Marcela snaps. "It's too early."

"I got Nate earmuffs," Celestia chimes in. "They're lined

with fur."

I die a little.

Marcela's face turns red.

"The food must be ready by now!" I exclaim, jumping to my feet. "Why don't we eat? I'm starving."

Right on cue, the buzzer sounds and Kellan smiles. "Perfect timing. Let's go get the food, sweetie." He strokes Marcela's hair and turns that gorgeous smile on her. It's fake and awful and I feel nauseous.

"If I weren't so hungry, I'd fake an illness and leave," Crosbie mutters.

"Don't you dare abandon me," I whisper back.

In order to keep Celestia and Nate apart from Marcela, Crosbie and I take seats on either side of the table, Celestia next to me, Nate next to Crosbie. This leaves only the opposing end seats for Kellan and Marcela, and once they've loaded the table with turkey, potatoes, cranberries, rolls, and the perfect gravy, they sit down. Crosbie and I now serve as a buffer between Marcela, Nate, and Celestia, and I figure Kellan can fend for himself, since he's wielding the carving fork and slicing the turkey like a pro.

"You're good at that," Celestia says. "And the turkey looks perfect."

Truth be told, it does look pretty good. As someone who has only succeeded in eating roast turkey twice in the past fifteen years, the fact that there's any turkey at all is noteworthy.

"Dark meat or white?" Kellan asks.

"Oh, I'm vegetarian," Celestia says.

Marcela mumbles something that sounds like *you have to be fucking kidding me.*

"But I brought some fake turkey," she continues, pulling a little plastic-wrapped lump out of her purse and setting it on her plate. "It's just as good!"

Kellan looks alarmed, but Crosbie quickly stands and extends his plate. "White or dark is fine by me," he says. "I'll eat anything."

"Me too," I say, shoving my plate forward.

We all proceed to load our plates in even more loaded silence, the quiet cut by the sound of Celestia sawing through what might just be a piece of gray putty. The only other items on her plate are half a dinner roll and a cranberry.

Marcela looks ready to have a conniption fit and when I see her mouth open to make some offensive remark, I blurt out, "So, Nate. Earmuffs. They must be handy on days like today!"

He's got a mouthful of food so he looks around, chewing as fast as he can. "Very warm," he agrees, the words garbled.

"They're fur-lined," Celestia reminds us.

"Isn't that weird?" Kellan asks. "Being a vegetarian and wearing fur?"

She stares at him. "How do you figure?"

"What did you get Celestia?" I ask Nate, sensing Marcela winding up again.

"An angel," he mumbles. "For her tree."

"Oh. That's nice."

"He said it looked like me," Celestia adds. "It's beautiful."

A lengthy, painful silence follows.

"What'd you two get each other?" Kellan asks eventually, using his knife to point between Crosbie and me, nearly taking out Nate's eye.

Crosbie and I both freeze. We hadn't actually talked about gifts, though I'd secretly gotten him something. I hid it beneath the passenger seat of his car, figuring I could text him on Christmas morning to tell him where to find it.

"That's a surprise," Crosbie says, taking a gulp of wine. "For...later."

"Yes," I say, as though I too, have not bought a gift. "Later."

"Huh."

"And you?" Celestia says. "What did you buy for Marcela?"

"Lingerie," Kellan answers promptly.

"I'm wearing it now," Marcela adds.

Celestia looks startled. "Oh. How…personal."

"How about you, Marcela?" Nate asks. "What'd you get Kellan?"

"A video game," she lies. I know they didn't get each other anything at all, since they're not actually in a relationship and this charade is fine so long as they don't have to spend any money.

"Oh," Nate says, doing an excellent-if-sarcastic Celestia impression. "How…personal."

Marcela glares at him.

"Kellan, this gravy is amazing," I say, pouring a little more than necessary on my potatoes. "Well worth all the taste testing."

"It's the white pepper," he replies. "Who knew?"

Nate polishes off his beer. "Who indeed?"

Celestia pushes away her plate, half her tiny food portion still sitting untouched. "I'm stuffed," she announces. "Do you have any Perrier?"

"Still no," Marcela snaps.

With Celestia just sitting there watching us placidly, the sound of everyone chewing suddenly feels incredibly loud. And as though we all hear it, we all start to chew faster, just so it's over.

"Why don't we play this new video game of yours?" Crosbie asks when the tension grows to unbearable proportions.

Kellan face goes comically blank. "It's…not here."

"Where is it?"

"At my place," Marcela supplies. "I bought a console so Kellan could be there all the time."

Nate snorts.

Crosbie shrugs. "Whatever. Let's play something else, then."

"Go ahead," I say. "Marcela and I will clean up."

"I cooked!" Marcela protests.

Now I snort. Marcela can't cook a piece of toast. She just wore the apron and stood next to Kellan for a few hours.

We all stand, the boys slumping on the couch to digest and blow things up, Marcela and I rinsing plates and loading the dishwasher. Celestia pulls out her phone and starts texting, and Nate wanders around, taking in the decorations.

"What's this?" he asks.

I turn to see what he's referring to and freeze. He's lifted the Christmas tree drawing to reveal the list of crossed off names underneath.

"It's a...list," Kellan says.

Crosbie pauses the game. "Kellan was trying to—" He breaks off coughing when Kellan elbows him in the ribs. My heart is pounding as I wipe my hands on a towel and hurry into the living room.

"Trying to track down an old friend," I finish. "To say hi."

Nate frowns at the list. "Why don't you know your friends' names?"

"It's been a really long time."

Celestia gets up to join Nate, frowning at the easel. "*Smells Like French Fries?*"

Kellan looks at me frantically. "I have a poor memory."

"*Backpacker One – Freckles?*"

"Er, yeah, she was sweet."

"Wasn't there dessert?" I ask desperately. "Didn't we buy cheesecake?"

"We certainly did!" Kellan says, jumping to his feet. "Who's ready for dessert?"

"We just ate," Crosbie says. "Let's wait a bit."

But Kellan's rushing into the kitchen. "Chrisgiving waits for no one."

Nate looks confused. "Who?"

"It's chocolate cheesecake," I try. "You're going to love it."

Celestia winces. "Ooh, is it dairy? I don't eat dairy."

Marcela pauses in setting the table to stick a finger down her throat and mock gag.

"Have some more wine," I say. "Or beer. Or tap water.

Let's all just go back to the table immediately."

Celestia shrugs and turns to sit down, Crosbie following. I'm halfway there when Nate says, "*Red Corset?*"

All of a sudden I'm doing my best statue impression, one leg in the air, arms mid-swing. I swear the whole room can hear the alarm bells clanging, the arrows that appear mid-air to point at me, shrieking "Guilty, guilty, guilty!" at the top of their gleeful lungs.

"She was an actress," Kellan lies smoothly, walking over to fold the Christmas tree drawing back down over that dreadful list and putting an end to the inquiry. "It was one of those historical plays where the women wore corsets."

"Hmm." Nate takes his seat and accepts a piece of cheesecake. I stare at mine like it's a lump of dirt and wonder how the hell I'm going to choke it down. "Didn't you have a red corset, Nora?"

Now I'm sure they can hear the alarm bells, because the room goes deathly silent for ten full seconds. Crosbie looks at me in surprise and I open my mouth to say something, anything, when Kellan beats me to it.

"Nora?" He laughs. "In a corset? I can't picture it."

"Have you ever even been on stage?" Marcela asks, nudging me when it becomes clear that I'm too stupid to play along. "Ever dreamed of being an actress?"

"No," I manage. "Never."

"Wrong girl," Marcela says firmly. "You're imagining things."

Nate shrugs. "Huh. Okay."

I pick at my cake but my lack of appetite is unremarkable, since everyone is eating very slowly, still too full from having inhaled their dinner.

Celestia resumes her texting and after a minute Nate puts down his fork and pulls out his phone, and I wonder what message she's sending. *Get me out of here? Do you think they have any Perrier?*

But that's not it at all.

"Aha!" Nate crows happily. "Here it is." He shows his

phone to Crosbie, who glances at the screen politely, then freezes mid-bite. I have no idea what he's seeing, but all the blood drains from his face and he's suddenly gripping his fork so hard his knuckles turn white.

"What is it?" Kellan asks.

I reach for his hand, but Crosbie moves it away. "Are you okay?" I try. But he won't look at me. He won't look at anybody.

"I knew you had a red corset," Nate says, oblivious. "Marcela texted me this after the May Madness party. Remember when you went there to get drunk after learning how bad your grades were? Then you said the party was no good so you left to go streaking down Main Street?"

I can barely breathe. "What are you doing?"

"She told me what was happening and I didn't believe her, so she texted me some proof," he continues, turning his phone so I can see the damage. And it's bad. It's so bad.

It's a picture of our clothes crumpled on the sidewalk, the corset gleaming red on top, a beacon of my guilt. It's like sliding the final block into a very precarious tower, and just for a second it stands there, announcing its presence, before it all comes crashing down.

Crosbie's breathing heavily. "Is it true?" he asks.

"Yeah," Nate answers, oblivious. "She got arrested and everything. You didn't know?"

Crosbie ignores him, eyes on me. "*Red Corset*," he utters. "Is *you*?"

I can't say a single thing to defend myself. I don't want to admit it but I don't want to lie anymore, either. In any case, it doesn't really matter what I do, because he knows the truth, even if he can't believe it.

"Did you know?" he asks, turning to look at Kellan. His eyes are pleading, begging his friend not to have known, not to have betrayed him. "Did you know it was her?"

Kellan's shaking his head helplessly. "I just… I didn't remember…"

I'm numb. Every part of me. I don't even feel the tears,

just see them splash onto my plate, the untouched cake, the ruined everything.

"What am I missing?" Celestia asks, breaking the spell.

But it's already too late, because when I finally look up Crosbie's seat is empty and his jacket is gone and the front door is slamming shut.

"No!" The word sounds strangled as I lunge from my seat to go after him. I stumble around the table and down the stairs, yanking open the door to a face full of freezing rain. My feet slip on the wet stone as I run to the sidewalk, but I can't see him. In seconds my hair is soaked and plastered to my head, my teeth chattering, temples aching from the cold. The streets are dark, abandoned on this miserable night, and when I call his name the only answer is a car starting up somewhere out of sight, the squeal of wheels on slush and ice, and then the fading growl of him leaving me.

chapter twenty

I stumble back into the house and close the door behind me, resting against it when I can't bear the thought of climbing the stairs and facing everyone. I'm numb from both the cold and the shock of what just happened. Of course he would find out this way. Of course he would find out at all. Of course. The truth always finds a way out, in the end.

"Nora."

I hadn't realized I'd closed my eyes, but now I open them to find Kellan standing at the base of the steps, a towel in his hand, his face a miserable mirror image of mine.

"He's gone," I whisper, taking the towel. I can't stop shaking, even as I try to do the responsible thing and wring the icy water from my hair.

"I'm sorry," he says.

"It's not your fault." The words come out automatically, but as soon as I hear them, I want to take them back. Of course it's his fault. It's his fault for pretending to be Matthew; I never would have shown up here that day had I known it was Kellan McVey's apartment. It's his fault for offering me free rent; I never would have moved in if I'd had to pay. It's his fault for saving that stupid list; Nate never would have seen it if we'd burned it with the rest.

But even as I try my best to get angry at him, I can't. Smarter, grown up Nora knows where the blame belongs, and unfortunately, it's on my wet, slumped shoulders. "I should have told him," I mumble, slouching onto the steps. Kellan hesitates a second before joining me, and though there's a foot between us, the distance is quickly covered by the pool of water seeping out of my sodden wool dress.

"When?" Kellan asks ruefully. "When would have been a good time to tell him something like this?"

I shrug and think about it. When, exactly? When we first met in this very entryway? When there was no earthly reason to believe he'd ever want to know—or even care? Should I have told him when I started to realize there was some kind of spark between us, even though the news would have most definitely extinguished any potential flame? Should I have told him when things got more serious, when the news was bound to hurt impossibly more?

"I don't know," I answer eventually. "I don't know. But I'm pretty sure I couldn't have done worse than this."

"Our first and last Chrisgiving," Kellan says with a sigh.

We quickly run out of commiserating things to say, but the silence lasts all of four seconds before angry voices begin to filter down from the living room.

"...obsessed!" Marcela is shouting. "Why couldn't you just drop it? Why are you *even here*?"

"I was invited!"

"*We* were invited," Celestia corrects.

"Who brings their own dinner to a dinner party?" Marcela demands. "And who, under the age of ninety, *wears fur coats*?"

"Would you get over the fur coat thing?" This is Nate. "You never gave her a chance. You're like a toddler who doesn't want a toy, but doesn't want anybody else to have it. It's time to move on, Marcela."

"Move on?" she squawks, outraged. "Move on from what, exactly?"

"This unrequited love you two have going," Celestia replies calmly.

A shocked pause, then both Nate and Marcela start sputtering. "We don't—We're not—There's no—"

"Stop kidding yourselves," she interrupts. "Because you're

certainly not fooling anyone else. Have a nice life, Nate."

"Cece—you don't—"

"You call her Cece?"

"Would you *shut up*?"

Kellan and I stand uncomfortably as Celestia descends, collecting her fur coat from the hook by the door and pulling on her boots. "Thanks for dinner," she says, opening the door and frowning as she looks outside. "And Happy Chrisgiving."

"Happy Chrisgiving," we echo uncertainly, watching as she exits into the storm, presumably to walk...somewhere.

"Oh my God, oh my God," Nate mumbles, hurrying down the stairs. He snatches up his coat and stuffs his feet into his sneakers, not bothering with the laces. "Nora," he begins, hand on the knob. "I'm so sorry. I don't know why I—I have to go catch—I just—"

I wave him off. "Just go."

He looks between Kellan and I, pained. "I had no idea."

I shrug. "You're not the only one."

Kellan winces at the reminder, and we both shiver as icy wind whips in when Nate leaves.

After a moment we turn to see Marcela hesitating at the top of the stairs. "I guess I'll go," she says awkwardly. "Unless you need..."

"I think we're all set," I say.

"Right."

We hover uncomfortably as she gets dressed and pulls her car keys from her pocket.

"Sorry about Crosbie," she offers.

"Sorry about Nate," I say.

"Sorry about Chrisgiving," Kellan adds, just to be included.

Marcela leaves and then it's just Kellan and I looking at each other until my teeth start to chatter.

"Do you think there's any point in driving to the Frat Farm?" I ask, wrapping the towel more tightly around my shoulders. It makes me think of Crosbie's Superman cape, which reminds me of watching him remove it the first night we'd slept together, and that makes me indescribably sad. I'm the world's worst superhero; the antihero of this dreadful story. The lamest villain.

Kellan shakes his head. "We can try, but he knows we'd go there. He was planning to head to his parents' place in the morning. He's probably driving over right now."

"Do you know the address?"

"No. Just that it's in Chatterly. I've never been."

"Me either."

The intensely awkward silence is broken only by the snap of my teeth clacking together.

"Go take a shower," Kellan says, placing a palm in the center of my back and urging me up the stairs. "Get warm. I'm sure… I mean, this thing… He knows you… We… I…"

"He knows everything," I say. "Too much, too late."

We stop in the living room and stare at that stupid easel, the flashing lights, the silly Christmas tree, the secret we tried to hide.

"We should have done this last time," Kellan says, striding over and tearing off the page of names. "But better late than never."

"It's just late," I say, trailing him as he grabs the lighter from the television console and heads into the bathroom. "Nothing's better."

He doesn't answer, just tears the paper in half and half again, crumpling each piece and tossing it into the tub. We're quiet as he lights the fire, the pages crackling as they catch. They burn quickly, turning into murky black ashes against the white porcelain.

When the fire is gone Kellan and I look at each other, and the only reason I know I'm crying is because the tears cut warm tracks over my frozen skin.

"I'm sorry," he says, as though the tears remind him. "For everything."

"Me too."

He smiles sadly, then turns and walks out the door, tugging it shut behind him. I strip out of my wet dress and wring it out in the sink, then climb in the shower and turn on the water. I'm so cold that even lukewarm feels searing hot, and I watch the ashes swirl around my feet as the water beats against my shoulders. Every drop hurts.

I thought this was over the last time we did this, but I was wrong.

Now it's over.

* * *

Breakfast the next morning is a torturously awkward affair. Kellan and I each have exams that start at one, so we're both home to study. When I stumble out of my bedroom shortly after eight, Kellan's already sitting down with a bowl of cereal. I'd much rather crawl back into bed and hide under the covers, but I can't afford to do any of the things I really want to do, so I stick some frozen waffles in the toaster and eat them standing up.

For a long time the only sound is the scrape of Kellan's spoon against the bowl and the crunch of my waffles.

"Sleep all right?" he asks eventually.

"I texted Crosbie a dozen times, no answer. I called too. No response."

Kellan stirs through the flakes until he finds a blue marshmallow. "Me too."

"You really think he went home? To Chatterly? In the storm?" The weather is now deceptively calm and clear, the sun out, the sidewalks dry, as though nothing had happened last night. As though everything is fine.

"Yeah," Kellan says. "I do. Wouldn't you?"

I think of my parents, living together but apart, making everyone miserable. "No." I polish off my second waffle and wipe my fingers on my shorts, then glance at the clock on the microwave.

"You're going over there?" Kellan finishes the cereal and stands. And, apparently, reads minds.

"I have to try. I mean, I know that news had to come as a

shock, but it was last year. We didn't even know each other. Maybe now that he's slept on it, he'll…it'll just…"

Kellan looks unconvinced, but shrugs anyway. "I'll come with you."

"I don't think seeing us together is going to help."

A long gap of silence grows as the words sink in.

Kellan clears his throat uncomfortably. "You're right."

"I should go alone. I'll bike over now, then head to the library to study before my exam. If he's at the Frat Farm I'll text you."

He nods. "Fine."

* * *

He's not there, of course. My knocking wakes up Dane, who is, for some reason, sleeping in a hammock strung up at the bottom of the stairs, and he confirms that Crosbie didn't come home last night. He's a little perplexed to learn that I don't know where my boyfriend is, but I hurry away before he can wake up enough to ask questions.

Last spring I'd nearly flunked out of Burnham, had sex in a closet with Kellan, streaked down Main Street, and gotten arrested. If I learned anything from the experience, it's how not to compound my mistakes. So even though what I'd really like to do is cry myself to sleep and bike all the way to Chatterly wailing "Crosbie, talk to me!" what I actually do is head to the library, crack open my books, and control the one thing that's actually within my power.

By the time I get home that evening, the apartment smells like fried chicken, Kellan's second favorite food.

"Hey," I say, finding him in the living room, eating straight out of the bucket and watching a hockey game.

"Hey."

"How'd your exam go?"

"I think it went well. Yours?"

"Pretty good."

I grab a microwave dinner out of the freezer and nuke it

for two minutes, then sit at the dining room table to eat.

"I guess you didn't find Crosbie this morning," Kellan remarks when the game goes to commercial.

"Dane said he didn't come home last night."

"Figured."

"Did you hear from him?"

"No. You?"

I shake my head. "Not a word."

Kellan takes a deep breath and sets the bucket on the coffee table. I watch him turn and steeple his fingers under his chin, deeply serious. "We should talk."

"We are talking."

"About...this." He gestures around the room.

I follow his arm and just see the apartment. "Okay."

He exhales heavily. "I really like you, Nora. You're a good roommate and a nice person and...yeah."

There's a pause, as though I'm supposed to return the compliment somehow, but I'm not about to offer him anything when I know there's a "but" coming.

"But," Kellan continues when I don't chime in, "Crosbie is my best friend. I don't know what's going to happen from here on out, but the one thing I do know is that there's no way he's going to keep being my best friend if you're living here."

My brows shoot up, and not just from the surprise of learning I'm being evicted. For once, Kellan's actually making a good point, and I'm a little alarmed I didn't think of it first. I open my mouth to reply but he plows ahead.

"It would just be weird," he adds. "And uncomfortable for everybody. And while I hope you and I will stay friends, I have to do whatever it takes to fix things with Crosbie. Bros before ho—roommates. Ahem. Roommates."

And there's the Kellan we know and love.

"Fine," I say, even as I'm wondering where the hell I'll go. It's not like Christmas is prime apartment-hunting season. "I'll look for something else."

He looks relieved, as though there'd been a chance I'd throw a fit. "Great. Okay. Good."

I eat the last limp piece of pasta from the cardboard container. "Great."

"I'm sorry, Nora," he adds, when I stand up to throw away my trash and head for my room. "For everything."

"Me too," I say.

* * *

"He threw you out?" Marcela looks like she's utterly confounded by the news.

"Not 'threw out,' exactly," I clarify, wiping down a table. "But the 'sooner the better' part was pretty strongly implied. The worst part is, I should have been the one to initiate the conversation. Obviously I should leave. I never should have moved in."

"There's no way you could have predicted how this would play out," she argues. "Was it your best idea to move in with Kellan McVey? No, of course not. But how were you to know you'd fall for Crosbie and that stupid little May Madness mistake would come back to bite you in the ass?"

I shrug. "Life's not fair." And it's really not. How is it that I hook up with five guys and one of them winds up being my future boyfriend's best friend and I end up the villain? How is it that Kellan can have sex with sixty-two women, catch an STI, and have his problems cured with a week's worth of antibiotics? Crosbie literally covered up his regrets with a coat of blue paint; I tried to keep mine under the radar but that blew up in spectacular fashion. It's the whole balance thing, all over again. In my effort to make up for being invisible in high school, I'd raced from the Nora Bora end of the spectrum right over to the Red Corset side. And for all my trouble to see and be seen, the only person who'd spotted me at all last year was a middle-aged peace officer with a flashlight and a frown.

"Enough about me," I say determinedly. "What's going on with you and Nate?"

Instead of their usual sniping, they've been studiously ignoring each other all afternoon, and Celestia has yet to make

265

an appearance.

Marcela studies her fingernails, painted to look like clouds. "Nothing."

"Nothing?" I narrow my eyes.

She holds up her hands defensively. "Nothing, I swear. But…"

I wait her out.

"But there's something to be said for having things out in the open," she adds hastily. "I mean, last year with the secret admirer stuff—it was easy to pretend I didn't know who it was. And I think it was easier for him to pretend he believed I didn't know. And this year, as bad as it's been seeing them together, it was easier than admitting that maybe I'd made a mistake not acknowledging him."

I blow out a breath. "Wow."

"Yeah. So, who knows what—if anything—will happen next. But you started fresh this year, and I'm going to start fresh in January. That's my resolution. No secrets, no mixed messages."

"You're going to tell Nate you like him?"

"No, of course not. But I'm not going to pretend I don't, either."

"I really feel like maybe you're missing the point."

She bites the back legs off a sugar cookie shaped like a reindeer. "Well, look what happened here. You and Crosbie put it all on the line, and that flopped."

"You're very sensitive."

"I'm just saying, maybe the truth is a little more than we can handle right now, but lying only makes it worse."

"You can say that again."

"And you can hear me say it," she says, "whenever you want, since we'll be roommates."

I stop polishing the silverware I'd picked up. "Come again?"

She licks the red sprinkles off the reindeer's nose. "Well, you're homeless, and I have a spare bedroom. What kind of friend am I if I don't insist on having you move in?"

"Are you serious?"

"Of course. It'll be a boy-free zone. Kind of like what you and Kellan had, except without all the lying and gonorrhea."

"You know how to woo a girl."

"I'm going to Tahiti for two weeks; I'll leave you my keys and you can move your stuff in. We're talking, what? A duffel bag and a milk crate?"

"*Two* milk crates."

"Look at you," she coos, chucking me under the chin. "All grown up."

* * *

To a perfect stranger, I'd look like anything but a grown up. In my efforts to keep my mind off Crosbie, I throw myself into studying, forsaking pretty much everything except my shifts at Beans, since I'll now need the money more than ever. My hair is in a perpetual straggly bun, my daily uniform is the same pair of ratty jeans paired with a T-shirt and a hoodie. I haven't made my bed since Chrisgiving, and the fitted sheet is just a crumpled ball lost under the duvet somewhere. It's only when the last exam is written and it's time to pack my bags to head home for the week that I survey the situation and realize what a mess I am. Perhaps it's for the best that Crosbie's been ignoring me since that awful night—if he came by and saw this, he'd hightail it right back out of here.

I blow out a heavy breath and grab my hamper, resolutely filling it with every washable item in the room. Every item of clothing, save the pair of sweatpants and T-shirt I'm currently wearing, every piece of bedding—nothing is safe. I march the entire thing into the kitchen and start what will probably be the first of five loads, doubling up on detergent. I won't lie: it's starting to smell, and I'm not going to take this mess with me into either the new year or my new apartment. It will be a fresh, clean start, in more ways than one.

My bus leaves at noon tomorrow and since Kellan's in California until January second, I've booked a ticket back for

New Year's Eve to give myself a day and a half to finish packing and get everything carted over to Marcela's before his return. With the room largely empty, there's no way to ignore the obvious, and I stare at my desk and bed until my lower lip trembles, and not just because it's sad to dismantle them only to rebuild them a week and a half from now. It's sad because they make me think about Crosbie; this whole room makes me think about him. Everything does. I've taken to leaving my phone in my sock drawer so I can't text him whenever the urge hits, which is still with embarrassing frequency. I know I can't afford to go down this depressing road, so I trudge back into the kitchen to collect Kellan's toolbox and decide the bed will be my first victim.

I drag off the mattresses and stash them in the living room, and that small act has my muscles burning and my breath coming in harsh pants, making me consider abandoning the bed altogether and crashing on the couch until I leave. But I don't. Loose ends are my newest nemesis, and I'm going to see this thing through. At least, that's the plan until I crouch next to the bed, wrench in hand, and spot the small red box on the floor.

I've definitely never seen it before. It's flat and square, not quite as large as a CD, the velvet smooth and soft under my fingers. The wrench clatters when I drop it back into the toolbox, but I barely register the noise over the thudding of my heart. I know this room was empty when I moved in; I know I have never seen this box before. Sometime between Labor Day and today, this thing…materialized.

Equally frantic parts of me are warring over whether or not I should hope it's something from Crosbie or just something Kellan accidentally tossed in here. He's forever throwing things from the couch into the kitchen, swearing he can land them in the sink. Why he would do that with a red velvet box—

Okay. I'm just going to open it.

I take a deep breath and lift the lid, feeling the strong fight of the springs, as though it's never been opened before.

When I see the fine gold chain bearing a tiny book pendant, I know this has nothing to do with Kellan. Nothing does. I've known this for a long time; the one person who needs to know it is the only one who doesn't.

If I were smarter and saner, I'd snap this box shut and leave it in Kellan's room, asking him to return it to Crosbie when—and if—he sees him again. But I'm not feeling even remotely smart or sane right now, and instead I lift the necklace from the box and study the delicate little book, half open to reveal dainty gold pages. It's small enough that I have to squint to read the characters etched on the cover, but when I finally make them out, I confirm what I have known for a while: I have made a huge mistake.

I love you.

The tears that have been threatening for days take advantage and pour forth, stupid and sloppy, until I'm just a sobbing mess on the floor. I cram the necklace back into the box and slide it away, as unreachable as the guy who put it here in the first place. It must have been a Christmas present; he must have brought it that last night and hidden it under my pillow, and sometime in the terrible aftermath it must have slid down between the mattress and the wall and gone unnoticed.

Until now.

Which is ironic, because now that it's found, everything it represents is farther away than ever.

The buzz of the washer finishing its cycle nearly gives me a heart attack, and I lurch to my feet and swipe at my eyes, grateful for something to do beyond sitting here weeping foolishly.

I stick the wet clothes in the dryer and load up another batch, then take a seat at the breakfast bar and stare at my room like it's the mouth of a dark, terrifying cave.

Poor Crosbie. Always working so hard to present the perfect, strong image to the world. The exercise, the studying, the sweet gestures no one saw because I insisted he remain a secret. He gets so much attention being the guy people think he is, but the guy at keg parties and on bathroom walls isn't the real Crosbie at all. It's the person behind those ideas, the guy who works so diligently to keep the wheels turning, that counts.

I, on the other hand, worked so hard to be seen that I let all the other things slip away. Study, be responsible, be honest, be kind. I didn't study; I got arrested. I lied to Kellan and Crosbie; I unfriended Marcela because I needed a scapegoat to justify last year's stupidity. Everything I did was to cultivate some ridiculous phony image, either a party girl or a studious homebody, but I'd never taken the time to shore up my defenses, to make sure the person inside was solid and sound. And to what end? The one person who finally noticed me saw past the façade to the real me and liked me anyway. Long before I was smart enough to realize it.

I think of Nate sending those gifts to Marcela last year, her not-so-secret admirer. I think of all the times he'd listened to us recount our weekend exploits, all the times he must have wished it were him in those stories, that he could be that guy. But still he'd loved her, supported her, admired her. Until he couldn't anymore. And then these past months, the furtive looks they'd exchanged, the not-so-significant others they'd paraded around when really it was the things they weren't saying, they weren't doing, that spoke volumes.

I think of my parents, their lives together but not, residing in separate halves of a home. They insist on presenting a united front for my benefit, but nobody benefits from this arrangement. When my back is turned they resume hating one another, a festering and unnecessary contempt that should have ended long ago.

We can scream and fight and cry and ignore, but really, it's the things we do when we think nobody's watching that reveal the most. Well, I'm done. No more messes, no more lies.

Starting now.

* * *

Snow crunches under the tires as we pull into the dingy bus depot in Grayson, Washington, and I see my parents fighting for top billing as they stand clustered with the small crowd gathered just inside the terminal doors. In typical fashion they'd both dressed in neon colors to try to stand out more than the other: my mother in pink, my father in yellow. I'm pretty sure I remember those jackets from an ill-fated ski trip when I was six. In any case, they're effective: there's not a single person on the bus who hasn't noticed them.

"Hi!" my mom exclaims, folding me in a hug when I enter.

"Hi," I say, the words muffled against the rayon fabric of her jacket. I extricate myself from her grip only to be pulled into my father's hug.

"How you doing, Nora Bora?" he asks. "Got anymore luggage?"

"No," I say, stepping away and hefting my backpack onto my shoulder. "Just this."

"That's not very much for a week."

"I don't need much." There's not a whole lot to do in Grayson, and given my non-existent high school popularity, I don't have many friends to catch up with or places to go. Unfortunately, the same can currently be said about Burnham.

"You look great," my mom says, leading the way to the parking lot.

"Thanks." I shiver in the damp air and zip my coat to my chin. Then I sigh as we reach the cars. Two of them. Parked side by side, ready for me to make a choice.

"Get in," they say, reaching for the passenger side doors of both vehicles.

"Were two cars really necessary?" I ask tiredly. "When we're going to the same house?"

"It's a duplex," my dad points out.

"It's the same structure."

"But two homes."

"Yes, I get it. But you're wasting gas." And truthfully—no matter who I choose, no matter the reason, someone's feelings are going to get hurt. There are only two sides in this equation, much like there are two sides in the duplex. There's no safe, neutral territory. Maybe that's why a comfortable middle balance is at once so appealing and so difficult to achieve.

"Fine," I say, when neither of them gives in. My dad is parked at the end of the aisle, which means the door opens wider so I can stuff my bag in easily. "I choose this car. See you at the two homes."

My mom looks wounded. "But I—"

"You wanted me to choose. I chose. Let's go."

They look startled as I sling my bag into the footwell and follow, buckling my seatbelt. In previous years I'd bemoaned their behavior and pleaded with them not to do things like this. It's not a competition. I love them both, as much as they frustrate me. But their unspoken war has more to do with each other than it ever has with me.

My dad seems pleased as we ride home, telling me about his current girlfriend, Sandy, who works at a gym, and their plans to go to Antigua in the spring. "Your mother's going to Mexico," he says, his tone almost pitying. "That's a little...done, don't you think?"

"Is Mexico 'done?'" I echo. "I don't know. I've never been."

He's been, three times. My mother's been as well. But I've never been invited.

We stop for a red light and he turns to look at me, expression serious. "Are you okay, Nora? You seem a little tense."

"It was a long bus ride, that's all." It's late afternoon but the sky is already growing dark. I feign a yawn and he seems to buy it.

We make our way silently through the center of town, the icy streets still busy as people finish up their last-minute shopping. It's Christmas Eve, so shops will be open for another few hours, and when we pass a grocery store, I sit up in my seat.

"Who has the turkey?" I ask.

"Hmm?"

"The turkey. Who's making it this year? You or mom?"

"Oh, your mother, I believe. Don't worry—I bought hamburgers, just in case."

We stop for another light, my mother idling right beside us. I roll down my window and gesture for her to do the same. "Do you have a turkey?" I shout.

"What?"

"Do you have a turkey?"

"Your father's making it!"

"He said you were!"

"Robert!" she yells past me. "You said you would get it!"

"I offered," he hollers back, "but you said I would lose it!"

"And then you said—"

I roll up the window on the argument. "Stop at Carters."

* * *

We end up with a small but obnoxiously overpriced bird that sits in the laundry sink in my mother's basement overnight, presumably thawing. I explain I'll be alternating sides of the duplex during my stay, starting with mom's house tonight so I can keep an eye on the turkey.

Christmas morning is the usual strained affair. My parents act as though everything is all right and I sit there in pajamas opening too many presents as they try to outdo each other with things like perfume and scarves and gaudy jewelry—none of which I would ever wear, but thank them for all the same. I think we're all relieved when the last gift is unwrapped and I head down to the basement to grab the turkey from its chilly bath.

Kellan had insisted on explaining the whole turkey process as he performed it, gross things like grabbing the innards that are stashed inside and sewing parts to other parts so it stays together. I skip the "brining," mostly because I don't know what brine is, and skim the recipe he'd texted me, mixing

273

up breadcrumbs and diced vegetables and a variety of spices rescued from the depths of my mother's pantry.

I gag a little as I stuff the bird and rub butter under its pebbled skin, then stick the whole thing in the oven. I threaten to go home immediately if this bird disappears for even one second, and both my parents promise to remain hands off. To be honest, they look a little frightened by my uncharacteristic decisiveness.

All too soon it's time for dinner. I make my way downstairs where I'm introduced to dad's girlfriend, Sandy, and Byron, mom's new boyfriend. Each relationship is still in its early stages, far too early for Christmas dinner with each other's ex, if their strained expressions are any indication.

For the first time in years, we sit down to a meal that involves actual turkey cooked in our oven. Everyone makes appreciative noises as my dad carves it up, and I feel a tiny, satisfied thrill when we start eating and no one pulls any supplementary food items from their pockets. It's already more successful than Chrisgiving.

"So," Byron says, peering at me over his glass. "You're at Burnham, is that right?"

"I am."

"My alma mater," my father chimes in, uninvited.

Byron just glances at him before returning his attention to me. "What are you studying?"

"I'm undecided."

"I thought this was your second year."

"It is."

My mom smiles reassuringly. "There's no timeline for finding your way," she assures me. "When you get there, you'll know."

Dad and Sandy scoff in unison.

"I'm sorry, Robert," my mom says tersely. "Is something wrong?"

"Wrong?" he asks. "No, Diane, nothing's wrong. Why would it be?"

"I—"

"Though there *is* a timeline," he continues. "It's four years. And each one costs a small fortune."

I cut my turkey into miniscule pieces and try to avoid eye contact. Though my grades—and, for the most part, my behavior—this year have been much improved, I still don't think they'd be thrilled to learn I'm newly evicted—or why.

"So what does one learn when they're 'undecided?'" Sandy asks, not unkindly. I'd really rather be eating under the table than having this discussion, but I recognize that she's just trying to deflate the tense bubble blooming between my parents.

I shoot her a tiny smile and recap my classes from this year and last.

"That's a very broad selection," Byron remarks.

"She's twenty-one," mom says dismissively. "Not everyone knows what they want when they're twenty-one. Sometimes you have to try on a few pairs of shoes before you find the ones that fit." She looks proud of her analogy, but my dad rolls his eyes.

"She's not Cinderella, Diane." Then he quickly glances at me. "Though you'll always be my princess."

Now *everyone* rolls their eyes.

"I have an engineering degree," he continues, undeterred. "Nothing wrong with that."

Mom narrows her eyes. "You edit cookbooks. Where does engineering come into play?"

"It looks good on a resume."

"You were a philosophy major in first year, and a biology major in second. You were undecided for quite a while, yourself, Robert. There's no rush, Nora." She pats my hand.

My dad scowls. "That's easy to say when you're not the one paying the tuition."

"You're the one who insisted she go to Burnham. Let her test the waters a little bit and find out what she really wants. When she's ready, she'll make her choice. Won't you, honey?"

I shift in my seat and think of Crosbie. "Yeah."

Dinner drags on interminably, and Sandy and Byron book

it out the door as soon as they're able.

"Well done, Diane," my father remarks, bringing dishes into the kitchen.

"Me?" she protests. "You're the one painting people into corners."

"How? By hoping our daughter actually learns something at college? Is having some expectation of her really that ridiculous?"

"I'm right here," I point out, standing two feet away with a stack of plates.

"You're making her feel bad!" my mom snaps.

"She feels fine," my dad retorts. "And maybe if—"

"Could we stop talking about how I feel?" I interrupt. "And maybe talk about how you two feel? For once?"

They freeze and turn, as though just now remembering I'm here. "Nora, honey," my mom says. "Everything is fine. We're just talking."

"Because we care," my dad adds.

"You're lying," I say flatly. "To me. To each other. To Sandy and to Byron. To everyone. You're stuck in this charade of pretending everything is okay because you think that's the best thing for me, but it's not. I'd really much rather have you be honest about everything, once and for all. Keeping this all bottled up is only making everyone miserable."

"We're not—"

"Just say it," I interrupt before they can start to argue. "Tell the truth. Put everything out in the open. And if you can overcome it, great. And if not, that's fine, too. It'll hurt, but you'll live."

I'm still living, after all, and I'm tired of these tortured holidays. Tired of swapping sides of the duplex and making small talk with strangers and never having any turkey. To date my efforts to be different have involved a fair bit of lying—to myself, to other people. It's time for the truth.

"I hate you, Robert," my mother says finally. "I just really hate you."

My dad looks stunned. "Diane! Nora is—"

"An adult," she finishes firmly, if a bit sadly. "She's an adult and just like she knows Santa didn't bring any of those gifts this morning, she knows this whole 'getting along' charade is just that—a charade. And a dreadful one, at that."

His mouth works, but nothing emerges until, "I suppose I hate you too," he offers grudgingly. "And I hate this duplex. You never mow your side of the front yard and it always looks lopsided."

"Oh, you and that grass obsession! At least I don't insist on walking up the stairs like an injured hippo—the whole house shakes."

"You beep the car four times to lock the door—four! It only takes one. How many people have to be disturbed..."

I snag an extra piece of pie and back out of the room, passing the dining table where the remaining turkey sits guilelessly on its holly-rimmed platter. It had taken far too long for us to have this dinner, and though it wasn't exactly the easiest meal to choke down, I can't help but think how many things would be different if we'd only had it sooner.

chapter twenty-one

Though it was only four months ago that I moved in with Kellan, it feels much longer when I make three round-trips through Burnham's quiet streets as I cart my things over to Marcela's. In addition to leaving me the keys to her—our—home, she'd also loaned me her car, and now I park at the curb and jog back up the steps to my—Kellan's—apartment to contemplate how best to get the long slats of the bed frame into the tiny trunk.

It's nine o'clock on New Year's Eve and everything else is already gone. I'd gotten home at three to finish packing and start moving, determined to wake up tomorrow in a newer, better place, both literally and metaphorically. But now, faced with the final pieces of the puzzle, I'm exhausted. I'd stopped in town for Chinese food on one of my runs, and now I slump on the couch with a carton of cold noodles and a glass of orange juice to see the ball drop in Times Square. Last year my parents and I had stood in the front yard to watch neighbors shoot off fireworks. They'd pretended it was because they had a keen interest in pyrotechnics, but we all knew it was because neither wanted to concede the holiday by going to the other's home to watch the countdown on TV.

The counting begins and ends and New York explodes in cheer, everyone kissing and hugging and smiling, happy and unburdened. I change the channel until I find an old black and white movie, wishing things were that simple, then mentally kicking myself for being so maudlin. Yes, I'm a twenty-one-year-old girl who's spending New Year's alone. Yes, I was recently evicted. Yes, I was recently dumped. But if I consider my list of goals for this year, "do not get evicted" and "do not get dumped" were never on it. I'm not flunking any classes and I haven't gotten arrested, so technically I'm still on track.

I turn to look out the window where a light snow has started to fall, sifting over tree branches and clinging to the grass. I don't know what the forecast is, but if I want to complete this move tonight, I can't waste any more time feeling sorry for myself. Not here, anyway. I can do it at my new apartment.

I throw the empty carton in the trash, rinse out my glass and stick it in the dishwasher, then start the cycle so Kellan comes home to a clean kitchen. Fresh starts for everybody.

I've just carted all the pieces of the bed frame down the stairs to the front door and am reaching for my boots when there's a sudden knock. I freeze, then slowly straighten. After a second, another knock. I already know Burnham is deserted. I'd passed only three other people on my trips back and forth from Marcela's apartment, and none of them have reason to visit me at nearly ten o'clock on New Year's Eve.

I rise onto my tiptoes to peer warily through the peephole. And for the second time in as many minutes, I freeze.

It's Crosbie.

Though I'm perfectly warm in my jeans and fitted wool sweater, my fingers are numb as I fumble with the deadbolt and twist the knob to pull open the door. Frigid night air rushes in and I shiver. Even though I knew it was him, I'm still stunned to see Crosbie two feet away, head ducked down against the cold, hands jammed in the pockets of his jeans. His puffy black jacket is zipped to his chin and he shifts from foot to foot, stopping only when he looks up to meet my eye.

"Hi," I say, when I can't come up with anything else.

He nods briefly. "Hey."

Whatever small, desperate hope had been blooming

quickly withers. "He's not here," I say, nodding over my shoulder. "He's not back until the second."

"I know." He's watching me, face expressionless, the shadows beneath his eyes deepened by the yellow porch light.

"Then what are you…" I shiver again. "Did you forget something? Do you want to come in?"

A slight hesitation. "Yeah."

I step back as he enters, scuffing his feet on the mat and closing the door behind him. Without the white noise of the night, it feels deathly quiet in here, the tension thick and painful. He finally looks away, taking in the familiar slats of wood resting against the wall. "What are you doing?" His voice is raspy and he clears his throat, looking embarrassed.

"I'm moving," I say, also looking at the frame. "To Marcela's. This is my last trip."

He nods and looks over my shoulder, up the stairs. "No kidding."

"No kidding."

More silence.

"Did you need something?" I ask when I can't take it anymore. "A video game or something? Why are you back so soon? There's no one else in town."

He meets my eye again. "I know."

My heart thumps so hard in my chest it feels like it'll bruise. "You know?"

"Yeah. I know."

"Then…what?" I think about all my unanswered texts. The apologies. The Christmas present. "The necklace?" I ask softly. "It's on the counter. I can get it. I was going to ask Kellan to return—"

"Not the fucking necklace, Nora."

I'm mid-turn, one foot on the bottom stair, when the quiet words bring me to a halt. There's no vehemence there, no anger, only sadness. Exhaustion. As though being angry has left him wrung out and raw. I know the feeling.

For a long, exposed minute, we just look at each other, and then I can't do it anymore. I blink away tears as best I can, but I feel them catch on the ends of my lashes and finally I give up and shrug helplessly. "I'm sorry," I say. "I texted you a thousand times, I left messages. I'm sorry, Crosbie. I'm so sorry. I don't have anything else to say."

His jaw flexes and he nods. "Right."

"Do you want me to say something else? To say I regret it? That I regret not telling you? That I regret going to that stupid party? Because I do. I regret everything. But how was I supposed to know you—I—this—" I gesture between us weakly, "was going to happen? I couldn't know—I didn't know—" I break off when the tears are too heavy and I taste them on my lips. "I need a tissue." What I really need is space. Because though I've spent the past two weeks wanting nothing more than to see Crosbie, talk to Crosbie, the reality of him is so much different now.

The reality of me is different for him, too.

I'm Nora Bora and Red Corset and everything in between.

I grab a tissue from the bathroom and mop up my eyes, dragging in deep breaths and willing myself to calm down. When I come back out, Crosbie's sitting on the arm of the couch, jacket unzipped. With the exception of the now-missing Chrisgiving decorations, the place looks pretty much the same. My life had been contained to my room, and unless he went to the door and peered inside, there's really no way to tell I'd ever been here.

I just stare at him. I don't know what else to do.

"It's not fair," he says, scuffing his socked toe on the hardwood floor.

I swallow. "I know."

He shakes his head. "It's not fair that I have a list I have to fucking paint over, and you have, what—five minutes in a closet?—that gets you a nickname and a witch hunt."

I'm not sure I'm breathing anymore. "Wh-what?"

"I mean, it's not fair that my girlfriend had sex with my best friend, but how could we have known?"

"Cros—"

"I was at that party, Nora. And I never saw you. You were wearing a fucking *red corset* and I never saw you. Then you show up here, trying to be invisible, and all of a sudden I couldn't see anybody else."

"Wh—"

He scrubs his hands on his thighs, as though his palms are sweaty. "I had to think about things. You broke my fucking heart that night. I know you didn't mean to, but it doesn't mean you didn't."

I wince. "I know."

His gaze travels across the room to the little red box sitting on the counter. "I guess you do."

"I'm sorry, Crosbie."

"I went home because I thought the distance would make it easier, that not seeing you would make it easier, but it didn't. I think about you all the time. I have, ever since September. And I tried going out, doing whatever, and I just couldn't stop thinking. I couldn't turn it off. Because I don't want to be that guy on the bathroom wall, anymore than you wanted to be the girl on Kellan's stupid list."

Even though I know we've been broken up for weeks, the thought of him going out and "doing whatever" still makes my heart crack in two. "Did you—"

He shakes his head, knowing exactly what I'm thinking. "I didn't mess around with anybody. I was home by nine every night. That's when my parents knew something was up."

"What did you tell them?"

"That there was a girl."

"What'd they say?"

He smiles faintly. "That it was about time."

"Did you tell them about…" I can't say the words. Now that they're out there, I can't say them anymore than I can take them back.

"No. Of course not. That's your secret to tell. Or not."

"I'd really rather not."

"Me either."

The silence stretches thin again.

"Crosbie." The word sounds scratchy. "Why are you here?"

He lifts a shoulder helplessly. "Because I wanted to see you. I always have."

"Even—"

"I got your texts."

I stop.

"All one hundred and fourteen of them."

I cringe. "I didn't—"

"It's okay. Kellan sent three hundred and twenty-two. Compared to him, you were completely uninterested in my well-being."

I laugh weakly. "Did he tell you he kicked me out? That's why I'm moving."

"Yeah. He told me."

"Did he tell you bros before hos?"

His eyebrows shoot up. "He said that? Out loud? To you?"

"Well, it was more like, *bros before ho-roommates*."

Now Crosbie laughs. "Smooth."

"I mean, I'm also leaving because I never should have moved in to begin with."

"I was here that first day," he reminds me. "When you realized you'd probably get to bump into me from time to time, you never really stood a chance."

"That's exactly what decided it."

More silence.

"Remember when you told me that you don't know how to balance things?" he asks eventually. "That it's one extreme or the other? Nora Bora or...Red Corset?"

I bite the inside of my lip and nod.

"You know what I was thinking?"

"What?"

"That on Halloween, we met right in the middle. That dog park, it's halfway between here and the Frat Farm."

My mouth opens then flaps closed, surprised. "That's very...insightful."

"I know. I also realized we were both in costume. You were this wild woman on the run, and I was, quite naturally, a superhero."

"Naturally." But my mind is whirling, zipping around frantically to pick up scattered pieces, putting together a new picture of that night. He'd been Superman, somebody's alter ego, the side the public saw. And when we'd gotten back here the cape had come off and he'd been Crosbie and I'd been Nora, and we'd just been ourselves. And that had been more than enough.

He studies his fingernails, then glances up at me. "Do you have anymore secrets, Nora?"

I shake my head. "No. Definitely not."

"Me either."

Beside me the movie ends, the programming promptly switching as the Chicago New Year's countdown begins.

"It's eleven o'clock," I say, startled into moving.

"Yeah. So?"

"So I told myself I was going to start this new year in a better place. Marcela's place, specifically. Without...you know."

"Me."

I gesture vaguely to the whole apartment. "This."

"You need a hand?"

"There's only the bed frame left."

"Come on, I'll help you. Where does Marcela live?"

"About five minutes from Beans."

"Okay."

It takes four trips to get the pieces wedged into both trunks, and even then Crosbie has to use a scarf to tie his closed, since the latch won't catch. The snow has picked up and the whole street is blanketed in white. He waits on the doorstep as I give the apartment one last once-over, turn off all the lights, and lock the door behind me.

We drive slowly through the powdery, dark streets, the fresh snow grinding under the tires. Crosbie trails me for the ten-minute drive, pulling into the adjacent space when I park at

Marcela's building.

We climb out of our cars and meet at the trunks. "This is it."

"I figured." He unties the scarf and scoops up the wood slats, then insists on carrying half of mine as well. "Lead the way."

Marcela lives on the third floor of a building that qualifies as "new" in Burnham, which means it's about fifteen years old. Her apartment is dated but spacious, and Crosbie nods his approval as we cross the threshold. "Nice."

"This is going to be my room." I lead him through the kitchen to a short hallway with bedrooms on opposite sides. He pauses at the door and frowns at the milk crates, the duffel bag, the mattresses I had nearly died getting here.

"This again?" he asks, arching a brow in my direction. "Square one?"

"Marcela has a wrench and a screwdriver," I inform him. "So…maybe she'll know how to reassemble the furniture."

He smirks and carefully places the wood slats along the wall, away from the wood pieces on the other wall that used to be my desk. "Go get these 'tools,'" he orders, shrugging out of his jacket. "And this time, pay attention."

I'm not about to look a gift horse in the mouth, so I whirl around and hustle into the kitchen to find the wrench and screwdriver in Marcela's junk drawer. By the time I get back Crosbie's got the pieces arranged on the carpeted floor, and he's kneeling between them, looking perplexed. "What'd you do with the screws?" he asks. It takes me a second to answer; he's wearing a black T-shirt and it's straining across his back, his biceps broad and defined.

I shake my head to clear it of lusty thoughts. "I left them in my car. I'll go grab them." I turn back around and hurry out the door before he can think this through. I'd be lying if I said I wasn't positively giddy that he's here. That he's…trying.

I reach the car and snag the plastic bags I'd stashed the screws in, then hesitate as I study Crosbie's car. The lock on the driver's side door is up, and before I can talk myself out of it, I'm rooting around beneath the passenger seat until I find the gift I'd hidden there before Chrisgiving. Maybe I'll give it to him as a thank-you for building my furniture. He'd given me something, after all. Even if I had to return it.

I get back to the apartment and join Crosbie kneeling on the floor in my room, handing him things as instructed, pretending to pay attention like I'd done the last time. "How'd your exams go?" he asks, holding a screw between his lips as he twists another one in.

"Okay, I think. Better than last year, definitely. You?"

He shrugs, and his shirt lifts up to reveal a swath of pale skin and his boxers peeking out from the top of his jeans. "Not too bad."

"That's good."

"Yeah. How was your trip home?"

I hesitate. "Ah…"

He stops working. "What does that mean? No turkey?"

"There was turkey. And there was…truth-telling."

"Truth-telling?"

"Yeah. I basically made my parents admit they hated each other."

"Do they? Did they?"

"Yes and yes. My dad's already looking for a new place."

"No way."

"Turkey's overrated."

"Or underrated," Crosbie counters. "As a truth serum."

I laugh. "Fair enough."

"How about Nate and Marcela? Are they going at it yet?" He turns his attention back to connecting the final pieces of the frame.

"I don't know," I muse. "I don't think so. Marcela said she wasn't ready to admit she was in love with him, but she's not going to pretend not to care, either."

"Where does that get them?"

I shrug. "Marcela's in Tahiti, so…paradise?"

He smiles and pushes to his feet, gently kicking the frame to make sure it's sturdy. "Grab the other end," he instructs, picking up the box spring. I do as I'm told and we wedge it into the frame, following with the top mattress. Crosbie sits down heavily, bouncing a few times, and it all holds up.

Then he looks at me.

"You know what I'm going to say."

"Happy New Year?"

"Jump on the bed, Nora."

"Remember what happened last time?"

He gives me a thorough once-over. "You look like you've lost some weight. It should be okay."

"I can't believe I ever missed you."

His smile fades slightly. "Did you?"

"Did I miss you? Yes, of course. You got a hundred texts."

"A hundred and fourteen, but who's counting?"

"Who, indeed." I take a breath when he stands and extends a hand to help me up. I'm perfectly capable of climbing into bed on my own, but I want to feel him again, even if it's just the coarse skin of his fingers against mine, the faint squeeze before he lets go. I stand in the middle and watch him as he leans against the far wall, folding his arms across his chest. His biceps bulge, his forearms look ridiculously strong—he's so sexy and I feel like such an idiot.

"I'm not—"

"Jump," he interrupts. "We have to make sure it's safe."

"I'll probably—"

He clears his throat and raises an eyebrow.

I grimace and give a tentative push with my toes. The mattress springs squeak, but nothing terrible happens. I stare at my socked feet and push a little harder this time, my heels coming off the slippery fabric, skidding a little. I bend my knees and try a bit more, glancing up warily, as though I'm in any danger of hitting the ceiling.

I'm not.

I inhale and tell myself I'm only going to do this once, just one big jump to show Crosbie that I can, even though by now I think he knows it.

I jump.

Nothing breaks.

I plant my feet and wait, fully expecting the mattress to come tumbling down or a neighbor to pound on the door, but it doesn't happen. I jump again and the mattress squeaks, but everything holds firm. I jump again, and again, and again, and when I look up Crosbie is smiling as he watches, sexy and amused and somehow knowing.

I brace a hand against the wall as I stop, the mattress wobbly under my feet, my breath a little unsteady as I curl a finger in Crosbie's direction. "Come on," I say. "Your turn."

"I've already had a turn."

"I just want to see that you know how to have fun," I say. "Isn't that what you said to me?"

"Did I?"

"Mm hmm."

"And what did you say?"

"I was like, 'Okay, great idea.'"

He laughs. "I've already built this thing twice. I'm not building it a third time. Get down here."

"Why?"

"Because I said so." He bends to collect his jacket from the floor, and my stomach sinks. Oh.

But then he pulls out the flat red box from his coat pocket and turns to face me, exhaling carefully. "You know what else I realized?" he asks quietly.

I step down off the mattress but don't cross the four feet that separate us. "What?"

"That we saw each other on Labor Day, Veteran's Day, Halloween, Chrisgiving, and now New Year's. But not Christmas."

I stare at the box he must have retrieved from the kitchen. "I know."

"I got you this. I put it under your pillow, but then…"

"I know."

"I thought a lot about it recently. I mean, fuck, I thought a lot about it since we met. I was really worried that I was in love with someone who was in love with someone else."

"I'm not in love with Kellan."

"I know."

"I—You do?"

"Yeah. A hundred and fourteen texts, remember?"

"That sounds like an awful lot. But if you don't think it's stalkerish or creepy, then okay."

"You helped me study," he says, trailing a finger around the edge of the box. "You gave me free snacks at the coffee shop. You pretended not to know about that *Hustler* in my pillowcase."

"What's *Hustler*?"

"You acted impressed by my magic tricks."

"They are impressive."

"And you helped me paint over that bathroom wall. Like the choices I made last year, the ones I regret, were okay. Because that's what happens in college. You make mistakes. And you learn from them."

I nod, hopeful and afraid of it.

"Some people streak down Main Street and get arrested," Crosbie adds as an afterthought, "but those are the really messed up ones."

"You were doing so well."

He smiles and studies the box. "What time is it?"

I check my watch. "Eleven forty-nine."

He sighs. "Do you want to wait eleven minutes for this so it's really perfect timing?"

I shake my head fervently. "I don't want to wait."

He extends the box. "Merry Christmas, Nora."

"Oh, what is this?"

He laughs, embarrassed, and steps on my toes, lightly. "Just open it."

Of course I already know what it is, but still my breath catches when I lift the lid to see the dainty gold necklace inside, the tiny book charm, the careful etching on the front.

"Did you put it on?" Crosbie asks, hooking a finger under the chain and lifting it out. "When you found it?"

I shake my head, unable to speak as he fiddles to open the clasp, then carefully fastens it around my neck. The gold book dangles into the V-neck of my sweater, and we both glance down as he strokes his thumb over the letters carved on the front.

"What do you think?" he murmurs. "Did I choose right?"

I nod mutely.

"Did you?"

Finally the words do come. "There was never a choice," I say, reaching up a hand to touch his face, the hair curled around the bottom of his ear, the tendon in his neck.

His smile widens and he dips his head to kiss me, but I push him back. "Hang on a second."

He freezes. "Seriously?"

"Yeah." I jog out of the room and retrieve his gift from where I'd stashed it behind a chair in the living room. When I come back he stares at the wrapped box, about the size of a board game, and slowly accepts it. It's dented in one corner and there's a tear in the paper and part of it's wet.

"What's this?"

"Your Christmas present. I hid it in your car before everything, but then..."

He studies me, then looks back at the box, curling his finger beneath the folded edge of the paper.

"It's not as nice as yours," I say hastily. "And I mean, it's kind of stupid. I know you don't need—"

"Shut up," he orders, pulling off the paper and letting it drop to the floor so he's holding the box. Large, sparkly letters printed across the top spell out "Magic Kit" and beneath that in block font reads, "Lovely Assistant! Astounding Illusions! (Assistant not included.)"

"It's, um... It's all tricks that require an assistant," I say, suddenly more awkward than ever. "I thought until you got more comfortable on stage, if you wanted, I could...assist...you. Or...whatever." I trail off as he just stares at the box, turning it over to scan the contents listed on the back. It's from a weird little store in Gatsby and the guy at the counter swore it would be well-received. He'd also tried to sell me what amounted to little more than a bathing suit and a pair of fishnets as my "assistant outfit," but I'd declined.

"Thank you," he says finally, lifting his head. I'm taken aback by the force of the emotion in his eyes, the sincerity, the intensity. He'd given me a gold necklace and I'd given him a *magic kit* and he's reacting as though that's anywhere near the same thing.

Still, all I say is, "You're welcome."

He sets the box on the mattress behind me and fingers the book charm again, looking at me. "You still want to be my assistant?"

"If you still want me."

"These will be the only secrets you can keep."

"I promise."

"You've got to take them to your grave."

"Oh, absolutely."

"All right, Nora. You're hired."

I can't help but laugh. "Fantastic."

"And…" He looks at me seriously and tugs on the necklace. "I love you. In case you can't read."

"Will you build my desk now?"

"Nora. I swear to—"

I press onto my tiptoes so I can kiss him. "I love you, Crosbie. Only you. I've never said that to anyone before, I promise." Then I tell him something he hasn't heard a lot, something he deserves to hear every day. "You're the first."

I feel him smile against my lips, his hand sliding around the back of my neck, fingers snagging as they slip into my hair. "Same here."

Outside, the fireworks start before I can reply. It sounds like a million tiny explosions, the display short but intense, and through the frosted glass of the window we can make out blurry washes of reds and greens and yellow rocketing into the sky, unfurling quickly before sinking away. Lovely, intense, ephemeral.

"Perfect timing," I say.

"Just like I planned."
"Is this part of the illusion?"
He smiles and kisses me. "No. This is real."

epilogue

I glare at Crosbie and plant my hands on my hips. "You went out last night," I snap.

"So?" He glares right back. "I can't see my friends anymore? We get married and all of a sudden *this* is supposed to be my whole world?"

I gasp. "As though *this* is so bad? I work hard to make *this* look nice for you!" I gesture around the stage, decorated to resemble a makeshift living room. It consists of an old armchair, an unplugged lamp, and a long wooden box on a raised table.

"I work hard to pay for all this! Not to mention *that!*" He points at the enormous fake diamond ring on the fourth finger of my left hand. "I deserve a little me-time!"

"Trust me," I bite out. "You will be getting more than a little me-time. Fine—go out with your friends. I'm going to bed."

"Fine."

"Fine!"

Crosbie storms off stage as I make my way around to crawl into the prop box, lying flat on my back, head sticking out one end, high-heeled feet visible on the opposite end. I close the top so I'm securely tucked inside, then wiggle my toes and give an exaggerated yawn before quickly falling fake-asleep.

We've rehearsed this a hundred times, so I don't need to

open my eyes to see Crosbie sneaking back on stage with a saw. Beans is packed, the shop standing room only as people piled in for the Valentine's Day Open Mic performances. As usual, there's lots of poetry and singing, but only one magic act. Crosbie did most of the show alone, but this—the finale—requires an assistant, so here I am.

Getting sawed in half.

The audience gasps and snickers as he locks the box then determinedly saws through the wood, and on cue my eyes fly open. "What are you—" I shriek mid-sentence, then launch into a very convincing death scene.

"That oughta do it," Crosbie announces when the box has been sawed clean through. He tosses the saw to the ground and separates the halves, showing that I have indeed been neatly cleaved in two. Though it's an illusion we've all seen before, the audience applauds uproariously, and it's all I can do to keep a straight face as I continue to play dead.

I hear Crosbie breathing as he rounds the table, checks for a pulse, nods his satisfaction when he doesn't find one, and moves the box back together. With great flair he unlatches the lid and I climb out, unscathed, and we hold hands and bow, the audience on their feet.

He leans over to kiss my cheek. "Happy Valentine's Day."

"You do know how to woo a gal."

We grin and bow one last time, then quickly move our props to the side for the next performers. Crosbie clutches my hand as we weave our way through the crowd, giving thanks and high fives as required, before ducking into the kitchen to grab two bottles of water and heading down the hall to the back entrance for some fresh air. Though my portion of the act lasts only six minutes, it was a nerve-racking six minutes and I'm sweating copiously, despite the fact that my assistant outfit is only a pair of thin black tights and little black dress that takes *little* very seriously.

"You were great," I say once we've caught our breath. "The trick where you throw the cards and grab the right one out of the air? They were stunned."

Crosbie watches me as he downs half his drink in one swallow. "You know they were only watching you," he says, wiping his mouth with the back of his sleeve before gesturing to my ensemble. "Who can blame them? I could barely concentrate."

I smile. "I'm proud of you."

He smiles back, embarrassed. "Thanks."

His nerves haven't eased much since the last time he performed, but as always, he's out there trying, doing his best, working his ass off. And though my "assistant" role was relegated to the shadows until the finale, I really don't care anymore. The spotlight is overrated. Being seen is overrated. If I have to pick quality or quantity, I'm going with quality every time. Because Crosbie Lucas is the best boyfriend I never would have guessed I wanted.

"What are you thinking?" he asks. He polishes off the water and launches the bottle into the nearby recycling bin for a perfect three-pointer.

"That you're a good boyfriend."

"Oh yeah? In what ways?"

"Mostly how you're so modest."

"Yeah, I'm pretty great."

"And you're smart."

"I'm brilliant, but close enough."

I scratch my chin. "And…you run really fast."

"Mm hmm."

"Um…I guess you're sort of attractive."

He makes a buzzer noise. "Wrong."

"You have good taste in girlfriends?"

"Wrong again. You were doing so well, Nora. When's your next meeting with the Dean? I'm going to tell him you're not progressing as we'd hoped."

I snicker. "Leave Dean Ripley out of this."

A chilly February wind blows through the alley, making us both shiver. We step back inside and head up front to check out the rest of the show, stopping abruptly at the kitchen door. On the other side, lingering behind the coffee counter, are

Nate and Marcela. They've been cordial since the Chrisgiving blow up, but to the best of my knowledge, nothing has actually happened between them. Now, however, they share a bowl of popcorn, their hands bumping when they reach in at the same time, glancing at each other for a long moment, then removing their hands and pretending to watch the show.

Ever so slowly I see Nate's canvas sneaker-clad foot slide across the inches separating their feet, stopping just short of actually touching Marcela's sparkly gold boot. After a second she shifts her heel, bumping her foot against his. They don't look at each other again, and they don't move.

"Ooh," Crosbie whispers, equally captivated. "Who needs sleight of hand when you have sleight of foot? Maybe I haven't given that guy enough credit. Maybe he does have game, after all."

We back away from the door, unwilling to interrupt. "Let's go out the back," I suggest. "Where are you parked?"

"Down the block."

Our coats and my purse are stashed in the storage room, and we snag them quickly and head out into the alley and around to the street. The plan is to go to Marvin's when open mic wraps up, so Nate had given us the okay to store our props here over night. I worked the first part of the evening but my shift ended when Crosbie's performance started, so it's okay for me to bail early.

"Do you think they'll ever get it together?" I ask. "The anticipation is killing me."

"Of course they will," Crosbie replies, reaching for my hand. "Has magic taught you nothing? What you don't see is just as important as what you do."

I think back to my belated epiphany. How sometimes it's the things we do when we think no one is watching that really matter. "You're right."

"Of course I am."

"Ha ha."

We reach his car and he gallantly unlocks the door and gestures for me to climb in. "Wait. Why are we getting in your car?" I ask. "Aren't we going to Marvin's?"

Crosbie checks his watch. "Show's not over for another half hour. We've got time."

"For what?"

"To go back to your place to bang our brains out."

"Ooh. Be still my heart."

He laughs. "Just get in."

I do as instructed and he closes the door, then rounds the front and climbs into the driver's seat. "Give me a hint," I order. We'd agreed not to do anything special tonight, so this feels suspiciously like I've been fooled.

"Hold your horses."

He starts the car and gives it a second to warm up, but before he can pull out, a car comes up alongside us, honking maniacally.

Crosbie groans. "Dammit."

I can't help but laugh as he rolls down the window to see Kellan leaning across the passenger seat of his car, not one but two girls squeezed into the front.

"Great show tonight!" he hollers. "You have to tell me how you did that thing with the glass of water!"

The girls echo the praise and Crosbie handles it smoothly, perfectly comfortable with the attention. It didn't take long for him and Kellan to get back to best friend status, so I still see Kellan from time to time. Things aren't weird but they're not entirely normal, either, and Kellan seems to have forgotten his vow to stop messing around. I'm not the person who moved into that apartment in September, and Crosbie's not the person I thought I met then, either. But Kellan is exactly who he appeared to be—no pretenses, no illusions. Maybe he'll change, and maybe not. Whatever he's doing seems to be working for him, and that's what matters.

He invites us to a Valentine's party at one of the sororities, but Crosbie demurs, saying we have plans. Kellan gives a lascivious waggle of his eyebrows, wishes us luck, and speeds off.

"Jealous?" I ask, when Crosbie exhales and watches them

go.

He looks over. "Of what?"

"Of that. Of the…variety."

"Are you kidding?" He pulls into the road and starts driving back toward Burnham. "I've got Nora the Nerd, Nora the Assistant, Nora the Convict, Nora the Party Animal… Your multiple personalities provide all the variety I'll ever need."

"I don't know what I see in you."

He flexes his arm, and even in the dim light from the streetlamps it's obvious he has very impressive muscles. "It's probably these guys."

I squint. "I can't see anything."

A few minutes later we reach the Frat Farm and find parking a couple houses down from Alpha Sigma Phi. The place is dark, the guys either at the open mic to support their friend or at one of the various parties around campus.

"A frat house," I whisper, getting out of the car and following Crosbie down the sidewalk. "How charming!"

He smacks my ass. "Just you wait."

He leads me inside and up the stairs to his room, unlocking the door and trailing me in. If I was expecting rose petals and mood music, I'd have been sorely disappointed. It's exactly the same as it always is, right down to the corner of the *Hustler* sticking out of his pillowcase.

"Here," he says, grabbing a pair of my sweatpants from the back of his chair and tossing them to me. "Put these on."

I frown. "I feel like this is going the opposite of how I pictured it."

"Patience, grasshopper. I have a point."

"Let's hope so. You know I like to sleep in these pants. You've got about five minutes before I crash."

He laughs. "I'll make it fast. Get changed and I'll be right back." He hurries out of the room and I hear him run down the stairs as I tug on the sweats over my tights. I hadn't taken off my jacket and since he hadn't either, I leave mine on, wondering what, exactly, the plan is.

298

I find out seconds later when he returns with a bouquet of roses. "Ta-da!" he crows, whipping the flowers out from behind his back.

"Seriously? We said we weren't going to do anything!"

"What's the point of having all these holidays together—even fake ones—if we don't celebrate properly?"

"Thank you," I say, accepting the bouquet and inhaling. "They're beautiful."

He winks at me. "You're beautiful. Now put those down and come on." He opens the window and the sweats start to make sense. I set the flowers on the bed and crawl outside, Crosbie right behind me. There's a blanket on the roof and we sit in the middle and curl the sides over our legs. Unlike Halloween, there's no one milling around the front lawn, no space between us, no attempt to find each other a perfect someone else.

"This is sweet," I say, resting my head on his shoulder.

"There are maybe five nights a year this place is quiet," Crosbie replies. "This is one of them. Lie back."

We recline, his arm around my shoulders, my cheek on his chest. The stars are out in full force, and for a long minute we just watch them. Not even the February chill can penetrate our lovely little fog.

"You take any astronomy courses last year?" Crosbie asks.

"No. You?"

"No. I don't know what the hell we're looking at." He fumbles in his jacket for something. "But I do know this." He passes me a manila envelope and watches as I open it, pulling out a piece of heavyweight paper with fancy script printed across the top. It's a Star Certificate, complete with coordinates for where new star *Nora Kincaid* can be found, and stamped with an official gold seal.

"Crosbie," I mumble, touched. "You…"

"I gave it some thought," he says, "and I know how desperate you are for attention. Now you're a star."

I shake my head. "You do the sweetest things. And then you ruin them by talking."

I feel his chest rumble as he laughs. "Happy Valentine's Day."

I moan. "My gift is not going to compare to this." We weren't supposed to get presents, so I'd only picked up something as a gag.

He lifts his head to peer down at me. "No? What is it?"

"A new copy of *Hustler* and then…some sex?"

"Both are acceptable," he says, patting my shoulder. "Also, 'new copy of *Hustler*' implies I have an old copy, and I think we both know I don't."

"My mistake."

He sits up. "All right. Let's go inside and start knocking boots."

I sit up too. "You're so romantic."

He grins at me, sexy and unapologetic and everything I never knew I wanted. "The last time we were up here, I desperately wanted to kiss you," he says, surprising me. "I'd wanted to for a long time, and this seemed like the perfect place. Then the next thing I know I'm pointing out guys for you to hook up with—"

"You suggested absolute losers."

"Yeah, well, I have my methods. Now look around."

I study the empty street, the dark houses, all the parties hosted at sororities on the other side of campus. There are no cars, no people, no distractions.

"What am I seeing?" I ask.

"Nothing," he replies. "You see what you want to see, and sometimes you see what I want you to see."

"We're probably on the same page with this one."

"We both want you to see me," he confirms.

I stroke his bicep. "How could I not see you? With all these huge muscles…" I sling a leg across his thighs and slide a hand under his jacket, over his stomach. "And this six pack…"

"It's an eight-pack," he mutters, eyes sliding shut.

"And this adorable messy hair…"

"Don't ruin it with the wrong adjectives."

"Fine, no more compliments. Just facts. I love you,

Crosbie Lucas."

"I love you too," he replies. He smiles and opens his eyes, his gaze trailing over my temple, my brows, my nose, my mouth, my chin. Just looking at me.

Seeing me.

Only me.

acknowledgments

If there's ever a time to realize how truly smart and talented your friends are, it's when you're trying to self-publish a book for the first time. Their help and encouragement has resulted in a final product of which I am very proud, and though I've thanked them privately, they deserve much more public praise than I can find words for. But I'll try.

Khoi Le: Friend, photographer, and graphic designer. I told him about my concept for a cover, sent him a dreadful mock up, and he made magic happen. He's also helped out with a bunch of images for my website, and never complains that I can't figure out how to determine what size a picture should be. This kind of friend (and graphic designer) is a rare and wonderful thing. He took the picture, made the cover, and outdid all my expectations. You can contact him through his website: http://khoistory.com. Thanks, Khoi.

Natalie Perret: I'm from Canada, Natalie's from New Zealand, and a long time ago, we met in China. Our friendship has traversed continents, oceans, and many years, and she is one of the few friends who is actually brave enough to read my books. This is her first time seeing an unpolished version, and she was generous enough to volunteer her time and her smarts to proofread for me. She was incredibly thorough and helpful, and without her you'd be reading things like "in appropriate" and "freeze booze." *Xie xie*, Natalie.

Elan Cross: How fortuitous that I made a new writer friend just as I embarked on this self-publishing journey. Having another writer to talk to and brainstorm with is something I have done without for a very long time, and Elan's editing hand helped get a lot of unwieldy sentences under control. Her vacillation between Team Kellan and Team Crosbie also told me I'd picked the right name for the book. Victory! Oh, this isn't about me? Thanks, Elan.

about the author

Julianna Keyes is a Canadian writer who has lived on both coasts and several places in between. She's been skydiving, bungee jumping and white water rafting, but nothing thrills—or terrifies—her as much as the blank page. She loves Chinese food, foreign languages, baseball and television, though not necessarily in that order, and writes sizzling stories with strong characters, plenty of conflict, and lots of making up.

In addition to *Undecided*, she is the author of four contemporary romances: *Just Once*, the story of a world weary socialite and a stubborn ranch foreman; *Going the Distance*, a love story set in China between a kindergarten ESL teacher and a former army interrogator; *Time Served*, the tale of an ambitious young lawyer whose perfect world is jeopardized when she reunites with her ex-con ex-boyfriend; and *In Her Defense*, in which a ruthless young lawyer realizes there's more to life than being the best...right? *The Good Fight*, book three in the Time Served series, releases in July 2016.

Connect online:

Website: www.juliannakeyes.com

Twitter: twitter.com/JuliannaKeyes

Facebook: www.facebook.com/juliannakeyesauthor

Printed in Great Britain
by Amazon